Charles Ligne

The Prince de Ligne

His Memoirs, Letters, and Miscellaneous Papers. Vol. 2

Charles Ligne

The Prince de Ligne
His Memoirs, Letters, and Miscellaneous Papers. Vol. 2

ISBN/EAN: 9783337169831

Printed in Europe, USA, Canada, Australia, Japan

Cover: Foto ©Raphael Reischuk / pixelio.de

THE PRINCE DE LIGNE

HIS MEMOIRS, LETTERS, AND MISCELLANEOUS PAPERS

VOLUME II

Catherine II

OLD FRENCH COURT MEMOIRS

THE

PRINCE DE LIGNE

HIS MEMOIRS, LETTERS, AND MISCELLANEOUS PAPERS

IN TWO VOLUMES
VOLUME II

WITH INTRODUCTION AND PREFACE BY
C.-A. SAINTE-BEUVE AND MADAME DE STAËL-HOLSTEIN

TRANSLATED BY KATHARINE PRESCOTT WORMELEY
ILLUSTRATED WITH PORTRAITS FROM THE ORIGINAL

VOLUME VII

NEW YORK
BRENTANO'S
PUBLISHERS

CONTENTS.

LIST OF

PHOTOGRAVURE ILLUSTRATIONS.

MEMOIR

OF

CHARLES-JOSEPH, PRINCE DE LIGNE.

I.

1786–1787.

THE JOURNEY TO THE CRIMEA.

[EARLY in 1786 the Empress Catherine determined to make a journey through her newly acquired dominion of the Crimea, otherwise called the Greek Kingdom of Bosporus, ruled by Tartar khans, but a dependency of Turkey, which ceded it to Russia in 1783. This journey was intended to be, and was, a triumphal progress, and the empress wrote to the Prince de Ligne inviting him to accompany her. Delays occurred, so that the start was not made till January, 1787, when the empress left Czarsko-zelo, attended by the principal personages of her Court, and accompanied by the ambassadors of France, Austria, and England, namely: Comte Louis-Philippe de Ségur, Comte Cobenzl, and Mr. Fitz-Herbert, afterwards Lord St. Helens. Prince Potemkin took charge of the arrangements and directed everything. The Sovereign of Austria, Joseph II., was invited to join the empress, and did so at Kherson. The King of Poland, Stanislas Poniatowski, met her on the way. The Prince de Ligne wrote a series of letters descriptive of this wondrous journey to the Marquise de Coigny, who shared them with his other friends at the French Court, where they created such interest and were so much talked about that they have since remained his best known and oftenest quoted piece of writing.

The following is the prince's reply to the empress's invitation to accompany her. In her letter of invitation she offered him certain lands in her new territory.]

The Prince de Ligne to H. I. Majesty the Empress Catherine.

VIENNA, February 15, 1786.

MADAME, — I have possessed for one week the letter which does me the greatest honour and gives me the greatest joy of my life. I have kissed it a thousand times, because the heart can see without the help of eyes. Blinded as I am for a time like Milton and Homer, — though not as mad as the one nor as garrulous as the other, — I recover, in order to express my thanks to your Imperial Majesty, I recover my sight, of which a terrible influenza had deprived me.

No one has disputed my birthplace, as they have that of the bard of an old wooden horse, and no one can doubt about the place of my death, which will surely be at the feet of your Majesty, from joy, excess of feeling, and gratitude, on the scene of your triumphs and beneficence. For myself, I much prefer being a victim to those emotions to being, like Iphigenia, that of the bigotry of my grandfathers.

However, as we do not really die of such sentiments, but, on the contrary, live upon them, I shall hope for an even finer death, — if, for instance, in the midst of our journey in Taurica, that superb, triumphal progress of your Majesty, some Tartar barbarian should disturb your *fêtes* by making an incursion, and mine should be the happiness to repulse the hated horde and buy with my blood before the eyes of your Majesty a little victory. What joy to fight for hearth and sovereign three thousand leagues from home and in Her presence!

Louis XIV., for want of having learned geography, thought himself the greatest king on earth, and was persuaded, at Versailles, that Franche-Comté was larger and more considerable than the peninsula of Taurica and the island of Kuban. How I delight in reviving those glorious names and glorious times known to us hitherto in fable only!

Elevation of soul, imagination, grandeur of ideas, seem to me like the sea which draws away from one place to bear itself to another; 't is thus they have insensibly attained the realms of your Majesty, to whom belongs the magic of Armida, painted by Quinault in that fine choir, which Gluck still farther embellishes. This permission to follow you to that fabled land is a favour as great as all the other marks of your generosity. I should hardly have been bold enough to solicit it, but ah! with what pleasure I shall profit by it!

I wish to take to Greece a few good Flemings, who are Greeks in agriculture. Perhaps their children in future years may become so in other ways, though their parents, heavy Belgians, are far indeed from the graces of the charming inhabitants of the loveliest land on earth.

What right have I to so much distinction and magnificence? I went to the most brilliant of Courts, I had the happiness to amuse myself for a time in that capital on the banks of the Neva. I saw, I admired, but I scarcely said anything; I listened, I was touched. I returned to the banks of the Seine and the Danube, but I could not tell one hundredth part of what I felt. The trumpet of renown and M. de Voltaire's clarion had already charmed the ears of all Europe with the recital of those marvels, and my little flageolet, worthy at most of the fields and the camp, could barely repeat it.

I shall plant in Taurica for the governor, the Maréchal Prince Potemkin, transparent apples, because they are to his liking, and the image of his soul, and I shall make, like him, English gardens upon my roofs; and thus, without being able to imitate the genius of that spoilt child of nature, I shall be his equal in attachment and gratitude to our good sovereign.

What a title that is! No one said in the olden time, of conquerors and great men of both sexes (if there were any) "our good king," "our good queen." Even the "good Henri" (who has suddenly, one hundred and fifty-five years after his death, been made the fashion by a comedy) came near flinging all Europe into fire and slaughter with his pretended *poule au pot.*

I place myself, therefore, at the feet of my good sovereign, and while awaiting the little statue for my garden in Iphigeniopolis, I shall preserve, sure that no stones can overthrow it, that greater one which I have long raised to her in my heart. That of Diana I shall fling down if I meet her; hypocrisy no longer suits me, and I am tired of hunting.

If I quarrel with our governor on the score of his effacing all pagan ideas with his Greek liturgy, your Majesty must obtain my pardon. [Prince Potemkin was fanatical for the Greek Church.]

I have the honour to be, with as much attachment, enthusiasm, respect, and admiration as ever, Madame, etc.

The Empress Catherine to the Prince de Ligne.

NOVEMBER 15, 1786.

MONSIEUR LE PRINCE DE LIGNE,—You will say that I write to you too often; but not only must I answer your last letter, but I think it necessary to tell you that I have at last fixed the time for my journey in Taurica. I shall leave here the first week in January, 1787, and I shall be eighteen days in reaching Kiev. There I shall patiently await the breaking up of the ice in the Borysthenes [Dnieper] and the arrival of those who will be ready to embark with me about the first of April. This will employ, as you see, two full months. I shall then lead you all to the land inhabited in the olden time, so they say, by Iphigenia. The name of that land will rouse imaginations; there are no fables they will not tell about my journey there. One thing is sure; I shall be charmed to see you once more.

I hope to bring with me a number of your acquaintances, and several ministers from countries at peace with me, in presence of whom no battles can take place; therefore sheathe, if you please, your combative inclinations. Besides, the governor-general is too alert to suffer Tartar incursions, as the Seigneur Iman Mansour can testify. The grand equerry threatened to play us a very ill trick; he was sick unto death, but is now convalescent.

You do not like the divinities of paganism, and show as little taste for Diana as you once showed here for Hercules and his club. Do you remember the rheumatism in my arm which made me so sullen every evening regularly at six o'clock, and which increased as the room filled up?

You are delivered from the danger of losing your eyesight; but if ever such a misfortune should happen to you, you will be the most clear-sighted blind man I have ever known.

I am not sure whether my Governor-general of Taurica will take your attack on Homer in good part; he sulked because I thought that Comte Stolberg had made a fairly good translation of that poet into German. . . .

If Louis XIV. thought himself the greatest king on earth it was because all the world exhausted themselves in telling him so. But what yard-measure did they go by? Geography was the one least favourable to him.

The Prince de Ligne to H. I. M. the Empress Catherine.

NOVEMBER 15, 1786.

MADAME, — I see with pleasure the happy day approach when your Imperial Majesty, crossing, with the sun, your vast domains, to illumine and vivify them (like that beneficent star which is your only rival), will shine in Taurica upon a new horizon. The mother of light is preferable to the father, and is not so dangerous as he whose strokes are feared, for those who approach your Majesty gain only benefits. Neither have I heard of his success in society; there is too much Phœbus in his conversation, while that of your Imperial Majesty leaves something behind it that makes us gayer, gentler, better informed, and better altogether. I think it must be jealousy, Madame, that makes your rival show himself so short a time in Petersburg.

My military residence in this country [Low Countries] is just ending. I shall go for a short time to Paris and Vienna before placing myself at your Majesty's feet in the uniform of your government, which I often wear with pleasure. Impossible to be a scamp in that green coat! My father was mistaken, and my tutors told a lie when they said that I should never be anything else.

The prospect of the voyage on the Dnieper turns my head; the happiness of seeing your Majesty from morning till night throughout that time makes me long for the journey. I shall reach Kiev as soon as I know the day of your arrival there.

Deign, Madame, etc.

The Empress Catherine to the Prince de Ligne.

PETERSBURG, Dec. 2, 1786.

MONSIEUR LE PRINCE DE LIGNE, — Your letter of Nov. 15th has just reached me and gives me true pleasure, — that of knowing that we shall meet again. My departure for Czarsko-zelo is fixed for January 2nd; thence I start on the 4th, and shall reach Kiev, please God, on the 25th, and shall there await the opening of the Borysthenes in order to embark; this will be, they say, in April.

Far from resembling in my course the brilliant image of the sun, as you suggest, we are taking all possible precautions to appear like heavy clouds. Each star that accompanies me is provided with a good, thick, black pelisse, and as, like all stars, my companions desire that their furred garment should have the same cut as mine, that model has become the affliction of everybody. I wish, myself, that it were already torn or lost, that I might hear no more about it. But this ill-humour will have passed, and the constellation of the Bear will have come by the time your friends have the joy of seeing you. I sing chorus to them.

I hope that the navigation of the Dnieper will prove prosperous, and I wish that you may not be bored.

Heads of Medusa, which petrify the moment they appear, are not good company; I have therefore avoided increasing their number. You will hardly know the grand equerry; at least he takes great pains, ever since his illness, by the arrangement of his hair to make himself look like a choir-boy. I suspect he has intentions to quell the Tritons of the Black Sea, for he has lately been breaking coursers for me that are more fit to swim than to gallop. He has travelled much since you saw him, and has even tried to go to the other world. You will find that he has benefited in every way, and has not forgotten his Chinese.

I hope that your eye will not suffer from the journey, and that I shall soon have the satisfaction of telling you by word of mouth the distinguished sentiments that I have for you, which differ entirely from those of your father and tutors, of which you inform me. I think you have more than one gift; those that I myself have the pleasure of knowing have given me a very particular esteem for you.

CATHERINE.

I request malicious persons who have read the "Private Life of Catherine II.," and another libel called her "Amours" not to believe them. There may be a few little things that are true in the accounts which have appeared of the journey of the empress to the Crimea; probably remembered and repeated by those to whom I told them. But as they are mingled with other things that are not true at all, I have resolved to publish the letters that I wrote during this journey. If her Imperial Majesty of all the Russias were still living, I should not publish her praises; when I sang them she did not hear them, nor will she now.

To Mme. la Marquise de Coigny in Paris.

KIEV, 1787.

Do you know why I regret you, Madame la marquise? It is because you are a woman unlike any other; and I am a man unlike any other, inasmuch as I appreciate you better than those who are about you. And do you know why you are a woman unlike any other? Because you are kind (though some people do not believe it), because you are simple, although you are witty; it is your language; you are wit itself; but you never run after epigram, it comes to you.

At fifty years of age you will be another Mme. du Deffand for piquancy, another Mme. Geoffrin for judgment, and a Maréchale de Mirepoix for taste. At twenty you possess the results of the three centuries which the ages of those ladies combine. You have the grace of an "élégante" although you have not taken to that profession. You are superior without alarming any but fools. Already as many noble sayings as witty ones are quoted from you. "Never take a lover, for that would be abdicating" is one of the profoundest as well as the most novel of ideas. Yet you are more embarrassed than embarrassing; and when embarrassment seizes you a certain rapid out-flowing little murmur announces it in the drollest way. You are the most amiable of women and the prettiest of boys; in short, you are that which I regret the most.

Ah! good heavens! what a scene before me! what a hurly-burly! What diamonds, gold, and stars and *cordons*, but not including that of the Holy Spirit! What chains, ribbons, turbans, what scarlet caps, either furred or pointed; the latter belonging to grotesque little beings who waggle their heads like those on your chimney-piece. They are called Lesghians and have come as a deputation (as have various other vassals) from the frontiers of the great wall of the Chinese empire and that of Persia and Byzantium. They are rather more imposing than the deputies from parliament or the assemblies of a little town, who are now coming a score of leagues by coach to Versailles to make some silly representation to the king.

Louis XIV. would have been jealous of his sister, or he would have married her, if only to have had such a splendid circle about him. The sons of the king of the Caucasus, of Heraclius, for instance, who are here, would give him more satisfaction than his five or six old chevaliers de Saint-Louis.

Twenty archbishops (a trifle unclean) with beards to their knees are far more picturesque than the king's almoners in their little neckbands. The escort of Uhlans attending a Polish great seigneur, who is on his way to see a cousin in the neighbourhood, has more of an air than the horse-police in their short jackets, who precede the melancholy coach, with its six sorry nags, of an official in a flat collar and big wig; and their glittering sabres with jewelled hilts are much more imposing than the white wands of the great officers of the King of England.

The empress received me as if, instead of six years, I had left her only six days ago. She reminded me of several things that sovereigns alone remember; they all have memories. There is something of the whole world here, and for all sorts of people: great and little politics, great and little intrigues, great and "little Poland." A few of the famous of that land, who deceive themselves, or are deceived, or deceive others, all very amiable — their wives still more so — are anxious to make sure that the empress does not know that they insulted her by the barking of their late Diet. They are watching for a glance from Prince Potemkin; difficult to catch, however, for the prince keeps the line between a squint and blindness. The women are soliciting the ribbon of Saint Catherine in order to wear it coquettishly and so make their friends and relations jealous. War is desired and dreaded. Complaints are made that the ministers of England and Prussia are inciting the Turks thereto. I, who have nothing to risk and glory, perhaps, to acquire, I long for war with all my heart; and then I say to myself: "How can you wish for that which will bring so many evils?" Then I stop wishing for it; but the remains of fermentation in my blood bring back my wishes, and the remains of reason again oppose them.

Ah! good God! what beings we are! Perhaps I shall have to write and tell you that —

> To see Paris again I can never pretend;
> To the night of the tomb I'm about to descend.

That idea affects me; for I want to see you; you are nearer to my heart than all Paris put together. — They have just come to fetch me to see fireworks which, they say, have cost 40,000 roubles. Those of your conversation are not as costly as that, but they do not leave us afterwards in the dulness and darkness that follow the other kind. I prefer your sparkles and your style of illumination.

To the Same.

FROM MY GALLEY.

This is fate, Madame la marquise. I left you in the midst of a dozen adorers who do not understand you, and I who do know how to understand you, shall have no chance to do so for a long time. I am twelve hundred leagues from your charms, but always mentally near your wit which returns incessantly to my memory. I see you, taking pains for the one or two of your adorers who comprehend you, and wasting yourself on others; but I do not see that your heart is engaged in all that. Two or three deceivers by profession tell you tales, but you are not their dupe. Two or three speculators flatter themselves they can make you take their shares in some scheme that is beginning to tangle. You take no share in anything but what amuses you; you adopt as your political opinions only those that inspire a piquant speech or a witty one. You laugh indifferently at all, — the *tiers* and the quart; methinks I have heard that underlined word pronounced already by some of your tiresome "Notables."

So the great men of America seem small to you in Europe; I myself do not find them, like Bordeaux wine, the better for crossing the seas. You say they wear you out, and you take the "liberty," of which they talk so much, to tell them so. And you do not like the Turgotins any more than you do the Turgotinesses; you would rather have wine-shops than "clubs," and good, dull minds than bureaux of intellect. Some of those men of intellect, *who have not said all their say*, and of whom we are warned, are excellent persons who will have to make themselves beasts to make you believe in their passions.

If he beside whom I am lodged at this moment goes astray it will be from good motives and too little logic. He is the only one indulging those ideas who will deserve indulgence. This dear Ségur is separated from me in this galley by a mere partition. How we talk of you! And what evil I tell him of certain persons of whom he thinks well, and to whom he is so superior! Beware of philosophy!—But I say once more, he is the only one who has nothing but praiseworthy intentions.

I think that this letter will be sent from Krementczuck. The name is not lyrical; but you must accustom yourself to many that none but Lulli and Rameau could make mellifluous. We are not traversing a land of nymphs and swains and vintagers; but you do not care for that, for you are not pastoral. The grandest sights, however, are before us. For example, from my splendid bed I can see Pérévóosloff, where that poor Charles XII. crossed the Borysthenes to hide in Bender. I await the end of our navigation to give you a better account of it. I never before embarked on any but small adventures, and I paddled my own boat then like others. Until I enter that of Charon, I shall never cease to love you and tell you so.

To the Same.

FROM KHERSON.

Cleopatra's fleet left Kiev as soon as a general cannonading informed us that the ice in the Borysthenes had broken up. If any one had asked, on seeing us embark in our great and little vessels to the number of eighty, with three thousand men in their crews, "what the devil we were going to do in those galleys," we should have answered, "Amuse ourselves, and — *Vogue la galère!*" for never was there a voyage so brilliant and so agreeable. Our chambers are furnished with chiné silk and divans; and when any of those who, like myself, accompany the empress, leaves or returns to his galley, at least twelve musicians whom we have on board celebrate the event. Sometimes there is a little danger in returning at night after supping with her Majesty on her galley, because we have to ascend the Borysthenes, often against the wind, in a small boat. In fact, one night there was a tempest, in order that we might have all experiences, and two or three galleys went ashore on a sand-bank.

Our Cleopatra does not travel to seduce Mark Antonys and Cæsars. The Emperor Joseph was already seduced into admiration of her genius and power. Cleopatra does not swallow pearls, but she gives them away plentifully. She resembles her prototype of antiquity only in a liking for costly navigation, magnificence, and study. She has given more than two hundred thousand volumes to the libraries of her empire. That is the boasted number of the library of Pergamos, with which the Queen of Egypt restored that of Alexandria; and as for fêtes, Kherson is indeed another Alexandria.

After those at Krementczuck given by Prince Potemkin, who caused to be transplanted into a really magical English garden exotic trees as big round as himself, we disembarked at the cataracts of Keydac, former capital of the Zaporoguas aquatic brigands. Here the Emperor Joseph II. came to meet us, and the fêtes were renewed on his arrival. What astonished and interested him most, for he is a great musician, were fifty *do*'s, fifty *re*'s, fifty *mi*'s, and so on; in short, a concert of notes in which many performers play one note only; this concert makes celestial music — for it is too extraordinary to be known upon earth.

I forgot to tell you that the King of Poland awaited us at Kanièvc on the Borysthenes. He spent three months and three millions in waiting to see the empress for three hours. I went in a little Zaporogian canoe to tell him of our arrival. An hour later the grandees of the empire came to fetch him in a brilliant barge. As he set foot upon it he said, with the inexpressible charm of his beautiful face and the soft tones of his voice: "Messieurs, the King of Poland has charged me to present to you the Comte Poniatowski." The dinner was very gay; we drank the king's health to a triple salute of all the artillery of the fleet. On leaving the table, the king looked about for his hat, and could not find it. The empress, more adroit, saw where it was and gave it to him. "Twice to cover my head!" said the king, gallantly, alluding to his crown; "ah, madame! that is heaping too many benefits, too much gratitude upon me." Our squadron was lying under the windows of the king, who returned to the house to give us a supper. A representation of Vesuvius, which lasted the whole night that we lay at anchor, lighted up the mountains and the plains and the river better than the finest sun at mid-day, gilding, or I should say igniting to a blaze all nature. We did not know that it was night.

The empress has never before known so well the charms of social intercourse; and, as there are two or three of us who do not play cards, she has sacrificed the little game she usually plays in Russia to give her something that appears like an occupation. The other day the grand equerry, Narischkin, the best and most infantile of men, spun a top into the midst of us, the head of which was bigger than his own. After much humming and many leaps, which amused us very much, it burst, with horrible hissing, into three or four pieces, one of which passed between her Imperial Majesty and me, wounded a couple of our neighbours, and struck the head of the Prince of Nassau, the invulnerable, who has had, in consequence, to be twice bled for it.

The empress said at table yesterday: "It is very singular that *you*, which is plural, should have come to be the rule. Why have they banished *thou?*" "It is not banished, Madame," I replied, "for Jean-Jacques Rousseau says to God: 'Lord, in thine adorable glory;' and God is thee'd and thou'd in our prayers; for instance: *Nunc dimittis servum tuum, Domine.*" "Well, then," said the empress, "why do you treat me with more ceremony? Come, I will set you the example. Wilt thou give me some of that?" she said to the grand equerry. "Yes," he replied, "if thou wilt hand me something else." And thereupon a deluge of thee-ings and thou-ings, each more funny than the others. I mingled mine with "Majesty," and *Ta Majesté* seemed to me the right thing. Others did not know what they ought to say. But in spite of it all, her thee-ing and thou-ing and thee'd and thou'd Majesty still wore the air of the autocratress of all the Russias, and of nearly all the rest of the world.

The empress permitted us, that is to say, the Prince of Nassau and me, as amateurs, and *perhaps* as connoisseurs, to go and reconnoitre Oczakow [that and Kinbourn were Turkish forts at the mouth of the Dnieper] and ten Turkish vessels, which have placed themselves, very uncivilly, across the

Borysthenes, as if to stop our passage in case their imperial Majesties should wish to go by water as far as Kinbourn. When the empress saw the position of the vessels marked on the little map that was brought to her she gave a flick with her finger to the paper and began to smile. I look upon that as a delightful *avant-courier* of a pretty little war we shall soon have, I hope. I thought the other day it must be for this that they ushered into the empress's cabinet, where the emperor had just gone, an officer of artillery, an officer of engineers, and Prince Potemkin.

"You are aware," said the empress the other day, "that your France is always, without knowing why, protecting the Mussulmans." Ségur turned pale, Nassau turned red, Fitz-Herbert yawned, Cobenzl wriggled, and I laughed. Really, it is not so; the matter in question was only one of building a magazine in one of the seven coves in the harbour of Sevastopol. When I talk of my hopes of war to Ségur he says: "But we shall lose the seaports of the Levant" [*les échelles du Levant*]. To which I answer: "There is nothing left for you to do [*Faut tirer l'échelle après vous*] after the ministerial folly you have just committed by M. Necker's general confession of poverty before that ridiculous Assembly of Notables."

"How do you think I succeed with the empress?" said the emperor to me one morning. "Wonderfully, sire," I replied. "Faith! it is difficult," he added, "to hold one's own against the rest of you. There is my dear ambassador, out of gratitude, kindness, liking for the empress, and friendship for me, always swinging his incense-pot, into which you throw grains for the rest of us pretty often; M. de Ségur pays her his very witty and very French compliments, and even that Englishman lets fly from time to time some tiny shaft of flattery, so epigrammatic that it is all the more piquant."

We have launched three vessels, and I amused myself by being launched in one of them. You understand, of course, that the one I was on was a vessel of the *ligne*. Gauzes, laces, furbelows, garlands, pearls, and flowers adorned the canopies erected on the shore for the two Majesties, which looked as if they had just come from a fashionable shop in the rue Saint-Honoré, but they were really the work of Russian soldiers, who are turned into milliners, sailors, popes, musicians, or surgeons, in short, into anything that is wanted, by a fairy wand — not that of a fairy as charming as you. Now I am going to think of your enchantments in the land of enchanters, for we are starting immediately for Taurica, where, if Iphigenia had been as amiable as you, she would never have been sacrificed — never, at least, in that way.

To the Same.

BARCZISARAI, June 1, 1787.

I expected to elevate my soul on arriving in the Taurica [Crimea] through all the great things, true and false, that have happened here. My mind was ready to turn itself, with Mithridates, to the heroic, to the fabulous with Iphigenia, the military with the Romans, the fine arts with the Greeks, to brigandage with the Tartars, to commerce with the Genoese. All those personages and nations are somewhat familiar to me; but lo! here comes another, and they have severally disappeared before the Arabian Nights. I am in the harem of the last Khan of the Crimea, who made a great mistake in breaking up his camp, and abandoning to the Russians, four years ago, the most beautiful country in the world. [The last Tartar khan, Saham Guerei, abdicated in 1783 his sovereignty in favour of Catherine II., to whom Turkey also ceded its supremacy. Russia thus became possessed of a strong position, from which she hoped in time to command the Danube, the Bosphorus, and the Euxine.] Fate has destined to me the chamber of the prettiest of the sultanas, and to Ségur that of the chief of the black eunuchs. My cursèd imagination will not shrivel with age; it is as fresh and rosy and round as the cheeks of Madame la marquise. In this palace, which partakes of the Moorish, Arabic, Chinese, and Turkish, paintings, gilding, inscriptions, fountains, and little gardens are everywhere; among them, in the very droll and splendid audience-chamber may be read, in the Turkish language, in letters of gold, around the cornice, these words: "In defiance of Envy, the whole world is informed that there is nothing in Ispahan, Damascus, or Stamboul as rich as this."

After leaving Kherson, we found marvellous camps of Asiatic magnificence in the middle of the desert. I no longer know where I am, or in what age I live. When, suddenly, I see mountains rise up before me and walk, I think it is a dream; it is really a stud of dromedaries, which, when they get up and walk on their great legs, resemble at a distance moving mountains. "Such as these," I say to myself, "are just what furnished the stable of the Three Kings for their famous journey to Bethlehem." Again I dream, methinks, when I meet the young princes of the Caucasus, almost covered with silver, on their dazzling white horses. When I see them armed with bows and arrows I fancy I am back in the days of the old and the young Cyrus. Their quivers are superb — you know none but those of Love, but the shafts in yours are gayer and more pointed. When I meet detachments of Circassians, handsome as the day, with their waists more tightly nipped into their corselets than that of Madame de L——; when I see Mourzas more daintily dressed than the Duchesse de Choiseul at the queen's ball,

Cossack officers with better taste in draping their scarfs than Mlle. Bertin, and furniture and garments of more harmonious colouring than Mme. Le Brun can put into her paintings, I am lost in amazement. At Stare Krim (where a palace was raised in which to sleep one night) I could descry from my bed all that is most interesting in two quarters of the world as far, almost, as the Caspian Sea. I think it was a part of Satan's temptation, for nothing finer could have been shown to our Lord. I could see from the same point on leaving my chamber, the Black Sea, the Sea of Azov, the Sea of Zabache, and the Caucasus. The guilty man who was eaten there (everlastingly, I believe) by a vulture had never stolen as much fire as you have in your eyes and in your imagination — at any rate, that is how your subtle and adoring weasel, the Abbé d'Espagnac, would put it.

Again I think I dream when, in a coach of six places (a triumphal car adorned with jewelled monograms), being seated between two persons on whose shoulders the extreme heat makes me often drop asleep, I hear, as I waken, one of them say to the other: "I have thirty millions of subjects, so they tell me, counting only males." "And I," says the other, "twenty-two, counting all." "I require," adds the first, "an army of six hundred thousand men, at least, from Riga to Kamtschatka." "With half that number," replies the other, "I have just as many as I want."

Ségur will tell you how much this impetuous imperial comrade has pleased him. In return Ségur has pleased the emperor. That monarch enchants all who see him. Freed from the cares of his empire he makes the happiness of his friends by his social qualities. He has only been slightly out of temper once, the other day, when he received news of the insurrection in the Low Countries. All those who own lands in the Crimea, such as the Mourzas, and others, like myself, to whom the empress has given estates, have taken an oath of fidelity to her. The emperor came up to me, and taking hold of the ribbon of my Fleece he said: "You are the first of this Order who have ever taken an oath with the long-beard seigneurs." I replied, "It is better for your Majesty, and for me too, that I should be with the Tartar seigneurs than with the Flemish seigneurs just now."

All nations and their greatest personages have been reviewed in that coach, and God knows how they were served. "Rather than sign the separation of thirteen States, as my brother George has done," said Catherine II., softly, "I would have shot myself." "Rather than throw up my power, as my brother-in-law has done by convoking and assembling the nation to talk of abuses," says Joseph II., "I don't know what I would have done." They were quite agreed about the King of Sweden [Gustavus III.], whom neither of them liked, and against whom the emperor had taken a prejudice in Italy on account, so he said, of a blue and silver dressing-gown with a diamond badge that the king wore. They both agreed, however, that he had energy, talent, and intellect. "Yes, undoubtedly," I said, defending him, because the kindness he has always shown me and the fine characteristics I have seen him display attach me to him. "Your majesty ought to prevent the shameful libel of treating as a Don Quixote a prince endowed with genius, who is good and lovable."

Their imperial Majesties felt each other now and then about these poor devils of Turks. They threw out suggestions and glanced at each other. As a lover of glorious antiquity (and of novelty as well) I talked about restoring the Greeks; Catherine of reviving the Solons and Lycurguses; I enlarged on Alcibiades; but Joseph II., who was more for the future than the past, and for the practical instead of the chimerical, only said: "What the devil should we do with Constantinople?" In this way isles and provinces were taken with ease as if it were all a mere nothing; but I said to myself: "Your Majesties will never get anything but trifles — and troubles."

"We treat him too well," said the emperor, one day, speaking of me. "Do you know, Madame, that he was in love with my father's mistress, and prevented me from succeeding with a marquise, lovely as an angel, who was the first passion of both of us?" There was no reserve between these two great sovereigns. "Tell me, did no one ever attempt your life?" — "I have been threatened." — "As for me, I receive many anonymous letters." — "Now this is a real confession that I am making to you, — charming details unknown to all the world," etc.

The empress said to us one day in her galley: "How do people make verses? Write it down for me, M. le Comte de Ségur." He wrote down the rules, adding some charming examples, with which she went to work. She made six lines, so full of faults that we laughed, all three of us. She said to me: "To teach you to laugh at me, make some directly, yourself. I shall not try any more; I am disgusted with it for the rest of my life." "That is right," said Fitz Herbert, "you had better keep to the couplet you wrote on the tomb of your little dog: —

"'Here lies Duchess Anderson
Who bit Monsieur Rogerson.'"

But the matter came back into her head at Barczisarai. "Ah! messieurs," she said to us, "I intend to shut myself into my own room, and you will see!" This is what she brought back to us, saying she could get no farther: —

"Sur le sopha du khan, sur des coussins bourrés,
Dans un kiosque d'or, de grilles entourés —"

[On the sofa of the khan, on the cushions downy,
In a golden kiosk, with lattices around me —]

You can imagine how we reproached her for not having got beyond *that*, after four hours of reflection, and so fine a beginning. Nothing is forborne in travelling.

This country is assuredly a land of romance, but it is not romantic, for the women are locked up by these villanous Mahometans, who never read Ségur's ode on the happiness of being deceived by a wife. The Duchesse de Luxembourg would turn my head if she were at Achmeczet, and I should write a song on the Maréchale de Mouchy if she lived in Balaklava. There is none but you, dear marquise, to be adored when in Paris — *adored* is the word, for there is no time to love there.

There are various sects of dervishes here, each more amusing than the others, called *Twirlers* and *Howlers;* they are Jansenists, as crazy as the old convulsionaries. They shout, "Allah!" and twirl, until, their strength being exhausted, they fall to the ground, hoping not to rise again till they enter heaven. To-morrow I am going to leave the Court to its pleasures for a few days, and ascend and descend on the other side the Tchatirdagh at the risk of my life, following the craggy bed of the torrents, in default of roads, of which there are none. I need to rest my mind, my tongue, my ears, and my eyes from the glare of illuminations. All night they rival the sun, which is only too hot on our heads all day. None but you, dear marquise, know how to be brilliant without fatiguing; I grant that gift to no one else — not even to the stars.

II.

1786–1787.

THE JOURNEY TO THE CRIMEA.

To Mme. la Marquise de Coigny.

PARTHENIZZA.

I send you, dear marquise, after copying it for you neatly, what I wrote on the spot in pencil at Parthenizza: —

'T is on the silvery shores of the Euxine, on the banks of its widest brook, down which pour the torrents of the Tchatirdagh, 't is beneath the shade of two great walnut-trees old as the world itself, at the foot of a rock on which still stands a column, sad relic of the Temple of Diana so famous for the sacrifice of Iphigenia, to the left of the rock whence Thoas hurled strangers — it is, in short, in the most beautiful and most interesting region of all the world that I write these words.

I am seated on cushions on a Turkey carpet, surrounded by Tartars, who are watching me while I write and casting up their eyes in admiration, as though I were another Mahomet. I see before me the favoured shores of ancient Idalia and the coasts of Anatolia. The fig-trees, palm-trees, the olive, cherry, apricot, and peach trees, all in bloom, shed the sweetest perfumes round me, and shade me from the rays of the sun; the waves of the sea are rolling to my feet their diamond pebbles. Behind me I see, amid the leafage, an amphitheatre of dwellings, those of my Tartar savages, who are smoking on their flat roofs, which they use for salons. I see their cemetery, the site of which, always chosen for the purpose by Mahometans, reminds me of the Champs-Élysées. This particular cemetery lies along the bank of the brook I mentioned; but just where the rocks and pebbles obstruct its course the brook widens a little on one side, flowing peacefully among the fruit-trees, which give to the dead their hospitable shade. This tranquil resting-place is marked by stones surmounted by turbans, some of which are gilded, and by cinerary urns, coarsely cut in marble. The variety of all these sights induces thought and disinclines me for writing. I fling myself back on my carpet and reflect —

No, what is passing in my soul cannot be conceived; I feel myself another being. Escaping from grandeur, from the tumult of *fêtes*, the fatigue of pleasures, and the two imperial Majesties of the North and West (whom I have left on the other side of the mountains), at last I possess my own self. I ask myself where I am, by what good chance I am here, and then, without my intending it, a recapitulation of all the inconsistencies of my life passes through my mind. I perceive that, being unable to be happy except in tranquillity and independence, which are in my power, and inclined by nature to laziness of body and mind, I have, all my life, agitated the first incessantly by wars, inspection of troops, and travels; while the second I have wasted upon persons who are not worth it. Gay enough within me, I must needs fatigue myself to be so for others who are not gay. I ask myself why, not liking restraint, or caring for honours, money, or favours, having enough of all to make little account of any, *why* I have, nevertheless, spent my life at all the Courts of Europe. Well, I remember that the paternal sort of kindness of the Emperor Francis I., who was fond of heedless young men, was what attached me first to him. Loved by one of his ladies, I stayed on at the Court, but I never lost that sovereign's good-will. At his death, in 1765, I thought myself, though still very young [æt. 30] a seigneur of the old Court, and was about to criticise the new one without knowing anything of it, when I discovered that the new emperor, Joseph II., was just as amiable and had qualities that made me desire his esteem more than his favour. Certain that he never liked to show preference, I could follow the bent of my inclination towards him; and while I blamed the too great rapidity of his operations, I admired three-fourths of them, and I always maintained the good intentions of his genius — as active as it was fruitful.

Sent to the Court of France in its brilliant period, to carry brilliant news, that of a battle won [Maxen, 1759], I never wished to return to that Court. Chance brought the Comte d'Artois to a garrison in the neighbourhood of another where I happened to be inspecting troops [1774]. He wanted me to go and see him at Versailles. I said no, I would see him in Paris. He insisted; spoke to me of the queen, our own archduchess, who, not long after, sent me a command to go to her Court. The charms of her face and of her soul, the one as white and beautiful as the other, and the attraction of that society made me henceforth spend five months of every year in her suite, without absenting myself for a day. Thus, idle amusement took me to Versailles; gratitude made me return there.

Prince Henry [of Prussia, brother of Frederick the Great] was visiting the battlefields. Philosophy and military instruction having brought us together, I accompanied him. I had the good fortune to suit him. Much kindness on his part, assiduity on mine; close correspondence, and rendezvous at Spa and Reinsberg. A camp of the emperor at Neustadt in Moravia attracted the then King of Prussia [Frederick the Great] and the present one. The former observed my admiration for great men and invited me to Berlin. My relations with him there, and the marks of esteem and kindness given to me by that first of heroes crowned me with glory. I escaped the cordial invitations of the two other kings of the North; the weak brains of the one having turned the too lively brains of the other in time to save me from the insipid amusements promised to me at Copenhagen and Stockholm. I was quit of them by giving *fêtes* to one king and receiving them from the other.

My son Charles married a pretty little Polish girl [in 1779]. Her family gave us paper in place of ready money; claims upon the Court of Russia. On my return thence I made myself, and was made a Pole at the Diet in Warsaw. A fool of a bishop (who has since been hanged), uncle of my daughter-in-law, took into his head that I was *au mieux* with the empress, because he heard she treated me well, and he persuaded himself that I should be King of Poland if I were naturalized. "What a change," he cried, "of the face of Europe! What happiness for the Lignes and the Massalskis!" I laughed at him. Nevertheless, I had a fancy to please that nation, then assembled for its Diet. I talked Latin; the nation applauded me; I embraced their moustachios; I intrigued for the king, Stanislas Poniatowski, who is himself an intriguer, like all kings who stay upon their thrones on condition only of doing the will of their neighbours and subjects. He was kind, amiable, and attractive; I gave him advice; and there I was, bound to him.

When I went to Russia the first thing I did was to forget what I went for, because it seemed to me indelicate to profit by the favour with which I was received to press a claim. The confiding and fascinating simplicity of Catherine the Great captivated me; and it is her genius which has now made me follow her to this enchanting spot.

I let my eyes wander over it; I allow my mind to rest: has it not just proved to me, by retracing the chain of circumstances which has always led me to do what I did not will to do, that I have no head?

The night will be delicious. The sea, tired with its motion through the day, is now so calm that 't is like a mirror; in it I see myself, to the depths of my heart. This evening hour is wonderful; I feel in my ideas the same clear light that reigns on sea and sky. Why — I say to myself — why am I now meditating on the beauties of it instead of enjoying the sweet repose of sleep, of which I am an idolater? Because I fancy that this region inspires me; that amid so many enchantments a thought may come to me that will do a good or give a pleasure to others.

Perhaps it was here that Ovid wrote; perhaps he sat where I sit now. His elegies were from Ponte, and there lies the Euxine. Certainly this shore belonged to Mithridates, King of Pontus, and as Ovid's place of exile is uncertain I have more right to believe it was here than, as the Transylvanians assert, at Caramischedes. Their claim rests solely on the words *Cara mia sedes*, the corrupt pronunciation of which they imagine makes the name I have quoted. Yes, this is Parthenizza; the Tartar accent having thus transformed the old Greek name, Parthenion, which means virgin. This is the famous Cape Parthenion, where so many things have happened; it is here that mythology exalts the imagination. All the talents in the service of the gods of fable have exercised their empire here. If I quit, for an instant, fable for history I discover Eupatoria, founded by Mithridates; near-by, in Kherson, I pick up fragments of alabaster columns, I find the remains of aqueducts, and city walls inclosing a greater space than Paris and London put together. Those two cities will pass away like these; in all, the same intrigues of love and politics; each believing that it makes a vast sensation in the world, while the very name of this land that these lost cities stood on, disfigured now into Tartary and Crimea, is passing to oblivion: a fine reflection for the self-important.

Turning round, I see my good Mussulmans on their roofs with feet and arms crossed, and I applaud their laziness. I find among them an Albanian who knows a little Italian. I tell him to ask them if they are happy, and if I can be of use to them; also, whether they know that the empress has given them to me. They make answer that they know in general that they have been parcelled out, but they do not wholly understand what it means; that they are happy now, and if they cease to be so they shall embark on the two vessels they have built for themselves and take refuge with the Turks in Roumania. I reply that I like lazy people, but that I wish to know on what they subsist. They point to a few sheep lying, like myself, on the grass. I bless the lazy. They show me their fruit-trees, and say that when the gathering season comes the kaimakan comes round from Barczisarai and takes half; each family sells two hundred francs' worth a year, and there are forty-six families in Parthenizza and Nikita, another little property now belonging to me, the Greek name signifying victory. I bless the lazy. I promise to prevent their being harassed. They bring me butter, cheese, and milk — not mares' milk, as it is among the Tartars. I bless the lazy, and return to my meditations.

Once more, what am I doing here? Am I a Turkish prisoner? Have I been cast upon this coast by shipwreck? Am I exiled, like Ovid, by some Court, or by my passions? I search, and say: Why, not at all! After my children, and two or three women whom I love, or think I love, to

Stanislas Poniatowski
King of Poland

madness, it is my gardens which give me the greatest pleasure in life; there are few as fine. I delight in working to make them still more beautiful. I am scarcely ever in them; I have never been there in the early flowering season, when all the little forests of rare shrubs are perfuming the air. I am two thousand leagues from all that now. Possessor of lands on the Northern Ocean, I am here in other lands, also mine, on the shores of the Euxine. A letter from the empress reached me from a distance of eight hundred leagues. She remembered our conversations on the noble ages of antiquity and she proposed to me to accompany her to this land of enchantment, this Taurica, to which she restores the name, and, in favour of my taste for Iphigenias she bestows upon me the site of Dian's temple, where the daughter of Agamemnon was priestess.

Forgetting at last all thrones, dominations, and powers, I suddenly experience one of those delightful annihilations that I love so much, when the mind rests absolutely, when we scarcely know that we exist. What is the soul doing then? I do not know; one thing is certain, its activity is suspended; but it has the enjoyment and the consciousness of its rest.

After that, I make plans. *Blasé* as to nearly all known things, why not settle myself here? I will convert my Tartar Mussulmans to the juice of the vine; I will give my dwelling the look of a palace, to be seen from afar by navigators. I will build eight houses for vintagers, with columns, and balustrades to hide the roofs. I planned a plan which would have been executed incontinently were it not for the war to which our festal trip gave rise.

What a pity — I say to myself, lying here — that the bigotry of the Greek religion has destroyed the noble remains of the worship of the gods, so favourable as it is to the imagination. However, these fine sites do still rejoice the eye with their white minarets, their tall, slim chimneys, shaped like needles, a species of Eastern architecture which gives its dainty style even to the humblest hut. My reflections which remind me of the ravages of time make me also think of my own losses. It occurs to me that nothing here below remains in a state of perfect stagnation; unless an empire enlarges, it diminishes, just as the day when we do not love more, we love less — What word was that I said? Love! Ah! — I burst into tears; I know not why; but they are sweet, — an overflowing of sensibility, though unable to determine its object. At this moment, when so many ideas are crossing one another in my mind, I weep without being sorrowful; but alas! — I say to myself as though I were addressing certain persons of whom I often think — perhaps I am sad, perhaps you are sad, because we are parted by seas, deserts, remorse, relatives, meddlers, prejudices. Perhaps I am sad for you who have loved me and never told me; whom I have left because I never divined your love. Superstitious slaves of duty, perhaps I am sad for you. The love of poesy, of the fields, our readings, our saunterings, a thousand secret bonds may have united us, although we never knew it.

My tears will not be stanched. Is it the presentiment of some heart-rending loss that I shall some day suffer? I put that fearful thought away from me; I pray to God, and say: This vague melancholy, like that we feel in youth, does it not foretell me some celestial object, worthy of my worship, which will forever fix my way in life? It seems to me as though the Future desires to unveil herself to me. Enthusiasm, exaltation are so nearly allied to the power of interpreting oracles.

Thus did the picture of my past and present and future

loves paint itself in my memory. Would that I could so recall the recollections of friendship! I have had friends, more than other men, because, having no pretensions to anything of any kind, my history is in no way extraordinary, and my merits are not alarming. Everywhere I meet the social friends with whom one sups and trifles daily, but have I ever found one who cares for me enough to make me feel the obligation? Earnestly do I desire to have that obligation to others; some have had it to me, and though they little felt it, I still had the pleasure from time to time of making them ungrateful. The fear of being ungrateful myself makes me often prefer the contrary extreme. A little insincerity in that line seems to me very pardonable. Without weeping over humanity, without loving or hating men too much (it is fatiguing to hate), I am not more satisfied with mankind than I am with myself. In examining myself I find but one good quality, — that of being very glad of the good that comes to others.

I judge the world; I watch it like the slides of a magic-lantern while awaiting the moment when the scythe of time shall lay me low. Nine or ten campaigns already made, a dozen battles or encounters seen from time to time, flit past me like a dream. I think of the nothingness of glory; ignored, forgotten, envied, attacked, revoked; yet a part of my life — I say to myself — is spent in seeking to lose it (that life) in chasing glory. I say nothing against my valour; that is brilliant enough, no doubt; but I do not think it is pure enough; there is clap-trap in it; I play too much to the gallery. I prefer the valour of my dear good Charles, who never looks about him to see if he is being looked at. When I examine myself further, I see a score of faults.— And next I think of the nothingness of ambition. Death has deprived me, or will soon deprive me, of the favour of several great soldiers and great sovereigns. Caprice, inconstancy, malignity may make me lose all hopes; intrigue, if it parts me from my soldiers, may cause them to forget me. But here, *here*, without regrets for the past or fears for the future I let my existence float upon the current of my destiny. I laugh at my paltry merit and my various adventures at Court and with the army; I am glad I am no worse than I am; and I congratulate myself especially on the great talent of making the best of everything for my own contentment.

Child of nature, and perhaps her spoilt child, I see myself as I am in the glassy calm of that vast sea which reflects my soul as a mirror reflects the features of a face. Already the veil of night is beginning to obscure the day; the sun is awaited on the horizon of another hemisphere. The sheep which browse about my Turkish carpet bleat to their Tartar masters, who gravely descend from their roofs and shut them up with their women, whom they have kept concealed the livelong day. The criers are calling to the mosque from the tops of their minarets. With my left hand I feel for the beard I have not; my right hand I lay upon my breast; I bless the lazy, and I leave them, as much astonished to see me their master as to hear that I wish them to be always their own.

I collect my wits, which have been so scattered; I gather together, as best I can, my incoherent thoughts; I look about me with emotion on these beautiful scenes, which I may never see again and which have caused me to spend the most delightful day of all my life. A fresh breeze, springing suddenly up, decides me against the boat, which was to take me round by sea to Theodosia. I mount a Tartar horse, and, preceded by my guide, I plunge once more into the horrors of the night, the road, the torrents, and recross the famous mountains to rejoin, at the end of forty-eight hours, their imperial Majesties at Kara-su-Bazaar.

Oh, Parthenizza! witching spot! you have recalled me to my true self. Parthenizza! never will you leave my memory.

To the Same.

FROM KARA-SU-BAZAAR.

I have quitted meditation, and return to active life. I found on arriving here fresh subjects for admiration; but before describing them, Madame la marquise, I wish to say a word to you about fidelity. Do not be alarmed by that word — it does not relate to you or me. It concerns a Tartar barbarian to whom I was confided for my trip in spite of the bad reputation and evil looks of those fellows. He would perhaps have robbed and beaten me had he met me, but as I was confided to his care he was ready to sacrifice his life to defend me. I escaped out of his sight for a few moments, while carving on a rock about thirty paces from the sea a name most dear to my heart; he looked about for me everywhere, and, believing me murdered, he was about to set fire to the adjoining village while waiting to know positively what had become of me.

On my return trip (in charge of my constable) I thought I was dreaming when I saw a house in the midst of an odoriferous desert, flat and green as a billiard-table. I thought still more I was deluded when I found it white, clean, and surrounded with cultivated ground, half orchard half vegetable-garden, through which ran the purest and most rapid of brooks. But I was far more surprised when from the doorway issued two celestial figures dressed in white, who proposed to me to seat myself at a table covered with flowers, on which were butter and cream. I bethought me of the breakfasts I had read of in English novels. These were the daughters of a rich farmer whom the Russian minister in England had sent to Prince Potemkin, to make attempts at agriculture in Taurica.

I now return to admirations and marvels. We find the seaports, armies, and fleets in the finest condition. Kherson and Sevastopol surpass all that can be said of them. Each day is marked with some great event. Sometimes a cloud of Cossacks from the shores of the Tanaïs [the Don] manœuvre around us after their fashion; sometimes the Tartars of the Crimea, faithless formerly to their khan, Sahem-Guerci, because he wished to train them into a regiment, have themselves formed a corps to meet the empress. We have crossed during many days vast, solitary regions, from which her Majesty has driven Zaporogua, Budjak, and Nogais Tartars, who, ten years ago, threatened to ravage her empire. All these places were furnished with magnificent tents for breakfasts, lunches, dinners, suppers, and sleeping-rooms; these encampments, decorated with Asiatic splendour, presented a most military spectacle. Deserted regions were at once transformed into fields, groves, villages; already they are inhabited by regiments, but they will soon be the home of peasants, attracted to them by the excellence of the soil. The empress has left in each chief town gifts to the value of a hundred thousand roubles. Every day that we remained stationary was marked with gifts of diamonds, balls, fireworks, and illuminations throughout a circuit of ten leagues. Forests on fire would appear upon the mountains, then the burning bushes, gradually coming nearer, were turned into vast pyres.

One other little remark about the countries we are crossing. The subjects of this empire, whom those of other nations are kind enough to pity so often, care nothing for your States-general; they request philosophers not to enlighten them, and the great lords not to permit them to hunt upon their lands. In spite of their quibbles about the Holy Spirit, they are not ill-treated by it, and are more intelligent than people think. They feel a need to kiss the hands of their popes, and prostrate themselves before their sovereign to show submission. In other respects they are slaves only in being restrained from doing harm to themselves or others; they are free to enrich themselves, which they do often, as may be seen by the splendour of the costumes of the different provinces. The empress, who is not afraid of seeming to be governed, gives to those whom she employs full authority and her utmost confidence; she denies no right, except that of doing evil. She justifies her magnificence on the ground that by giving money she obtains a large return. She justifies the great number of offices she has created in her provinces by declaring that in that way specie is made to circulate, fortunes are increased, and the seigneurs are compelled to stay on their estates, instead of flocking to Moscow or Petersburg. If she has built in stone two hundred and thirty-seven towns, it is, she says, because villages built of wood are always burning and costing her a great deal. If she has created a splendid fleet in the Black Sea, it is because Peter the Great loved the navy. She has always some such modest excuse for the great things which she does. No one has any idea what a pleasure there is in accompanying her.

Adieu, dear marquise. Already I hear millions of Allahs echoed to the Orient by the worthy Mussulmans for our safe return. One learns to howl with them, in time, and I catch myself occasionally invoking Mahomet like the rest. May he shed upon your lovely face the dew of his benedictions, that it may ever be as fresh as the flowers of dawn.

To the Same.

KAFFA, THE ANCIENT THEODOSIA.

The charm still lasts, but it nears its end. This is a great city, remarkable for its mosques, baths, ancient temples, old commercial marts, and harbour, — in short, for the remains of a grandeur which is about to be restored.

I entered several of the cafés and several shops. I saw foreigners from distant lands: Greeks, Turks from Asia Minor, manufacturers of weapons from Persia and the Caucasus. There are no civil people, I said to myself as I watched them, but the peoples who are not civilized. They all assume a gentle air, which is more or less respectful, when they meet. Their language is noble, like Greek or Spanish; it has neither the hiss, nor the coarseness, nor the drawl, nor the sing-song, nor the vulgarity of the European languages. A Tartar would be much astonished, on arriving at the city of urbanity and grace *par excellence*, to hear the coachmen on the boulevard talking to their horses, or the dames of the Market conversing with their neighbours. And what a contrast between the insolence, avarice, and filth of the nations of Europe and the friendly good-humour and cleanliness of this people! Nothing is done without being preceded and followed by libations. The libation with which the barbers regale their customers is a little extraordinary; they take their heads between their knees and let the water of a fountain flow over them.

I have seen but one woman, and she was a princess of the blood, the niece of the last khan, Sahem-Guerei. The empress, before whom she unveiled, hid me behind a screen. She was beautiful as the day, and wore more diamonds than all our women in Vienna put together, and that is saying a good deal. Otherwise I have seen no female faces but those of a battalion of Albanian women, from a little Macedonian colony established at Balaklava: two hundred pretty women or girls, with muskets, bayonets, and lances, with Amazonian breasts and long hair braided gracefully, who came to meet us, to do us honour and not from curiosity. There are no gapers in this country; gaping belongs, with impertinence and flattery, to civilization. No one has either run after us or run away from us. They look at us with indifference, not disdain, and even with a sort of benevolence, when we stop to ask questions.

If the monks were not beginning to be persecuted (the result of tolerance in the philosophical countries), I should say thank God there are no mendicants or capuchins in these lands. The worst bed of the poorest Tartar (none of whom ever ask or ever want charity) is a fairly handsome Turkish carpet with cushions, spread upon a wide board. The new population of this superb amphitheatre on the shores of the Black Sea, will be a very happy one; the former inhabitants who lived in the neighbourhood of the salt marshes were constantly exposed to the plague. If ennui, which insensibly invades society through the wits and the gifted women who have entered it, if this ennui, I say, becomes too great in Paris, even in your salon, escape, dear marquise, and come here; I will receive you better than my predecessor Thoas.

To the Same.

TULA.

Alas! here we are on our way back. Do you know that I was on the point of loving you in Asia, and of writing to you from Azov? A cursèd prudence of doctors and ministers (in neither of whom does the empress believe) prevented our leaving Europe — if what we have lately seen can be called Europe, for it resembles it little enough. I know it is not the fashion to believe travellers, or courtiers, or any good told of Russia. Even those Russians who are vexed at not having come with us pretend that we are deceived, and deceiving. They have already spread about the ridiculous story that cardboard villages were set up along the line of our route for hundreds of miles; that the vessels and cannons were painted images, the cavalry horseless, and so forth.

For the last two months I have been throwing money out of window; this has happened to me before, but never in precisely the present way. I have already distributed, it may be, millions, and this is how it is done. Beside me, in the carriage, is a great green bag, like the one you will put your prayer-books in when you become devout. This bag is filled with imperials — coins of four ducats [a gold ducat, two dollars]. The inhabitants of the villages and those from ten, fifteen, and twenty leagues round line our route to see the empress, and this is how they see her. A good quarter of an hour before she passes, they lie down flat on their stomachs and do not rise for a quarter of an hour after we have passed. 'T is on their backs and on their heads kissing the earth that I shower a rain of gold while passing at full gallop, and this usually happens ten times a day; my hands are soiled with my beneficence. I have become the grand-almoner of all the Russias. He of France throws money also through his window, but it is his own.

I know very well what is trickery: for example, the empress, who cannot rush about on foot as we do, is made to believe that certain towns for which she has given money are finished; whereas they are often towns without streets, streets without houses, and houses without roofs, doors, or windows. Nothing is shown to the empress but shops that are well-built of stone, colonnades of the palaces of governors-general, to forty-two of which she has presented silver services of a hundred covers. In the capitals of the provinces they often give us balls and suppers for two hundred persons. The furs and gold chains of the wives of the merchants, and the sort of grenadier-caps the people wear adorned with pearls show wealth. The costumes of the gentlemen and ladies in these vast halls are a fine sight. The provinces of the East wear brown and gold and silver; the others red and sky-blue.

In this place [Tula, still famous for mathematical instruments and cutlery of all kinds] is one of the finest manufactories of arms that can be seen anywhere; besides this, they work in steel nearly as well as they do in England. I am loaded with presents that I do not know what to do with. The empress buys everything, to give away and at the same time to encourage manufacture. I have a stool, an umbrella, a table, a cane, a damascened dressing-case; all of which are very useful to me, as you may suppose, and very convenient to carry about.

"See," says the empress to me sometimes, pointing to fields in the governments of Karskoff and Kursh as well cultivated as in England, with a population almost as numerous, "see how the Abbé Chappe[1] never *saw* anything through the wooden windows of his carriage, closed on account of cold; and how wrong he was in saying that there were 'nothing but deserts in Russia.' I will not warrant that some village seigneur, abusing his power (which might happen anywhere), may not have produced, whip in hand, the cries of joy to drown the cries of misery. But as soon as such seigneurs are complained of to the governors of the provinces, they are punished; and certainly the hurrahs we have heard along our route were shouted heartily and with very smiling faces.

[1] Inventor of aerial telegraphy. His first attempt was made in 1793.

As I have quitted the empress from time to time and made various trips, I have seen many things that the Russians themselves do not know: superb establishments in process of building, manufactories, villages well built, streets laid out in lines, surrounded by trees, and watered by brooks. All that I tell you is true; because, in the first place, I never tell lies except to women who are not like you; and next, because no one here reads my letters. Besides, we never flatter people whom we see from six in the morning till ten at night; on the contrary, one is sometimes out of temper with them in a carriage. . . . I remember one day we were talking of courage, and the empress said to me: "If I had been a man I should have been killed before I was a captain." I answered, "I think not, Madame, for I still live." I noticed that after taking some time to understand what I meant, she laughed softly to herself on perceiving that I had corrected her for thinking herself more brave than I and so many others. Another time I was disputing with her very seriously about the Court of France; and as she seemed to be putting faith in certain pamphlets that were being circulated in foreign countries, I said to her almost sharply: "Madame, they lie at the North about the West, and at the West about the North; we should no more believe the sedan-bearers of Versailles than your isvostchiks in Petersburg."

We look upon the rest of our journey as a trifle; unhappily, we have only four hundred leagues more to do. We have required throughout six hundred horses for each relay. All the carriages are filled with peaches and oranges; our valets are drunk with champagne, and I am dying with hunger, for everything is cold and detestable at the empress's table. She never sits there long, and if she has anything agreeable or useful to say she does it so slowly that nothing is hot except the water we drink. One of the charms of this country is that the summers are more scorching than they are in Provence. In the Crimea I came near suffocating from the fumes of the brazier one breathes. Another charm of the country is that we get no news of your little Europe from any of you. I do not believe my letters reach you; and I shall receive none from you if, as I hope, war will be declared one of these days with the good Mahometans. I am in haste to fight, my dear marquise, that I may see you all the sooner; meantime I adore you as a divinity without seeing you.

To the Same.

MOSCOW.

Here is one more letter. This city, which gives me in some respects an idea of Ispahan, looks as if five or six hundred country châteaus' of great lords had come, on rollers, with their villages, to unite and live together. Look in the geographies, dictionaries, and books of travel for all that relates to Moscow and say I wrote it to you. What you will not find there is that the greatest seigneurs of the empire, tired of the Court, are living here, finding fault and growling at their ease. The empress only knows of this in bulk and does not want to hear of it in detail; she does not like the police and their system of domestic spying. "What do you think of these gentlemen?" she said to me. "Fine ruins," I replied, looking at three or four former grand-chamberlains, generals-in-chief, etc. "They do not like me much," she said, "I am not the fashion in Moscow. Perhaps I was wrong towards some of them; there may have been misunderstandings."

The empress was no longer Cleopatra at Alexandria; besides, Cæsar had left us and gone home. Romance had disappeared and left the sad reality. Alexis Orloff had the courage to tell her Imperial Majesty that famine had appeared in several of the provinces. The *fêtes* were stopped. Beneficence displaced magnificence; luxury yielded to necessity. No more money was thrown, it was now distributed. The torrents of champagne ceased flowing; thousands of bread-carts succeeded the boat-loads of oranges. A cloud obscured for a moment the august and serene brow of CATHERINE THE GREAT: she shut herself up with two of her ministers, and only recovered her gayety as she got into the carriage.

If you knew our archbishop you would love him distractedly, and he would return your love. He is named Plato, and is worth much more than the other, whom they call divine. What proves to me that this one is Plato the *human* is that yesterday, when leaving his garden, Princess Galitzin asked him for his blessing, and he gathered a rose, with which he gave it to her.

If I were a La Rochefoucauld or an Albon, or even a young man of the Court, for they are beginning to be learned, I would tell you of the culture of the soil and the finances of the empire; but I have not the honour of understanding such matters. Oh! as to finances, I do know something of those; I know that for sturgeon of the Volga, veal of Archangel, fruits of Astrakan, ices, confectionery, and wine of Constantia I have paid to the crown enormous sums.

Ask pardon for me of your pedants, the enemies of abuses; I am now an abuse of this country and I find myself all the better for it, and others too. Our abuses in the good and true monarchies are of great benefit to the many; suppress them and you will see the Pugatcheffs[1] revive. May

[1] Pugatcheff: the leader of a rebellion which threatened to be a revolution in Russia.

Heaven preserve you from that! but you are rushing towards it with great strides. It might perhaps have been better never to have taken M. de Calonne; but he ought certainly to have been allowed to finish what he began. An able man, who knows what he is talking about, said to me the other day that the Deficit which had turned, very inopportunely, the head of your good king, was a mere washerwoman's bill, to be paid in a week if desired. Had society never sounded that tocsin against the Court, had the queen never pardoned those pretty little Parisians for screaming against her when she did not get them a bishopric or a regiment for their lovers, the dangerous and ridiculous discontent of the present moment would never have come about.

It seems to me now as though I were to see you tomorrow or the day after. I have already come eighteen hundred leagues nearer to you; there are but twelve hundred more to reach you. Therefore, *au plaisir de vous revoir*, dear marquise, or, to write you from Constantinople, should these affairs continue to embroil themselves. I say nothing about the state of my heart. Yours is a lottery; I have put into it, and I have paid for my tickets in ready-money; on one is written "admiration," on another "adoration," on the third "joy of my life."

I really think I am beginning to be a trifle *précieux;* and that is neither in your style nor in mine. This certainly has an air of the map of the Pays du Tendre, but we should lose ourselves, you and I, in that country. All hail this land if we were here together. It is better to be Tartarian than barbarous, and that is what you are very often to your adoring Court. Remember him who is most worthy to belong to it; though lovers are always oppressive; those in good faith are too interesting; those who play at love are too interested. I like my condition of foreigner everywhere;

Frenchman in Austria, Austrian in France, and Russian in all countries. That is the way to succeed and to make one's self happy.

The moment has come to quit fable for history, the East for the North. I keep the South in my heart for you—what think you of that piquant little fancy? It has at least the merit of being truthful.

III.

1787–1788.

THE WAR OF RUSSIA AND AUSTRIA AGAINST TURKEY.

[WAR between Russia and Turkey was declared in the autumn of 1787, the Porte being the aggressor by imprisoning the Russian ambassador. A secret agreement had been entered into by the empress and Joseph II. during the Crimean journey; but the Prince de Ligne, believing that the emperor would be slow in declaring war on his side, asked and obtained permission to serve meantime as general in the Russian army under Prince Potemkin, with the additional duty of keeping the emperor informed of the movements of his allies. He joined that army then encamped at Elisabeth-Gorod, north of Kherson, in November, 1787, the fortress of Oczakow being to the south, at the mouth of the Dnieper, where it falls into the Black Sea. He soon became discouraged at the lethargic conduct of the war; and after fretting over it for more than a year he secretly requested the emperor to recall him. During the campaign of 1789 he was second in command of the Austrian army under the emperor and Maréchal de Lacy, and to him was owing, in a great measure, the taking of Belgrade.

The story of this war is given chiefly in the letters that he wrote to Joseph II. during his campaign with Prince Potemkin. In his own narrative prefacing those letters he gives a fuller account than that contained in the letters to

Mme. de Coigny of the origin of the war, and of how the emperor was enticed and persuaded to take part in it. A series of letters to Comte Louis-Philippe de Ségur, French ambassador at Petersburg, contain (vol. vii. of his Works) a more lively and personal account of the prince's stay with Potemkin than is given in his letters to the emperor (vol. xxiv.).

The Prince de Ligne's eldest son, Charles, served with the emperor during the campaign of 1788, and distinguished himself greatly at the taking of Sabacz. After the death of the emperor in February, 1790, he joined the Russian army then operating on the Danube under Maréchal Suvaroff, and again distinguished himself at the taking of Ismaïl. After the death of Joseph II., the Prince de Ligne returned to the Low Countries, then in revolt against Austria under the influence of the French Revolution. He was the hereditary Seneschal or Governor of the province of Hainault, of which Mons is the capital town, Belœil being within a short distance of it.]

Nothing in the way of relation can have a greater stamp of truth than what I shall here say about the campaign of 1788 against the Turks. My letters to Joseph II. are themselves its history. They need only to be sewn together, with preambles and a few portraits and anecdotes, to make them a very interesting whole.

The enemies of Prince Potemkin had assured his sovereign that her army was only on paper; they even denied the existence of the light-horse cavalry. So that when, on the Borysthenes, fifty or sixty squadrons galloped to meet her all glittering with silver and steel, she was amazed at the sight. She said to me: "Those wicked people! how they tried to deceive me! Why, *there* is enough to snap our fingers at the Turks." Then, looking at the portrait of Peter I. as usual, she said, with an air that dictated my answer, "What would he say? what would he do?" It will not be doubted that my desire to please and to make war inspired my reply. "But the French?" she said. "They have just made their public confession," I answered, "in that Deficit which Necker has announced to the Notables. Poor devils! they may perhaps have a revolution. Besides, M. de Vergennes is dead, and the Archbishop of Toulouse, whom they talk of as the next prime minister, has no house of business of his own in Constantinople." "But the Prussians?" she said. "Let us make haste," I replied; "the emperor can take Belgrade, and your Majesty Oczakow, Bender, and Akermann before King William knows that there is any question of war."

Prince Potemkin, who was dying to command an army in order to get the grand cordon of Saint George, talked to me incessantly about the war. The emperor arrived at Kherson in my carriage, which I had sent for him, and said to me the next day: "It seems to me these people want war. Are they ready? I don't think they are; and, in any case, I am not. And what do they expect to get? I have just seen their fleets and their fortresses, and they are only sketched out to throw dust in one's eyes. Nothing is solid; it has all been done in a hurry, and very expensively, to humbug the empress." I, who did not see so accurately as he, and was dazzled by the passing of so much artillery and such superb regiments and by what I was told of magazines and munitions, assured him that I thought the Russians were ready. What was singular is that the emperor was seduced himself by the same sights, of which he was not the dupe when he saw them alone. The cleverness of showing them again in presence of the empress, the quantity and importance of the military objects presented daily before him, the magic of this journey of six thousand versts, seemed to proclaim a power he blamed himself for having misjudged.

Potemkin thought that the moment had come to explain matters to the emperor. He went to see him one morning and told him about the pretended wrongs the Court of Russia had received from the Porte — which was being insulted constantly by M. de Bulgakoff and a crowd of little scamps of consuls, of whom the Porte complained quite mildly. The emperor answered with generalities, personal attachment to the empress, fidelity to his engagements, and so forth. Prince Potemkin is timid, and easily embarrassed. He did not say all that he wanted to say, so he begged me to speak to the emperor and complete that which he had only begun.

I did not fail to do so. "I don't see exactly what he wants," said his Majesty. "It seems to me that when I do as much as I did in helping them to get the Crimea, that ought to be enough. What would they do for me if I should have war with Prussia some day or other?" "Everything, Sire," I said; "at least they promise it; they even say everything your Majesty may want in this affair." "What I want is Silesia, and war with Turkey will not give me that," he replied. "Well, we'll see; we'll see."

I have related elsewhere all that was done to intoxicate the empress. A cloud of Cossacks from the Don arrived like a whirlwind and enveloped our carriage in the deserts of Perekop. The empress supposed them eight hundred leagues distant. An armament of Tartar guards, all young Mourzas, with splendid figures superbly dressed, appeared as suddenly to escort the empress on her approach to Taurica. And when, close to Inkermann they parted, as if by a fairy wand, into two columns and revealed the fleet of Sevastopol, this final draught of champagne went to her head. She rose suddenly, during dinner, looked at us with fire in her eyes, and said: "I drink to the health of my best friend," motioning to the emperor. Kissing of hand on his part. Embrace on hers. Great hopes of war in me and the Prince of Nassau. Embarrassment in Ségur, fearing to play a poor *rôle* in it all; philosophic indifference in Fitz-Herbert, one of the most amiable of Englishmen; uncertainty in Comte Cobenzl, trying to read in the eyes of the emperor; and great curiosity in all the courtiers.

Prince Potemkin, who had kissed hands also, and made believe weep with joy and gratitude, kept up the salvos of the fleet incessantly, in order to keep our heads turned.

"Do you think," said the empress to me, one day, "that if your dear master, my dear ally, were hindered by some of his neighbours, I could carry on this affair by myself?" "Undoubtedly, Madame," I replied. "But he will want to share your glory, much more than your conquests, for, thank God! we are in need of nothing." "What have you done? what have you done?" cried Cobenzl, to whom I told all this. "Prince Potemkin is too much in a hurry; there are many political considerations to be faced. After that, we may see about it."

"If it were not for France," Potemkin said to me, frequently, "we might begin at once." "So I think," I replied; "but your infantry, cannon, munitions, magazines?" "All ready," he replied; "I have only to say to a hundred thousand men: March!"

"What is this mania of yours," I said to Ségur, "for protecting such ignorant people, and such bad company as those Turks?" "Balance of Europe; justice, for they have given no real cause for complaint, though we are told they have every day; our commerce in Smyrna; the seaports of the Levant, — those are good reasons enough, it seems to me," replied Ségur.

"What are all these romances?" said the emperor, as our journey was nearing its end. "They want to go to Constantinople. What are we to do with Constantinople?" "Make it a Greek republic," I said, laughing. "Don't you remember," said the emperor, "the joke of the late King of Prussia, who wrote to d'Alembert, that the name of Constantine given to a little grand-duke meant that they would seat his little person on the throne of Constantine? That has not put an end to the project," he added. "But you may believe me that when we get there and have to take it, they will be more embarrassed than I. However, that woman is lucky." See how cabinets and cafés deceive themselves! They and the world at large imagine wiliness and diplomacy in everything and judge the actors wrongly. The meeting of the King of Poland with the empress, and hers with the Emperor of Austria, passed exactly as I have related them.

Catherine again showed me the portrait of Peter the Great on her snuffbox, and said: "What would he say? what would he do?" "He would atone," I said, "for his horrible capitulation on the Pruth." Thus it was that I contributed, without suspecting the result, to the harm that has been done. Thus the gallantry of Ségur, the piquant indifference of Fitz-Herbert, which only made his little praise the more delicate, the flattery of some, the sycophancy of others, intoxicated this great princess. It only proves the undesirableness of women upon thrones, even more than in society. Homage is so lavished upon them that they make no distinctions as to its value; they receive it all as sovereigns. The Russian bishops and archbishops, flatterers by profession, awaited the empress at the doors of all the churches, incense, moral and physical, in hand, and told her, in the name of God, that she was invincible, and that her subjects were in great prosperity; the truth being that throughout her empire a frightful famine was raging, and that her infantry, whom Prince Potemkin took good care not to show her, had been so ruined by mismanagement, cheatery, and theft, that it actually did not have the munitions of war.

I was on the point of leaving Petersburg in the middle of July, when the empress told me she was expecting a courier from Constantinople with news of the outbreak of the war, or else of the overthrow of the Grand Vizir. I waited a month longer. War did not come. I was to leave on a Tuesday. Sunday we heard that M. de Bulgakoff [Russian ambassador to the Porte] was in the Seven Towers. I never was so pleased since I came into the world. I went to see her Majesty to congratulate her. What was my astonishment to hear her say: "I shall defend myself, but I can do no more. I am attacked. I shall do the best I can." I could only suppose that Prince Potemkin had written her depressing and alarming letters, as if the Turks were coming to burn Czarsko-zelo, and also that he did not have everything as ready as he had said he had.

The empress asked me what I thought the emperor would do. "Can you doubt, Madame," I said, "that he will promptly send you his good wishes, and perhaps his troops? but as the former are more portative than the latter, I think his letter will come first." In fact I so little expected the troops to arrive promptly that after committing many a folly in my life I now committed a stupidity: namely, that of requesting his Majesty, Joseph II., to allow me to be employed for him in the Russian army, and to correspond with him from there, in order that plans for the campaign, the concordance of the two empires and the various enterprises might be concerted, consulted over, and executed conjointly. Too late I heard that he was about to open the campaign with 100,000 men, and that I was appointed lieutenant-general-in-chief, with the command of the artillery, and that of the whole army in the absence of the emperor and Maréchal de Lacy. I tried to withdraw my request. Too late! the empress was not willing; the emperor took me at my word. I reached the Russian army Nov. 1, 1787, and then begins the period of my correspondence with the emperor.

I am confiding; I always believe that people like me. I thought that Prince Potemkin, who had so often assured me of his regard, would be charmed to see me. I did not notice his embarrassed manner when I first met him. I fell on his neck and asked: "When shall we take Oczakow?" "Eh, my God," he said, "there are 18,000 men in the garrison, and I have not as many in my whole army. I lack everything; I am the most unfortunate man if God does not help me." — "They told me you had already begun the siege, and I have travelled night and day to get here." "Alas!" he said, "please God the Tartars may not come down here and put everything to fire and sword. God has saved me so far (I shall never forget it); He has permitted that I should gather what troops I have behind the Bog [river flowing into the Euxine]. It is a miracle that I have kept what territory I have till now." "Where are the Tartars?" I asked. "Why, everywhere," replied the prince. "Besides, there's a Seraskier with a great many Turks near Akermann, 12,000 in Bender, the Dniester guarded, and 6000 in Choczim."

There was not a word of truth in all this; but how could I suppose he meant to deceive one of whom I believed he was in need? If I was unfortunate in the whole of this politico-military mission I deserved it. I was, as Maréchal Neipperg said at the peace of 1739, like Lucifer, hurled down by my pride, for I thought that I commanded the two Russian armies.

I told the prince that I had dissuaded the empress from sending a fleet to the Mediterranean, which would cost a great deal and yet not serve the purpose in hand. Though she told me this project the moment that she conceived it he wanted me to believe that it was his. Some days later, forgetting this, he told me that he had written to the empress not to send that fleet. "But that is just how she acts, that woman," he said, "especially when I am not there; always gigantically! And why did she answer Prussia so gruffly when he offered her thirty thousand men and money? Always her cursèd vanity!"

"Here," I said to the prince, "is a letter from the emperor in which is a plan for the whole war. It shows the operations in the mass; it is for your different corps to detail it all, according to circumstances. His Majesty instructs me to ask you exactly what you propose doing." The prince replied that he would give his plan to me the next day in writing. I waited one, two, three, eight days, fifteen days. At last his plan of campaign was sent to me, and I never had any other. Here it is: "With the help of God, I shall attack everything that comes between the Bog and the Dniester."

At last [June, 1788] I found a lucky pretext to get away from that encampment of filth at Elisabeth; another week and I should have died of it. The prince was sending me to the devil. Sometimes we were on good terms, sometimes on bad; often at daggers drawn, and then again I was a prime favourite, playing, talking, or saying nothing; but always on the watch till six in the morning to get him to utter some reasonable word that I could send for the emperor's guidance. At last, I could bear no longer the fantastic moods of this spoilt child; worn-out by such horrible and unheard-of inaction, I went to see why Maréchal Romanzow [commanding one wing of the Russian army at Jassy] was not doing more than Prince Potemkin; having gone through my mourning with the one, I hoped to get something, at least, from the other.

The marshal, as amiable as the prince was surly, overwhelmed me with caresses and promises. The pair were only agreed on one point, and that was to deceive the emperor and not begin their campaigns till July, by which time they expected that the whole Ottoman force would have flung itself upon the Austrians. I did not even succeed in quarrelling with Romanzow, in spite of the fact that I proved to him he had made me six false promises. He pressed me in his arms, laughed, wept, pitied himself and me, and went on with his little tricks as before.

I returned to the prince and his melancholy army; he being then at Alexandrowska, not knowing how to begin his campaign, having been fifteen days in crossing the Bog, and making, since then, the very shortest marches he could manage.

It was at the camp of Novo Gregori that we heard the news of the [naval] victory of the Prince of Nassau over the capitan-pacha. The prince sent for me, embraced me, and said: "This comes from God. Look at that church; yesterday I consecrated it to Saint George, my patron, and the news of this victory at Kinbourn comes the next day." At the end of several weeks of marching and countermarching about a bridge which they did not know where to place to cross that cursèd river, we again found ourselves on the heights of Novo Gregori, where we received the news of two more naval victories of the Prince of Nassau. "Well, my friend," said the prince to me, flinging himself on my breast, "what did I tell you of Novo Gregori? Here it is again. Is it not signal? I am the petted child of God" [*l'enfant gâté*]. Those were his very words; and I repeat them here to make known the most extraordinary man that ever lived. "How fortunate," he added, "that the garrison of Oczakow is running away. I march at once; will you come with me?" "Can you doubt it?" I cried. And we started.

Instead of going straight to the fortress, which I counted on reaching with the whole cavalry force in two days, we spent three by the water side, catching and eating fish, and we went to pay a visit to the victorious fleet. Still, we had, sooner or later, to arrive at Oczakow. The prince summoned the place to surrender. No one had left it as he had been led to believe. The pacha did not do him the honour to make any reply to his summons.

Nassau brought us an old Dutch colonel of engineers to support his opinion, which was to assault the fort at once on the sea side. Instead of which, he was ordered to fight a fourth naval battle and burn the town. The morning before this was done Potemkin said to me: "This dog of a fortress hampers me." I answered: "And it will hamper you a long time yet if you don't go to work more vigorously. Make a false attack on one side and jump in on the other by the intrenchment. Get in pell-mell with all you can; it is an old fortress and you will have it." "Do you think," he said, "that this is like your Sabacz, defended by one thousand men and taken by twenty-five thousand?" I answered that he ought to speak with respect, and imitate an assault made by the emperor in person with two battalions and vigorously carried out under a storm of fire on all sides. The next day the prince, having brilliantly established in person a battery of sixteen cannon on open ground not five hundred feet from the intrenchments, and thus made a diversion for Nassau's fight, remembered our conversation of the night before, and while the bullets were raining round us he said, laughing, to Comte Branicki: "Ask him if his emperor was any braver at Sabacz than I am here." It is most true that this sham half-attack was hot, and no one was ever more nobly and gayly valorous than Prince Potemkin. I loved him that day and the next three, when he was in the greatest danger during the siege. I told him I saw plainly it was necessary to fire cannon at him to get him out of his ill-humour.

After that everything was charming for a few days. As I supposed they were going to employ the usual means of reducing a fort, — that is to say, a strong assault, or a regular siege, which in this case would have been an affair of a week or so, — I took part in all the skirmishes, because I had never yet seen the fighting of the Turks. We took and lost the pacha's gardens several times. Once my horse fell with me, either from fright or the wind of a ball; and my faithful aide-de-camp, Bettinger, major of my own regiment, shared in the fight for fear he should miss anything; though he said it was playing to the gallery, for there was no common-sense in it all.

On one occasion I made a useful excursion; or rather it would have been useful if the self-sufficiency of my prince had not prevented him from following the advice. I made a reconnoissance close up to the fort on the Liman side and the intrenchment on the side of the Black Sea, discovering the range of the forty cannon by drawing their fire upon me one after another. I then proposed the action which will be found in my letters, but was neither listened to nor even heard.

My letters from Elisabeth-Gorod will sufficiently show that, whether from policy, want of will, or incapacity, the campaign was lost before it was begun. What follies, whims, and childishness, what anti-military things did I not see during the period of five months that I remained before that paltry place! I tried to ignore them; but I suffered, like a musician when he listens to instruments that are not in tune. In a moment of great impatience, when I thought the prince suspected me of wishing to take the command of the army from him and overthrow him at his Court, I made him some reproaches that touched him. I had had the moderation not to mention to either of the Imperial Majesties, or to their ministers, the ridiculous things that were said and done by the prince, and I never complained to any one, though perhaps I had better have done so. But it is impossible for me to do harm to any one, certainly not to a man who had formerly shown me such friendship, who might still retain it at the bottom of his heart, and who had, moreover, procured me so many kindnesses from the empress. The blame that truth requires me not to conceal here will do no harm to him when these words are read, for they will not appear until he and I are no longer in this world.

I wrote him a sharp letter, and ended by telling him that I should leave the next day. He wrote me in reply the gentlest, tenderest, most naïve letter that was ever written. Nothing could better prove that if he be, as indeed he is, the most inconsequential of men, he is also, at times, the best of men; sometimes our quarrels were like those of a lover and his mistress.

I was so worn out, so weary of the scenes of that theatre of iniquity, that I longed to get away. My son Charles arrived with despatches from his Majesty the emperor, commanding me to join him in Vienna, and I quitted forever, with pleasure and with regret, the armies and the empire of Russia, where I had met with so much personal kindness, but where my zeal for the glory of our mutual arms caused me such great ill-humour; but for that, I should have been most happy. The empress was too clear-sighted not to perceive my displeasure. I had not written her a single letter throughout the whole campaign. If I had only once written praises of Prince Potemkin and of his operations, I should have been overwhelmed with estates and diamonds. Catherine would even have been glad, I think, had I deceived her. It would have been more comforting to her to think that all went well. [Here follow some of the prince's letters to the emperor during that campaign so-called.]

To H. I. Majesty Joseph II.

PETERSBURG, October 14, 1787.

I thank his Majesty for the proof he deigns to give me of his confidence by employing me in the Russian armies; and I take the liberty of saying I should never have solicited that employment had I known of the two favours he had graciously done me: that of appointing me Feldzeugmeister, and of employing me in his army of Hungary which he commands in person; not foreseeing the vigorous promptitude with which he has come to the support of his ally.

But if I have the happiness of being useful to him, it will be a compensation for having lost the honour of serving under his own eye. If I find the need of help to make his Majesty's intentions successful I shall appeal to his ambassador, Comte Cobenzl, requesting him to solicit the empress to order the co-operative action which is so wisely indicated in the instructions of his Majesty.

ELISABETH-GOROD, November 15, 1787.

This is merely to inform his Majesty of my arrival, and to say to him that this army not being initiated into the science of details I shall often have difficulty in obtaining the statements I need for his information. But in spite of that, I shall send him as well as I am able the strength and position of the various corps. Prince Potemkin, to whom I have given an extract of his Majesty's letter (as I did to the empress before my departure) appears to intend to execute his Majesty's plan. That which I have debated with him against Choczim seems to me to concern the Russians more than the Austrians, but I have promised to present his project and to send a small Austrian corps to occupy Krayova, because he assures me that the slightest act of hostility on the part of his Majesty the emperor would take off, morally and physically, the Grand Vizir's head, the latter having assured the Divan that his Majesty would not advance.

I have advised Prince Potemkin to take advantage of the ice to surprise Oczakow, which the chilly and neglectful Turks are guarding very ill. I believe, for I have reconnoitred in a little boat very close to the fortress, that a hundred men could scale the wall and open the gates to a column which should cross the Bog.

I am not able to get any real enlightenment as to the destination of the army under Maréchal Romanzow; all I know is that he is now on his estates about four hundred versts [300 miles] from his troops.

I send herewith to his Majesty a note written by Prince Potemkin, in which, without sufficiently explaining himself as to the siege of Oczakow or the length of time he expects the siege to last, he pledges himself to cross the Bog as soon as the season allows, and attack whatever Turks he finds between that river and the Dniester. He thinks the Mussulman army will assemble near Godzabey, that Inkermann will then fall of itself, after which he can march on. This he explained to me in giving me the Note; and he is anxious to justify himself to his Majesty for being forced to keep the defensive by his total lack of provisions and his distance from his base of supplies, — not having, he says, expected this sudden declaration of war.

To Comte Louis-Philippe de Ségur.

ELISABETH-GOROD, December 1, 1787.

Here I am, my dear Ségur, in the Russian uniform of a general-in-chief which gives me great pleasure, a Turkish sabre at my side, and, while awaiting service as general or volunteer, with an Austrian pen in my hand, — a sort of diplomatic jockey to that best of ambassadors, Cobenzl, who thinks night and day of the glory of the two empires. I am very happy to be able to serve them both in different ways: *consilio manuque.* Meanwhile behold me in a little chamber one foot shorter than myself, where I might from my bed open the door if it could be shut, make the fire if I had any wood for the stove, and close the window if it did not have paper instead of glass, and no sashes.

Separated from the whole world, without letters to write or receive, I drive away the memory of all I have left three thousand miles away from me and make myself romances of success of another kind. I say to myself sometimes: "The queen's balls begin perhaps to-day," — yes, but to-morrow we will drive those Tartars across the Bog, which is now frozen over. Once it was called the Hypanis. What a charming name for history! Even the Ingul, which flows near this place, is more piquant than the Seine.

Enjoy the presence of the sun, the ineffable happiness of

admiring Catherine the Great and of seeing her daily. I could never have left her but for her sake. I go to fight her enemies, but I do not leave her in the midst of mine. In a few days I will continue this letter: but as the days are very long here that may mean several months.

To H. I. M. Joseph II.

ELISABETH-GOROD, January 15, 1788.

This is to render his Majesty an account of my fears as to the great loss of time, and also as to the subject of my letter to Comte Cobenzl, and the remedies that ought to be applied. I take the liberty of asking whether it is true that the Court of Petersburg has sent his Majesty an account of its forces and a plan of campaign.

I have to say that there is no Turkish army anywhere, not so much as the smallest corps; there are no troops except the garrisons of Oczakow, Bender, and Choczim, and the number of those is exaggerated. I had the honour of informing his Majesty that five Turks had been captured; six others have been killed by a party of Cossacks, but they had to ride one hundred versts the other side of the river to do it. I beg also to inform his Majesty that I have received a plan of campaign, rather less vague than the last, which promises the capture of Oczakow in the month of June, after three weeks' siege, covered by Maréchal Romanzow, who will cross the Dniester by way of Bender; and if Prince Potemkin suffers severely by the siege and assault, he will advance to the Danube and be covered in turn by the prince.

The latter has informed me that whenever he approaches sufficiently near to the army of his Imperial Majesty he intends to send him two regiments of Cossacks, for he noticed in the Crimea how much he admired those troops.

I communicate herewith to his Majesty the news from

Constantinople, which the prince sends me, together with the reports of the spies. His arrangements are now good for supplies and hospitals. I add an account of the cost of forage, which I have advised should be put under two heads instead of three.

I have only to congratulate myself on the friendship of the prince, which still continues, though I sometimes try it severely by my obstinate desire to begin the campaign, to which I urge him vigorously for the sake of his own fame, in which I am so much interested that I shall be very sorry if he spends more consecutive months in Elisabeth-Gorod doing nothing, for it will injure him much in the eyes of Europe.

To the Same.

Still at Elisabeth-Gorod, February 10, 1788.

Sire, — I am going to risk many things. But *zelus domus tuæ comedit me.* Your Imperial Majesty will not expect to receive counsel from me, and I should not venture to send it if I were not sure of being long without seeing you; I hope, however, it will have been followed and forgotten between now and then.

Europe is muddling things in such a way that there is no time to be lost in taking advantage of some circumstances and preventing others. The King of Prussia is irritated because the empress sent him word he had been too short a time upon his throne to pronounce upon the interests of others, and that he ought not to think, like the republic of Holland, of settling the affairs of three empires, and handling them like Poland.

Your Imperial Majesty could prevent Poland from delivering herself up to him if you would deign to write me an ostensible letter, promising that two of the co-partitioning powers would arm against the third if the king attempted to obtain the very smallest *starostie*. Under pretext of using them against the Turks, I have persuaded Prince Potemkin to give me forty thousand muskets for the Poles if they wish to make a confederacy supported by the two imperial Courts. Several Polish grand seigneurs with whom I have communicated on this subject are only waiting for this support to choke the Prussian party. All I ask of them is to *be Poles*. Prince Tchervertinski, who is as ardent as he is enlightened, agreed with me yesterday that for his compatriots to be otherwise would be the ruin and the end of their nation. I tell them always: "Do not look to Vienna, Petersburg, Berlin; if you want to get free from the Russian yoke do not put yourselves under one more dangerous."

I have pledged myself that your Imperial Majesty will induce the empress to lessen the abuses of authority which her generals and ministers commit, often unjustly, on the Poles. This would be good policy, and good morals too. Before I meddled in politics I should have put morality before policy; but I see now the latter wins.

I am here exactly in the position of a child's nurse. But my nursling is large, strong, and perverse. Yesterday he said to me: "Do you think you have come here to lead me by the nose?" "Do you think," I answered, "that I should have come if I did not think so? Lazy and without experience, what could be better for you, dear prince? Why not let yourself go to a lover of your fame and the glory of the two empires? You lack so little of being perfect; but what can your genius do unless aided by friendship and confidence?" The prince said: "Make your emperor cross the Save and I will cross the Bog." "How can you," I said, "stand on ceremony, as if you were entering the door of a salon? But my emperor will make way for you; he has a

Turkish army in front of him, and you have none." "Do you think," he remarked, "that he would give us crosses of Maria Theresa and receive our Saint-George for those who distinguish themselves in both armies?" I saw he was coming to that. He has a mania for Orders. He has only about a dozen. I assured him that Oczakow would be worth our grandest cross, and Belgrade, if he made it easier to your Majesty to capture it, would win him Saint-Étienne. I beg your Majesty to confirm this hope; and if our Roman Catholicity could set itself aside in his favour as to the Golden Fleece, he would be wholly ours.

Your Majesty alarms me by what you deign to write me on the subject of France and Flanders. Both countries must have greatly changed during the two years that I have lost sight of them if an army of fifty thousand men assembled near Paris, and a "Vive le Roi!" gayly shouted in France, and firmness shown in Flanders, cannot restore and preserve order. Take off the head of a monk, a burgomaster, a brewer, and one of the conscript fathers, and you will save the other heads from the poison breath of England and Prussia, and the scaffold.

If your Imperial Majesty maintains the three bodies which compose the State Assemblies, and the essential principles of the Constitution, none but intriguers and false patriots who for selfish ends desire to make trouble will remain. It was this assurance that I begged your Majesty, as you will remember, when we were at Barczisarai to allow me to take to the Belgian Assembly, and I believe that I could then, if allowed to abandon a few innovations for the benefit of the country, have pacified everything in ten days.

I beg your Majesty to avert from my head the indignation of the Council of war and the Chancellerie; however willing I may be to do so I have nothing to write them, for we are doing nothing. Moreover, the intimate and very true friend of your Majesty does not wish that what she writes to me should reach your ministers: for instance, her remark (which I repeated to your Majesty) that if I would induce you to send the Prince of Coburg into Moldavia she would give her imperial word that we should have Choczim and the Raya at the peace — such peace as they can make!

She is impatient, and wishes the war could be hurried, because she is not sure but what the King of Prussia is working on the hot and crooked brain of the King of Sweden. One thing is certain; if something is not done to stop those impertinent threats and representations of the French nation and the impotent projects of the Flemish malcontents the whole of our part of the world will shortly be in flames.

Prince Potemkin gives me news brought back by his emissaries at Scutari, but I never guarantee his facts, because that great child is capable of being very wily. The other day I reproached him for our inaction, and soon after a courier arrived with news of a battle won in the Caucasus. "Behold!" he said to me, "you say I do nothing. I have just killed ten thousand Circassians, Abyssinians, Immorets, and Georgians; and I had already killed five thousand Turks at Kinbourn." "I am charmed," "I said, "to find we have so much glory without ever suspecting it." I have informed him of the wretched condition of his cartridges. If we had provisions we should march; if we had pontoons we should cross the rivers; if we had bullets and balls we should lay siege; nothing has been forgotten but those items; the prince has ordered them to be sent with post-horses; this style of transportation and the purchase of munitions are costing three millions of roubles.

I place at the feet of your Majesty the zeal and personal attachment of, etc.

P. S. In spite of all the weaknesses of my commander-in-chief he has one rare merit in this country, — sincere attachment to the house of Austria.

To the Comte de Ségur.

February 15, 1788.

No news; no appearance of the promised Tartars. But the Prince of Nassau has arrived from Paris. His tenacity in negotiation as in cannon may bring us something; his reputation, consideration, and logic, though he never had the time to study, may serve our wishes at this important crisis. Meantime, did I not see him two days ago, sabre in hand, saving my life? He is never two days together like other people. This is how it happened. I am getting over an attack of fever (for luckily there are no doctors here), and having heard of the sun I was awaiting its arrival to be cured. Nassau guided me out of this melancholy fort. My servants carried me, laid me down on the grass, and went away; while I went to sleep in the sun. A snake which the first warm rays brought back to life, as they did me, coiled itself about me. I heard a noise. It was Nassau striking something as hard as he could, cutting it into twenty little bits, which all wriggled though separated from each other.

They brought in to-day a few Turkish prisoners, as stupid as the Turks of an Opera ball. In fact I cannot get it into my head that they are not masks, and that we are really at war with them. The prince has had a unique idea, that of forming a regiment of Jews, which he calls his Israëlowsky. We already have a squadron which is all my joy, for their beards, which fall to their knees because their stirrups are so short, and their terror at being on horseback, make them look like monkeys. You can read their uneasiness in their eyes, and the long lances which they hold in the most comical manner make you think that they want to mimic the Cossacks.

Jews have never been in vogue since God abandoned them. That is why Christians have nothing to do with them; philosophers, on the other hand, have never given them a thought, apparently because their faces are not pleasing to them. The world is supposed to have a horror of the Jews on account of their religion; it is really on account of their appearance. If Christians have neither the cleverness nor the kindness to drag them out of the state they are in and make something of them, I wish for the sake of their happiness (for they make me laugh and pity them every day) that some one with influence would persuade the Grand Turk to give them back the kingdom of Judea, where they would probably behave better than they once did. The degree of degradation in which the European governments leave the Jews, their poverty, their filth, their bad food, the noxious air of their synagogues and their streets perpetuate their faces and figures, so that one may truly say: Jacob *genuit* Isaac like unto himself. They certainly do have stigmatized faces, and, being full of faith in the prophecies, I am convinced they deserve them; but they might look less so if, besides being condemned of God, they were not chastised by men. That is what makes them cheats, cowards, liars, and base. Those four qualities stamped on their faces do not beautify them. But they are not thieves, or assassins, or wicked, nor are they ever seen in places of debauchery. Give them a station or an asylum, and they will cease to be what they are. Why not settle with the pope (if he still exists) and Holy Scripture, and see how far one might go with regard to the Jews without falsifying the Prophets? — which is, however, impossible.

Yesterday I won six hundred ducats at *dames* [draughts], there being no other sort of dames here to occupy me. Adieu. I can say, as the husband to his wife, I have no one, and no one has me; I hope that is true of you. When I hear something interesting I will — no, I will not write it to you, because I remember I am on public business and ought to be discreet. So far our secret has been well kept. Good-night.

To H. I. M. Joseph II.

April 6, 1788.

SIRE, — It really seems as if we were about to bestir ourselves a little; the grass which is beginning to appear has induced a corps to cross the Bog (which it ought to have done long ago) in order to cut off the communication between Oczakow, Bender, and Godzabey, whence the former obtains its reinforcements. I am constantly told that the campaign will be better than I thought, and I believe it.

Maréchal Romanzow wrote to Prince Repnin asking to be told privately what he was to do, and what Prince Potemkin's intentions were. Repnin could not tell him. The slowness in making preparations has caused the Prince of Nassau to lose six good weeks, and it will be three more before he gets what he needs in order to attack Oczakow. And that delay, I think, is what they want to get time to cross the Bog and make believe it is that move which compels the surrender of the fortress.

Prince Potemkin complains of the ministry at Petersburg; he says they do not send him proper accounts of what they are doing in this or that affair, and also that they deceive the empress. There is, in fact, so strong a cabal against him that I should not be surprised, from certain things he tells me when much discontented, if he did not finish this campaign.

I think I have contributed a little to stir up the King of Poland, without in any way committing your Majesty's name. The king has asked for the sanction and advice of Russia in forming a Confederation. He writes me that they have not answered him from Petersburg. They are losing time that would be precious in preventing a most important scheme. The pretext of defending Poland from invasion by imaginary Tartars, of whom there is so much talk and no appearance, will suffice to arm that country.

I learn with much feeling that your Imperial Majesty was pleased with the conduct of my regiment at Brussels. I venture to take the liberty of assuring you that if it had been there on the 1st of May of last year its fidelity and its zeal for the sovereign would have prevailed over the efforts of the *canaille*, who profited by that fine word "prudence," ridiculously used in place of the means afforded by the Ligne regiment, which does not understand "affairs."

I am greatly in hopes that within three weeks we shall quit this Elisabeth and cross the Bog. The Prince of Nassau left us to-day to command the flotilla off Kherson. This, at least, I have accomplished. He knows very well that he can burn the Turkish fleet (which has now been given time to collect here), but not fight it. He has five floating batteries, eight galleys, fifteen gun-boats, and a quantity of other vessels well supplied with cannon. Therefore he can silence the guns of the fortress, avoid the fire of Hassan Pacha's redoubt, and rake the great intrenchment constructed by the French. He expects to make a breach large enough for General Suvaroff, protected by his guns, to open the attack on that side. Meantime they are furnishing him with what he wants, and I hope that in a month he can at last begin the bombardment with a cannonading of red balls.

The jealousy felt here at seeing a volunteer — German, French, or Spanish, it matters not — in charge of all this is extreme, and will increase when it becomes known that Potemkin has persuaded the empress to take Paul Jones into the service of Russia as major-general and vice-admiral. He will arrive here next week; an excellent acquisition, so they say. We shall see; but I think him only a corsair.

Immediately after the taking of Oczakow I intend to avail myself of your permission to move to the army of General Romanzow, which is then to march to the Danube, and there execute, as I hope, all that I have proposed on the part of your Imperial Majesty to unite the armies and give a final defeat to the Ottomans. Prince Potemkin will, apparently, content himself with covering the march of the convoys and the province of Ekaterinoslav.

It is impossible for me not to place at the feet of your Majesty my gratitude and my deep emotion at what you deign to tell me of your satisfaction with the zeal of my good Charles. In spite of your omnipotence you could not possibly have granted me a greater benefit than that of those three precious lines. I venture to assure you that he is worth more than I; and it will be a great consolation to leave behind me a subject who may, perhaps, be so fortunate as to be of service to his Master.

I have the honour to be, etc.

IV.

1788–1789.

THE TURKISH WAR CONTINUED.

To the Comte De Ségur.

ELISABETH-GOROD, May 8, 1788.

Ah! my friend, let me weep a moment, while you read this: —

KLENACK, April 25, 1788.

We have taken Sabacz. Our loss has not been considerable. General Rouvroy, whose worth you know, has a slight wound in the breast which prevents his wearing clothes and going out. Prince Poniatowski was shot in the thigh; the bone was not touched, though the wound is of consequence.

But I must, my dear prince, tell you of something else which will give you the more pleasure because you will recognize your own blood in it. It is that your son Charles has, in a great degree, contributed to the success of our enterprise by the infinite pains he took to trace out the line of intrenchments for the placing of the batteries. He was also the first to climb the parapet and show the way to others. I have therefore promoted him lieutenant-colonel and conferred upon him the Order of Maria Theresa. I feel a true pleasure in giving you this news, from the certainty I have of the satisfaction it will be to you, knowing as I do your tenderness for your son, and your patriotism.

I leave to-morrow for Semlin, etc.

JOSEPH.

What modesty! the emperor never mentions himself. He was in the thickest of the fire. And what grace and kindness in the account he sends me! The beginning of the letter was only instructions, reflections, etc., and then this, which made me burst into tears.

The courier who brought it saw the emperor facing with good grace the musketry fire in the streets of Sabacz; and Maréchal de Lacy himself tearing down a palisade to place a cannon to bear upon a tower from which continual fire was made upon my Charles, and so protect his assault. The marshal would have done the same for any other, I am sure, but it had the air of personal and paternal kindness to Charles.

The marshal was a little tired, and the emperor fetched him a barrel and made him sit down, while he and the generals stood around him and did him a sort of homage.

Here is a letter from Charles himself: —

"We have Sabacz. I have the Cross. You will feel, papa, that I thought of you as I went up first to the assault."

Was ever anything more touching than that? Why was I not near him to grasp his hand! I see that I have his esteem in those words, "I thought of you." Would that I had better deserved them!

I am too overcome to write more. I embrace you, dear count.

To H. I. M. Joseph II.

May 13, 1788.

Expressions fail me; all that I can say to your Imperial Majesty is that you dispose henceforth of our entire existence. Our blood, our fortune, our life are ours no longer — happy if I could buy with mine the same success beneath your eyes when your Majesty will have the goodness to recall me from here, where matters, being now in train, can go by themselves. My happiness in what your Majesty has deigned to say and do for Charles is lessened by regret that I could not be with him upon that parapet, where the name, the activity, and the presence of your Majesty did more than even the cannon. I envy Charles and all others of that splendid expedition.

Her Majesty the empress wrote yesterday for the first time on the subject of delays. Why did she not do so earlier? And she does it now only at the instance of our ambassador, to whom I made remonstrance openly through the Russian couriers, because I hoped to have my letter read — for it is all the same to me now to quarrel, or be on good terms as I please. It is not becoming in me to give advice to your Majesty, but you will pardon my excess of zeal. There is such jealousy, malice, and ignorance, so little eagerness to do, so many pretexts for not doing great things on the offensive line, that, in my opinion, in order not to have the whole Ottoman force flung upon our troops, there is nothing to be done but to make a good peace as soon as your Imperial Majesty, after taking such places as you want, can get the rest by treaty.

Russia feels the weakness of her colossus [Potemkin]. She will be content if no demand is made upon her for the Crimea, if an arrangement can be made about the Caucasus, if she obtains Oczakow and is able to give the name of Oczakowski and the grand cordon of Saint-George to Prince Potemkin. She wants nothing more; neither Moldavia nor Wallachia; and if she could get Bender and Choczim rased, so that the navigation of the Dniester shall be free to her, she will have everything she desires. All her fine projects of driving the Turks out of Europe and turning Constantinople into a republic have vanished.

Apropos of Orders, I do not know what was in the head of Prince Potemkin the other day, but on his table where he was making designs with diamonds, I saw a splendid Golden

Fleece, worth a hundred thousand roubles. Was that to tell me it should be mine if I would write to the empress and say that all was going well? Or did he mean me to understand that he should give it to himself if your Majesty bestowed that Order upon him? The empress, astonished at receiving no letters from me, sees plainly enough that I am too grateful for her past kindnesses, which I owed in the first instance to Prince Potemkin, to complain to her of him, and also that I am too truthful to write her that he could not do more than he is doing. So I think no longer of my claims on Russia through the marriage of Charles with a Massalska,—claims for which I made my first journey to Petersburg. I think I shall have no difficulty now in avoiding gifts of diamonds and peasantry as I had last year.

To the Same.

May 21, 1788.

The English and the Prussians have an envoy with the Turks to make them do something in the interests of those countries. I pity him with all my heart, for his position is as thankless as mine. The conduct of the Turks is quite as extraordinary as that of the Russians. There is no appearance of their troops; not the smallest little *corps d'armée* between the Bog and the Dniester; our Cossacks meet no one, though they ride about everywhere, especially of late. The Greeks are desirous of arming and entering the service if any opportunity is given them. Neglected by the empress, forgotten by Potemkin (who has kept a deputation of two hundred waiting about here for over two months), they have now come to me to say that your Imperial Majesty may count upon them. I did not commit myself, for I know there is no trust to be placed in them. As I would rather lose my money than the credit of my influence, I gave five hundred ducats to a very intelligent young man named Arthur Görgi to enable him to take to your Majesty his little colony, which desires to establish itself in the Banat [province of Hungary].

To the Same.

IN CAMP BEFORE OCZAKOW, July 19, 1788.

SIRE, — I fully expected that our false attack by way of diversion, which made us see how easy the intrenchments were to carry, would be the prelude to a real attack on the morrow. It was plain that the battalion of chasseurs, with which I was, could easily get a footing there, and that the infantry, in the confusion that reigned in the town, might have entered by way of the enemy's camp. Every one in the tents within the line of intrenchments had fled. I saw this myself.

But instead of this prompt action, we are to wait for the heavy artillery (which the empress detained under the idea of difficulties with the Court of Berlin), in order to lay a regular siege, although there are no engineer officers here to conduct it. Owing to sickness, which prevails and increases, we have only about 10,000 effective infantry, who are melting away under the filthiness of this camp, and 25,000 Cossacks and light-horse, with 30,000 men for the 120 siege guns now on their way, and the supply trains. Thus it will be two or three weeks yet before the siege begins.

I have had the honour to send your Majesty an exact account of the strength of this army, the horses and men of which are in fine condition! 200 per battalion on the sick-list; but that will not last long; if they continue to be as ill-treated as they are now they will all be dead soon. A few are dragged along in those English carriages your Majesty has seen, — without surgeons or medicaments; when they get worse they are sent back to Wagenburg; if dangerously ill to Elisabeth, and die on the way.

As for provisions, the troops carry them with them; they are called portative. The cavalry horses, also those for the artillery, are good; the oxen, which are used for food and draught both, are very good. There are provisions enough, thanks to biscuit and fast-days, to last the campaign; also there is flour enough for each soldier to now and then make his own bread.

As for the soldier himself, he is always a model of punctuality, cleanliness, patience, obedience, good-will, and good service, though no one takes care of him. I have never yet seen a drunken soldier, or a quarrelsome, argumentative, or negligent one. No one ever drills either the infantry or the light-horse. There is no forming in line; no standing motionless; but they keep their distances pretty well. They march by fours in these vast plains; and the columns find means to intersect one another to enter camp. Camp is always taken so that one face of the square is to the Liman, and the other turns its back to the enemy — if there is an enemy.

I have already had the honour of telling your Majesty of the great inconvenience caused by the scarcity of pontoons. The four hundred and fifty feet width of the Bog cost us twelve days. There is no communication with Kherson except by the Liman, the navigation of which is so dangerous that the other day, returning with Prince Potemkin from the fleet, we came near being drowned, and Paul Jones and Nassau had water to the knees in their boat. The Prince's army is pretty well paid; that of Romanzow is not paid at all. The colonels, who did not report that they had four hundred men and horses less than they are credited,

Prince Potemkin

have advanced the 30,000 roubles they will draw for them, with which they pay their actual force, and the empress will pay the colonels when she can. Her funds are exhausted, and her credit so low that in changing a bill of 100 roubles into small paper one loses ten roubles. It is impossible to make a foreign war in this way. The seductive curtain which covered the lack of real means is now, unfortunately, raised, and foreign Courts will soon see what is no longer a mystery in this country. Always the superfluous, never the necessary.

The Prince of Nassau proposed to Prince Potemkin to demolish the remains of the Turkish fleet, now sheltered under the walls of the town, and to burn the latter, urging, as I did also, that an assault be made at the same time on the land side. This fourth battle did Nassau as much honour as the three former. At half-past three o'clock in the morning a diversion was made with four big siege guns, which are all we have while awaiting the hundred and twenty now on the way. They also brought up twelve 12-pounders and a few mortars; which did not make a very grand effect. But Prince Potemkin, with all his cavalry under fire from the fort, made a great demonstration to impress the enemy with the idea that he meant to invest, and should attack any and all who came out. He placed his cannon himself on the open plain, without so much as a ditch or any sort of defence, and stood by them, almost within range of the musketry from the intrenchments, — the glitter of the diamonds round the portrait of the empress which he always wears at his button-hole drawing several shots. He has a noble valour, and his presence animated the artillery-men, who aimed well.

This little combat on land, that on the Liman, the blowing up of the vessels, the town in flames, all seen at the same time from all points, made a sight superbly horrible. The battalions of chasseurs, exposed from head to foot, showed a fine composure. Prince Potemkin reconnoitred the fort thoroughly, helped by the Cossacks who were burning and pillaging the suburbs. The fortress could have been taken then with the utmost ease. In vain I told him so; he would not believe me. As general-in-chief, known to be so, and wearing the uniform, I offered to lead the troops in, without avail. Instead of that he named me in his report as having figured well among the bullets that fell around him like hail!

August 3, 1788.

The Rear-admiral Paul Jones has to-day, for his first exploit, passed with his three frigates to the other side of Hassan Pacha's redoubt, and captured a boat without a crew. There is reason to think he owes his reputation to a desire to enrich himself. He has not yet done what he could have done; he only serves to hinder Nassau and encourage the prince, who does not like the latter to risk anything.

It will not be your Majesty's fault if these delays allow time for the Turks to send a land force to trouble us and perhaps compel us to abandon the siege. I do not know why some of those Moldavian detachments do not come down for that purpose; Maréchal Romanzow would let them through. We live from day to day and apparently no arrangements are being made for victualling the army. The next campaign will be without money and without credit in a foreign land. Discipline, that good mother of the Russian armies, is already relaxing; the men have taken to firing about their camps like the Turks. I have noticed a queer fashion the Turks have in sending their 3-pound shot into our camp, which is little over a mile distant. They wrap them up in quantities of rags and fire them from their

24-pounders. They seem to have plenty of provisions, and though the capitan-pacha can do nothing, his presence so encourages the men that the morning after his arrival they shouted to our guards: "Stoupay, Moscow." They will defend themselves well; and sooner or later those intrenchments will have to be rushed.

I forgot, apropos of the siege, to tell your Majesty that, M. de La Fayette having sent me what he called a French engineer named Marolles to manage the siege, I took him to Prince Potemkin. "How soon do you want the place taken, general?" he said. "Why, as soon as you can," replied the prince. "Have you a copy of Vauban," said my original, "or Cöhorn? And I would also like Saint-Rémy, to brush up what I have forgotten, or I may say never known; for I am only an engineer of bridges and highways." The prince, who is always kind and amiable when he has time, began to laugh and said: "Go and rest after your journey; don't kill yourself with reading; I'll send you something to eat in your tent."

To the Comte de Ségur.

CAMP BEFORE OCZAKOW, August 10, 1788.

Here in my tent, on the shores of the Black Sea, on the hottest of nights which prevents me from sleeping, I go over in my mind the extraordinary things which are passing daily before my eyes. I have seen four naval battles won by a volunteer who has had nothing but glory and brilliant adventures since he was fifteen years of age; brave as a lad, and the prettiest little aide-de-camp of a general who worked him hard; then lieutenant of infantry, captain of dragoons; courteous knight, avenging the injuries of women, redressing the wrongs of society; in the midst of the stormiest youth, but always of the better species, leaving, to make a tour of the world, his pleasures, for which he found a momentary compensation in the Queen of Otaheiti, and in killing monsters like Hercules. Returning to Europe, he was colonel in the French service of an infantry regiment, commander of a regiment of German cavalry, without understanding German, leader of an expedition as captain of a ship, half-burned and sunk, in the service of Spain, major-general of the Spanish army, a general officer in the service of three countries (of which he did not know the languages), and the most brilliant vice-admiral that Russia has ever had.

Nassau-Siegen by birth, become Nassau-Sieger by exploits — for you know that Sieger in German means Conqueror in French — he is recognized in Madrid as an ancient grandee of Spain, though he did not know it, and everywhere as prince of the Holy Roman Empire, which nevertheless has given his principality to others. If injustice had not deprived him of it he might, at least for a time, have wasted his impetuous nature on wild boars and perhaps on poachers, though his taste for danger would soon have told him what his value was for war.

What is the secret of his witchery? His sword is the wand of the sorcerer. His own action the dictionary to his words and sciences, and that sword is still further his interpreter by the successful way it points to the shortest method of attack. Two eyes, more or less large, which he sometimes makes as terrible to his friends as to the enemy, complete the explanation of him. His manœuvre lies in his *coup-d'œil;* his talent in the experience that ardour has made him seek; his science in his short, concise, clear orders, given on the day of battle, easy to report, easy to comprehend; his merit in the precision of his ideas; his resources in the grand and well-marked character to be read in his face, in his successes, and in his courage, unequalled, both of body and mind.

I see the commander of an army, who seems to be lazy and works without ceasing; who has no desk but his knees, no comb but his fingers; always in bed and never sleeping day or night because his ardour for his sovereign, whom he adores, incessantly agitates him; while a single cannon-shot, which does not come nigh him, makes him wretched with the thought that it costs the lives of some of his soldiers; timid for others, brave for himself, pausing under the fierce fire of a battery to give orders; more Ulysses, nevertheless, than Achilles; uneasy before danger, gay when in it, sad in pleasures. Unhappy because so fortunate; *blasé* about everything, easily disgusted; morose, inconstant; a profound philosopher, able minister, splendid politician, child of ten years old; never vindictive, asking pardon for a pain he may have caused, quick to repair an injustice; believing that he loves God, fearing the devil, whom he imagines the greater and more powerful of the two; with one hand giving proofs of his liking for women, with the other making signs of the Cross; his arms in crucifix at the feet of the Virgin, or round the necks of those who, thanks to him, have ceased to be so; receiving benefits innumerable from his great sovereign, sharing them instantly with others; accepting estates, returning them to the giver, or paying her for them without ever letting her know it; gambling incessantly or else never touching a card; preferring to give than to pay his debts; enormously rich, yet without a penny; distrustful or confiding; jealous or grateful; ill-humoured or jovial; easily prejudiced for and against, returning as quickly from either extreme; talking theology to his generals and war to his archbishops; never reading, but sifting those with whom he talks, and contradicting them in order to learn more; presenting the most brutal or the most pleasing aspect, manners the most repulsive or the most attractive; with the mien of the proudest satrap of the Orient, or the cringing air of Louis XIV.'s courtiers; a great appearance of harshness, very soft in reality at the bottom of his heart; fantastic as to his hours, his meals, his sleep, his tastes; wanting all things like a child, able to go without everything like a great man; sober with the air of a gourmand; biting his nails, or apples, or turnips, scolding or laughing, dissembling or swearing, playing or praying, singing or meditating; calling, dismissing, and recalling twenty aides-de-camp without anything to say to them; bearing heat as if he thought only of a luxurious bath, laughing at cold, apparently able to do without furs; always in a shirt and no drawers, or else in a uniform embroidered on every seam, feet bare or in spangled slippers, without cap or hat (as I saw him once under fire); in a shabby dressing-gown or a splendid tunic, with his three stars, ribbons, and diamonds as big as my thumb round the portrait of the empress which always attracts the bullets; bent double, huddled up, stunted when in his own room; tall, his nose in the air, proud, handsome, noble, majestic, or seductive when he shows himself to his army with the air of an Agamemnon amid the kings of Greece.

What is his magic? Genius, and then genius, and again genius; natural intelligence, an excellent memory, elevation of soul, malice without malignity, craft without cunning, a happy mixture of caprices, of which the good when they are uppermost win him all hearts; great generosity, grace, and justice in his rewards, much tact, the talent of divining that which he does not know, and great knowledge of men.

I see a cousin of the empress [Prince of Anhalt-Bernberg] who has the air of being a mere young officer, with his modesty and his sublime simplicity; who is, for all that, everything, and chooses to seem nothing. He unites all talents and good qualities; a lover of shots and duty; doing the double of what he has to do; making the most of others, and attributing to them what is due to himself; full of delicacy of soul and mind; a refined and very sure taste; gentle, amiable, though nothing escapes his notice; prompt in repartee, also in execution; rigid in his principles; indulgent to me only, but severe to himself and others; prodigiously well-informed; a veritable genius for war, joined to the greatest and noblest of valours, — in a word, to my thinking, perfection.

I see a phenomenon from your country, and a charming phenomenon: a Frenchman of three ages, — the chivalry of one, the grace of another, and the gayety of the present day. François I., the Great Condé, and Maréchal de Saxe would have been glad of a son like him. He is as giddy as a bumble-bee in the midst of the liveliest cannonading; noisy, a pitiless singer, yelping his songs, the finest airs of the opera, at me; fertile in the wildest quotations; more original still in proposals and actions, and in the midst of it all, marvellously clear-sighted. Guns do not intoxicate him, but he glows with a pleasant ardour, as one does at the end of a supper. It is only when he wears an Order and gives his little counsel or takes some care upon him that he waters his wine. Always French in soul, and, it may be, a trifle vain, he is Russian in the example which he sets of subordination and good deportment. . . . Amiable, beloved by all, and what one calls a charming fellow, a brave fellow, a seigneur of the good tone of the Court of France, — *that* is what Roger Damas is.

I see Russian soldiers to whom they say, "Be that," and they become it; learning the liberal arts as "the doctor in spite of himself" took his degree; Russians who are made in a moment into foot-soldiers, sailors, chasseurs, priests, dragoons, musicians, engineers, comedians, cuirassiers, painters, and surgeons. I see Russians who sing and dance in the trenches from which they are never relieved under the heaviest cannonading and musketry, in the snow, in the mud, clever, clean, attentive, respectful, obedient, and always trying to read in the eyes of their officers what they want, in order to forestall it.

I see Turks who pass for not having common-sense in war, but who fight with a species of method; scattering widely so that the artillery and the fire of the battalions cannot be directed upon them. They themselves aim marvellously well; firing always at collected objects, concealing their own manœuvres, hiding in all the ravines, hollows, and up the trees; or else advancing in small bodies of forty or fifty with a flag, which they run very fast to plant and secure the ground. The first line fires kneeling and goes to the rear to reload; and thus they succeed each other. This they keep up, running forward with their flag and their revolving line. They form a species of alignement for these flags so that none of the little bodies covers another. Frightful howls, cries of "Allah!" encourage the Mussulmans, frighten the Christians and, with the addition of a few chopped-off heads, have a really terrible effect. Where the devil did my father and three uncles, who all fought the Turks, get the idea that they marched, as the geese fly, in a triangle, or like the *cuneus* of the ancients? I have never seen anything to make me think that such a fashion ever existed.

Do they know in Petersburg of the death of Ivan Maximo, whose rhyme and reason inspired you with that choice couplet,—

> "His heart may be given to virtue,
> But his face is a picture of crime"?

He was killed behind us, by a cannon-ball which passed between Prince Potemkin and me.

To the Same.

CAMP BEFORE OCZAKOW, Sept. 15, 1788.

All things remain *in statu quo.* Nothing is done, or even planned. I turn my mind as much as may be to other things, and Europe is indeed so thoroughly muddled at this moment that it is high time, as I think, to reflect about it. France writes; unfortunately our empire reads. The soldiers of the Bishop of Liège are in full march against the bankers of Spa. The Low Countries are revolting, without knowing why, against their sovereign. Soon, no doubt, they will begin to kill each other in order to have more liberty and happiness. Austria, threatened in her very bosom, is feebly threatening her friends and enemies, whom she scarcely knows apart. England — which never agrees with England! — has a majority in favour of Prussia, who is already firing shots in Holland. Proud Spain, who once upon a time fitted out armadas, is uneasy if a single English vessel sails from port. Italy is afraid of her lazzaroni and free-thinkers. Denmark is on her guard against Sweden, and Sweden against Russia. The Tartars, the Georgians, the Immorets, the Circassians are killing the Russians. Our journey to the Crimea exasperated the Crescent. The pachas of Egypt are fighting the Turks. "To arms!" they are crying everywhere. I do not cease to be an observer; and although I am an actor in the present scene, I take that and all that is happening about me as a mere kick in the ant-hill. What are we more than ants, poor human creatures that we are? . . .

To H. I. Majesty Joseph II.

CAMP BEFORE OCZAKOW, October 8, 1788.

I am so grieved at the condition of your Majesty's health that I cannot refrain from satisfying my heart by describing what has passed within it since I received the letter of September 27, with which you have honoured me. Your health gives me far more anxiety than the Turks, as to whom there will certainly soon come some occasion to get the better of them, and the first will lead to others. It is not my talents that I desire to offer to your Majesty, but my willingness, my activity, and the assurance that I will never abandon my post while I live. The most horrible hole, or dreadful cavern, or the worst of defiles to guard will seem to me delightful winter-quarters if I can be useful in your service; and in any country, with any number or any kind of troops that may be intrusted to me, I will answer for the zeal with which I will command, and the readiness with which I will go wherever ordered.

After all these months before Oczakow I am about to start again for the army under Maréchal Romanzow, whence Baron de Herbert writes me that I may be able to help him to accomplish something if the enemy is allowed in Wallachia — so easy for the Russians to occupy! At any rate, it will be a diversion, and if none is made this empire will be dishonoured in the eyes of all Europe. I leave on Sunday. Seeing that I cannot obtain sufficient influence over Prince Potemkin's mind, — not more, in fact, than others, — I separate from him on good terms, and with much regret on his part, which may be useful under other circumstances. Perhaps at a distance and by letter my advice and solicitations may have some effect. His frigates have arrived, but he does not yet attack. Meanwhile, the capitan-pacha is daily receiving reinforcements and will, apparently, undertake some enterprise. He has, at the present moment, ninety vessels, having repaired those which were disabled in the four engagements of last summer.

They have made the Prince of Nassau pay dear for his

victories. Part of his fleet has been given to Paul Jones (in addition to the latter's own three frigates), to whom the prince intends to intrust the chief commission for the bombardment whenever it takes place. In spite of a private letter from the prince, who feared the wrong-headedness of Paul Jones, the latter has refused to salute the flag of the vice-admiral, — which M. de Nassau since then has not raised; announcing that he shall leave the moment that Oczakow is taken.

To the Same.

JASSY, October 22, 1788.

SIRE, — I found Maréchal Romanzow on my arrival full of the utmost good-will, which may or may not continue. He has almost promised me to attack the Turks at Roboïai-Mohilai. As it is impossible to trust a single word in these armies I will not guarantee that his whole army will pass the winter in Moldavia, but I think I can assure your Majesty that he will leave a large part of it, — half, I hope, between the Dniester and the Pruth, and half between the Pruth and the Serith.

As it is impossible for me to have any illusions as to the Russians or to hope any longer, I venture to take the liberty to assure your Majesty that if one of your corps does not make, in the direction of the Danube, the diversion that we had the right to expect of our allies, things will go on as they are now. The reasons, true or false, about the lack of supplies and the antechamber intrigues, of which the Russians are thinking much more than they are of the enemy, will continue to keep them useless to us. Her Majesty the empress knows nothing of what is going on; she is ignorant, though I have written it *by post* to our ambassador, that her troops have made the most shameful of campaigns. She is thinking only of rewarding them, preparing ribbons and medals for battles that will never be fought. Even the taking of Oczakow at this late day will not make much change in the situation.

To the Same.

JASSY, November 18, 1788.

At the end of a month without news from Prince Potemkin, a courier arrived yesterday. Maréchal Romanzow tells me that the Prince of Nassau had started for Warsaw, Paul Jones for Petersburg, Dolgoroucki for Moscow, Branicki for Bielaczerkew. The capitan-pacha still remains. The prince writes that he believes he shall be obliged to come to an assault. The courier says the troops are in a miserable plight; as may well be believed with no wood to burn and far from everything.

Cadet Beniatsch has this moment returned, bringing me the letter from Semlin with which your Majesty has honoured me. The chief object of his mission is accomplished, which was to see your Majesty himself and bring me an exact account of your health, which I hear with the utmost joy is better.

I have the honour to be, with the keenest sentiments of gratitude for what your Majesty has deigned to say to me in your last two touching letters, and with as much attachment as respect, etc.

To the Same.

JASSY, November 30, 1788.

I can never sufficiently express to your Majesty the double happiness you have given me: that of allowing me to return to you is the greatest; and next is that of being informed of your permission by my son Charles, who is as much attached to your Majesty as I am myself. I shall profit shortly by the greatest favour I could have received; that is, as soon as I have received certain information, which it will be wise for me to obtain before leaving; although, in truth, little more is needed than that which I have given your Majesty in my last two letters concerning an empire from which there is nothing to hope and will be nothing to fear for a very long time. No plan of campaign is possible until the taking of Oczakow or the raising of the siege. Moreover, Prince Potemkin, who makes no reply either in words or writing, will never explain himself, being firmly resolved to do, as he told me himself, only what he chooses, and never what any one, even the empress, orders him to do.

To H. I. M. Catherine II.

Jassy, November 30, 1788.

I cannot take a sheet of paper large enough to tell your Imperial Majesty that I leave your person with a regret that you alone could imagine, if you did yourself justice — the only justice that you never do.

When one is gay one takes a little sheet of paper and scribbles it over with a wretched pen, and perhaps a few paltry verses; but alas! this is prose. Charles has just arrived with a letter from the emperor in which his Imperial Majesty has the kindness to recall me to himself, that I may have the happiness of serving under his own eye.

I shall carry back to Hungary the two most beautiful dreams of my life, — my journey to Petersburg, and that to Taurica. I must await a time more tranquil to go again to the feet of your Majesty; but I shall dream in that direction as soon as may be after endeavouring to give to his Imperial Majesty, under his own eye, some proofs of my zeal for the two empires.

I have the honour to be, with boundless attachment and respect, Madame, etc.

The Empress Catherine to the Prince de Ligne.

PETERSBURG, December 2, 1788.

MONSIEUR LE PRINCE DE LIGNE, — In order to take leave of me on departing from Jassy, you have written me, November 30, a letter on a sheet of paper as large as those used in the public offices for discharging employés. When I saw the size of that missive I thought it an evil omen, and I found I was not mistaken. Certainly, after a prolonged visit of two years one ought not to think it strange that a person who is not condemned to live among us should leave us; but still, there are people in the world from whom we cannot part without regret.

It is your son who draws you to the army of the emperor, to serve, you tell me, under his Majesty's own eye. Valour, honour, happiness, and fortune will no doubt guide your steps. Be assured of the sincere interest that I shall take in the brilliant successes that you cannot fail to obtain.

If our campaign among the arid rocks of Finland has not been wonderful [she was then at war with Sweden], at least we have lost no battle, and not one inch of the soil that belongs to us. I was brought up to love and respect republics, but experience has convinced me that the more people we get together to reason, the more unreasonable is what they say.

To Prince Kaunitz [Austrian Prime Minister].

JASSY, December 15, 1788.

I have executed the orders of your Highness with regard to the ill-advised malice of the Russian emissaries among the Montenegrins, or rather in those who sent them there.

Allies who wish to be friends (they are often the one and not the other) should keep an eye on blundering officers

That is why I wrote very seriously to the Prince of Coburg to punish the officer who summoned Choczim. "Distrust the Russians," he said to the pacha; "do not surrender to them; they are barbarians."

It is to avoid all asperities, which are very prejudicial to the service, that I have interrupted my correspondence with the empress; I could not have kept myself from telling her that I was apparently taken by her people here for a Turkish spy. In order not to have an accusing air, and yet to show matters of friendly complaint, I wrote the other day to M. de Ségur *by post* saying that they did not place confidence enough in me.

I can be employed in political affairs as an *enfant perdu*, and disavowed as much as any one likes. That is how I said one day to Prince Potemkin that if he would march along the shores of the Black Sea to the Danube, and make Romanzow march to Bucharest, I could succeed in making him Hospodar of Moldavia and Wallachia. "I scorn it," he replied. "I bet I could be king of Poland if I chose; I have already refused to be Duke of Courlande. I am much more than all that." "Well, at least," I said, "make those two countries (Moldavia and Wallachia) independent of the Turks at the peace; let them be governed by their boyards under the protection of the two empires." To this he replied, "We will see about it."

Your Highness will remember, no one better, the moral of the fable of the lark and her fledglings. We can depend on none but ourselves; and I believe we have these allies only to make sure that they are not entirely our enemies. If M. de Loudon were here with twenty thousand men he could do the task I have urged upon Romanzow. If we began by Belgrade or even Orsowa, joined to what has been already done in Bosnia, I will answer for it the war would be finished by next June. Such operations would draw the whole strength or rather weakness of the Ottomans upon us, and then my colossus might bestir himself. He is an emblem of his empire, — a mine of gold and arid steppes; but my Potemkin is the better fed colossus of the two; the other dwindles as it enlarges.

May God preserve to the world the great and immortal empress. But as that can be only in history, I think we ought to manage with extreme care the grand-duke, who, while he reforms a million of abuses, spends millions in generosities and is prompt, ardent, and capable of work, changing too often his opinions and his friends ever to have a favourite or a mistress, may prove very much to be feared some day, if his mother leaves him the empire. I think that if she has time she will leave it to the little Grand-Duke Alexander, for she alienates her son from public affairs as much as she encourages her grandson by the attention she gives to forming him herself, young as he is, for government. His father at the present moment is altogether Prussian. But that may only be as M. le Dauphin was pious, because Louis XV. was not. However, he is extremely fickle; albeit during the short time he wants, or loves, or hates anything, it is with violence and obstinacy. He detests his nation, and said to me once at Gatschina that the Russians were scoundrels who wanted to be governed by none but women.

I have succeeded in three things only: first, in making them give the fleet to the Prince of Nassau, who took or burned thirty-six vessels large and small, killed or drowned five thousand men, and captured 578 cannon; and next I made Potemkin cross the Bog, and Romanzow the Dniester. I may also put Choczim into the list of my military exploits morally, because it was by dint of sending couriers that I made them attack; and I have also obtained the assurance of the empress that it shall be ours at the peace — such peace as they can make.

I beg your Highness to continue your kindnesses, the habit of bestowing which ever since my childhood makes you so often call me "my son." I feel that title in the respect and tenderness that I devote to you.

To the Comte de Ségur.

Before the Camp of Roboïai-Mohilai, otherwise Jassy, where I have my headquarters, December 18, 1788.

I expected to have told you long before this of an easy victory over the sultan, prince *in partibus* of the Crimea, over Ibrahim-Nazir and the Seraskier of Ismaïl. I counted on the fête of Saint Gregory, Prince Potemkin's patron, but alas! I am still a *vox clamans in deserto.*

The Turks, who always, just like game, have the same runs and the same burrows, collect at the beginning of every war in the camp of Roboïai-Mohilai. This time they had the cleverness to place it sideways so that they could easily have been attacked and beaten. But now the fifteen or twenty thousand men, who were made to pass for fifty thousand, have departed. I find myself in a land of enchantment after Servia, the country of the Nogais and Budjaks, Tartary, and the neighbourhood of Bessarabia, from which I have just emerged. A long and dreadful winter in a hut placed in the middle of a redoubt full of snow and mud, without anything to look at but the sky, the sea, and a stretch of plain three hundred leagues long, followed by a campaign of six months doing nothing, was surely enough to make me think this place most delightful.

After I departed from Elisabeth-Gorod I never saw a house or a tree, except those in the pacha's garden close to the intrenchments at Oczakow. I went under fire from the fort guns and kissed some of those trees, I had such pleasure in seeing them; I even gathered and ate some of their apricots. Water as green as the dead bodies of five thousand Turks was all we had to drink for five months, except the water of the Black Sea, which is not so salt as other seas. Imagine therefore my happiness when I came upon a charming fountain on the heights that overlook Jassy. I kissed the water before I drank of it. I devoured it with my eyes before I wet my lips, which for so long had been moistened by nothing so delicious.

I am lodged in one of those superb palaces which the boyards build in the Eastern style, more than one hundred and fifty of which rise high above the other edifices in this capital of Moldavia. Charming women, nearly all from Constantinople and of ancient Greek families, sit negligently on their divans, their heads lying back or supported sometimes by an alabaster arm. The men who visit them almost lie at their feet. A very short, scant skirt only slightly covers their charming shape, and a gauze scarf defines the pretty outlines of their throat and bust. They wear upon their heads a stuff that is either black or scarlet in the shape of a turban or cap, glittering with diamonds. Pearls of the purest white are on their neck and arms, round which they sometimes wear strips of gauze studded with sequins and half-ducats. I have seen as many as three thousand worn by one lady. The rest of their Eastern apparel is of stuffs embroidered in silver and gold and edged with the choicest furs; so are the costumes of the boyards, which only differ from those of the Turks in the cap that they wear above the red fez, which looks somewhat like a turban.

The wives of the boyards, like the sultanas, always hold in their hands a sort of chaplet of diamonds, pearl, coral, lapis lazuli, or some rare wood which serves them for attitudinizing, like the fan of our women. They flirt it and display their agile fingers, the nails of which are dyed red, telling their beads, as it were, and having invented (so I am told) a vocabulary for their lovers. I fancied I caught the looks of two or three husbands curious to know whether I could understand the pretty alphabet of gallantry. The hour for a rendezvous could easily be given in that way; but how obtain the rendezvous itself? Seven or eight of the boyard's serving-men, and as many young girls waiting on the wives, are always in the apartment. Their costume differs only in richness from that of their masters and mistresses. Each and all have their own department. One brings, as soon as you enter to make a visit, two or more pipes; another a saucer and little spoon with rose confectionery; a third burns perfumes or scatters essences which make the salon fragrant; a fourth brings a cup of coffee; a fifth a glass of water; and this is repeated in the houses of twenty boyards if you go to see that number in one day; and it would be considered a great impoliteness to refuse these civilities.

The weather is warm. I dress like the boyards. I often go among them to think without distraction, for I know only a few Wallach words and no modern Greek, which the ladies speak, despising the language of their husbands. But, in any case, the boyards speak little. The fear they have of the Turks, the habit of expecting evil, and the tyranny which the Divan at Constantinople and the hospodar exercise over their minds have brought them to a state of unconquerable sadness. Persons assembling every day in one another's houses have an air of awaiting the fatal bowstring. One hears it said repeatedly, "Here my father was slain by order of the Porte," or, "There my sister was killed by the prince's order."

When I say that I go among the boyards to think, I mean that I go there not to think; for at the fourth pipe I become a Turk; I am nil; I have no ideas; and perhaps it is the best thing for me, being so far away from you and all I love.

Constantinople gives the tone to Jassy, as Paris to the provinces, and the fashions arrive more quickly. Yellow was the favourite colour of the sultanas last year, and it is now the reigning hue among the women of Jassy. Long pipes of cherry-wood having superseded in Constantinople the jasmine-wood pipes of the past, all we boyards are smoking through cherry-wood too. A boyard never goes out on foot; in that he is quite as lazy as a Turk.

The ladies might dispense with having so much stomach; but it is so well recognized here as being a great beauty that a mother excused her daughter to me for having none. "It will come in time," she said, "but now it is really mortifying; she is as slim and straight as a reed." The costumes and the Asiatic manners make the pretty ones prettier, but the ugly ones frightful; though ugly ones, to tell the truth, are rare. It has happened to me once or twice, in consequence of the way the women curl themselves round, to mistake them when the room was dark for pelisses thrown aside on the divan.

The daughters of the boyards are shut up like the Turkish women in harems behind wooden lattices, often gilded, through which they may look at men and select their husbands; but the men may not see their wives until after the very slight ceremony of the Greek church has been performed.

I have just given a charming fête, which succeeded delightfully. A hundred boyards and their wives to supper and a ball; at which they danced the pyrrhic, and other

Greek, Moldavian, Turkish, Wallachian, and gipsy dances. Those dances show the origin of an amusement which in itself would be stupid were it not for its object. Dancing can have but two motives: rejoicing after victory, and voluptuous pleasure in peace. These dancers held each other by the hand. Sometimes they circled round, but usually they faced each other; they gave each other looks; parted, returned, approached, I hardly know how; looked again, listened, divined, and seemed to love each other. I thought it a very sensible dance.

Nothing in the least resembles the situation of these people. Suspected by the Russians of preferring the Austrians, suspected by the Austrians of being secretly attached to the Turks, they long for the departure of the first two as much as they dread the return of the third. O you statesmen! arbiters of the fate of these poor mortals, in whose hands you have often put arms, repair the evils that you have done; you are more responsible than we, the military, who are but the executors of your decisions. Serve this humanity and benefit the policy of your empires by leaving these poor Moldavians at peace. Their country is so fine that all Europe will cry out if you attempt to dismember it; make them independent of their Eastern tyrants, let them govern themselves, and in place of their hospodar (who is forced to be a scoundrel or a despot to pay court to the Ottoman Porte) give them two boyard governors, removable every three years. Those men, returning to their class at the end of that time, will not dare to abuse their authority, for they would pay dearly for it afterwards.

When peace comes let the mediating Courts endeavour to frame for them a code of laws, very simple and, above all, not traced out by the hand of philosophy, but by good, honest, legal minds, who know the climate, the nature, the religion, and the manners and customs of people and country. Such a code would give sovereign authority to the two great and powerful seigneurs chosen to administer the laws.

What an opening that is, my dear Ségur, for your soul and your mind! Become a Montesquieu and a Louvois if you can, without ceasing to be a Racine, Horace, and La Fontaine. Work for my poor Moldavians in some good way, whatever it may be. They treat me so well! I love everything about them; especially their language, which recalls their descent from the Romans. It is an harmonious mixture of Latin and Italian. They say *szluga* for "I wish you good-day;" *formos coconitza* for "a beautiful girl;" *sara bona*, "good evening;" and *dragua-mï* for "I love you;" which I can say to you in twelve languages, trusting that you will say it to me in good French.

[The prince had scarcely left the Russian armies in December, 1788, before Prince Potemkin stormed Oczakow and took it at the end of one hour and a half. It seems incredible that he should have waited a whole year and allowed (as we have seen) all his chief commanders to disperse, besides incurring untold expenses, before reducing a place which took so little time and gave him so little trouble to capture. The Prince de Ligne on receiving the news wrote immediately to the Empress Catherine to congratulate her. This is her answer:]

To the Prince de Ligne.

February, 1789.

By your letter of January 16, which I have just received, I see the joy you feel at the taking of Oczakow. The Maréchal Prince Potemkin tried, as was proper, all measures before coming finally to an assault. The most convenient time for the operation was, undoubtedly, when the Liman, being frozen over, made the water side inaccessible for reinforcements to the besieged, and the place once captured, this allowed time to take all necessary precautions for the future. But the impatience of young men full of courage, half-heads, three-quarter heads, envious persons, and open and secret enemies, is, in all such cases, quite intolerable, and from it the marshal has had much to suffer, — a fact that does him the greatest honour in my eyes. Among his other great and good qualities I have always seen that of pardoning his enemies and doing them good; in that way he wins a victory. On this occasion he has beaten the Turks and those who have criticised him in one hour and a half. Persons now say he might have taken Oczakow sooner: that is true; but never with so little inconvenience.

This is not the first time among us that the sick have left the hospitals to rush to an assault. On many a great occasion I have known the same thing happen. I can tell you more than that: Last summer when the King of Sweden attacked us suddenly, I sent word to the villages of the crown domains to give me recruits, and I said that they must estimate for themselves how many they could send. Well, what happened? A village of one thousand males sent me one hundred and seventy-five fine recruits; another of four thousand sent two hundred and fifty; a third, of Czarsko-zelo, where there are three thousand peasants, sent four hundred horses with men and waggons for the transportation of munitions. All of them made the campaign in Finland. But that is not all. The neighbouring provinces, and then, little by little, all the provinces offered me, this one a battalion, that one a squadron; the city of Moscow alone would have put ten thousand men into the field had I allowed it. Our people are warrior-born, and our recruits are drilled in a trice. The nobles, young and old, have all served, and when the occasion called for it not one said no to anything; all have rushed to the defence of State and Country; and no effort was needed to make them do so.

V.

1789–1790.

TURKISH WAR CONTINUED: SIEGE OF BELGRADE.

After leaving Moldavia, Bessarabia, and Tartary at the close of the last campaign I passed a very happy and tranquil winter in Vienna, without letting myself think much about public affairs. No one talked of them to me, seeming unaware that I had had much to do with them for the last two years. This did not signify to me. Now and then I passed from ear to ear the necessity of reinforcing the Princes of Coburg and Hohenlohe and sending them to Bucharest, taking care also to send munitions and supplies into Wallachia, to cut off the head of Mauro-Jan, and march to the Danube. For a year I had vainly urged (at a distance, it is true, because at a distance one has more boldness in telling the truth to sovereigns) that the Banat and Transylvania could never be properly covered except by that operation.

I arrived at Semlin from Vienna about the middle of the month of May, 1789, and there I found an armistice going on, rather badly made, and not too well kept, and very ill-defined; sufficiently so to displease the Russians, to whom it seemed that we wanted to send them the Grand Vizir, and useless to us, because the inundations of the Danube and other rivers presented insurmountable obstacles between the main body of the Turks and ourselves. The honest, virtuous, and enlightened Maréchal Haddick commanded the army.

There was talk of laying siege to Belgrade, and so much was said about it that I concluded it would never be done. It vexed me to see provisions getting daily into the city, which was almost without any, while we were prevented by this armistice from capturing them, which, with my Servian guerillas, would have been so easy. [Belgrade is on the Danube at its junction with the Save; the citadel stands on a rock 100 feet high on a tongue of land formed by the two rivers, and was one of the strongest fortresses in Europe; Semlin is on the Save within sight of Belgrade.] I groaned over that armistice, which was injurious from a military and political point of view, and ridiculous from others. But I profited by the time to reconnoitre the environs. One day I took an escort of hussars and Servian free-lances and reconnoitred to a long distance beyond Belgrade and far into the enemy's country. We had plans and very fine drawings, but not one of the draughtsmen had ever seen the place. I admired the passion shown for marching in squares to get through a country so broken, unequal, and full of defiles, in order to besiege Belgrade.

But all this was so uninteresting that I kept no record of what happened through May, June, July, and August, which latter month came near killing me. My corps, which had a force of 30,000 men, was reduced by sickness to 15,000. One hundred men a day sent to the hospitals was thought to be a small matter. I, who did not know what it was to be ill, had a fever for seventeen consecutive days; this happened unfortunately at a time when Turks on the one hand and our generals on the other did not give me a moment's peace. The first persisted in marching a battery up the other bank of the Save just to fire a few shots and then retire. The latter insisted on giving me advice, which I returned by advising them not to give it, and to stop their fears about my breaking the armistice with the two cannon I had posted beside my bridge over the Save. I repaired the great redoubt of Semlin, strengthened the ramparts, and added some other works. Sometimes I gave myself an alarm during the night, to make sure that everybody knew his place.[1]

During the latter part of this time Maréchal Loudon, having superseded Maréchal Haddick, who was recalled without any one knowing why, was eating his heart out at Weiskirch. The enemy was in the Banat. Loudon awaited the final orders of the emperor to make or not to make the siege of Belgrade. He was furious at being prevented from going to Banjaluka after taking Berbir and conquering the whole of Bosnia, and he saw the difficulties of the locality, the season, and the continual sickness among the troops. He assembled all his principal generals for a council of war. On that day I had such a violent attack of fever that it was impossible for me to be present, but I wrote my opinion, and perhaps the heat of my paroxysm was communicated to my reasons against the siege. Maréchal Loudon approved of them; but the emperor apparently did not, for soon afterwards the siege was resolved upon. "Cost what it may," he wrote, "I wish you to take Belgrade."

I wished it too, but I wanted Servia cleaned out previously, to get Abdy Pacha off our hands and so be able to take Belgrade in three days. I wrote, as I say, this opinion of mine to be read at the council of war at Weiskirch, and then sent to his Majesty, who was perhaps not pleased with

[1] The prince enters into close details of all his dispositions throughout this campaign and his reasons for them. They are too minute and professional for these pages, and perhaps too antiquated for modern warfare; but the Duke of Wellington read and studied these and the prince's other military works with interest. They are contained in vols. i., vii., xiv., xvii., xix., xxiv. of his Works. — Tr.

it. But the Truth was a rival in my heart to the sovereign I loved, and carried the day on all occasions when it concerned the honour of our arms; as for my life, that was wholly at his service. I saw the obstacles so plainly, and so did Maréchal Loudon, — though the event proved against our expectation, — that it was quite impossible for me not to endeavour to make others see them.

Fever, Turks, and generals continued to torment me so that I do not know how in the intervals between delirium and chills that lasted five hours, I managed to give and dictate orders. In the midst of it all the enemy attacked and burned two of my vessels. I ordered up the fleet to where their shot could reach the town, and the 18-pound guns of my repaired redoubt created great alarm there and did some damage. This brought the generals down upon me. Already I had had representations that I was breaking, as they called it, the armistice. "But my vessels, gentlemen," I replied; "what do you say to those?" "They were attacked and burned in spite of Osman Pacha," said the general who was particularly charged to remonstrate.

Three days later the town of Belgrade fired a broadside at the town of Semlin; it did look, I must acknowledge, a little like reprisals. My shot had grazed, I believe, the house of the pacha; his flew past my windows and went further. What looked like open war was the insulting advance of two Turkish sloops close up to mine on the left arm of the Danube. The latter fired, as it had orders to do; on which the Turks advanced and brought up seven other vessels. My son Charles saw it all from my window and rushed, with the excellent, brave, intelligent Baron de Bolza, my adjutant-general, and Langendonck, one of my aides-de-camp who always thrust himself wherever there were cannon-balls or musketry. They jumped into a boat and I was sure then that the fight would be hot.

I was not exactly like Louis XIV., who, says Boileau, complained that his grandeur tied him to the shore. A terrible attack of fever held me at my window; from which, nevertheless, I commanded the naval battle by shouting with all my might, *Alla larga!* and *Avanti!* to the frigate "Maria Theresa" and my other vessels. As they were not able to stir, I only cracked my throat and greatly increased my fever. But what increased it still more was the fear that fire or water would play some bad trick on Charles, who is by way of being too much of an amateur. But he got off happily and bravely, as usual. The fight was lively. We fired more than six hundred cannon-balls. I never knew the enemy's loss; but we sank the two sloops that first advanced; I saw them early in the fight retiring.

This was a good time to make the pacha explain himself; but I don't like explanations — either with women or the enemy. If I had complained of these insults, the pacha might have sent me back a dozen decapitated heads, and we should have lost the right to cross the Save with an army without giving ten days' notice. The singular part of it was that all this time my stupid old Osman Pacha kept writing to me most tenderly as to certain affairs we had together about prisoners and armistice. I replied and always signed myself, "Your good neighbour and friend." After this affair I continued to write to him and he to me. I still have all his letters, but very few copies of my own.

To the Comte de Ségur.

IN MY HEADQUARTERS AT SEMLIN, June, 1789.

I might have written to you last winter about things you did not know, or since then about things that you do know; but I never write with pleasure unless I can receive an answer within a few hours. In Paris I never wrote to the other side of the bridges; and this was why, floating with you on the Borysthenes and separated only by a silken partition in the splendid galley of that triumphant and magical journey, I wrote and received a morning greeting in a moment.

A species of armistice, or I might say social agreement, leaves me free to give the Turks (in a superb tent as Turkish as they) delightful concerts on my bank of the river. All the garrison of Belgrade come out to listen to them on the opposite shore. Like the King of Spain who for forty years had a certain air of Farinelli's sung to him daily, I make them play to me every night *O cosa rara!* — which thus ceases, as you perceive, to be a rare thing. Beautiful Jewesses, Armenians, Illyrians, and Servians are present.

When the Turks pass my frontiers I punish them. Osman Pacha thanks me, and says he can't make them obey him. As I like better to tease him than to be fooled by excuses, I fired a little *feu de joie* the other day in commemoration of one of our small victories in Moldavia, but I loaded the guns with ball to avenge a sentinel of mine whose head they had cut off. The thing succeeded. Eight inquisitive persons were killed at the foot of the redoubt. The pacha seemed to think it was quite natural. I hoped he would have been angry. I myself never complain when a few shots are fired at me in play as I take my walks. But a lieutenant-colonel of one of my advanced posts on the Pantschowa side, disapproved of their treating one of his officers in that way and complained to Aga Mustapha, who answered as follows: —

"I salute you, neighbour Terschitz. You say there is an armistice. I know nothing about that. You talk to me of the Pacha of Belgrade. I am not dependent upon him. You offer me help in case I need it. Learn that the Sublime Porte does not allow me to need anything. All I want is to drink your blood. You tell me that I can trust you. Know that in these days no one should trust any one. I salute you, neighbour Terschitz."

Here is the answer I sent him in neighbour Terschitz's name, —

"I salute you, neighbour Mustapha. Your letter is very Turkish. I am glad, for I was thinking there were no Turks. You say you want to drink my blood. I don't care about drinking yours. What is the blood of an aga? Do what you like, and come when you can. I have given my people orders to take you prisoner at the first opportunity. I should like to see you. Good-bye to you, Aga Mustapha."

I did a rather giddy thing the other day. I had to write to Osman Pacha about a courier from M. de Choiseul who occasionally sends me one. I carried the letter myself; that is to say, I went, accompanied by my interpreter, in a little boat with a white flag (sign of wanting a parley) to the foot of the citadel, ostensibly to deliver the letter, but really to reconnoitre the side on which the attack will be made, as I hope, a month or two from now. I had plenty of time to examine everything before a boat with a dozen men, whose faces were either splendid or villanous (for there is no medium among the Turks), came out to look at us and take my letter, which I presented as being sent through me by myself. I was very cajoling and used all the thirty Turkish words that I know. Two or three of their moustaches smiled; but the others frightened me horribly by examining me. I remembered that they might have seen me firing at eagles and wild-duck under their noses on the Save. I was wearing a huge white cloak and a shabby slouched hat. I heard them ask my interpreter who I was. He replied that I was the secretary of the Seraskier of Semlin for French correspondence. The most villanous-looking of the Turks, with an infernal face, snatched my letter from me abruptly, saying he would take it to the pacha. I was quits for a few moments' uneasiness, but I got away by force of oars as fast as I could.

Adieu, my dear Ségur; I leave you to see ten fine battalions of reinforcements just sent to me from Austria. May I soon make use of them! I wish they would let me cross the Save to Sabacz, just to see if there is really such a being as Abdy Pacha, of whose coming I am constantly warned; likewise of that of the Pacha of Trawnick and the famous Mahmoud of Scutari. I should like to sweep the plain up to the very cannon of Nissa. If it were not for the uneasiness this Abdy Pacha gives us, things would go on much better.

I embrace you with all my heart.

After the last letter of the emperor, Maréchal Loudon made all arrangements to cross the Save on the 15th of September. I felt that I must take quinine in order to take Belgrade. I took it; for I was nearly at my last gasp, — and grew worse. They ordered me change of air and I started September 1 for Kergedeck, a Greek monastery in the mountains near Carlowitz. There I should have recovered entirely, but knowing the marshal's promptitude of mind and action I grew uneasy, and left at the end of eight days to rejoin the army, with a weakness of the legs and a stiffness in the knees which never left me as long as I remained in that cursèd region.

I had guessed right; instead of crossing on the 15th, the marshal had changed to the 14th, and then he suddenly came down to the 12th because the report of a scout made him believe that Abdy Pacha was on the way with thirty thousand men. True or not, it was what he might be (and

Maréchal Loudon

it is very surprising that he never came). The marshal, with that quickness of mind I mentioned above, which sometimes led him to think aloud, said to those about him, what any other man would have said to himself: "Shall I, or shall I not cross the Save?"

Some generals present gave it as their opinion — at this moment when it was impossible to hold back, all was too far advanced, everything had to be chanced and all efforts doubled — some generals, I say, answered not to cross. Mack, who is not a general but deserves to be, and Colonel Bourgeois, gave it as their opinion that we ought to cross. This recalled to the marshal's mind the emperor's last words, and he said: "Very well, let us cross," in his simple way, as if he had not already formed his decision. Ten minutes later he added, with flame in his eyes: "Messieurs, the first step is now to be made. I warn you, it is conquer or die." Then, pointing to the ground before Belgrade, "There," he said, "it is *there*, in that corner, that we will settle the fate of the monarchy."

It is surprising that the emperor persisted in doing, in the month of October, what he would not do in June, when the fall of Belgrade would have entailed that of Orsowa, Widdin, and Nissa. Policy, apparently, had something to do with it; and when one sees such precious moments in war sacrificed to politics it puts one out of temper.

With two fine marches the army was across the Save, and the marshal made his famous attack on the two villages called the Faubourgs. I protected him with six hundred 24-pound shot. It was then that the Comte de Browne, at the head of four columns, which he cleverly divided, got possession of the Ratzenstadt, and displayed such valour, coolness, and talent that after the siege M. de Loudon, who had seen all three qualities in him, said to me: "There's a man we must push, to put him soon at the head of armies." During the engagement the marshal kept writing to me to fire fast, and Collercdo to fire slow, and Pellegrini to fire straight. I obeyed the first, for it was more in my line; besides, it electrified me, and I electrified others.

The weakness of my legs and the stiffness of my knees made me more of a general than a soldier while the intrenching was going on; but perhaps this did more for our success, because my head worked better. That is, if I had been in health I might never have left the trenches; as it was, I was there all day. I went to see every work as soon as finished, and decide on others and place them. One day, half carried by two subalterns, and dragging myself along, I helped to lay out the redoubt of the Donawitz, after which I passed a dreadful night in the trenches. I did not sleep, day or night, and there was not a quarter of an hour that M. de Bolza was not up and about to second or forestall my intentions. Poor Dettinger was ill, and ill of being ill and unable to follow me everywhere as at Oczakow; but he did me many services whenever his strength allowed. As for Langendonck, he took it as his business to rush through balls and bombs to be useful to me; and he passed enough nights in the trenches to kill him, as the enemy did not choose to do so.

I was very much pleased with the valour of the engineer and the artillery officers, both; but it was the devil and all to make arrangements with them because of their professional jealousies and the division of authority. Any one who knows Colonel d'Arnal will not be surprised at this; he was full of the most distinguished talents, but also of ancient prejudices; brave and intelligent but rather impracticable, deaf, and a little blind. Colonel Funk kept everything going, with unequalled intrepidity and valour. The first quality led him to face anything, and led others, by his vigorous example, to do likewise, under the hottest fire, and sometimes the continual fire, of the enemy; the other made him spend every night through three whole weeks in the works, rendering me the utmost service, for he often did what the infantry should have done.

The essential point of our position was the Sauspitz. I placed a detachment in the underbrush on lines I marked out myself, beginning at a distance of about one hundred and fifty feet from the intrenchments, and I made a road, so that in case the Turks attempted to occupy the Sauspitz, two battalions could be brought up instantly. Collecting all my strength I went several times alone, sometimes with patrols of sharpshooters, through the underbrush of the Sauspitz, to reconnoitre the most difficult ground of all, and the most necessary to study in order to station troops and protect ourselves from attacks on that side; for the enemy would surely, except for these precautions, have got a footing there.

My greatest merit in my own eyes is for having secured, little by little, this piece of ground by cautious manœuvring; had I tried to do so by force, I should only have become involved in ridiculous skirmishing, like that of the previous year; I should have wasted my time instead of completing my works, which would, moreover, have been impossible if the enemy could have hidden a thousand men in the holes and coverts of that underbrush.

When it became a question of establishing the redoubt at the mouth of the Donawitz, I assembled my generals and the officers of the Engineer and Artillery Corps, the majors of the trenches, and the commissaries, in order to regulate the number of workmen, the affairs of the laboratory, the depots, the tools, the army-waggons, etc. There are a thousand things needed for a siege, of which no one could form an idea unless he had commanded at one, all of which required the most assiduous attention. I did nothing for three weeks but attend to these matters; besides which, I had to purvey for the marshal's whole army. I was told that I should find everything had been prepared for the siege during the previous year. As for that, the fascines had been burned, the rats had eaten the bags that held the earth, the gabions had not been filled; there was no supply of munitions or of any of the things most necessary, but much thwarting from the country itself and from the Departments of Engineering and Artillery, and endless requisitions and writings. Five hundred ducats which I paid among the people of the neighbourhood, to buy, persuade, and reward, did something. There were no arrangements for the wounded. Rusty cannon-balls exploded when they left the guns, and killed my own men, — in short, a hundred thousand vexations which would have been fatal hindrances to any one less obstinate than I.

The marshal saw plainly that he had no great resources in his army of any kind; and he knew from the first that a tremendous fire from my side, and the quickest possible, could alone ensure success, because the batteries of his attack could only touch the parapet *à cornes* of the enemy's works and, slightly, the embrasures, those works projecting too little to be battered from anywhere except the crest of the covered way. But it was certain that all our bombshells from the Sauspitz were crushing men and houses; not a shot missed.

I had ordered that the battalions on the left and two on the right should fire at different angles. I gave the direction of the powder magazines to my four 100-pound mortars; for I believed that, even if they did not succeed in crushing in the roofs, they might blow up the buildings by falling on some thread of powder scattered by careless hands.

I gave orders to the artillery to dismount the guns that were firing upon us. "That is no matter," said d'Arnal, "let us help the others." "No," I said, "let us help ourselves first; silence those guns." And silenced they were, so thoroughly that we could go the whole length of the intrenchment and drag a powder-waggon in broad daylight. In fact, what could resist our infernal torrent of fire? Here is the number of the balls and bombshells that I discharged from the Sauspitz: 5662 balls, and 6083 bombshells.

It was decidedly that which took Belgrade; for the batteries of the three marshals could only touch, as I have said, the crest of the parapet and the embrasures. It only remained to surmount the covered way, uncover the base of the wall, and batter a breach. This Maréchal Loudon was about to do when the fort surrendered; and it was from his recognition of all this that he deigned to attribute in a great degree to my zeal and the manner in which I had pressed the work the taking of the place.

I was all on fire myself for that Being, who was more of a demigod in war than a man. Urged by him I urged on others. Bolza watched and flew; Funk fired; Maillard rushed forward. I thanked, I begged, I ordered, I threatened; all went well; and all was done in the twinkling of an eye. Here is the charming note the marshal wrote me:

Before BELGRADE, October 8, 1789.

I give myself the honour of informing your Highness that the garrison of Belgrade surrenders on condition of a free passage out, that this capitulation is settled, and that our troops will this day occupy the enemy's works.

Owing a great part of this fortunate result to the efficacious manner, so conformed to our purpose, with which your Highness employed your energies, which have largely contributed to that result by the attack made on the side of your Command, I shall lay before the eyes of his Majesty the very ample praises that your Highness so well deserves.

LOUDON.

He did as he said; and it is to him I owe the honour of being a commander of the military Order of Maria Theresa. The star which I received eight days later, that favour due above all to Maréchal Loudon, is the thing that has given me the greatest pleasure in all my life.

To the Comte de Ségur.

BELGRADE, October 18, 1789.

Here we are, in this rampart of the Orient, of which we have opened the gates, not with the rosy fingers of Aurora, but with the red hand of fire. The boldness and promptitude of the passage of the Save, the rapidity of the march and of the entrance to the old lines of Prince Eugène, the audacity of the reconnaissance, made to the stockade itself, all that was the work of fifteen days worthy indeed of the finest days of Maréchal Loudon. He fired our heads, we fired off the Turks' heads, and I dismounted their guns. He attacked Belgrade on the right bank of the Save, and I on the left bank, where I was the eagle of the Jupiter whose thunderbolt I hurled.

What a source of reflections! Hardly had the word "capitulation" been uttered before ten thousand of the conquered mingled with as many conquerors. Ferocity gave place to gentleness, anger to pity, the wiles of war to sincerity and good faith. They all took coffee together, they sold, they bought. The Turk, honest in his marts, fixes a price and delivers his goods hidden in the casemates, goes about his affairs, and receives his money without eagerness if he happens to meet his purchaser. Philosophers, without being aware of it, the rich proprietors are calmly smoking on the ruins of their houses and their fortunes. Osman Pacha, the silly old governor of Belgrade, smokes in the midst of his Court, ranged ceremoniously round him, as if he still commanded the place and were not expecting a *capidgy-bachi* from Sultan Selim demanding his head — which he does not possess, for he lost it at the sound of the first gun. The beauty and variety of the rich and striking colours of the janissaries, the caps of our own grenadiers, the turbans of the spahis, who are not at all cast down though beaten, their splendid weapons, their horses, proud as themselves, their firm air, never abased in spite of misfortune, the shores of the Danube and the Save lined with these picturesque figures, all these things refresh the eye and delight the soul. But it was rather sad to see them carrying away the bodies of men, horses, sheep, and oxen which they could not bury during the siege. One smelt, all at the same moment, death, burning, and attar of rose — for it is extraordinary how they mingle sensuous tastes with barbarism.

Who wants to know what the Turks are? Here it is; very different from the idea that most people have of them. They are a people of antitheses: brave and cowardly, active and lazy, libertine and devout, sensual and hard, delicate and coarse, dirty and clean; keeping in the same room roses and dead cats. If I speak of the great men of the Court, army, and provinces I shall add: haughty and base, distrustful, ungrateful, proud and cringing, generous and thieving. Of all these qualities, good and bad, the good preponderate in the bulk of the nation; they depend on circumstances, and are always covered by a crust of ignorance and stolidity which prevents these poor people from becoming unhappy. It is quite clear that, if they were not under the yoke of masters who strangle them to get their sons and daughters or their wealth, they would not be so familiarized with customs which give them a barbarous character.

They scarcely smile; they answer with their heads, or eyes, or hands and arms; they never move without dignity, but they seldom speak. There is nothing common or vulgar about them, either in what they say or in their manners. The little servant of a janissary, though his feet and legs are bare and he has no shirt, is jaunty in his way, and has a more distinguished air than the young seigneurs of the European Courts; the poorest of the Turkish soldiers have nothing to clothe them, but their damascened weapons are dazzling in the sunlight. I have seen them refuse two hundred piastres, fearing less to die of hunger than of shame.

The Turks are capable of gratitude and respond to good treatment; in all the circumstances of their lives, in war as elsewhere, they keep their word; all the more, as one of them once said to me, because they do not know how to write.

The Turks have some resemblance with the Greeks, but far more with the Romans. They have the tastes of the one and the habits of the other. Their works are charming, full of good taste, and suggestive of ideas; those ideas, when they have them, are refined and delicate. They show a polished mind in the little that they say or write. They are grave like the Romans, and will not take the trouble to either laugh or dance; Ibrahim-Nazir, whom we have driven from Moldavia, had five or six very pretty slaves, superbly dressed, who surrounded him on horseback. The Turks explained to me that they liked beauty, and it was very agreeable to them to be waked in the morning by handsome figures bringing them their coffee, their pipe, their sherbet, their aloe wood to burn, their amber perfume, and their attar of rose. They scorn our ways of having a common sweeper or a confidential old valet to make our fire and open our curtains. They are always lying down, like the Romans, who, I doubt not, had divans like the Turks, on which they ate and passed their days. The tunics and slippers of both nations prove that neither liked walking.

There is no fury and anger like that of the cold and phlegmatic natures. The Turks, like the Romans, especially the Turks of the present day, make vengeance a business; in other respects they are gentle. They never argue and never quarrel. The Romans, if popular government did not always bring with it party spirit, intrigue, jealousy, and their accompanying crimes, would have been very worthy people; and if the opposite extreme, the despotism of a sultan and of two or three of the great officials, did not terrify them incessantly the Turks would also be among the best people in the world.

Ignorant from laziness and from policy, superstitious by habit and calculation, they are guided by natural and lucky instinct. What would the peoples of Europe be if their prime ministers were soap-dealers, their high-admiral a market-gardener, and a lacquey the commander-in-chief of their armies? Where else will you find men equally fit to fight on foot, on horseback, or on the water, clever in all they undertake, and individually intrepid? Stations and conditions being all mixed up, no one being classed, it follows that each man has a right to everything, and awaits the place to which his destiny allots him.

Observers, travellers, spectators, instead of making trivial reflections about the nations of Europe, who are all pretty much alike, should meditate on those which derive from Asia if they want to find something new, fine, grand, noble, and very often reasonable.

The marshal has asked on my behalf for the cross of commander of the military Order of Maria Theresa; and the emperor has already sent it to me. They say they are satisfied with my promptitude, and especially with the effects of my last bombardment, which decided the Turks to capitulate. Nothing was wanting to my happiness except the arrival of Abdy Pacha to relieve the place. It would have been a keen pleasure to me to cross the Save, assist in beating the pacha, and then return to continue my attack.

I would have written to you during the siege but I was afraid my letter might become posthumous, and I did not wish to tell you what was in my head before I knew whether the enemy would leave it on my shoulders. Adieu, friend of my heart.

I remained for some little time at Belgrade, and then was on the point of starting for Vienna, when certain reasons, which I was too careless to fathom, induced the Emperor Joseph II. to send me orders to choose my winter quarters at either Effleck, Belgrade, or Peterwaradin.

To Maréchal de Lacy.

BELGRADE, December, 1789.

It is not to enhance my value, my dear marshal, for to do my duty costs me nothing, that I wish to tell you that I am battered with proposals to put myself at the head of the Flemings. [The Austrian Low Countries, under the influence of the French Revolution, were then in a state of revolt and so continued until December, 1790, when the Austrian army re-occupied Brussels and subdued the insurgents.]

I have answered only once, to say that I shall not answer at all. I endeavoured to make them see the folly and the impotence of their revolt (thanks to their poor heads); for they could perfectly well have prevented the passage of the Sambre on one side, and that of the Dyle on the other by means of its rocky banks, which are on their side. After having proved to them that they did not know how to read aright the manifesto of the worthy archduke, I added that I thanked them for the provinces they offered me, but that I never revolted in winter.

I did not even honour Van der Noot with that poor joke, and I never answered his summons to go and defend our privileges, nor his threats of what would happen to me if I did not go instantly.

I beg your Excellency not to say a word of all this to the emperor, whom I pity for having, perhaps, thought that I was taking some part in the Belgian revolt; — for that, I imagine, is the reason why I am kept here in a species of exile. As he easily recovers from any wrong impression that he takes, I am sure that he will soon come out of this idea and retract his order that I am to choose my winter quarters at Belgrade, Effleck, or Peterwaradin.

If I have to remain here I will avenge myself by remaking what is called "Prince Eugène's road," a fine communication between Semlin and Belgrade, and I will complete a canal begun by the Romans in Syrmia; I will employ my whole *corps d'armée* in that way.

The *tefterdar* whom I have with me as a hostage, and who, forgetting Mahomet, pretends to mistake Hungarian wine for sherbet, told me the other day that the ministers of England and Prussia were desperately anxious that the war should continue. Those two powers, by their infernal and little understood policy, want to make Austria lose the Low Countries, and England wants to make Frenchmen lose France. I wish they would make haste in Vienna and conclude a peace. I know very well that women, abbés, and idlers in cities never want peace. But even if we had all Bosnia (very difficult to conquer because of the castles of a Mussulman feudality whose very names are unknown) we should be none the richer. Let us be content with Novi, Sabacz, Belgrade, and Choczim, and let Russia be content with Oczakow. Let us attend to the most pressing thing of all, namely: extinguishing the conflagration in the Low Countries and preventing that in France. Soon it will be too late.

They can't think of anything at Petersburg until they make peace with Constantinople. The day it was known that Bulgakoff was put in the Seven Towers the empress was almost sorry. She is a sovereign for history, not for romance, though people do not think so. Prince Potemkin, who was both, has completely given up the romance.

France will be punished by means of her sin; she will be punished for having assisted America to revolt, and for having encouraged Turkey in its enmity to Austria. The poor Turks, knowing little of what is going on in Europe, think that their allies will support them! The English will repent themselves of not supporting the throne of the unfortunate and virtuous Louis XVI. My God! how I pity the poor queen in the Tuileries. The details that your Excellency gave me of that arrival in Paris made me burst into tears.

The enlightenment which may have come to the emperor, or the need that he had of me, as I was his only field-quartermaster-general during this whole campaign, made him send me an order to leave my exile.

To H. I. M. Joseph II.

BELGRADE, December, 1789.

SIRE, — I am overjoyed with the permission that your Imperial Majesty grants me to place myself at your feet and remain in Vienna until I lead into Moravia, or, as I hope, into Silesia the army that returns from Syrmia. I am more sensitive, Sire, to favour than to disfavour. The care I never ceased to give to the siege of Belgrade, and the fever which quinine could not conquer, kept me from dwelling on the grief I should otherwise have felt from that terrible phrase in your Majesty's letter: "Expect proofs of my displeasure; I have neither the habit nor the will to be disobeyed."

I remember that you thanked me, Sire, eleven years ago in Bavaria for my conduct. This time your Majesty orders me, by return of my courier, to send no more letters, because the foreign ministers are so watchful for news. If I did send my aide-de-camp it was because the Comte de Choiseul wrote me from Constantinople begging that I would forward very safely and very promptly his important despatch to the Marquis de Noailles, who was to impart it to Prince Kaunitz.

I beg your pardon, Sire, for not being more uneasy at your anger. The reason was that I know your justice well. I have deeply regretted the cessation of the letters so full of confidence and affection which your Majesty wrote me last year; but I have never doubted the return of your kindness, even after the reception of your stern order to choose my winter quarters at Belgrade, Effleck, or Peterwaradin, instead of returning to Vienna to recover my health. I said to myself: "That untimely journey of my aide-de-camp to the Low Countries at the height of the revolt may have made his Majesty think that I was taking part in it, and forming relations with the malcontents. This cannot last; his Majesty will bethink himself, and will then feel that such a thing is impossible."

During this time I have been taking my revenge upon you, Sire. I wrote to the Queen of France, entreating her to send you Dr. Seyffert, whose great talent is to cure the very ill from which your Majesty suffers. I hope that he arrived in time, or else that your Majesty no longer needed him. Nothing can concern me more, Sire, than your glory and your life, for which I would give my own; which I will expose all the more readily before Neiss if you will permit Maréchal de Lacy, as he ardently desires, to command under the walls of that fortress, and prevent the king from meddling in our affairs, and playing the mediator, which appears to be his mania.

I had, as will be seen above, received orders to conduct a part of the army into Moravia for the ensuing campaign, for the purpose of putting ourselves in opposition to the desire shown by the King of Prussia to lay down the law to us. During the time that my regiments were assembling and marching I remained in Vienna, where I was very well received by the emperor; who thanked me for all I had done, and kept me two hours talking with him, ill as he was, during which time he said to me such touching things that I shall never forget them as long as I live. I tried in vain to recover my health, which was not restored for more than fifteen months. This, however, did not prevent me from fulfilling all my functions during the species of campaign that followed in 1790.

[The Emperor Joseph II., died in February, 1790; and with him the Prince de Ligne's public and military career came to an end, — except for a brief period before 1795, during which he returned to his hereditary government of Hainault. Whether this was caused by personal prejudice against him in the minds of the succeeding emperors, Leopold and Francis, whether a suspicion still hung about him of sympathy with the Belgian revolutionists, or whether (which is more likely) the fact of his being a Belgian and more French by nature than Austrian, made the Austrian government after the final loss of the Low Countries in 1795 unwilling to employ him, — the fact remains that, although he regretted it sincerely (as we shall see), he was never again in active service.]

VI.

1790.

VIENNA: JOSEPH II: HAINAULT.

To H. I. M. the Empress Catherine.

VIENNA, February 12, 1790.

He is no more, Madame, he is no more, the prince who did honour to mankind, the man who did most honour to princes. That ardent spirit is extinguished like a flame whose substance has burned away; that active body lies between four planks that forbid its action. After watching with his precious remains I was one of four to bear him to the Capuchins. Yesterday I was not in a state to render to your Imperial Majesty an account of this sorrow.

Joseph II. died as he lived, with firmness; he ended as he began, with the same methodical spirit. He directed the procession of the Holy Sacrament when they brought it to his deathbed; and he lifted himself up to see if all were as he ordered. When the last and most cruel blow fell upon him [the death of the Archduchess of Würtemburg], the blow of fate which completed his sorrows, he said: "Where have you placed the body of the princess?" They answered, "In the Chapel." "No," he said, "that is my place, and you would be obliged to disturb her; put her in some other place where she can lie tranquilly."

These details give me strength; I thought I could not continue such a tale. He chose and regulated the hours for the prayers which they read to him. As long as he was able he read some himself; and he seemed in accomplishing his Christian duties to be arranging his soul as he always wanted to arrange his empire, by himself. He made the physician who told him the truth about his state, a baron; he loved him so much that he begged he would follow his body to the grave, asking him to tell him as nearly as he could the day, and even the hour, when he should descend into it.

The emperor said to me a few days before his death, on my arrival from the army of Hungary, which I had just led into Silesia: "I was not in a state to see you last night. Your country has killed me; Ghent taken was my death-blow; Brussels abandoned is my death. What an insult to me!" He repeated several times the words: "I die of it: one must be made of wood not to die of it." Then he added, "I thank you for all you have done for me. Loudon has said much good of you to me. I thank you for your fidelity. Go to the Low Countries; bring them back to their allegiance; and if you cannot do that, stay there: do not sacrifice your interests to me, for you have children."

All those words so deeply moved me and are so engraved upon my memory that your Majesty may feel sure there is not one that was not his. My conduct will be my answer; it is useless to repeat my words, which were choked with tears.

"Did any one shed tears while I received the sacraments?" he said to Mme. de Chancloss, whom he saw a moment later. "Yes," she answered, "I saw the Prince de Ligne in tears." "I did not think I was worth all that," the emperor said, almost in a tone of gayety.

Madame — shall I say it, to the shame of humanity? — I have seen four great sovereigns die, and they have not been regretted until a year after their deaths; during the first six months men hoped, during the last they grumbled. This was so when Maria Theresa died. Men little feel at the time the loss that they sustain; their minds are full of the new reign. It will be a year before the soldier will say: "Joseph II. faced many a cannon-ball in the dike of Beschania, and many a volley of musketry in the suburbs of Sabacz; and it was he who bethought him of the medal for Valour." Yes, it will be a year before the traveller will say: "What noble establishments for schools, hospitals, prisons, and education!" the manufacturer: "What encouragement!" the labourer: "He laboured himself;" the heretic: "He defended us." The presidents of all departments, the heads of all bureaus will then say: "He was our head-clerk and our superintendent both;" the ministers: "He killed himself for the State, of which he was, he used to say, the first subject;" the sick will say: "He visited us;" the citizen: "He beautified our cities by making promenades and open squares;" the peasant and the servant will say: "We could speak to him as often as we chose;" fathers of families: "He gave us advice;" his own social world: "He was safe, agreeable; he talked pleasantly, he had wit in his conversation; we could speak to him frankly about all things."

I am talking to you, Madame, of his life, when I meant to tell you only of his death. Your Majesty said to me in the carriage as we drove to Czarsko-zelo some ten years ago: "Your sovereign has a mind that always turns to the useful; there is nothing frivolous in his head. He is like Peter I., he allows you to contradict him, he is not offended by resistance to his opinions; he wishes to convince before he orders." To exhibit his portrait before I myself continue it, I send your Majesty a letter which he wrote to the Maréchal de

Lacy on the day of his death. It will show you two persons at once.

Ah! Madame, it is fortunate for the consolation and honour of this earth that your Majesty, by your health, system of living, age, and gayety have still some forty years to stay upon it.

I am, etc.

From H. I. M. Joseph II., written on the day of his death.

VIENNA, February 9, 1790.

MY DEAR MARÉCHAL DE LACY, — Nothing but the impossibility of writing these few lines with my trembling hand would induce me to use the hand of another. I see approaching with great strides the moment which must separate us. I should be very ungrateful if I left this world without reiterating to you here, my dear friend, all the feelings of gratitude which I owe to you for so many reasons, and which I have had the pleasure to testify before all the earth. Yes, if I have become something, to you I owe it; you formed me, you enlightened me, you made me know men; and, besides that, to you the army owes its formation, its influence, its consideration.

The sureness of your counsels under all circumstances, that personal attachment to me which never failed on any occasion, little or great, all that, my dear marshal, makes me feel I cannot sufficiently reiterate to you my thanks. I have seen your tears flow for me; those of a great and wise man are a noble apology. Receive my farewell. I embrace you tenderly. The only thing I regret to leave in this world is the very small number of friends, of whom you are most certainly the first. Remember me, remember your most sincere friend and affectionate

JOSEPH.

If to obtain the title of Great it sufficed to be incapable of littleness, we might say Joseph the Great; but I feel that more than that is needed to deserve the name: it needs a glorious reign, dazzling, fortunate; illustrious exploits in war, unexpected enterprises, superb results, possibly fêtes, pleasures, and magnificence. Circumstances refused to Joseph II. all brilliant occasions to make himself known. I cannot flatter after death any more than I can in life. He was not a great man, but he was a great prince, and the first among the first of them. He never abandoned himself to love or to friendship; perhaps because he felt himself strongly inclined thereto. Often he mingled too much caution with his affections; he checked himself from confidence, because he saw how other sovereigns were misled by their mistresses, their confessors, their ministers, or their friends. He checked himself on indulgence, because he wanted, before all things, to be just; he made himself stern, in spite of himself, meaning only to be strictly correct. His heart might perhaps be obtained without deserving it, but no one ever missed his esteem who deserved it.

He was afraid of seeming partial in the distribution of his favours; he granted them without adding to them cordiality of manner; and he refused them in the same way. He expected more than nobleness on the part of the nobility, and despised it for the lack thereof far more than he did the other classes. He desired the greatest authority in order to keep from others the right to do evil. He deprived himself of all the enjoyments of life in order to teach others to work, for what he hated most of all was an idler. He was out of temper for a moment if any one made him a representation or gave him an answer that was rather sharp; he would rub his hands, and then turn round to listen, reply, and after that discuss the matter as if nothing had happened. He was miserly with the property of the State and generous with his own: but "generous" is not the word; it should be "beneficent."

He could be the sovereign, and he held his Court well when absolutely obliged to do so. At such times he gave to the Court (which for the rest of the year had the air of a convent or a barrack) the pomp and dignity of Maria Theresa. His education had been, like that of many sovereigns, neglected by dint of being over-cared for; they are usually taught all except that which they ought to know. Joseph II. in his youth did not promise to be agreeable; but he became so, suddenly, after his coronation at Frankfort. His journeys, his campaigns, and the society of a few distinguished women ended by forming him. He liked confidences, and was very discreet, though he mingled in everything. His manners were extremely agreeable; never did he show any pedantry. I have seen him write, on one of those great cards he always carried in his pocket, moral lessons of gentleness and obedience to a young girl who wanted to quit a mother who made her furious; or music lessons to another, because, having been present at those given by her master, he was not satisfied therewith.

In society he saw instantly if any one was annoyed by him about some order, or enterprise, or punishment; and he would take great pains to set himself right with society by redoubling the charms of his conversation and his gallantry to women; he would give them a chair, open the door, or close a window for them. His courtesy was his safeguard against familiarity. He fully understood little shades and distinctions; he did not have that affability of which so many other sovereigns make their stock in trade, and which serves them to mark their superiority; he concealed what he had of it in many ways. He related a story gayly and with much natural humour.

He knew neither how to eat, nor how to drink, nor how to amuse himself, nor how to read anything but public documents. He governed too much and did not reign enough. He played music for himself every day. He rose at seven in the morning and while he dressed he would sometimes laugh and make his chamberlain laugh, but always without familiarity; also his surgeon and his other attendants, who all adored him. From eight to twelve he walked about among his various departments, where he dictated, wrote, and corrected everything himself. In the evening he went to the theatre.

Passing from his own apartment to the cabinet he usually met some twenty, thirty, even to a hundred poorly dressed men or women of the people; he took their statements, talked with them, comforted them, and answered, by writing or otherwise, the next day at the same hour, and he kept their complaints secret if he found that they were not just. He wrote badly only when he took pains to write well; his sentences were then very long and diffuse. He knew four languages perfectly, and two others fairly well.

His memory, spared in his youth, became, perhaps for that reason, extremely good later; he never forgot a speech, or a face, or a matter of business. He would walk up and down his room with the person to whom he gave audience, talking to him almost with effusion and a smiling air and holding him by the elbow; then, as if repenting this, he resumed his grave air. Often he would interrupt himself to put a stick of wood on the fire, or to pick up the tongs, or look out of the window. He never broke his word. He laughed at the evil that was said of him. He alarmed the Pope, the Grand-Turk, the Empire, Hungary, Prussia, and the Low Countries. The fear of being unjust and making human beings unhappy by carrying out by force of arms projects he had already begun often stopped them.

He knew very well in Vienna before he travelled in other countries that his Court was not as brilliant as that of Versailles, and that the ocean and the Mediterranean bore other vessels than those of the Danube. The things that most struck him, though without amazing him, were the port of Marseilles and the canals. Assuredly he could never rival them, but his three hundred thousand well-disciplined soldiers, the crops and wine of Hungary, the few taxes of the country, and the esteem of his people consoled him amply for what he could not have. The ill-humour that he sometimes showed was caused chiefly by foolish or indiscreet questions that people put to him, or by pleasures they wanted to give him against his will. "Maréchal de Mouchy," he said to me one day in Paris, "forced me to go to the theatre; I would not forgive even the Maréchal de Richelieu for that." Some one asked him if he were in favour of the English or the Americans. "It is my trade to be a king," he replied. When they asked him if there were good actors in Vienna, what their names were, whether he could see the waves of the Black Sea in Vienna, and whether he shot as well as Louis XIV., it made him laugh, but did not amuse him. When the Maréchal de Broglie took up a whole evening while people present hoped to hear the emperor talk (which he did extremely well), in telling him about his little victory at Bergen, it made him laugh because it disappointed the audience. He answered with pleasure the most ridiculous questions of the common people; and one day when he chanced to have trimmed his own beard an innkeeper's wife asked him, as he got off his post-horse at the inn door, what office he held about the emperor; to which he replied: "Well, sometimes I have the honour to shave him."

It is to the turmoil in the blood of Joseph II. that we should attribute the uneasy restlessness of his reign. He never finished or polished any one of his works; and his only blame is to have merely sketched everything, good and bad. I think I have mentioned elsewhere that, Lord Malmesbury having asked me at the beginning of his reign what I foresaw of it, I replied: "He is a man who will always have small desires which he will never satisfy. His reign will be a continual wish to sneeze, or, if you prefer it, it will be an erysipelas, like that of the body to which he is subject."

Without this restlessness, this constant agitation which brought him to the grave, he would have been the best of sovereigns. He said to me one day that he was worn-out with work and could do no more; even his eyesight failed him. I reproached him for such excesses, to which he replied: "What else can I do in this country (Austria) devoid of mind, without soul, without zeal, without heart in the work? I am killing myself because I cannot rouse up those whom I want to make work; but I hope I shall not die until I have so wound up the machine that others cannot put it out of order, even if they try to do so."

One day, when I was on duty as one of thirty-six adjutant-generals, rather than chamberlains, an Italian priest with a singular face, very wicked if it was not crazy, begged me to announce him to the emperor. I would not do it. At a time when, like a child, he wanted to have a finger in everything, a capuchin came to me for admittance in order that he might implore his Majesty to permit his monastery to sing through its nose, he having forbidden the reverend fathers from psalm-singing in their usual style.

I was the lieutenant-general commanding the troops in the Low Countries, under the orders of a worthy man who had more soul than head, and would willingly have let me do as I wished [Archduke Albert of Saxe-Teschen], when I started for the famous journey in Taurica. Never would the first motions of a revolt have taken place had I remained with my command. If the friendship felt for me in the Low Countries had not sufficed to stop them, a single threat on my part would have made their instigators tremble, and a single cannonade (had I been absolutely forced to that), charged with powder only, would have annihilated them. We should have seen no national cockade and no volunteers after that.

It is always some imaginary good which begins these revolutions; if there is any real good, it can only be attained in the first week; popular troops become ridiculous the following week, and dangerous the week after. The principle of arming the citizens against the populace only extends the power of the latter. The distance between them is not great enough to prevent their interests, ambitions, drunkenness, and frivolity from bringing the two classes into sympathy; there is little difference between them except in their coats, that are more or less fine and more or less ragged. I could have healed all, if the emperor had been willing to let me start from Barczisarai (though to my great regret) when I asked him to do so. He told me a few days before his death that he repented not having sent me there directly after the siege of Belgrade; I should then have arrived before the taking of Ghent; he also said that he regretted not letting me go, as I wished, from the Crimea in 1787, when the news of the first troubles reached him. That was the moment when the troubles began, and when all might easily have been stopped. But no, the populace was allowed to learn it had a stronger arm than it thought, and no one was there to show it that a head was the stronger.

I paid my court to the new emperor [Leopold II., brother of Joseph II.], who though still young was old, thanks to two campaigns and the training he had had from Joseph II., and I took the liberty of saying to him, with regard to the Low Countries, that vigour would exempt him from rigour; and that six months of firmness at the start would consolidate his reign forever.

[The policy of Leopold II. was, however, to keep at a distance the friends of his brother the late emperor. The Belgian insurgents having been subdued, and the Austrian army reoccupying Brussels in December, 1790, the Prince de Ligne returned to the Low Countries to preside, in his capacity as hereditary governor of Hainault, over the States-general of that province, which he opened, after a triumphal entry into Mons, the capital, with a speech of which the following extracts will give an idea.]

Messieurs, on seeing me here among you, it will be impossible for you to doubt that it is your happiness that recalls me. Not the happiness which you have thought you enjoyed, for I see nothing worse than your late situation, but that which will now, if you are willing, be born again in our native land. . . .

What was it that the emperor asked of you? A more reasonable criminal code: work at it now yourselves; a simpler administration: take that duty upon you; no doubt it will displease individuals by lessening costs of justice, free travels, free tippling, holidays, commissions, deputations, law-suits, chicanery, and the costly collection of taxes at the expense of the provinces in general and the citizens in particular. Meet the emperor's views instead of opposing them; and enlighten me wherever you can. . . .

It is shameful for our country that we do not ourselves fill up our Wallon regiments, which have done us so much honour by help of foreigners who are fortunately inspired by our *esprit de corps.* There are not eight thousand soldiers of our own nation in our ranks; and the country itself, to prevent a rigour prejudicial to our interests, should encourage recruiting instead of hindering it, and raise our force (partly perhaps as a State militia) to sixteen thousand Wallons perpetually under arms. . . .

Instead of this, what have you had among you? Dull calumnies, stupid enmities, silly suppositions about conscriptions, punishments, taxes to 40 per cent, despotism, invasion of private property, etc., and foolish edicts for the last two years. I' say nothing of the Oracle of the nation (I mean that to our shame), the ridiculous Van der Noot, and all the honours that have been paid to him. He was the lawyer whose memorial I corrected when, with fictitious warmth and a jargon and reasoning all his own, he attacked the unjust judgment of the Council of Brabant. "I shall go," he said to me, "and carry to the foot of the throne a history of our own laws which favour iniquity, and complain to his Majesty that his government protects such decisions. The sovereign," he added, "should come to the help of his people." Those, I give you my word of honour, were his words said to me; and yet when the sovereign came he was the one to lead against him. . . .

Examine for yourselves the actual facts, and see if we have not needed a new code and a new system. Have you not heard your merchants groan at the brutality and want of knowledge of those who have shackled the commerce of every man, and consequently that of the whole country?

Who among us has comprehended how to wisely balance the rights of export and import? See the prejudices which have in the past hindered our commerce with a nation that desired it — a nation that was till *recently* the most fortunate in Europe. What is it that has kept the Dutch and the Genevese from settling among us? Your intestine troubles, your bickerings, your libels, so ill-written, your fears, so ill-founded. Who has done most wrong to this country but the country itself? Let it therefore repair its wrong-doing and inform me of whatever it may judge necessary to bring back abundance and calmness to our midst: I charge myself with fulfilling it. . . .

And since I speak of myself, permit me to remind you that my ancestors, who always held anarchy in horror, were the sole ones to keep our country true to its sovereign when the United Provinces were about to be lost to him. May I, in like manner, have the great consolation of uniting you with those who govern us! Had I not gone to the Crimea with the Emperor Joseph and the Empress of Russia, I should have stopped your rebellion either by speaking to you as a zealous and sensible compatriot, or if that failed, as an Austrian general, with cannon (without balls) which would have killed you with fear.

I remind you also that I have often resisted in your favour, not the power of his Majesty, which I have regarded as just and enlightened, but that of his government. I stood firm against its acts of despotism, such as the killing of horned cattle, the grant of the herring fishery (now become a monopoly), the establishment of government prisons, which I prevented in Hainault, and that injurious and impossible canal which it sought to make. At the risk of being disavowed by the government, I compelled the Dutch, weapons in hand, to respect your dikes and your property; and I have often received from you a thousand benedictions and most touching proofs of your good friendship.

I am here now to give you another proof of mine. Believe me, messieurs, I am an impartial judge, a zealous citizen, a Wallon soldier who never learned in the field the art of dissimulating. It is truth that my voice utters, trusting that it may, while there is time, bring light to your souls.

I have never done harm to any one, no matter who. Perhaps if I had been malicious others would have done better by me. I have seldom had, however, to complain of any one; but I do remember just here a libel which a man, named, I think, Masson, a sort of lawyer at Nivelles, put forth about me. I had the greatest trouble to prevent his being punished for it; and as it was, he thought best to leave the country for several months; which proves, even more than his pamphlet did, how little he knew me.

Among other shafts that I have forgotten, he said in this libel (the only writing of the kind that I know of, for no songs or epigrams were ever circulated against me) that on my entry as Governor of Hainault I had the air of an old sultan surrounded by his harem, with whom I occupied myself exclusively, and that I had been fool enough to believe in good faith the acclamations of "Long live the patriot prince!" That last accusation was quite true. It happened in the church where I took the oath. I accepted those vivats as I had the others, never thinking for a moment that the shouters meant malice.

As for the sultan part, that does me too much honour. It is quite true that during the slow and wearisome procession some very pretty girls threw bouquets into my carriage, and as the crowd detained them close beside it I thanked them a great deal and told them I thought they were charming.

The only reproach about my procession which was not altogether ill-founded is that it seemed to him more fantastic than magnificent. The war had lately ended, and that, together with the revolution in the Low Countries, had caused me to spend and lose a great deal of money. I could have run in debt to gold-lace my servants on every seam; but I thought the people would be better pleased with me if I did not make too much display. I had, however, two Turks, four hussars, several Russians and their beards, a Tartar with two dromedaries, and they were enough to procure me his ingenious comparison with Tamerlane, or the Emperor of China, for I do not remember which of the two he thought I resembled.

It was quite unfortunate that the archduchess [Maria Christina, daughter of Maria Theresa, who governed the Low Countries conjointly with her husband, the Archduke Albert of Saxe-Teschen] became extremely cold to me about this time, almost without my knowing why, and chose to take tragically, as a want of respect to her whole family, a blunder made in addressing a letter which was certainly awkward. My adjutant, Dettinger, put upon a letter I had written to Archduke Albert the address of my wife, and on my letter to my wife the address of the duke,—I being at the time absent from home. It so happened that I had proposed to the Archduke Ferdinand and his archduchess to come and stay at Belœil; and I had given the same invitation for the same time to the royal highnesses of Brussels. Now I said in my letter to my wife which was sent to Archduke Albert, speaking of the Milanese royal highnesses: "We shall soon be relieved of this archiducal caravan" [*post-zug*]. That stupid nonsense, which was good neither to write nor to read, *mansit alta mente repostum*, and so alienated from me the mind of the little Court that the archduke did not ask me to serve under him, as he otherwise would have done. The archduchess is quick-tempered, but she does not get over her vexation quickly; and in that way she does injury to the great qualities she has derived from her mother. The archduke is good, and has much military knowledge, but, nevertheless, I should have been useful to him. Perhaps there would even have been no battle of Jemmapes, or the battle might have ended differently. Perhaps the Duke of Brunswick, with whom I should have had to treat, would have remembered our friendship and the fact that I could penetrate his mind. He said afterwards that I was the man best fitted to have ended that war; to which I replied that he ought to have said so louder and sooner.

Archduke Albert is the best-trained soldier and has the most military erudition in the Austrian army. His Memoirs are worth more than his memory, which is often at fault. But let him appear in the open on horseback, and surrounded by many persons, and any one would say that all he knows and sees marvellously well in his cabinet has vanished.

One night, soon after my return to the Low Countries, I was sleeping at my government house [in Mons], where, for forty years, apparitions, so they said, had been seen, and I heard such a noise on my door that it seemed as if it must open or fly to pieces. I rang the bell. Angelo, my *valet-de-chambre,* came and opened the door, and says to this day that he saw a tall white figure moving away, which he might have pursued, if terror and his legs had allowed him. My orderly corporal was sleeping in the antechamber. I heard nothing more, and went peacefully to sleep.

When the Emperor Leopold II., thanks to two persons who called themselves my friends, gave me the go-by in not making me marshal at his coronation in Frankfort, I requested him, in German, through the Council of War, and in the curtest and most insulting manner, to accept the resignation of all my offices. He was alarmed by that; but a curious circumstance had even more effect upon him. I, who seldom dance, danced that night by accident in his presence, at a ball given by the Neapolitan ambassador. I did more, without being aware of it. Louise Hardegg having come up to take me out for a *galop* (it often happens that lookers-on are taken out in this way when they least expect it), I dashed my sword to the ground, with an immense clatter of chains and buckles, almost at the feet of the emperor. I was not even thinking of him, it was pure gayety, having just heard that Charles was coming back to me from Ismaïl, covered with glory, and wounded but not dangerously. The emperor was furious, although, having sucked in Italy the milk of dissimulation, he controlled himself enough to assure me (on the Thursday after) that he should make me marshal on the following Sunday. I am not a marshal yet, and I do not care; but, to make the Court feel it, I never appear there except on days of ceremony and obligation, for my two Orders of the Fleece and Maria Theresa, and then in the uniform of my regiment, not choosing to wear that of a general officer.

When a good solid injustice is done to me I tell of it, and after that I think no more about it; but this one I will here prove by two letters, full of promises and falsehoods, which have lasted many years. The letters I have kept only to laugh at. Here they are: —

H. I. M., Leopold II., to the Prince de Ligne.

VIENNA, December 29, 1790.

MON PRINCE, — Although I try to keep my papers in order, and do not lose them as a general thing, I have lost

one for which I am very sorry. It is the one which you sent me through the Council of War. I have always done you justice in my heart. If you had done a little more justice to me, you would have felt sure that your advancement, desired, deserved, and promised, could not be delayed for long, and only on account of complications which concern your brother officers.

However, that is all past now, and it is better to say no more about it. You must keep your present offices; you shall have others in due time and we shall be as good friends as we were before. I am persuaded and convinced of your zeal and attachment to my service and person; and you should be equally convinced of the esteem and consideration with which I am your affectionate

LEOPOLD.

The Archduke Francis[1] *to the Prince de Ligne.*

VIENNA, October 29, 1790.

MON PRINCE,—Pardon me that I have delayed so long in answering your letter, which I did not receive until yesterday. The exposition which you make to me of the situation in which you find yourself, and the demand that you make concerning it, are more than just. You may be sure of the zeal with which I shall interest myself in this just cause, more especially for your sake, *mon prince*, whom I esteem personally, and who have given the most evident proofs of your zeal and attachment to all our family. Be assured that my father, and all of us, recognize it, and for myself in particular, I only desire an opportunity to prove to you the sentiments with which I shall never cease to be your very affectionate FRANCIS.

[1] Succeeded his father, Leopold II., as Emperor of Austria in 1792; elected Emperor of Germany July 5, 1792.

What a moment it is when we behold suffering and dying a great man, whom so often we have seen laughing at death only to fall into its hands finally like any common mortal! Maréchal Laudohn called death to come to him, because of the awful sufferings which the incompetency of a surgeon had caused him.

The day before he died he recognized me. The door was open and he saw me in his antechamber; he called me in a dreadful voice, and he who always spoke to me in German attempted to speak French and said: "Dear Prince de Ligne, I am terrible." It was true, but not what he meant to say. He wanted to make me understand that he suffered terribly. It is impossible to give an idea of what I felt. I wanted to cast myself on the hand of that old and honourable soldier to kiss it before he died. I choked, and was forced to leave the room.

He had all the simplicity of a child and the credulity of a dupe. An intriguing fellow persuaded him he was a Scotchman and made him sign himself London, instead of his right name, such as I have written it above, and as he himself had always written it till then. His wife made him a Catholic in the same way; that is, he believed he was one without knowing much of religion. Perhaps he is all the more saved.

There is no one who has not written and arranged to suit himself the causes of the French Revolution: the bigots say it was because of the Encyclopedia; the clergy, because the king did not take a distinguished confessor through whom they could have governed him; the ministers, because he did not abandon himself to their guidance; the courtiers, because they were not sent on foreign embassies; the parliaments, because they were made to feel they were not like the Parliament of England (where, moreover, they have but one); the men of letters, because there were none of their profession in the ministry; lawyers, because, they said, the Constitution was so often changed; authors, because they were not encouraged at Court; merchants, because no fêtes were given; the peasantry, because they could not get relief from the *corvée* and the salt-tax; and I, observer and man of the world, who belong to none of the foregoing classes, having seen all these things very closely, divide the causes under two heads, viz:—

1. Fools, villains, men of intellect.
2. Errors, horrors, and stupefaction.

That is the synoptical history, or whatever you choose to call it, of revolutions, in France or elsewhere, in morals, opinions, politics,—in all of them, egotism.

VIENNA, October 16, 1790.

To him whom I thought the best of friends, the most amiable of men, the philosopher the least philosophical, a most distinguished man of letters, a brilliant dragoon officer, with time and opportunity the most honourable of courtiers, and the most enlightened of ambassadors, who since—but *then* he was all that—

LOUIS SÉGUR,[1]—Your signature is not anonymous, and yet it is not yours, for it is the stamp of error.

Your "we shall come safely out of this" alarms me. The

[1] The Comte de Ségur, the trusted friend of Marie-Antoinette, attempted to play a mediating part between the queen and the revolutionary instigators, and was, naturally enough, distrusted by all. The above letter answers one in which Louis Ségur, dropping his title, had expressed his new opinions. After the date of this letter Louis XVI. sent him as ambassador to the Court of Berlin; where he made himself, justly or unjustly, more distrusted than ever. He returned to Paris shortly before the king's death, and continued to live in its neighbourhood until after the 18th Brumaire, when he attached himself for the rest of his life to Napoleon.—TR.

vile and stupid audacity of men without honour who attacked your excellent father, and the little respect they showed for his services and his infirmities, will (I said to myself) prevent my friend, if nothing else could do it, from rushing into their arms. Alas! I was mistaken. When one knows as I do the warmth of your soul one cannot but fear its exaggeration and its love of imaginary good, letting go of the good that is possible.

Greece had sages, but they were only seven. You have now twelve hundred, at eighteen francs a day, who are, unperceived by themselves, the by-word of Europe, — sages without a mission, except for their own interests, without training in affairs, without knowledge of foreign countries, without a general plan, without public interest (although that term is made to cover many a private one), without elevation, and without respect for a nobility which, in its brilliant days, was both useful and beloved! I know that they reckon on the ocean which can protect, but only in a country it surrounds, the makers of laws and phrases.

But how will France "come out of it"? Suppose, to her sorrow, there are more of these unchained philosophers, haters of pleasure and enjoyments, who assure you that their children will be deaf to the cries of happiness and love (which alone is sufficient to destroy equality). Will a nation so young, so lively, so excitable, which is now engaged in strewing thorns among its roses, will such a nation be restrained by the bits of a riding-school? I will suppose a dreadful event, unforeseeable and yet possible to "tiger-monkeys" as M. de Voltaire called Frenchmen: they might overthrow the king; but never the monarchy. Though a Bourbon might not return at once, perhaps the handsomest, bravest, most amiable, and best liked of Frenchmen might some day mount that throne, once shaded by laurel and myrtle. If so, a sceptre of iron would be needed to prevent a return to horrors. Behold the result of liberty!

The very names of your sages of to-day, they who think the universe has its eyes fastened on them, will be effaced. Plato is not good to follow, my friend, either in love or in republics. Diogenes would have broken his lantern in France. Are you made to be men, you children — the prettiest children upon earth? If the kings, to vindicate the majesty of thrones, desire to crush you, I defy you to get time to prevent it. You will need time and a great deal of it to collect your bodies and your hearts and minds in the field. I know your nation is warlike and capable of great things through its superiority in talents of all kinds; but I believe and hope that the other nations will not be so unskilful as to give you time. "Let us," the Great Catherine writes me, "let us, the four or five surrounding Powers, draw a cordon against that country as against the plague." And with all those powers armed to the teeth upon your frontiers, your commerce and communications stopped, you will be obliged either to kill each other in civil war, or do as your neighbours tell you.

Farewell, then, noble verse and song; farewell, divinest Poesy, witty and spicy epigram, and all those madrigals so French! Adieu, lovers and gallantry! Virgil, Horace, Ovid might have been stern and mediocre men if deprived of softness, pleasures, flatteries, and abuses. You will all be very wearisome; and you yourself are not beginning ill.

Come, leave a country that is always either above or beneath its part; where the destruction of arms proves how little they will bear them; where escutcheons are broken, noble mottoes erased, and the spirit of chivalry is departing. Quit a country where the storm now muttering without and within will fall of a sudden in thunderbolts and lightning. Your pretended reason is a will-o'-the-wisp that lures you to the precipice. Quit a land where the more superior you are, the more you will be envied, thwarted, stopped, and the less you will be believed. Come away, to return only when Frenchmen are once more amiable; and do not be the only one to do so.

Use the contemptible friends you ought never to have made to get out of all this; and after trying all you can to make them see more clearly, have yourself appointed ambassador to Vienna, whence you may be able to restore something, at least, to a state of safety — for already I see that crimes will be judged necessary by those men to maintain themselves. What a horrible expression! Crime a necessity! Evil to individuals for the general good! Alas! I shall never again behold your Paris, already stained with the blood of unfortunates. Judge what will be the aversion of Europe if more is shed.

Ah! Louis Ségur, let that baptismal name you have just so adroitly revived recall to your mind the great days of the great Louis. Give your hand to Louis XVI. to help him to reascend his throne, not to descend from it. Be more royalist, all of you, than he. You ought to say to him: "One fall leads to another fall." What will become of you, gentlemen, if that fall is total and if you are reduced to govern yourselves? Under what auspices are you marching now? The dames of the markets have taken the place of the Longueville, the Chevreuse, the Montbazon. I believe that *you* will never foul yourself in that awful sink-hole of Paris, but you are in it up to your knees.

Come out of it, my friend, I conjure you; and say before you leave: "Messieurs, your national debt and your deficit are no more than a laundry bill. Protect your priests, they will return it to you. Your king has been too kind; your queen too indulgent to the enemies she has had."

Think of it, Louis Ségur, there is still time. If you do it successfully, or even if you try to do it, love me as before.

PRINCE DE LIGNE.

The Comte de Ségur is rightfully a man of letters. He is more accurate than his brother the vicomte. His so-called history of Frederick-William is excellent, except as to Poland, about which he is mistaken. From too great eagerness for the visionary good of which his heart, ardent with love, and his mind, ardent from imagination, led him to embrace the shadow, he was mistaken in his adopted ideas, mistaken too, in a measure, about his country. But his sensitiveness, his horror of the crimes committed and of those who committed them, the good he said and desired for the king, and the great dangers he ran in consequence, have given him more claims than ever upon our interest. Esteemed by Joseph II., the friend of Catherine II., amiable, simple, though perhaps with an air of not being so, easy to live with, unspoilt by his successes in society ever since he came into the world, distinguished in his career, he became a philosopher in another direction than that in which he had commended philosophy to me. But it was not long before true philosophy made amends for the errors of the false, the source of which in him was pure as the soul in which it rose. I here confirm all the good that I have ever said, thought, and written of him; and I abjure my mistake in having thought his wrong-doing so considerable.

VII

1790–1792.

BELŒIL: THE FRENCH REVOLUTION: CASANOVA.

It was a very touching sight to me to see Monsieur [the Comte de Provence, afterwards Louis XVIII.] arrive at Coblentz and unite himself with all the French *émigrés* around the Prince de Condé and the Comte d'Artois. I urged them to march instantly into France, without arms, or nearly so if they did not have them, and try ladders or a secret understanding with some fortress on the frontier. Had they done it France was saved. The Comte d'Artois and the Prince de Condé had fifteen hundred gentlemen of France with them at Coblentz and at Worms, and could have done it. But the Comte d'Artois said to me: "There is to be a coalition of the Powers for us." I replied: "They will deceive you and deceive each other and be deceived." He said: "They will not let us assemble in force with arms." To which I answered: "They are laughing at the Elector of Mayence, who is supporting you, monseigneur; they say you are eating your uncle of Trèves out of house and home. Does that look like supporting you? Come into my little empire, where no one gives orders but myself; come, with all your *émigrés* and jump into Marienburg, which is only half a league off, the next day. When it is known in France that you are in a fortress they will trust you and rally round you, and you will be master of France."

So I said at that time; since then, what? Fools, aided by scoundrels who began to take their places by first associating with them intimately, declared war on five Powers at once, the weakest of whom could have beaten their army, which at that time scarcely existed. Here begins the scene of crime on one side and blunders on the other. One might make a calendar of those blunders to take the place of the saints in our almanac and of vegetables in that of the French; beginning: for January 1, Siege of Kehl; such a day, recrossing of the Sambre; another day, entrance into Champagne, and so on.

All the astonishing and brilliant successes of the French armies in the later campaigns were due to the fervour and activity of young generals and to masses and levies of national militia, soldiers for war only, under a great discipline, solely for essential objects; these did splendid service out of vanity and the desire to recover the respect of the world which they knew they had lost in other ways.

It cannot be denied that Frenchmen, on whichever bank they were, did prodigies of valour. Let us go back to the source and follow the development of the republican army, which has ended in being that of an absolute monarchy, called a Directory. Too much honour was done to it in supposing that its leaders had a plan. The proof that they had none, and that circumstances alone gave them one, which developed by degrees as the Coalition made blunders, is that they declared war before the army actually existed. Two corps alone, one of fifteen thousand men, another of seven thousand, began it, and were routed, as every one knows, the first by three hundred, the second by six hundred men. During two campaigns the French fought little and badly. It was not till the close of 1793 that they got together eighty thousand men; by that time the first mob of soldiers bribed from the old army had disappeared; a second mob behaved better; though such pillagers, savages that they were, shouting and roaring the Marseillaise, their generals as ridiculous as they were atrocious, making the conquered countries laugh and weep,—such men were not yet a true French army. At last the purified mass of the nation appeared, in 1794, and not till then. Bravery and intelligence soon enabled it to be organized, and made it manageable and victorious. It became a true army, and several armies, whose warfare was that of men of intellect. Talent took the place of the guillotine, Jourdan, Moreau, Pichegru, made their appearance, and finally the conqueror and pacificator, Bonaparte.

In the beginning the French had too many enemies to meet, too great an extent of territory to attack or defend, to be as strong as their opponents. But they have always had an advantage in their method of employing troops. Their armies of sixty thousand men have beaten armies of seventy thousand, because twenty thousand attacked ten thousand.

The French in the olden time did great things through the honour and gallantry of their nobility and the science of their generals; but once thwarted or defeated they could not recover themselves, and Paris was often their only rallying-point; Ramillies, Rosbach, and Minden were all disastrous in their results. The republican army of to-day brought intelligence only to the war, but it proved to be their means of superiority. They never gave or accepted battle; knowing how apt they were to be routed, they were careful not to expose themselves to it. They never pursued, knowing that they were liable to commit great follies in pursuit. Whenever, in the beginning, they felt they had the under side they retired and took up another position, from which their enemy again had the trouble of dislodging them. Their cavalry, which could only be ill-mounted and ill-trained, was never known to come openly in contact with the superb and more numerous columns with which it would have had to deal. There were none of those splendid charges of twenty or thirty squadrons, in which the French would have been knocked over in a moment; no march, on the day of the fight, of ten battalions in line of battle. Such charges would never have succeeded with men of intellect, but they do with men of war. The young men of a Court are impetuous. Those of a savage republic are not; it was death behind them that made them ready to face death before them. The savageness of a system, without which that republic would not have held together a week, was able to keep the armies in hand and to cast an impenetrable veil over plans of campaign and methods of executing them.

From Athens, France has been to Sparta, passing through the country of the Huns; beginning with Catiline, there has been something of Sylla and Attila. But the republican armies would never have become what they have since been, if the Coalition had startled them in the beginning by numbers, which it would have been so easy then to bring on, and by an unexampled rapidity. I do not like to quote myself, but I said on the day of the declaration of war that what we ought to do was to thunder and stun [*tonner et étonner*]. Instead of that, we went into the war relying on three maxims: (1) England will never allow France to keep the Low Countries; (2) Italy is the grave of the French; (3) The French are never lucky this side of the river.

The French have spent a treasury of money, but for it they have treasures in artillery, munitions, fortresses, plans, maps, and the fullest information. Moreover, they have the good fortune to hold the offensive, while the defensive, to which we are so unfortunately confined, is only training them the better to war.

Rome was taken by Brennus, and would have been by

Hannibal had he made a few more marches. Rome was never victorious except when she was out of her own country and far from its frontiers. The men of intellect in the French army, beaten when attacked, took their defeats as lessons. Correcting the faults they made, they took good care to make no others. Examine the changes which time produced in their method of getting the best out of their soldiers. The leaders knew well that enthusiasm never lasts of itself very long; they preserved it as long as they could by hymns. When Dumouriez entered my town of Mons he went straight to the State House to sing the Marseillaise devoutly. When they saw that the soldiers could no longer be duped in that way they permitted them to wrangle in the ranks and to pillage. When it was found that puffed up by their successes they needed this no longer, the greatest silence and the most severe discipline were enforced.

Great results occupied the minds of the generals, rather than glory. They felt that in a cause like theirs there was no place for heroism of the sort of Gaston de Foix and the Great Condé. Nearly all of them were gloomy or savage; soldiers who little resembled Frenchmen. No need for knights to command them; they required only intrepid leaders, doggedly cool and setting a good example under fire. Well-fed, having all he wanted to drink, encouraged by rapine, intoxicated by license, bold through impunity, the soldier sometimes won great advantages, which he kept through the strict order that the generals succeeded at last in establishing. Benefits, encouragements, and compliments were distributed for such successes, but terror was the pendant for all those to whom blame could be imputed.

Even before I saw all this I used to say that Montesquieu was wrong in not declaring that terror made republics, inasmuch as they can only exist in name because they are not that in fact. Crime gave the French republic birth; the most Oriental of despotisms sustains it. God grant it may have virtue for six months, and then it will be destroyed.

H. I. M. the Empress Catherine to the Prince de Ligne.

PETERHOF, June 30, 1791.

MONSIEUR LE PRINCE DE LIGNE,—If the extreme size of your last letter gave it somewhat the appearance of a kite, its contents in twenty very distinct paragraphs had the air of a definitive treaty. I must be pardoned for thus mistaking it in times when my mind is fully occupied with such matters, having heard of nothing else for ten or twelve months, without however advancing to their settlement by a single square inch.

I say nothing of the magic lanterns in Warsaw, where they are shouting with might and main for the Jesuits, of whom you seem to think a good deal. I often used to tell my great and good friend Comte Falkenstein (whom I shall regret eternally) that I was preserving the species intact in order to have the satisfaction of giving them gratis to the Roman Catholic countries. You may have noticed that the King of Prussia offered them at a ducat apiece.

You must find great pleasure in seeing people fight, since you are advising all the world to do so. So far, thank God, your advice has not been followed. If all that you predict to me happens, I fear those cannons will keep me from making cannons on my billiard table at the Hermitage. Society has danced at the latter place this winter with heart and soul, as your cousin Comte Stahremberg has doubtless told you. Also there were plays before and after supper, and masked balls, to which everybody rushed under pretext of amusing the Alexanders and Constantines, but everybody was delighted to be there, myself among the first, and the question was, who was the best disguised?

After that, tell me that the grand equerry is wrong when he proves with his usual physico-comical rhodomontade that gayety is a proper thing to give the soul, whereas gravity, sadness, and especially monotony freezes to the marrow of one's bones! Do you not think it singular that I should admit this of monotony?

But I have much else in my head. For instance: I am thinking that the Academy ought to found prizes for answers to two questions, namely: What have honour and valour (precious synonyms to ears heroic) become in the minds of present citizens under a suspicious government, jealously proscribing all distinctions? — whereas Nature herself has given to the man of intelligence pre-eminence over a fool, and ordained that courage be founded on strength of body or of mind. Second prize for second question, namely: Have we any need for honour and valour? If these are needed, emulation must not be proscribed, nor must it be shackled by its inveterate enemy, equality.

I rejoiced for a moment over the news which reached us here that the royal family were safely out of Paris, their deliverance effected by eight thousand gentlemen of France. But my joy was of short duration when I learned that the escort had made no resistance to the municipality of Sainte-Menéhould. It is to be supposed they were not mounted at the moment; but henceforth I despair of ever seeing them so.

I am much gratified by the confidence you show to me. You will always find in me the same *bonhomie* that you seem to value. I am convinced that my grandsons, who are now skipping round me, will have as much. Alexander is four inches taller than I, and his brother comes up to his shoulder. If you could see them I think you would be pleased with them.

To H. I. Majesty Catherine II.

BELŒIL, September, 1791.

MADAME, — I can get the better of your Majesty, it seems, only in the size of my paper; but if I can get the better of you in anything I am more powerful than all the other Powers of the earth, who cannot even equal their model in beneficence, justice, generosity, and grandeur of soul. My letters being long on the way, your Majesty can always be comforted, on receiving one, with the thought that you are rid of me for the next three months.

It is impossible for me not to answer your letters at once. I devour them, and then, for fear of losing them, I hide them in a *sachet*, called a portfolio, — though I dislike the men of portfolios. I write your Majesty what comes into my head; if I wrote what passes in my soul it would be an expression of feeling, or of admiration, which would bore you; and as ennui is the only sovereign of whom you are afraid, it is also the only one with whom you keep affairs *in statu quo* before that enemy can attack your Majesty. . . .

I have told several English and Prussian ministers that with Sevastopol well below Oczakow and Kinbourn (distant more than seven versts), under the cannon of which is the Vervalter, they do not know what they are talking about when they declare that Oczakow is the key of the Black Sea; and I have expressed myself on these various Peaces made by clerks in offices, who, without instruction from generals and those who fought the war, decide boundaries and make concessions without knowing the geography, military or political, of the region. It is, however, from the cold bureaus of clever men that treaties have emanated from the time of King Nimrod — who certainly did not make his in the name of the Holy Trinity.

I have seen the King of Sweden lately, with more interest than ever before. He told me rather humorously that if he had been king of another country he should not have been so headstrong and perhaps not so brave. "Sire," I said, "as a gentleman perhaps, and as a knight — " "Ah! that is just it," he said, with his amiable vivacity; "but as a soldier, to be King of Sweden one *must* take that style." "I can imagine, Sire," I replied, "that your two Gustavuses and Charles XII. have rather spoilt the profession." "I cannot reign," he went on, "except by the opinion they have of my personal character; and I had to show my subjects, more than the enemy, that I did not fear danger. My power is nothing compared with that of my neighbours. It was necessary, therefore, that I should have it said: 'If the King of Sweden commits certain follies, Gustavus III. maintains them and repairs them.' Perhaps I have sometimes unreasonably considered myself affronted; but the empress respects those who will not bear affront. But what do you know about it? what has she told you, or written to you?" "Nothing, Sire," I replied, "I have not seen her since your war. But when she sent me your manifesto, the mention of Pugatchef seemed to me to have irritated her, and the moderation of your Majesty in not having helped that rebel to dethrone her did not please her." "That was a bit of temper on my part," he said warmly, "of which I repented; but I did not repent the war. I wanted to know if I had means and talents for it. I have perhaps been spoken of with eulogy; I occupied the stage. There is more glory in resisting Catherine II. than there was in Charles XII. beating Peter the Great." In the king's talk, rather too abundant perhaps, there is always wit, piquancy, and an intermediary

The Comte d Artois

shade between talent and genius. He burns to command armies if war is made upon France; but who would intrust him with the command? I tried to get the idea out of his head with a bit of flattery, telling him what Cineas said to Pyrrhus [that to fight against the Senate was to attack another Hydra]. Finally, the successor of the Catholic, roaming, and eccentric Christina asked me twenty times over if I thought he had lost ground in your Majesty's opinion. I reassured him, and told him there were two ways of winning it and keeping it, — valour and good faith.

After having stopped the fermentation in my double government, civil and military, by telling them that there is none; after laughing at the cowardice, the politics, the dilapidation of the Van der Nootists, and the pretended royalism of certain scoundrels called Vonckists, and having put down those who carry their noses too high, I shall go and pass the winter in Vienna, if I am not fortunate enough to be sent, with some assistance, to preach the religion of kings in France. May that sermon be quick and strong, to finish the sooner. Thunder and stun — that is what I say always. May Heaven preserve us from a delay which shall give that nation time to collect itself and train for war. What your Majesty said to me about drawing a cordon round it as if it had the plague is fine. Let them make or unmake themselves by civil war; that is their affair.

Mine is now to end this letter and leave your Majesty to yours; assuring you of the respect, etc.

I was perhaps the innocent cause of the massacres at Lyons, because I instigated in that town the hissing of Collot d'Herbois, a miserable actor, who was oppressing a very good one, Chevalier, whom I protected. It is well-known that the former declared he committed those crimes to avenge himself on the town of Lyons for the insults he had received there. Among other disasters of which I have reason to fear I have been the involuntary cause, I must place that of having brought about the misfortunes of Poland by inducing the Empress Catherine to receive Ignatio Potocki very badly at Kiev. I had promised King Stanislas to do this; on which Potocki flung himself and all the compatriots of his region into the arms of the King of Prussia. Hence the constitution of May 3 and the consequences that followed.

During the first days of the emigration, a most touching scene occurred one evening in the theatre at Tournay, to which I had driven over from Belœil by chance. The piece they were playing was "Richard, Cœur de Lion." The audience saw me in my box much moved by the air *Ô Richard! ô mon roi! tout l'univers t'abandonne*, and they applauded to the skies. Frenchwomen, old and young, sprang up in their boxes, the whole pit was filled with young French officers who sprang upon the stage as if to the assault, crying out: "Vive le roi! vive le Prince de Ligne!" I could not restrain myself. There is a scene in the play where they vow to avenge the poor imprisoned king; I advanced, applauding, as if to take my part in doing so. In fact, I was then in hopes that I might really do so, for it seemed likely that I should be thus employed. That movement of mine caused more applause, which only ceased that all might wipe their eyes, which were bathed in tears.

Sixty-four of the best gentlemen of France, very interesting men, occupied one of my châteaux at the beginning of the emigration in 1791, and they afterwards wrote me a most touching letter when they left it. What might not that gallant and brilliant youth have done had it been launched at once into the kingdom, where at the worst a civil war would have prevented a foreign war? But it is none the less true that subsequently many Frenchmen became aristocratic and believed that they made themselves noblemen by emigrating; so that in this way the Republic has created almost as many as it has destroyed. Not one of these self-made nobles, insignificant though he be, but thinks himself the equal of a Montmorency because he serves, he says (though without serving), the Throne and the Altar!

It was thought by others as well as by myself at the beginning of the French Revolution that I should probably play a part in the armies of the Powers opposed to it. I received a letter from a club in Maçon, signed by a M. d'Aumbrat, a former brigadier whom I had known, informing me that I should be put out of the way and Belœil burned if I attempted to be an aristocrat.

While on a tour which I made through my province during the short time that the Low Countries remained in possession of Austria, a certain M. de Lacombe entered my room without having himself announced and said: "Monsieur, I am a Jacobin, but tired of being so. In order that there may be no more of them, I am about to return to France with proofs of malversation and treachery on the part of certain of my comrades, commissaries to Saint Domingo, which will get them guillotined; I shall thus gain the confidence of the Convention. Having done that, how would you wish me to betray it? As a general in Paris, or with the army? Commanding a fortress, or in the councils? It is all the same to me. Do you want a party in France for yourself personally? There is one for the Duke of York, and one for the Duke of Brunswick; but you are better known and liked than either. They say much good of you, monsieur, in France, where it is known that you have passed a part of your life."

I thanked him for his offer of royalty, which I abdicated on the spot, and then, not feeling absolutely sure that he was a madman, I advised him to get Lille restored to the Austrians as a means to inspire confidence in his powers. I never knew what became of him, nor whether he was or was not sincere in desiring to produce some revolt in Paris. I have a dim remembrance that I read his name soon after in a list of the guillotined.

I have given the portrait of a remarkable man, well-known to me, Giovanni Casanova, in my Works, under the name of Avanturos [vol. xxv. p. 87]. He was a man of great intelligence, force of character, and knowledge. He avows himself in his memoirs to be an adventurer, the son of an unknown father and a bad Venetian actress. Those memoirs, to which, among other things, his cynicism gives a high value, though it will forever prevent them from seeing the light, are dramatic, dashing, comical, philosophical, novel, stupendous, inimitable. They were written in 1790 at the castle of Dux in Bohemia, and are prefaced with the motto, *Volentem ducit, nolentem trahit*, which, he remarks, unfolds to the reader his style of thought. He read them to me himself at Dux, but I did not observe the dates of the singular events of his life sufficiently to give a chronology of them, except that he was born in 1625. Epigrams, songs, ribaldry, indiscretions of all kinds, gabble about governments, love, jealousy, imprudences, silken ladders, bribed gondoliers, adventures of all sorts and all kinds — Casanova denied himself nothing.

He played the seigneur in a coat of gray lutestring flowered in silver, a very large collar of Spanish point, a plumed hat, a yellow waistcoat, and breeches of crimson silk. He would have been a very fine-looking man if he were not so ugly. He was tall, built like a Hercules, with an African tinge; keen eyes full of intelligence, but emitting at all times so much irascibility, uneasiness, and spite as to give him an air of ferocity. You could sooner make him angry than gay. He laughed little, but he made others laugh; and he had a way of saying things, between that of a numskull and a Figaro, that was very diverting. There was nothing he did not know, except the things he plumed himself on knowing, such as the rules of dancing, those of the French language, of taste, society, and *savoir vivre.* He was a fountain of knowledge; but he quoted Homer and Horace till you were sick of them. He had feeling and gratitude; but if you displeased him he was malignant, peevish, and detestable; a million of ducats could not buy back the smallest little jest made upon him.

He believed in nothing, except that which is the least believable; for he was superstitious in every possible way. Fortunately he had honour and delicacy, and if he said, "I have promised God," or "God wills it," there is nothing on earth that he was not capable of doing. Here is his own confession of faith and ethics as I found it in his memoirs: —

He had friends, he says, who did him good, — to them he was grateful; and enemies on whom he did not revenge himself because he could not, but whom he would never have forgiven as long as he lived if he had not forgotten the harm they did him; a man forgets an injury but does not pardon it; he only forgets it. Pardon comes from heroic generosity of mind; forgetfulness from weakness of memory, or gentle indifference; sometimes from a need of calmness and peace; for hatred in the long run kills whoever indulges it. He is a theist; but of the right kind; always certain of the action, never discontinued, of an infinite, immaterial, all-powerful God, author of all forms, and master of Nature.

Knowing that His essence is incomprehensible, he has never submitted it to the examination of his feeble understanding. He dares only contemplate it. He knows it is not matter; and although he himself is in all things like it, he nevertheless has nothing in common with it. He knows that God does with him as He will; he does not know how, but he does not doubt it, and he pays Him homage in adoring Him. He adores Him at all moments by addressing to Him mental prayers, which he has ever found consoling and efficacious.

Casanova's stupendous imagination, the vivacity of his native land, his journeyings, the countless careers he had followed, his firmness under the repeated loss of every moral and physical good, made a rare man of him, and one valuable to have met with, worthy of even consideration and friendship from the very small number of those who found grace in his sight.

Passing through Nuremberg on one occasion he gave himself the name of Steingalt, which came into his head at the moment, and from that time forth he added it to that of Casanova, to make himself a nobleman, he said, without incurring obligation to any sovereign. This was after his escape from the Janissaries, who seized him in the streets of Constantinople for laughing at the Sultan. There was talk of impaling him; but Turks are slow and he was quick; he got away from them and swam to a ship just sailing for Venice. There he met his two brothers, also arriving from foreign parts. "What have you learned?" Casanova said to them. "From the conversation that ensued," he remarks, "I judged that one of them would never be anything but a ninny, and the other a lunatic." The lunacy of the latter was the genius of painting, which, developing soon after, has made him one of the most celebrated battle painters of his time, supplanting Le Brun, Van der Meulen, Houd, and Bourguignon. The prediction about his other brother, who died in Dresden, was better verified.

Casanova's adventures in Venice are too well known for me to relate them here. I shall only say that they were all certified to me as true by the Venetians themselves. After he escaped from the horrible and inhuman prison under the "leads" he wandered far. Arriving in Paris he bethought himself of Cardinal de Bernis, the only person he knew there, having met him in Venice. His money was gone. The cardinal asked him if he had any, and gave him a post in a lottery office which was worth about eight or ten thousand francs. But what was that in Paris? He spent thirty thousand on opera-dancers, equipages, liveries of a great Italian seigneur of the worst taste, suppers, and a fine establishment: somebody had to pay for it all. He chanced to meet with one of the greatest ladies of the kingdom, Mme. d'Urfé, who was taken with his large eyes, his singular voice, and the bronzed skin of his country. He supped with her; talked magic, astrology, and cabala in a reasonable manner; made light of the first two, but said he was strong on the third. "Shall I give you a proof?" he said. "Have you anything to ask for at Court? I can tell you what answer the minister will make." Whereupon he made calculation with words, letters, circles and Scripture numbers, and assured her that Cardinal de Bernis would speak to the king and cause her demand to be granted in spite of the difficulties he might make to it. Then he went off to the cardinal and told him the whole story. Bernis laughed like a madman. "Let us talk about Venice," he said. Casanova reminded him of certain verses the abbé had written there — very good, but very loose. "Forget them, my friend," said the cardinal. "I am on the verge of being turned out, as it is." In fact he lost his place a few weeks later, and Casanova lost his; but not before Mme. d'Urfé's affair was successful. Behold Casanova crowned with benefits! He taught her the cabala, and more than a hundred thousand crowns went into his pocket.

After this he went to Ferney; and the first thing he did was to quarrel with M. de Voltaire by letting him know that the "Henriade" was far below "Jerusalem delivered," and he himself still farther below Ariosto in the "Pucelle." In spite of which, he interested M. de Voltaire for a while; but happening to praise Jean-Jacques at a moment when the latter had raised all Geneva against him, they parted company mutually displeased with each other. Casanova became suspected by both the parties who have always divided that little republic, and went to England. There he had the most piquant love and benevolence adventure that I ever heard of; but I do not remember it well enough to tell it in detail. His fortunes were then at a very low ebb, and what could be more innocent than to seek to build them up? He sees the daughter of a rich banker named Hop. He pleases her; goes to her father's house and pleases him still more. To amuse them he plays cabala; chance makes all his promises succeed, and the cry is "Prodigy!" Mr. Hop says nothing, pretends not to believe, and asks if a certain vessel that he names (which was thought lost) would return from the Indies. Casanova figures, calculates, thinks, and predicts "in a week." Mr. Hop goes out and insures its safe arrival for two hundred thousand florins. The insurance people accept gladly. Returning, Mr. Hop embraces Casanova. "You have caused me to win two hundred thousand florins this day," he says to him. "How?" says the other, not understanding. "By your cabala; I have just insured the safe arrival of the ship." Casanova, frightened, cries out: "Go back, go back, if there is still time; I may be the cause of your ruin, and what a return for all your kindness! I am a most unlucky man! My cabala is only a joke; there's no such thing as the cabalistic art." "Oh yes, there is," says Mr. Hop, slyly; "that is only your modesty. I am certain of the fact." Happily for both, the vessel did actually arrive in port the next day. Mr. Hop wanted to take him into his business, and the daughter wanted to marry him. But Casanova said he did not wish to do them harm, and tore himself away from love and commerce, assuring them that the acquisition of an adventurer was not desirable in their family. Mlle. Hop was in deep distress at losing him for a husband, and could only be consoled by her father presenting him through her hands with a very considerable sum of money.

A vessel was at that time setting sail for Lisbon, and Hop having given him letters of recommendation, he went there and was well received by his old friends and preceptors, the Jesuits. Thence he proceeded to Spain. What a land for Casanova! Serenades given, or dispersed by him; philosophical crusade (ill-managed) against bull-fights; doubts on religion; scoffs at the grandees, always short in stature, upon whom he looked down from the height of his great figure; rivalry in love with monks,—in short, ten times more than was needed for an *auto-da-fé*. Happily, the daughter of a nobleman cobbler with whom he lodged, who was in love with him, warned him in the nick of time, and he took refuge at the Russian embassy, the secretary of which was just starting for Petersburg and allowed him to escape in his private carriage.

It is to be remarked that during the seventeen years that Casanova roamed the world he never had a passport, a letter of credit, or one of recommendation—except from his Hop. His adventures in Madrid were not of a kind to induce the

Russian ambassador, though allowing him to travel with his secretary, to give him any to Petersburg. "Well," thought Casanova, "here I am at the end of the world, in the hottest and the coldest of countries with nothing but my device, *Volentem ducit, nolentem trahit;* perhaps I can get employed in some capacity at the Court of Catherine, secretary, lover, librarian, *chargé d'affaires* somewhere, or the governor of a great seigneur. Why not? Casanova is made for all great places."

At the close of one of those Northern summer days when there seems to be scarcely any night, the empress was walking in the garden with all her Court, when she saw a figure, rather strangely dressed, Italian as it seemed to her, and she guessed it was the man whose name she had seen on the police reports.

Casanova was gazing at a statue with a contemptuous air. "Apparently it does not please you, monsieur," she said to him. "No, madame, it is out of proportion."—"It is a nymph."—"A nymph! what sort of nymph is that? it has no attributes."—"Are you not the brother of the painter?"—"Yes, madame; but how did your Majesty know that? and how is it that you know that dauber?"—"He has genius, monsieur, and I think a great deal of him."—"Genius! you may say fire, colouring, and rather fine grouping; but design and finish are not in him."

The empress passed on laughing; but hearing that with the little money that remained to him he was keeping a gambling table at a café, she had him informed that that was not the way to recommend himself to her favour, and that she could not employ him.

After this he departed for Berlin. "I'll talk to the king," he said to himself, "about Algarotti as if I knew him; and say harm about German literature, which I don't like, and know as little about as he does himself. I 'll ask him for a place."

Accordingly he presented himself as the man who had escaped from the leads of Venice. "Is all that true?" asked Frederick the Great. "No other man than your Majesty could ask me that with impunity. I have never lied." "You must abhor your country." "Not at all" — whereupon he regaled the king with his endless paradoxes on governments and laws. After which all the classic authors (on whom I have never known any one as strong as he) were passed in review. Frederick was pleased with him for a moment, and asked for still further details about Venice. But Casanova must needs assert that Maupertuis was a poor astronomer, and d'Alembert a poor geometrician, Voltaire nothing of a poet, d'Argens very little of a philosopher, the Abbé de Pradt a bad theologian, La Mettrie a bad doctor, Beaumelle a bad critic, Diderot a bad writer, and König a pedant.

Frederick began to think he was not the man for him, but he said to himself: "I will try to employ him. He certainly has wits and knowledge. He might be useful to me in some of my establishments." So the next day he sent for him.

"Have you patience," he asked, "and order?" "Very little of either, Sire." "Have you money?" "Hardly any." "So much the better; then you will be satisfied with my small salary." "I must be, for I have spent a million." "How did you get that sum?" "By the cabala, Sire; I knew the past and I predicted the future." The king began to laugh. "So you are an adventurer, are you?" "Yes, Sire, and if I catch fortune now by the tip of her wig I 'll not let go again." "You will not find fortune with me. However, follow me to my school of cadets. There I have a quantity of incapables, pigs, stupids, governors, masters, preceptors — I don't know what to call them myself. I should like to improve them. Come." So Casanova went.

He asked the first preceptor he met what his salary was. "Three hundred crowns," was the reply. "Mercy!" thought Casanova, "this is not my affair! However, I 'll see what there is to do." The king passed in review a line of governors; found they were pigs, as he had said, ill-combed, ill-clothed. He shook his cane at two who answered his questions badly. Then he went to the dormitories, found them in a filthy condition, and ordered the head-governor into the Stockhaus, that is to say, the guard-room.

Casanova trembled in all his limbs lest he should be sent there too in case he refused so delightful an office, and when the king turned to offer it to him, behold, he was not there. He started the same day for Warsaw, and sent Frederick word that on the whole he preferred leads to irons. . . .

I cannot now remember where else Casanova went to play the knight and the wandering Jew, for he was a little of both; the gates of all towns and courtyards and castles were more or less closed to him; but I do remember that he came to Vienna before his brother Francesco established himself there. He took advantage of the good-natured way in which the emperor received all comers. Joseph II., who forgot nothing, and knew everything about each individual, said to him: "You are, I think, the friend of M. Sangouri." "Yes," replied Casanova, "a Venetian noble." "I do not think much of that," said the emperor; "I cannot respect those who buy nobility." "And how about those who sell it, Sire?" Joseph II. changed the conversation, not willing to be engaged along that line, and soon withdrew, little pleased with his visitor.

About the year 1784 Casanova went to Paris for the last

time. My nephew, Waldstein, took a fancy to him at the Venetian ambassador's, where they met at dinner. As Waldstein makes a pretence of believing and practising magic, he happened to mention the collar-bones of Samson and Agrippa, and all that sort of thing, which comes very easily to him. "To whom are you telling it?" cried Casanova. "*O, che bella cosa! Cospetto!* I am familiar with it all." "Well, then," said Waldstein, "come to Bohemia with me. I start to-morrow."

Casanova, at the end of his money, his travels, and his adventures, agreed; and thus it was that he became the librarian of a descendant of the great Waldstein [Wallenstein]. As such he passed the last fourteen years of his life at the castle of Dux, near Töplitz, the Chantilly of Bohemia, where, for six summers, he made me happy with his imagination, as lively as at twenty, his enthusiasm for me personally, and his useful and agreeable information.

But it must not be supposed that in this tranquil haven, opened to him by the benevolence of Comte Waldstein to save him from the storms of life, there were no storms of his own making. Not a day went by without a quarrel in the household about his coffee, his milk, his macaroni, as to which he was very exacting. The cook had forgotten his polenta; the equerry had given him a bad driver when he wanted to come over and see me; the dogs had barked all night; guests had arrived unexpectedly, and he had been obliged to dine at a small table; that hunting-horn had torn his ears with its shrill notes (or its false ones); the vicar had plagued him by trying to convert him; the count did not say good-day to him first; he had not been presented to a man of importance who had come to see the lance that was run through the body of the great Waldstein; the count had lent a book out of the library without informing him;

he had made a bow on entering the salon such as Marcel, the great dancing-master, had taught him sixty years before, and somebody had laughed; he had done his steps in the minuet at the late ball, and somebody else had laughed; he had put on his plumed hat and his suit of gold silk with his black velvet waistcoat, and his paste diamond buckles on his silk stockings, and the company had all laughed. "*Cospetto!*" he cried; "canaille that you are! You are all Jacobins! You are wanting in respect to Monsieur le Comte, and Monsieur le Comte is wanting in respect to me not to punish you. Monsieur le Comte," he said, "I have stabbed the stomach of the great general of Poland. I am not a nobleman, but I have made myself a noble." The count laughed; grief the more. The next day Waldstein went to him with a pair of pistols, said not a word, but looked at him gravely and offered a weapon (expecting to die of suppressed laughter). Casanova wept, embraced him, crying out: "Shall I kill my benefactor? *O, che bella cosa!*" and fell to talking magic and macaroni.

But how was it possible to endure such persecutions? God commanded him to leave Dux. Without believing in God quite as much as he did in death, he always declared that everything he did was by God's order. God ordered him now to ask me for letters of recommendation to the Duke of Saxe-Weimar, who was my intimate friend, to the Duchess of Saxe-Gotha, who did not know me, and to certain Jews in Berlin. He went away secretly, leaving a farewell letter for Waldstein, very tender, proud, honourable, and cross. Waldstein laughed and said he would come back.

So it proved. They made him wait in antechambers; nobody would give him a place as governor, or librarian, or chamberlain. He said the Germans were all oafs. The

Duke of Saxe-Weimar received him well, but he instantly became jealous of Goethe and Wieland — very naturally. He declaimed against the literature of the country, and in Berlin against the ignorance, superstition, and rascality of the Jews to whom I had sent him; from whom, nevertheless, he drew bills of exchange on Waldstein, who laughed, paid them, and embraced him on his return.

Enchanted to see us again, he related most amusingly the vicissitudes he had passed through, to which his sensitive pride gave the name of humiliations. "I am proud," he said, "because I am nothing." But a week after his return the troubles began again. Strawberries were served to everybody before they were to him; and, to crown all grief, his portrait, which he had thought had been carried off after his departure by one of his admirers, was found in a dark closet.

Thus he passed five years more, fretting and distressing himself, and groaning over the conquest of his unhappy country and the vanished glory of his superb Venice, which had so long resisted all Asia and Europe. His appetite diminished daily, but he regretted life very little, and ended it nobly towards God and man. He received the sacraments with grand gestures and many phrases, and said: "Great God, and you, the witnesses of my death, I have lived a philosopher, and I die a Christian."

His brother Francesco [the painter] was also a singular man. I often reproached him for the cannon smoke by means of which he evaded finishing his military work properly. He also made the heads of his horses too small and too arched; but this was because his lay figure of a horse was so. I once asked him why, in one of his great pictures at the Palais Bourbon, he had painted my great-grandfather, on a gray horse, running away with all his might, when in point of fact he was made prisoner at the head of his infantry after doing marvels with the cavalry at the battle of Lens. Thirty years later he made a fine picture for the Empress of Russia, — a portrait of Joseph II., surrounded by his great generals, Lacy, Loudon, and others. What was my amazement, when the picture was exhibited, to find myself among them, and a very good likeness too. My comrades were hurt. "Why," I said to Casanova, "did you cause them pain in that way?" "I did it," he said, "to repair the wrong I had done to a Prince de Ligne in 1648."

Princess Hélène Massalska

VIII.

1735–1795.

THE FAMILY HISTORY.

[It will be observed that in his memoir and papers the Prince de Ligne says little of his domestic affairs; and this omission, taken in connection with the very conventional character of his marriage, would naturally lead readers to suppose that his home had no part in his life. So far from that, he had a large family, by whom he was greatly beloved and petted. As he does not himself make mention of this, except in the one sentence already quoted, "I have known but one united family, and that is my own," this chapter on his domestic life is here added. It is taken chiefly from the works of the Baron de Reiffenberg and M. Lucien Perey mentioned in the list of authorities on pages 42 and 43 of Vol. I. of this book. If a little repetition occurs here and there the reader must kindly consider it unavoidable.

The house of Ligne, one of the most illustrious in the Low Countries, possessed from the 12th century the peerage of Baudour, and from the 13th century the hereditary dignity of Seneschal, or Governor, of Hainault. Jean III. of Ligne received from Maximilian of Austria in 1498 the collar of the Order of the Golden Fleece; and his son, Antoine, created Prince of Mortagne by Henry VIII. of England, whom he had valiantly served, was surnamed "the great Ligne Devil" on account of his bravery. In the 16th century a younger son of the family founded the house of Arenberg, since so distinguished. The Lignes bear: or, a bend gules, with the motto, *Semper stat linea recta.*

The father of Charles-Joseph was Claude-Lamoral de Ligne, and his mother was Elisabeth-Alexandrine-Charlotte, Princesse de Salm, who died at his birth or soon after it. His own style and titles in full were as follows: Charles-Joseph, Prince de Ligne, d'Amblise, and the Holy Empire, Marquis de Roubais and de Dormans, Comte de Fauquemberghe, Baron de Werchin, Belœil, Antoing, Cisoing, Villiers, Silly, and Herzelles, Souverain de Fagnolles, Seigneur de Baudour, Wallincourt, and other places, Chevalier of the Golden Fleece, Commander of the Order of Maria Theresa, Grandee of Spain of the first-class, first Ber of Flanders, peer, Seneschal and Marshal hereditary of Hainault, Field-marshal of the Imperial armies, captain of Trabans, colonel-proprietor of the Wallon infantry regiment, Saxe-Gotha, and chamberlain to their Imperial Majesties.

He has told us about his youth in so fresh and boyish a manner that we need nothing further to bring him before our minds. He says in one of his letters that he began his fragmentary writings at the time he entered the army in 1752, being then seventeen years old; also that his "Journal of the Seven Years' War" was partly written on horseback, and that many of his other writings were the solace and amusement of his horrible winter quarters in the villages of Bohemia.

As soon as he became the master of large means, on the death of his father in 1767 (being made a lieutenant-general about the same time), he travelled much in the summers, to England, Italy, Switzerland, and the eastern parts of Europe; but he has left no record of these journeys, beyond the slight description of the gardens of England in his "Coup d'œil sur Belœil." When he was not travelling he lived at

Belœil, dividing his winters between Brussels, Vienna, and Paris until 1774, when he went, as he has told us, to Versailles, returning there for five months every year till 1787, the year of the Crimean journey; after which he never saw Paris or Queen Marie-Antoinette again.

The family home was at Belœil, with establishments in Brussels and Vienna. The great hôtel de Ligne in Brussels (where the prince was born) was close to the Church of Saint-Gudule; a street was afterwards opened past it which bears, or bore, the family name. There he set up a printing-press, and he also had another about the year 1780 at Belœil, which was used, as we shall see later, to great advantage by his son Charles. Married in 1755 to the Princesse Françoise de Lichtenstein, she gave him first two daughters, Princesse Christine and Princesse Euphémie, and then, to his great joy, in 1759 his eldest son Charles, at the news of whose birth we heard him say: "Ah, how I shall love him! if I return alive from this war, how I shall love him!" The death of this young man, whose nature was brave and tender, and his mind and acquirements remarkable, was the great sorrow of his father's life. A second son, Louis-Eugène, who died at Belœil May 2, 1812, two years before his father, is the ancestor of the present Prince de Ligne; he served with honour and distinction in the Austrian armies. Besides these there were two sons, Albert and François, who died young, and a third daughter, the Princesse Flore.

In a preface to one of his short essays the prince says: "Christine, who is an enthusiast, found much prettier things in the 'Voyage autour de mes poches' than are really there. Flore, who is a lazy girl, agreed with her. We were driving to Euphémie's château; Christine was reading the book in the carriage; I could not say anything against that, because she reads very well and is very useful. But I did say:

'Do you not see that the merit of a book of that kind belongs to the writer who first imagined the idea of it? After the "Voyage autour de ma chambre," which gave rise to a second, and then a third, everybody knows what is coming.' 'Well,' said Christine, 'if it is so easy, write one yourself.' 'Yes,' said Flore, 'and put in all the nonsense you like, but begin it to-morrow,'—and here I am, doing so. I do not know which of the two naughty girls it was who added: 'We expect something dreadful.'"

In 1779 a proposal was made for the marriage of Prince Charles, then just twenty years of age. The widow of the Prince de Ligne's uncle, whom he mentions in his memoir as a "very narrow-minded little marshal," the Princesse de Ligne-Luxembourg, was at that time living in Paris. As lady of the palace to the late Queen of Spain (daughter of the Regent) she had received from Louis XV. an apartment in the Tuileries. Her contemporaries declare that her face was the ugliest ever seen, fat, shiny, never rouged, of a livid paleness, supported by three tiers of chin. The Duchesse de Tallard said of her that she looked like a guttering tallow-candle. But she was kind and good, and took an interest just at this time in a bewitching little Polish princess, Hélène Massalska, an orphan, in the guardianship of her uncle, the Prince-Bishop of Wilna, who was being educated in Paris at the convent of the Abbaye-aux-Bois under the careful supervision of Mme. Geoffrin.

The elder brother of the Prince-Bishop, Hélène's father, had married a Radziwill. The Massalskis and the Radziwills were the two great rival families of Poland; the Massalskis supported the faction of the Czartoriskis, assisting the latter to put their nephew Stanislas-Augustus upon the throne in concert with Russia. The Radziwills, on the contrary, sworn enemies of the Czartoriskis, defended the old system of the Polish republic, and were very hostile to Russian influence and the election of Stanislas-Augustus. The Prince-Bishop of Wilna, to whose guardianship Hélène and her brother Xavier had been committed, was compromised in the recent revolution in Poland, and he was, moreover, a gambler who had lost in three years one hundred thousand ducats. Besides this, he paid from his privy purse the costs of his soldiery, the Massalski legion of sixteen thousand men; so that he was constantly in need of money, although the Massalski territorial possessions were immense.

Prince Radziwill, Hélène's uncle on her mother's side, equipped and maintained in his towns and castles a force of twenty-eight thousand men. The struggle ended for the time being in the triumph of Russia, the Czartoriskis, and Stanislas-Augustus. Prince Radziwill was exiled and his property confiscated to Russia. Thus Hélène's fortune on both sides, great as it was, was in jeopardy.

In 1777 a rumour of her beauty, her name, her wealth crept out from the walls of the Abbaye-aux-Bois, and suitors began to appear. The first was the Duc d'Elbœuf, Prince de Vaudemont, second son of Prince Charles-Louis de Lorraine, Grand equerry of France, and his mother was a Rohan. The negotiations for this marriage were carried on by the Marquis de Mirabeau, father of the more famous man of that name. Meantime the Princesse Hélène, who issued occasionally from her convent to appear at the juvenile balls of the Duchesses de Mortemart, de Chatillon, de Choiseul, and others, had met and liked Prince Frédéric de Salm, a young man of charming face and manners, the bearer of a great name, the possessor of a magnificent house on the Quai d'Orsay, who was not only worthless in character, but a proved coward. Of these last-named points Hélène was at first ignorant.

As a marriage of this kind was inadmissible, and the young princess refused to consider the Duc d'Elbœuf or any of her other suitors, the Princesse de Ligne-Luxembourg bethought her of the son of her husband's nephew, the young Prince Charles de Ligne. Prince Charles, judging by the following reply to his great-aunt, was not very ardent for the marriage, but his mother took up the matter warmly and requested the princess to continue the negotiation.

To the Princesse de Ligne-Luxembourg.

March, 1779.

I have received, my dear aunt, the letters that you have had the kindness to write me, and I sent them at once to my father. There will be difficulties, as far as I can see, about the affair in question. We are all impressed with your promptitude in taking up the matter that interests you, and with your other kindnesses for our family, for which we reiterate our thanks, my dear aunt.

The young lady [*la petite personne*] seems to me rather determined, and not very delicate in her choice, as she prefers Prince Frédéric de Salm, who has so bad a reputation. All this is provided the uncle has not decided already, for it takes so long to receive answers.

Accept, my dear aunt, etc.

CHARLES DE LIGNE.

The friends of Princesse Hélène feigned to ignore her preference for the Prince de Salm (although she openly showed it); they dwelt on the exceptionally brilliant position of the Princes de Ligne in Vienna and the Low Countries, and assured her that the well-known liking of the Prince de Ligne for the Court of France would certainly make him give her an establishment in Paris, for he adored his son and would wish to have him near him. But, they added, it would be best not to make that a condition of her consent, as it might oppose the wishes of the Princesse de Ligne. Thus urged, Hélène withdrew her positive refusal and asked for time to make her decision, which was all the more readily granted because Prince Charles and his father were then with the Austrian army in Bavaria.

Prince Charles had been trained at the famous military school in Strasburg for four years; on leaving it, at the age of sixteen, he entered the service of Austria as second lieutenant of engineers. His preference was strongly for the artillery, but he accepted the engineers to please his father. At the moment when these negotiations for his marriage began, the war between Austria and Prussia about the Bavarian Succession had broken out. The young prince was with the army under the emperor and Maréchal de Lacy; his father, as we know, was with that under Maréchal Loudon, and they wrote to each other constantly. Here is one of the father's letters: —

June 26, 1778.

Well, my engineer, so you are still fortifying, but not fortified, I see, in your respect for the genius of engineering.

The emperor has been here to make what might be called his grumble. He said he wanted real war, but did not think he should get it. "Who will bet?" he said to us. "Everybody," replied Maréchal Loudon, who is very much out of humour. "Everybody is nobody," said the emperor. "Well I, for example," said Maréchal de Lacy. "How much?" asked the emperor, who expected a bet of twenty ducats or so. "Two hundred thousand florins," replied the marshal. The emperor made a diabolical face, and felt that he had received a public lesson.

He has been very amiable to me. He is always afraid we

should play the teacher to him. He was much pleased with my troops, and told me much good of you, my dear Charles, whom he has seen to work wonderfully well. He has just gone; I see him still from my window.

I laugh at myself and others when I think that, unappreciated, I know I am worth more than people think. Here I am drilling every company myself. I crack my throat in commanding six battalions at once. There is not a *kaloup*, as they say in Bavaria, meaning a wretched hut, containing no more than four soldiers, that I do not visit myself, to taste the men's soup and their bread, and weigh their meat to be sure they are not cheated. There is not a man to whom I have not spoken and given vegetables or something else; there is not an officer I have not had to dinner, trying to electrify them all for this war. My comrades do not do that sort of thing, and they are very wise, for no one finds fault with them. Not one of them cares about this war; they talk in the most pacific manner to young men, expecting with time to make them good and zealous generals in that way! That is very well, they will be generals-in-chief sooner than I, and that is very well too.

If an infantry officer may be allowed to embrace an officer of engineers and a genius for work, I embrace you, my boy. I am charmed that you get credit for doing well those worthless works. Adieu, *my* excellent work; adieu, my masterpiece — almost as good as Christine.

The Bavarian war being at an end, the Prince-Bishop thought it time to obtain through the Princesse de Ligne-Luxembourg some definite information as to the property of the Prince de Ligne and the settlements he would make on the marriage. The reply to these inquiries came promptly from the mother of Prince Charles.

The Princesse de Ligne (Lichtenstein) to the Princesse de Ligne-Luxembourg.

You do not doubt, I hope, princess, the tender sentiments that I feel for you; those of gratitude which I owe you at this moment cannot add to them.

I have the honour to send you a statement of the property of M. de Ligne. As, for a year past, he has placed his affairs in my hands, I signing for him and drawing his revenues, M. de Ligne himself giving me a receipt for all the money he receives from his estates, I can guarantee to you the correctness of this statement.

I know my husband's tender feeling and confidence towards you, princess, too well not to be certain he will agree to any arrangement you may think proper to make in regard to our son. I shall venture to request, madame, that if you think twenty-five thousand francs too small an income for the immediate establishment, you will yourself fix the sum; because, as I only need one year to put our affairs in proper order (the public has been pleased to think them far more disordered than I have found them), I can promise to agree to any arrangements you may make for our young people. They will have no other trouble in obtaining their income than to give their signatures every three months. I have made it a law to myself, in regulating our affairs, to regard as sacred the times fixed for the payment of incomes and pensions.

It may ill become me, my tenderness for my children blinding me perhaps, to praise our son to you; but I think, from what those who have known him for years at Strasburg and in the army tell us, we have every reason to be satisfied with his character.

Deign not to relax the kindness you feel for him or your

efforts to contribute to his happiness; you will thus make mine; for I regard as such his establishment and the presence of my children about me.

Receive, princess, my homage, and the assurance of my respect, etc.

Hélène, however, was recalcitrant, and Prince Charles was certainly very cold, as appears from the following letter in reply to those of his aunt, in which he does not even speak of the marriage: —

My dear Aunt, — Though peace is made, the congress is not over; my father is very much annoyed, for he is detained in a wretched village to bore himself with nothing to do. He will certainly go to Paris as soon as he can, and I envy him the pleasure of seeing you, my dear aunt.

Permit me to assure you of the tender and respectful sentiments with which I shall be all my life, etc.

The marked coldness of the young prince is easily explained by the fact that from his earliest years he had cherished a deep affection for a friend of his childhood, which was destined to be never wholly effaced. But being accustomed to obey his mother in all things, the thought of disobeying her now does not seem to have crossed his mind. The Princesse de Ligne saw in Hélène's wealth, and her isolation from all parentage, which would naturally make her adopt the family of her husband as her own, exactly what she wanted; and to bring that result about, she chose to ignore the secret feelings of her son.

The Congress of Teschen being over at last, the Prince de Ligne returned, but leisurely, not hurrying himself. He writes to the Princesse de Ligne-Luxembourg from Vienna, as follows: —

They tell me, princess, that all goes well, thanks to your kindness. They say that you have done me the honour to write to me. I have not received your letters. They tell me also that I ought to write to the bishop. I beg you to send him this letter.

If you have any orders to give me, send them to Munich, *poste restante;* I shall receive them as I pass through.

All the information that I obtain from Poland appears to conform to our views.

I place myself at your feet, princess, and beg you to be convinced that my gratitude will equal my tender and respectful attachment.

PRINCE DE LIGNE.

As for Hélène, having been brought at last to consent to the marriage, she took more interest in the promise of certain *girandoles* (enormous diamond earrings worn with court dress) than she did in her future husband. She had no near relatives in Paris, so the marriage was celebrated at the Abbaye-aux-Bois, to the great joy of her schoolmates. In her journal she relates that when Prince Charles approached her he slipped into her hand his wedding present, an annuity of six hundred pounds sterling: "I thanked him," she says, "with a smile and a pressure of the hand, — the first I had granted him." The whole family returned at once to Belœil, where the bride was welcomed with one of the prince's ideal fêtes, ending with a marvellous illumination of the gardens and park. "It is not night," said Hélène, "it is silver day."

Hélène was now to know for the first time the meaning of family life, and she could not have seen it more favourably, for the Lignes lived together in an unconstrained intimacy, blest with gayety and tenderness. In her convent the little princess, with the natural selfishness of childhood, had thought only of herself; she was now to see the daily little sacrifices of brothers and sisters which a look or a kiss reward and make easy. Of all the members of the family her father-in-law and her sister-in-law Christine were the ones she liked best. The Princess Christine, married for the last four years to Prince Clary, was the eldest and favourite daughter of the Prince de Ligne, "his masterpiece," he called her. She was goodness, grace, and affability personified. Gifted with a sound judgment and perfect tact, she would have been an affectionate and charming guide for her young sister-in-law at the dawn of her womanhood, if that office had not been already taken by the princess-mother who was very jealous of the right, and would have yielded it to no one.

The Princesse de Ligne played a most important part, if not in the heart of her husband, at least in that of his home. The prince, who always recognized his wife's merits, treated her with great respect and the utmost friendliness. "My wife," he said, "is an excellent woman, full of delicacy, good-feeling and nobleness; she is not at all selfish. Her ill-humour passes quickly, and her eyes are suffused with tears for a mere trifle. There is no unpleasantness about her, for she has an excellent heart." Perhaps it was not very difficult for the prince to take her ill-humour easily, for he did not suffer from it; but it was not so easy for the children. It must be admitted, however, that there was some cause for the unevenness of her temper, for not only was her husband openly unfaithful to her, but he was constantly entangling his affairs, and in spite of his enormous fortune he would often have been seriously embarrassed had it not been for the constant and judicious care of the princess in managing their property, and in balancing expenses with revenue. However, in spite of the rather difficult character of the princess, the unalterable good temper and gayety of the prince made the home a delightful one; he was, and this is a very rare thing, as amiable there as he was in society.

The life at Belœil when the prince was present (during his frequent absences the princess held sterner rule) was gay and animated. Visitors abounded; they came from Brussels, Paris, and Vienna. Not only did the prince keep open table for all who liked to come there and pass the day, but a number of apartments were kept ready for unexpected visitors, who often remained for a length of time. Among these guests we find the names of the Viceroy Prince Charles de Lorraine, the Prince de Conti, the Comte d'Artois, the Polignacs, the Chevalier de Boufflers, the Chevalier de l'Isle, a very intimate friend of the prince, who figures in the correspondence of Mme. du Deffand and many others.

It must not be thought, however, that the life of the Lignes was all amusement. They knew how to mingle pleasure with serious occupations. Their mornings were given to study; music, drawing, art, and literature occupied them each in turn. The prince had hardly risen before he went, book in hand, to read and write on Flora's isle, or else to direct the various works about his property, all of which had a useful or a poetically fantastic object. His poetry too, or — what shall we call it? — his fatal facility for scribbling verses on any topic must have taken quite a serious portion of his time. There are quatrains and triolets and rondels, and madrigals and pastorals and idylls, — usually addressed to friends on some trivial social circumstance, and seldom of greater length than thirty or forty lines. The prince took great satisfaction and put all his vanity (which he might justly have spent, but did not, upon other gifts) into scattering these poems broadcast among his friends; and it may fairly be asked whether the reputation for frivolity which clung to him all his life was not caused by this rain of rubbish, which certainly did him great injustice. But here comes in, as if to rebuke this judgment, the affection that his family felt for him. His son Charles, leaving, in his most affecting will, directions for placing his bust in a certain room at Belœil with the portraits of his friends around it, adds: "I beg my father to compose and cause to be engraved on the pedestal verses which shall tell the happiness I have had in that society; but he must not praise me; and beneath each portrait he must write the portrait in verse of each person." Alas! Belœil was no longer theirs when the time came to obey the will.

The prince's printing-press was a matter of great interest to him; the books that bear the Belœil stamp are now much prized by bibliophiles. A complete list of them will be found in M. Lucien Perey's charming memoir of the Princesse Hélène Massalska, from which this account is taken. The "Coup d'œil on Belœil" was first printed on this press by Charles de Ligne, who made the quaint little drawing for its titlepage, which is on the last page of the Belœil chapter in Vol. I. of the present edition. He printed also his father's shorter poems, and that may have been one reason why they rained so profusely. Here is one which gives a fair idea of the best of the prince's verse; though it is not a very close translation.

Walking one evening in the woods at Belœil we lost our way in the darkness. My daughter-in-law, Hélène Massalska, pointing to a star, advised us to follow it, which we did, and soon reached our home.

We wandered far;
We lost our way, the night fell fast;
Heaven showed a single star,
And lo! we reached our home at last,
Led by the Star.

Was it the star
That shone before the Eastern Kings,
Or Love's resplendent star?
I think, remembering certain things,
That was the star.

To Helen's side
The star of Love will surely lead;
Follow thy heavenly guide
O happy lover — blest indeed
By Helen's side!

Prince Charles was a passionate lover of paintings, and he found time, in spite of his other studies and his military service, to make a noble collection of original drawings by the great masters, both old and modern. He was a fine connoisseur and drew well himself; he even undertook to engrave a number of the rare drawings of his collection, and for this purpose he sent for the famous engraver Bartsch, who came to Belœil and gave him lessons. Hélène took an interest in these tastes of her husband, and while he worked she classified the drawings (of which there were more than six thousand), and studied under his direction the manner of each master, so that she was soon in a fair way to become an enlightened amateur.

These intelligent occupations filled the mornings until the half-past three o'clock dinner, at which the family and their numerous guests, with the officers of the prince's regiment, assembled. After dinner and an hour's subsequent siesta, the company resorted to the gardens, where there were bosquets for all, in which to walk or dream or group as they pleased. Sometimes they went for long excursions on horseback or in carriages to the forest of Baudour, and in the evenings, with lights and music, they floated about the great lake or the rivers and canals of the park.

Prince Charles, without taking an active part in the general amusements, lent himself very readily to enjoy them; but his mind was serious and wanted food. He was particularly interested in all scientific discovery, and watched at this time, with great attention, the progress of a new aërial invention by Charles Pilatre de Rosier and the Montgolfiers; in other words, the making and working of balloons. He made two ascensions in what was called a "montgolfière" (on the principle of a fire-balloon), one from Paris in November, 1783, and another from Lyons in the following year. A few months later he constructed a balloon at his own expense and sent it up successfully from Mons, having invited a large company to see the sight, then a great novelty, among them the Duc and Duchesse d'Arenberg and many distinguished personages from the Courts of Brussels and Versailles, who all stayed at Belœil after the ascension.

But after a while Hélène, who liked Flanders so long as her father-in-law was there to invent fêtes and take her to the Brussels Court in a superb gilt carriage with panels in vernis-Martin, painted by the greatest artists in Vienna, began to pine for Paris and to urge the gift of a home there. The princess-mother strongly objected, feeling the dangers for a pleasure-loving and beautiful young creature whose husband, being in the Austrian service, might be forced to leave her to herself for months together. But Hélène, who said of herself that she was obstinate as the pope's mule, carried the day, and a house was bought for her in the Chaussée d'Antin.

The next step was a presentation at Court and the Princesse de Ligne-Luxembourg very readily agreed to introduce such a charming niece; but Hélène was not satisfied unless she could appear with the honours of war, that is to say, with those of the *tabouret.* Now this distinction was granted only to certain claims. Those of a grandee of Spain

sufficed to obtain it. The Prince de Ligne possessed that dignity, and Hélène persuaded her husband to ask his father to cede it to him. It was no slight matter to make the request, and the young prince shrank from the awkwardness of doing so, especially as he was forced to couple it with another for money, beautiful toilets and jewels and furniture having absorbed the revenues of the young couple. However, unable to resist the wishes of his wife, Prince Charles took his courage in both hands and wrote the letter. Here is the father's characteristic reply: —

VERSAILLES, September 10.

It is a droll thing to be married, is it not, my dear Charles? But you will come out of it all right. It is only fools who do not know how to make the best of that state. Meantime you have a pretty little wife, who will do you no discredit, and can be your mistress. Though you and I and all of us, from father to son, have borne the name of Lamoral (I do not know whether he was a saint or not), I am neither moral, moralist, nor moralizing enough to preach; but I laugh at those who do not believe in my morality, which consists in making others happy. I am sure that is yours also. Without having a regiment of principles, that is one of four or five I hold for the second education. As for the first, you know I always told you that to be a liar and a coward would make me die of grief. Assuredly, my boy, you learned that short lesson thoroughly.

Well, now let us go to business. Take as much money as you want, or as my men of business have or can get; there is one thing settled. Your uncle, the Bishop of Wilna, who thinks that you and I might be kings of Poland some day, wants us to be naturalized; well, we will go and be naturalized; another thing settled. Our aunt in the Tuileries wants your wife to have the *tabouret*, and she wants to go to Versailles, and to compass that I am to cede you the grandeeship. I have already written to the King of Spain and the minister; third thing settled — except that I shall take cold getting out of my carriage at the gate of the courtyard, for they only let in the carriages of grandees, as at the Luxembourg.

What annoys me is to hear persons of intelligence talk such nonsense as they do; men talking of war who never saw anything but a drill, and bad at that; women calling themselves disinterested who, by dint of tormenting the queen (a thousand times too good for them) and the ministers, have contrived to snatch pensions; and other women talking sentiment when they have had a score of lovers. And besides these the plotters, the self-important, the malignant! Sometimes my blood boils at it all, but ten minutes later I forget it. This life of Versailles is charming to me; true château life. Adieu. I embrace your wife, and also your mother for having had the wit to make me a Charles like you.

P. S. *À propos*, I have it in my head to make a bosquet for my Charles with a fountain, on which shall be carved the name of Hélène and a cradle for the babes. As soon as I can leave Versailles I shall go and work at it and tell you, *tutti quanti*, that I love you with all my heart.

But the result of the life in Paris was disastrous. Hélène, received everywhere, at Chantilly by the Prince de Condé, at Petit-Bourg by the Duchesse de Bourbon, at the Temple by the Prince de Conti, was soon in a whirl of pleasure and coquetry, a whirl in which the more solid nature of her husband made him feel, and seem, out of place. Before long Hélène compared him with the gay young men about her; his taste for study and the rather German romanticism of his mind were indeed a contrast to their light and superficial volatility. With the thoughtlessness of her years and nature Hélène decided in her own mind that he bored her, and if she had not feared to offend his father, she would have made him feel it even more than she did. His position in Paris was a difficult one. The son of a brilliant father who was always the first in society wherever he went, Charles was reduced to a secondary and almost an eclipsed position. This would have cost his modest nature nothing in itself, but he was soon made to feel that it injured him in the eyes of his wife. He had not loved Hélène when he married her, never having seen her, but he soon attached himself to her as his wife with a feeling that was almost paternal. He allowed her great liberty at Belœil, seeking all the while to develop her serious tastes (always liable to be smothered by her passion for pleasure), and was just succeeding when the three years in Paris came to undo his work utterly.

It was during the last of those years that his father went to Russia and the Crimea with the Empress Catherine and Joseph II. Before his return Maréchal de Lacy, foreseeing the Turkish war, recalled Prince Charles from Paris, and about the same time the Ligne family at Belœil, alarmed by the outbreak of the first Belgian revolution, went to their Vienna home for safety. Hélène, who disliked Vienna and its society, would fain have stayed in Paris, but dared not ask her husband to allow it. She had at this time an infant daughter, named Sidonie, her only living child, another having died at its birth. Late in the winter of 1787, Charles de Ligne was ordered to his post as major of engineers with the army in Moldavia, and we have already seen how in April, 1788, he distinguished himself at Sabacz. He had scarcely left Vienna before his wife wrote to ask his permission to visit her uncle, the Prince-Bishop, in Warsaw, alleging that important business required her presence to settle it. He gave the permission readily, on condition that she would leave the little Sidonie with its grandmother. Hélène started at once and never returned, nor did she communicate in any way with the Ligne family; she never saw her husband again, or her daughter until the latter was a woman and married. The story of the rest of her life, which does not enter into this history, is one of tragic passion, and is well worth reading in the memoir already mentioned. It is enough to say here that on the death of Prince Charles she married Comte Vincent Potocki, to whom she was passionately attached, but whose love for her seems to have been more mercenary than sincere.

After receiving Joseph II.'s letter on the taking of Sabacz, the Prince de Ligne writes to his son as follows:

Elisabeth-Gorod, May 12, 1788.

What shall I say to you, my dear Charles, that you do not know already as to what I have felt on receiving a letter from his Majesty full of kindness and grace? That letter is worth more than all the parchments, title-deeds, diplomas, and patents — food for rats! In it there are expressions so touching for both of us that although I am getting rather too big to cry, it is impossible to prevent it every time that I read those words. All the generals and officers, Circassians, Zaporoguians, Tartars, Germans, Russians, Cossacks, etc., have come in crowds to say delightful things to me which I shall never forget.

The father and tenderest friend of my Charles is assuredly much touched by the honour that you have done yourself, but General de Ligne has suffered devilishly. Ah! my boy, imagine what a moment it would have been for both of us could I have been the first whom you helped up the parapet which you yourself had been the first to mount!

Good God! what it is to be so far away! I who could have coolly seen you shot in the arm in Bavaria, I am anxious as a woman now. . . . Don't you think now, my Charles, that I was right to want you in the engineers? The engineer corps wanted *you*, I know that. But are you sure you are not a trifle wounded and will not tell me? Never let a courier of his Majesty start without a letter to me.

During the next campaign, when the Prince de Ligne returned to the Austrian armies and commanded before Belgrade, Prince Charles, as we know, was with his father. After the convention which Austria signed with Prussia at Reichenbach to conclude her part in the Turkish war, Prince Charles, foreseeing inaction, asked and obtained permission to enter the Russian service, to the great regret of his father. He made the campaign in Bessarabia under the orders of General Suvaroff, and was specially appointed by him to direct a part of the operations of the too famous siege of Ismaïl. He was the first, as at Sabacz, to mount the parapet, after an assault of ten hours, followed, as volunteers, by the Duc de Richelieu, Comte Roger de Damas, the Comte de Langeron, and others.

The joy of the Empress Catherine on receiving the news of the taking of Ismaïl was very great. Her first characteristic thought, as usual, was to reward the victors. She sent Prince Charles, among others, the cross of her Order Saint-George with the following letter: —

To Prince Charles de Ligne.

January, 1791.

Monsieur le Prince de Ligne: It is useless to tell me that all men are equal when experience shows me daily that they are not, and that some are strong and some are weak. But the fact which gives me still greater conviction is that I know races in which valour and military virtues are perpetuated from father to son. Such is yours, Monsieur le Prince de Ligne. Born of a father who is as brave as he is amiable and full of knowledge, you have inherited his fortunate gifts, you have made them shine in the eyes of those illustrious warriors with whom you shared the dangers of mounting, without an open trench, without a battered breach, the formidable fortress of Ismaïl, where a whole army of enemies to Christian men were awaiting you. The *corps d'armée* which took the place was small in number, but great in zeal and courage.

The Order of Saint-George, having for the basis of its statutes the laws of honour and valour,—precious synonyms to heroic ears,—is always by its institution eager to count among its valiant knights whoever gives proof of those military virtues. Receive, Monsieur le Prince de Ligne, the cross of Saint-George and the cordon which I send you. You will wear it, if you please, around your neck, in token of your exploits in my service. Receive them also as a mark of my esteem and affection; which your actions have won you, and your honourable wound deserves [he was shot in the leg but paid no attention to it during the assault]. Continue to give to the world an example, both useful and necessary in these days, of virtues perpetuated in illustrious races from father to son long faithful to their legitimate sovereign. On which I pray God to preserve you in His most holy keeping.

Catherine.

Immediately after the taking of Ismaïl the empress began negotiations very secretly with the Turks. Prince Charles, cognizant of what was going on, asked and obtained leave of absence. He announced his return to his father, who replies: —

VIENNA, February, 1791.

My God! my Charles! dear Charles! you are coming back to me! I cannot recover myself. I don't know how I can embrace you, or where your great nose will go, or where I can ferret mine. I must kiss that wounded knee; perhaps on my knees before you — or before Heaven.

The Emperor Leopold had granted, December 2, 1790, an amnesty to the Belgian revolutionaries, and before long all trace of the late troubles disappeared. After remaining in Vienna long enough to rejoice in the return of her son, the Princesse de Ligne went back to Belœil to repair the injury done to their houses and estates, which had been abandoned to the revolutionists since 1787. Early in 1791 the Prince de Ligne, accompanied by his son, made his grand entry into Mons as hereditary Seneschal and Governor of Hainault, the particulars of which we know already. The Lignes passed the next summer at Belœil, happy in being once more united and tranquil in the place they loved so well, with little thought that never again would they be there together. It was then that the father put up his obelisk "to my dear Charles for Sabacz and Ismaïl."

Meantime the terrible march of the French Revolution was advancing, and the *émigrés* were beginning to collect in the Low Countries. At first they clung about the border land, and it was not till all hope of a quick return was lost that they went to Vienna, London, Poland, and Russia.

Prince Charles solicited and obtained his return to the

Austrian army with the rank of colonel of engineers. He was appointed in February, 1792, to the army corps of General Clerfayt; the commander-in-chief of the Austrians being Duke Albert of Saxe-Teschen (the husband of the Archduchess Christina), whose headquarters were at Mons.

The Emperor Leopold died in March. An ancient custom, descending from the time of Charles V., required that each new emperor should be inaugurated and take the oaths as Count of Hainault in the cathedral church of Mons. This was done by proxy, and Francis II. appointed Charles de Ligne to represent him. It happened that the latter, being engaged with the enemy all night, arrived in Mons at full gallop, black with powder and heated with the combat, only just in time to don a grand court uniform and jump into his carriage to head the procession and go through the ceremony. The next morning he was back in camp, glad to have ended a rôle that was out of keeping with his simple modesty.

Three months went by in galling inaction. July 25 the Duke of Brunswick, commander-in-chief of the allied armies of Prussia and Austria, issued his well-known manifesto. In September, the month of the massacres, the French army occupied Nice and Chambéry; and Dumouriez's victory at Jemmapes, November 6, was followed immediately by the French occupation of Belgium.

Meantime it was in September that Dumouriez determined to prevent the Allied Army from gaining possession of the defiles of the Argonne. He occupied all the principal passages save one, the Croix aux Bois, which was thought to be so insignificant that he defended it with only two battalions of infantry and a squadron of horse. The Duke of Brunswick saw an opportunity of carrying the place, and General Clerfayt intrusted the attack to Prince Charles. Dumouriez, informed of the danger, sent up reinforcements.

Six times was the passage taken by the French and retaken by the Austrians. The young prince saw that it was necessary at any cost to capture a murderous battery and he headed the charge. Eight men were killed in the front rank and he, the ninth, rushed forward and fell dead with a bullet through his brain, September 14, 1792.

His father's anguish was unspeakable. The body was taken to Mons, but it chanced that the prince had just left the town, being summoned to Vienna. In his memoir he briefly tells how Maréchal de Lacy broke the truth to him and his inmost heart at the same time. As long as he lived he could never speak of his son without tears.

"Alas! I would not comprehend Maréchal de Lacy when he said to me that dreadful word, *Dead;* or perhaps I could not. I fell unconscious, and he took me in his arms. I still see the place where he told me that my Charles was killed. I see my poor Charles himself as he brought me daily, at the same hour, his good and blessed face to lay it against mine. Fifteen days earlier I had dreamed he was shot through the head, and had fallen from his horse, dead. I was anxious for five or six days, and then, because we always treat as weakness what is often a warning, or perhaps an instinct of nature when there is affinity in the blood, I drove away the dreadful thought, which was only too surely verified."

On hearing of this cruel loss the empress wrote to the Prince de Ligne immediately.

September 30, 1792.

MONSIEUR LE PRINCE DE LIGNE, — Among the many and divers misfortunes of this summer, or rather of the past year [Prince Potemkin had died suddenly in October, 1791], one of those which have caused me the most pain, which has wrung my heart doubly, triply, is the loss you deplore. If by the share that I take in this sad event you can be comforted, be assured that my regret equals the esteem which the noble qualities and the valorous actions of Prince Charles, your worthy son, inspired in me. The country ought to regret in him one of its true defenders. That poor Germany is in greater need of heroes firm and unfaltering in their principles than of timid or crafty negotiators, for she runs a risk of being engulfed in a whirlpool of incalculable woes.

What astonishes me is that neither floods, bombshells, nor famine of supplies have prevented Custine, Dumouriez, Montesquieu and gang from going where they choose. How comes it that it rains for the one side and not for the other? Why are not both sides mired? Grass and wheat are growing beneath the feet of the rebels, while those who fight them die of hunger. These are enigmas of which the Mercury of the coming month should give us the solution, or the method. Alas! alas! alas!

I have a consolation very miserable for one who truly cares for a great and noble cause: it is that they misconstrued and went against all that I proposed, with the result we see. My heart bleeds when I see the princes of the house of Bourbon and the French nobles abandoned as the reward of their devotion to the cause of the kings, and dying of hunger and misery without shelter and without resources. That example is not encouraging, assuredly.

In the midst of this happy family life of the Prince de Ligne, — for it was happy even after the fall of this terrible blow, because it was without bitterness, — a tragic little story is revealed, very faintly and delicately, in his son's last will. It may be told here because it can now have no effect but that of moving us to tender pity for those whom it concerns.

Among the young women of Vienna was the Comtesse Kinski, born Theresa Dietrichstein, a connection of Prince Charles, with whom he had been intimate from childhood. She was very beautiful, with an intelligent mind and a good heart. Her brother, Comte François Dietrichstein, was also the intimate friend of Prince Charles; in fact, the two had been brought up together. The parents of Comtesse Theresa and of Comte Kinski arranged the marriage of their children without consulting them, and they had never seen each other when Comte Kinski, who was quartered in Hungary, was brought to Vienna in time only for the marriage. Immediately after the ceremony he took his wife to their house, kissed her hand, and said: "Madame, we have obeyed our parents. I leave you with regret; but I must inform you that I have long been attached to another woman, without whom I cannot live. I go to rejoin her." His post-chaise was ready and he left her. A hard position; neither maid, nor wife, nor widow, with a lifetime before her.

If, during the few months that Prince Charles was in Vienna, between his unfortunate residence in Paris and his departure for the army in Moldavia, his life-long affection for his childhood's friend (now in so cruel a position — his own heart wounded and mortified) brought about a secret tie between them, no sign of it appeared upon the surface; the conventions of social life were strictly observed. But his will, written shortly before his death and beginning, "As I shall probably be killed," contains the following clauses: —

"I will that my heart be folded in a handkerchief worn by her I love, whom I beg to give it for this purpose. As she has always had my heart throughout my life, I wish that after my death it may be as content as a heart can be apart from her whom it treasures; that is to say, with something that belonged to her. I beg her to embroider in one corner of the handkerchief the word, *Alone;* in the second, *Tenderness delightful;* in the third, *Indissoluble;* in the fourth, *September* 21, 1787, and the date of my death.

"I. All my collection of engravings and of original drawings to be sold to the highest bidder. . . . If one of my family desires to possess it, he can take it at a price not less than one hundred thousand German florins; for the drawings being recognized as originals and there being nothing mediocre in this collection, it is really priceless. This sum, which is wholly mine and independent of the inheritance my heirs should have, and which I leave to them according to law, is to be divided thus: eighty thousand florins in trust for my natural daughter Christine. . . . I make my sister Christine her guardian; in default of my sister Christine, I appoint Mme. la Comtesse Theresa Dietrichstein, formerly married to Comte Kinski. I also bequeath to the little Christine the portrait of her mother by Leclerc and the chain I wear round my neck, which has upon its hasp the words 'These links [*liens*] are dear.' I beg her never to part with it but to wear it in memory of me and of the person who gave it to me."

"VII. I bequeath to Madame de Kinski, *née* Dietrichstein, all the framed engravings which I have in my apartments at Belœil, also the chain that I wear round my neck, which came to me from her best friend; it is for this reason that I venture to ask her to wear it all the rest of her life, remembering that it came from a person whose whole happiness was in that of Madame de Kinski, of which I am so convinced that I can assure her of it."

This last clause is among twelve others, making bequests of various treasured things, so that it does not stand out markedly.

No wonder that the Prince de Ligne, remembering his own marriage (though that was not unhappy), and the mournful marriages of his son and his son's dearest, should declaim, as he does in his "Scattered Thoughts," against the system of conventional unions.

A few short weeks and the prince and his family, lately so happy, were to see their beautiful home and their splendid fortune lost to them. The French armies occupied Belgium and the property of the prince was confiscated. Coming at the time it did the blow fell almost lightly. The news reached him in Vienna. "Who will pay my debts?" he said. and then he talked of other things.

He never saw his Belœil again, but he did not pine for it; he made himself a little "perch" elsewhere, and was happy and still made others happy; the one great blow of his life appears to have dulled the sense of other pain. There is not a word in his writings or in the records of other persons to show that he ever gave his changed fortunes a regretful thought. He grieves that he was not employed in the army; but those regrets would have been as keen, perhaps more so, had he still possessed the lavish means of other days. He had the art of happiness, and he practised it, although his greatest joy was taken from him.

IX.

1793–1800.

"REFUGE" IN VIENNA: THE EMPRESS CATHERINE.

WHEN Belgium fell into the hands of the French after the battle of Jemmapes, the Prince de Ligne shuddered lest Belœil should be pillaged, and all the relics of his son, and the obelisk raised to him in the gardens, destroyed. Fortunately the commander of the detachment sent to occupy the château was a former quartermaster in the prince's regiment, now a captain in the French army. He had but one thought, that the château and estate of his old general should be religiously protected. When the Prince of Coburg recovered Brussels after the battle of Neerwinden, the Prince de Ligne returned to Belœil, but only for a very short time. Belgium was retaken by the French in July, 1794, and the prince, now a poor man, settled permanently in Vienna, exchanging his former splendour for a little house on the ramparts, which he called his "parrot's perch," it having but one room on each floor; the first a dining-room, the second a salon, the third a library, which was also his bedroom.

His daughters, the Princesse Clary, the Comtesse Palffy, the Baronne Spiegel (Flore) had their own homes in Vienna, but were always in attendance on their father. The Princesse Clary (Christine), accepting the bequest of her brother Charles, had tenderly brought up his daughter, who was legitimatized by the Ligne family immediately after his death, and bore their name, but without a title. She grew up a sweet young girl, affectionate, and the idol of her grandfather; the family called her Titine, and she married, after the prince's death, Comte Maurice O'Donnell, the son of one of his oldest friends. Sidonie, the daughter of Prince Charles and Hélène Massalska, was brought up with Titine, and affection was strong between them, although they did not know of their real relationship. Hélène, who had married in Warsaw Comte Vincent Potocki four months after the death of Prince Charles, made no inquiries for the daughter she had abandoned until she lost her other children, when, for family reasons, she proposed and carried out a marriage between Sidonie and the son of Comte Vincent by a former wife, who was still living, and whom the count remarried on Hélène's death. She did not see her daughter until after the marriage had taken place. The whole history is a painful one and involves details which have no place in a memoir of the Prince de Ligne, although at moments the wisdom and kindliness of his conduct appear very brightly. It says much for him and for his family that Sidonie was brought up to love and respect her mother, to whom she says, in the first letter that she wrote to her: "All that I have heard of you increases my desire to know you; my aunt Clary shares my wish and bids me say that had she known you were in Dresden she would have gone to see you. Do contrive, my dear mamma, to let me know you soon. It is terrible to have reached the age of nineteen without knowing a mother, especially when I know that that mother is so kind, so amiable, and possesses all good qualities. My first and last thought daily is of you."

It is pleasant to know that out of this strange and at first sight unnatural marriage came happiness. The young people loved each other. Here is a little picture which Comte Francis Potocki drew of his new family in a letter to a friend written after his marriage: —

"The prince is tall and strong, his figure majestic, his manners noble and full of ease. His white hair, curling and slightly powdered, surrounds his handsome face, which is scarcely wrinkled. He has a charming smile with an expression of kindliness mingled with a little mischief and shrewdness. His mouth is large and gracious; his broad, intelligent forehead expresses serenity. His glance is quick; sometimes his eyes flash fire; everything about him indicates frankness. He is not loved, he is adored by his friends. His family have a veritable worship for him; no one escapes the fascination of his person and his mind. He always wears the uniform of the Captain of Trabans [the highest military post about the Court], and on his breast the cordon of Maria-Theresa with the Order of the Golden Fleece.

"The Princesse de Ligne has been extremely beautiful. She was married very young to the prince, to whom she has given the following children: Prince Charles, Christine, Princess Clary, Prince Louis, Euphémie, Comtesse Jean Palffy, and Flore, who is soon to marry Baron Spiegel, an officer highly thought of in the Austrian service. The Princesse de Ligne accustomed herself to her husband's infidelities, and was led to attach herself elsewhere; but she has never had more than that one inclination, and in that the senses have never had a part. The prince loves Comte ——, and treats him as his nearest friend, certain, as he surely is, of the perfect innocence of his relations to his wife."

Prince Louis de Ligne, the second son, here mentioned, was tenderly beloved by his father, but circumstances took him while still very young from the prince's side. Queen Marie-Antoinette put him, though a mere child, into her own regiment called the "Royal-Allemand." This was done to oblige his father, her friend, or at least it would seem so from the following letter:—

H. M. Queen Marie-Antoinette to the Empress Maria Theresa.

VERSAILLES, July 26, 1776.

The Prince de Ligne makes me a request about which I cannot refuse to speak to my dear mamma. He has much property in France and has just won a lawsuit which secures to him some that was contested. He fears, with reason, that he may not be master of enjoying it out of France. He desires to establish his second son in France; but before allowing himself to do so, he feels that he ought to have the permission of my dear mamma; and for that he has begged me to ask you. If you will have the kindness to permit it I will put the child into my regiment, until better can be done for him.

Thus Prince Louis' military career was widely different from that of his brother. His promotion was rapid. He entered the Orléans regiment, and the fatal 10th of August found him a lieutenant-colonel on Dumouriez's staff. He passed at once with the Duc de Chartres into the Austrian army, and became aide-de-camp to General Clerfayt. He distinguished himself at the battle of Jemmapes, where he had two horses killed under him, and was made captain in his father's regiment of grenadiers by the Archduke John, who had seen him, with his own eyes, dash into the French lines to recover the flag of his company which he brought back in safety.

At the battle of Hohenlinden, December, 1800, he commanded the regiment of the Archduke John and behaved in a most intrepid manner. At the head of a battalion of grenadiers, whom he inspired by his own example, he tried to cut his way through a body of the enemy; but was wounded in two places, left for dead, and taken prisoner. He was about to be shot as a deserter when General Ney saved his life by writing his name as Eugène instead of Louis, which wilful blunder prevented the authorities from establishing his identity. He was set at liberty in January, 1801, and joined his family in Vienna a month later. He was his mother's favourite child, and strongly resembled her, being very handsome. He was married to the Comtesse van der Noot de Duras, by whom he had three children, only one of whom survived. This son, named Eugène in memory of the circumstance that saved his father's life, was the grandfather of the present Prince de Ligne and died in 1880, having been ambassador to France and president of the Belgian senate. In 1803 Bonaparte, then First Consul, removed the sequestration placed in 1793 on the estates of the house of Ligne; but the prince, having formerly owned property in France, was considered as an *émigré.* He therefore formally renounced his property in the Low Countries in favour of his son Louis, to whom the estates were then restored by the First Consul, on condition of his becoming a citizen of France (his father remaining a German prince), and binding himself to free Belœil and its dependent properties from the debts charged upon it. Prince Louis died in 1812, more than two years before his father, and Belœil, around which so many poetical and historical memories cluster, is still the ancestral home of the family.

Let us now return to the prince himself. Here is a letter to a former secretary (for the days are gone when secretaries and adjutants abounded), replying to some affectionate inquiries as to how matters were going with him.

"I never used to ask you, any of you, how my affairs were going in the olden time, and I never knew. But you ask me how they go, and I have come to know about them now. Those balls of three or four hundred people, my riding-school, my gardens, the masquerades, the scenery, decorations, and costumes of my theatre, my opera of the Samnites, suppers for fifty, dinners for four hundred French officers when they came to see me manœuvre my regiment — all that never made me ask what it cost. What did I care for a few hundred ducats more or less if they did honour to Mons, or showed affection to the Comte d'Artois, I may say to the queen, and respect to the king?

"But *now* I catch myself telling my people, if by chance I give a tea at my 'refuge,' to make it very simple, no ices, no cakes, no fruit, except plums — the least expensive fruit in Vienna. I laugh when I succeed, by dint of a fib or two, in selling a few copies of my voluminous works. But my privations amuse me; I make fun of my avarice. My house, rose-coloured like my ideas, is the only one now open in Vienna. I have six dishes for dinner, five for supper. Come who will, and sit who can. When the sixty persons who frequent me arrive at the same time, my straw chairs do not suffice; and then they stand in flux and reflux, like the pit of a theatre, till some go away. There are always some good talkers among the foreigners, the only sociable ones. The talk turns on Poland, Russia, England, little on Italy, little on the old France, never, naturally, on the France of to-day.

"I do not go to Court, nor to the assemblies; I refuse great dinners and I live content. I rather like to play the grand seigneur in the streets of Vienna, on horseback behind the emperor's carriage on occasions of ceremony, when I take the office of grand chamberlain. I arrange with some coquetry my collar and ribbons, which Roger Damas calls in his charming way the 'bouquet of honour.' I do not wear my uniform of lieutenant-general, only that of my regiment;

and when I am appointed to carry the emperor's children at their baptism and people ask me why, when all the Court are in gala costume, I answer, 'I have made myself an arch-duke.' I might regret my existence of two or three hundred thousand florins a year, my beautiful Belœil, the finest of forests, and the possibility of being within twenty-four hours in Paris, London, the Hague or Spa, and the military and civil government of my interesting province, *but* the fear of one quarter of an hour's painful reflection keeps me from ever thinking of it; if now and then it crosses my mind, I only rejoice that I have no affairs — not so much as my will to make."

Besides the little house on the ramparts of Vienna, he had another, an old monastery given to him by the Emperor Leopold, on the Kalemberg, otherwise named the Leopoldberg, a hill, almost a mountain, close to Vienna and overlooking the Danube. He called it his "refuge" his "little Belœil," and on the wall that faced the river he inscribed these words: —

> "Without remorse, without regret, without fear, without envy,
> I watch the flowing of the river as flows my life away."

Here he went several times a week in an old landau with creaking springs and wheels, drawn by two aged white horses weary of life and known to all the town. The slowness of this singular equipage formed a most amusing contrast to its owner's vivacity. Behind it stood a Turk with a bronzed face, six feet tall, an inheritance from his son Charles, whom he had taken into his service on the death of the young prince. Ismaïl's feeling for him was nothing short of adoration.

In the quiet of his mountain, where, as he said, "I can live my own life," he prepared his thirty-four volumes of "Mélanges Militaires, Littéraires et Sentimentaires," about which he remarked: "I know very well that my title 'Mélanges Sentimentaires' is open to criticism; I know it is not the thing to say. But I wish to express the sentiment of sensibility and the sentiment of opinion. It is a composite word that I have invented, and must be forgiven. I could not say *sentimental* nor *sensible*. 'Sentimentaire' strikes me as having more sense in it." The prince, as this sentence shows, was strictly an amateur in his literary work. The reader has seen in the foregoing chapters how admirably he could relate the scenes in which he had played a part, how delightfully easy and graphic were his letters, and how keen (though kind) an eye he had for the characteristics of the persons with whom he had to do. He read with great interest, and very intently what he did read, but his range was limited and was always that of a dilettante. In his writings his range is wider; it covers much, but still with the same inconsequent and amateur quality. His thirty-four volumes (which are small and do not contain as much as their portentous number would indicate) came out by degrees and bear upon their titlepage the words: "From my Refuge on the Leopoldberg near Vienna. Sold in Dresden by the Brothers Walther, 1795," — up to 1811.

One by one the friends of his greater days became a memory: Maria Theresa, Joseph II., Frederick the Great, Lacy, Loudon, and, saddest of all, Marie-Antoinette. But one friend still remained, and she was true to him. No sooner did the empress hear of his total loss of fortune than her first characteristic thought was to help him, but to do it so delicately that his pride could not suffer. She wrote to propose to him the sale of his property in Taurica (that which she had given him), not to herself, but to Comte Zouboff, the governor of the province. To this proposal he replied as follows: —

To H. I. M. the Empress Catherine.

AT MY REFUGE, April, 1794.

MADAME, — Again I have occasion to see that your Imperial Majesty understands all things. You give, buy back, re-give, sell, re-buy and give again, and thus through many channels a rain of benefits is made to fall upon your empire. . . . Here, then, is a good affair for the Governor of Taurica and for me; but he does not know that I am grasping. Let him be informed therefore that I will never sell him a certain rock upon that property, the rock to which I went through water to my waist that I might carve thereon the name divine of Catherine the Great, and also the divine name of the lady of my thoughts at that moment. I beg your Majesty's forgiveness for that, but the letters were very small, and perhaps they are now effaced. Your Imperial Majesty can see that rock in the drawing that I gave you of Parthenizza with a plan for building upon it, which I should certainly have carried out if it had not been for Insuff-Pacha, to whom Russia owes so much for the enhancement of her glory.

I will, I insist, I claim that the rock be called, "Rocher Ligne" — no mediation, no intervention against that!

It is thus that I learned at a certain Court how to make treaties. H. M. Joseph II., "of glorious and eternal memory," as your Majesty says truly in writing of your worthy friend, promised me vines of his own Tokay, and vineyard-dressers. I am sure that our excellent and well-beloved ambassador Comte Razumoski, who is strongly attached to Comte Zouboff, will do all that is necessary to procure them, if the latter wishes it — unless it should now have become impossible. If the guileless and virtuous Sultan Selim compels your Majesty to go to Constantinople, I shall follow with my three buttons on the sleeve of the green coat which I still have, and love with all my heart.

Plans of campaign are being made here; but I fear that before our troops pass the Rhine and the Danube the regicides will have crossed the Meuse, the Sambre, and the Lys in three considerable masses towards three distant points, and before the necessary concentration can be made to prevent it they may jump, in Russian fashion, into the intrenched camp at Maubeuge, — a thing I have begged all winter that our armies might do, those infamous carmagnoles being then massed on the Rhine or in La Vendée. But for the last two years I preach in vain. My kingdom is not of this world now, and I do not wish that it should be, because things would have to be much worse and a fourth campaign necessary before they would come and seek me — who do not know how to force myself, either on whom or how to do it.

I have but one favour to ask my sovereign; it is that she will thank me for not taking the liberty to write to her as often as I desire, and that she will continue to me her kindness, so precious to my heart, which for fourteen years has been filled with the same sentiments towards her. Those of admiration have been there for thirty years, but afterwards came gratitude, and the warmest of enthusiasms,— adoration.

From H. I. M. the Empress Catherine.

CZARSKO-ZELO, October, 1794.

MONSIEUR LE PRINCE DE LIGNE, — If I have not answered your last letter for six months, excuse me; I have only followed illustrious examples who, when affairs were pressing, taught me that if they said a courier would start in eight or ten days that meant, in politics, eight or ten months; but a good household goes on all the same. I am, satisfied with mine, especially now that we are worn-out with fêtes and toils; first for our peace with the Sublime Porte, and secondly for the marriage of Alexander, my grandson — it was Psyche wedded to Cupid!

During these fêtes arrived to us the ambassador of the Grand Seignior, who did not do honour to the finances of Sultan Selim, — his suite being ragged to the last degree and deprived of those articles of habiliment hitherto considered necessary to a decent man. But no matter for that: on the first day they declared to me a possible third war. That is easy; he can have it if he wants it. The Turks are not like Christian powers; they usually make their plans of campaign in the autumn, which gives them plenty of time to think them over; meantime the grapes ripen of themselves.

As for Czarsko-zelo, which is, according to your idea, in a fair way to possess all my caprices, I have lately made a gentle slope which leads down to the colonnade of the garden; also an open rotunda, supported by thirty-two columns of Siberian marble. I want to see running on the grass of that slope my grandsons and their wives and children, — the latter when the former have them.

The Governor of Taurica, Comte Zouboff, will send you the money which he has drawn from the sale of Parthenizza and Niscita. I don't know whether he will employ for that purpose the Israelite in whom you have confidence, or whether the latter is dead and buried.

The empress, confident in the prince's judgment on gardens, would sometimes, during his stay in Russia, ask his advice about those of Czarsko-zelo. He was seldom of her opinion because, as he remarked, she had all the tastes and no taste. He was particularly given to laughing at a river, so-called, which she had caused to be made through the grounds, calling it an "imperial imagination." One day a workman was drowned in it; as soon as the empress saw the prince she announced the fact, adding, "What do you say to *that?*" "Oh, the flatterer!" exclaimed the prince. The empress was fond of proving in her letters that her "little household," as she called her empire, was orderly and well managed. In spite of the immense extravagances of her Court, she had in her nature a spirit of order and economy; but she never could endure the idea that reform in these directions should bear upon others and not upon herself. On one occasion when the grand-marshal urged her to abolish a great abuse in a perquisite of wines given on certain occasions, she stopped him with the remark: "I beg you never to propose to me the saving of candle-ends; it may be a good thing in itself to do, but in me it would be an impropriety." Nevertheless, she accepted honestly reforms that bore upon herself only, and whatever might be the plans on which her heart was set, such as the erection of public buildings or the purchase of works of art, she resisted her desires firmly when money was lacking. "Get thee behind me, Satan, or give me roubles," she said, in a mournfully comic tone, on one occasion when greatly tempted.

Although she wrote to the Prince de Ligne twice a year habitually, his last letter remained unanswered for eighteen months. Distressed by her silence he wrote her three letters during this period, of which the following is the last.

The Prince de Ligne to H. I. M. the Empress Catherine.

VIENNA, April 13, 1796.

MADAME, — If *alas!* were not the saddest of words I would begin and end thus the last letter I shall have the honour of writing to your Imperial Majesty, for I think you do not wish to have any more. Formerly I deprived myself of that honour, or rather I checked myself in taking it, for fear I should abuse the kindness that answered me so promptly. But having none of your precious and sacred writing in my hand or upon my lips for eighteen months, I fear it means what Joseph II. of glorious memory wrote to one who tormented him about his memoir: "No answer, no answer."

For fifteen years I have never been six months without enjoying that ineffable happiness. This is the fourth letter in eighteen months that I have taken the liberty to write to your Majesty; and the first sad one of more than sixty that you have deigned to accept with your gracious good-will.

Mme. Le Brun, who bears it, may be the best painter there is in the world, but she cannot paint my pain. The loss of my fortune was not very hard to me, because I expected it, — knowing the workmen who were to ruin so many countries and cross so many rivers the wrong way. But the loss of my most precious, agreeable, and honourable of correspondents is worse to me than the loss of Belœil.

I have given that name to a little pavilion ten feet in diameter which I have built upon a rock of the mountain that I call my Refuge; so that loss has been repaired.

I still know all that concerns your Majesty. I know that you enjoy that *imperturbable* health, — the quality that I always ascribed to your soul. Mine, without possessing it through strength of mind, has it in relation to events, because I am sickened with intrigues and blunders which have made what might have been an easy war a disastrous one.

I think incessantly of the days that are gone; I regret those moments when I took my homage to the feet of your

Majesty, hearing you, seeing you, and admiring you,— seldom done on closer view of any one, but reserved for you, Madame. It is a true regret that I now express, unhappily from afar, begging your Majesty to believe it, and to receive once more, etc.

H. I. M. the Empress Catherine to the Prince de Ligne.

CZARSKO-ZELO, July 3, 1796.

M. LE PRINCE DE LIGNE,— Other times, as M. de Betski used to say when he had his mind,—other times, before condemning any one it was usual to take the trouble to hear them. You are very decisive; because I have not answered you for eighteen months, you think that I do not wish to have your letters. Other times, before coming to that conclusion it seems to me it was customary to listen for a little word from those interested, especially from old friends of fifteen years' standing. . . .

Would you have had me write to you, "Alas! alas!" and fill my letters with the troubles, and with my perfect discontent at all that was going on in public matters? Could I have written, with the gall in my mouth, wearisome criticisms that would only have increased your own dissatisfaction? No; I prefer to seize the present moment to answer you, when a gleam of hope lights up my imagination. I fancy I see that all the evil which has been done may lessen and turn to good in a flash, that evil and wicked machinations can be foiled easily, and a return be had to the immutable principles of the cause of kings by recognizing without delay King Louis XVIII., and so enabling his faithful subjects to employ suitable means to form a nucleus for that cause in France. . . .

The new king will not want for ways and means; the rest is his own affair, not ours. You will then come out of your ten-foot refuge and return to Belœil. We shall cease to grieve for the days that are gone. Mme. Le Brun, after having painted the Grand Duchess Elisabeth, wife of my grandson Alexander, and the eldest of my granddaughters, who are both very pretty, will return to France with the rest of the *émigrés;* after which we shall write to each other letters as gay as they once were.

Adieu. Keep well, and be assured of my unalterable manner of thinking of you. CATHERINE.

[This was the last letter the Prince de Ligne received from the empress. She was seized with apoplexy November 17, 1796, and died without regaining consciousness, in the sixty-seventh year of her age. The prince was staggered by the blow. With the empress disappeared the last living link to his brilliant past; and, more than that, it was a loss to his affections. Immediately after her death he wrote the following portrait of her, which will be found in vol. xx. of his Works.]

Catherine the Great (I hope that Europe will confirm this title which I have given her), Catherine the Great is no more. Those words are dreadful to utter. Yesterday I could not have written them; but I shall try to-day to present the idea that should be formed of her.

This sketch of her traits, or rather all these collected traits, of little importance in themselves, have no pretension, and are only related here to enable the reader to form for himself a portrait that is fairly like her. What I write is just what comes into my head at this moment, to occupy my heart, still shocked by this terrible announcement.

Her personal presence is made known in painting and in narrative, and is almost always well presented.

She was still handsome sixteen years ago. It was plain that she had always been beautiful, rather than pretty; the majesty of her forehead was tempered by the eyes and the charm of her smile, but that forehead told all. Without being a Lavater one could read there, as in a book, genius, justice, honesty, courage, depth, equanimity, gentleness, calmness, firmness. The breadth of that brow revealed the faculties of memory and imagination; there was room there for all. Her slightly pointed chin was not absolutely advanced, but it was certainly far from retreating, and had much nobility. The oval of her face was not well defined on this account; though the face itself was infinitely pleasing for the frankness and gayety that dwelt upon her lips. She must have had a fresh complexion, and a beautiful bust; the last, however, only came to her at the cost of her waist, which once was slender almost to breaking; but in Russia the women grow fat very fast. She was cleanly, and if she had not had a fashion of drawing her hair back when it ought to have fallen lower and accompanied her face, she would certainly have looked better.

One scarcely perceived that she was short. She told me, in her slow way, that at one time she had been extremely quick, — a thing of which it was impossible to form an idea. Her three bows, in masculine fashion, *à la Russe*, were always made on entering a room, precisely in the same manner; one to the right, one to the left, the third to the middle, in front of her. Everything about her was measured and methodical. She had the art of listening; and so great a habit of presence of mind that she seemed to be understanding when perhaps she was really thinking of something else. She never talked for the sake of talking, and she brought the best out of those who talked to her. Nevertheless, the Empress Maria Theresa had far more witchery and fascination. She gratified and allured much more than the Empress Catherine at first sight, being herself led on by the desire to please every one in general, and by her grace, which gave her powers that were more or less studied. Our empress charmed; the Russian empress allowed the much less powerful first impression that she made to deepen. They resembled each other in one thing, namely: though the universe should crumble at their feet, *impavidas ferient ruinæ.* Nothing on earth could have made them give way. Their great souls were armoured against reverses; enthusiasm flew before one and marched behind the other.

If the sex of Catherine the Great had allowed her the activity of a man, able to see everything for himself, go everywhere, and enter into all details, there would not have been a single abuse left in her empire. Apart from these details she was greater, beyond a doubt, than Peter the Great, and she would never have made his shameful capitulation at the Pruth. Anne and Elisabeth, on the contrary, would have made commonplace men, whereas, as women, their reigns were not without glory. Catherine II. united the qualities she found in them with all those that made her the creator, rather than the autocrat, of her empire. She was easily a greater statesman than either of those empresses; she never risked anything, and, victorious or peace-making, she never met with a single reverse.

The empress had all that was good, that is, all that was grand, in Louis XIV. Her magnificence, her fêtes, her pensions, her purchases, her pageantry resemble his. She held her Court better; because there was nothing theatrical or exaggerated about it. But what an imposing scene was that mixture of the rich Asiatic or military costumes of thirty different nations! People trembled at the sight of Louis XIV.; they were encouraged by that of Catherine II.

Louis was drunk with his fame; Catherine sought hers and widened it without ever losing her head. Yet there was enough to make her do so amid the fairy-tale of our triumphal and romantic journey in Taurica, with its surprises, fleets, and legions, its illuminations, its enchanted palaces, its gardens created for one day only, and she herself surrounded by homage, seeing at her feet the hospodars of Wallachia, the exiled kings of the Caucasus, the families of persecuted princes, who came to ask for help or an asylum. Instead of having her head turned by all that, she said to me, when we visited the battlefield of Pultawa: "See what empires hang by; one day decides their fate. Without the blunder the Swedes made on this spot which you gentlemen are pointing out to me, we should not now be here."

Her Imperial Majesty often talked of the *rôle* she had to play in the world, but she knew it was a *rôle*. In any other, and in whatever class she had been obliged to play one, she would still have acquitted herself as well, because of her sound judgment. But the *rôle* of empress suited best her countenance, her bearing, the elevation of her soul, and the immensity of her genius, as vast as her empire. She knew herself; and she knew what merit was. Catherine chose her servitors with a cool head, putting each man in the place that fitted him. She said to me one day: "I often laugh alone to myself at the fright of a general or a minister when I treat his enemies well. They are not mine for all that, I say to myself. I employ them because they have talent; and I scorn those who imagine that I should not make use of men whom they don't like."

She often balanced the favour of some by that of others, who redoubled their zeal in consequence and observed each other more closely. It was apropos of her ways of making herself served and being led by no one that I once wrote to her: "There is much talk about the cabinet of Petersburg; I know of none so small, for it is only a few inches in dimensions; it extends from one temple to the other, and from the root of the nose to the roots of the hair."

On leaving one of the governments she had visited, the empress was still paying compliments and thanks and making presents as she got into the carriage. I said to her: "Your Majesty seems very well satisfied with those people." "Not at all," she replied; "but I always praise out loud and scold quite low."

She never said any but good things (I could cite thousands), but never a witty one. "Is it not true," she said to me more than once, "that you never heard me utter a *bon-mot?* You never expected to find me so stupid, did you?" I replied that it was true I had expected that my wits would have to be perpetually under arms before her, and that her conversation, in which she permitted herself everything, would be all fireworks, but, as it was, I preferred her careless talk;—which grew sublime when it touched on noble facts of history, of feeling, of grand ideas, or of government. "What sort of looking person did you suppose me to be?" she asked. "Tall, stiff, eyes like stars, and a great hoop." This amused her whenever she thought of it, and she often reproached me for it. "I thought," I added, "there would be nothing to do except admire; and admiration is wearisome." It was the contrast of simplicity in all she said in social life with the great things that she did that made her so piquante. She laughed at paltry things, quotations, nonsense, and amused herself with nothings.

"Is n't it true," she said to me one day, "that I should never have wit enough for Paris? I am convinced that if I had been one of the women of my country who go there

Peter the Great

in travelling the Parisians would never have asked me to supper." She called herself sometimes, "your imperturbable," because once, when we were speaking of the qualities of the soul, I told her that was pre-eminently hers. The word, which took her a quarter of an hour to pronounce, rolling it out with her majestic and sonorous slowness, amused her much, especially when, to lengthen it still more, she would say, "Have I, then, imperturbability? But what can you expect?" she added. "Mademoiselle Gardel never taught me any better; she was one of those old French governesses, a refugee. She taught me enough to be married in my own neighbourhood: but Mademoiselle Gardel and I, we never expected all this."

Remembering this, she said in a letter that she wrote me while a naval battle during the last war with Sweden was going on [1788]: "It is to the booming of cannon which shakes the windows of my residence that your imperturbable writes to you." I have never seen anything as prompt or better done than her arrangements for that very unexpected war, written by her own hand, and sent to Prince Potemkin, during our siege of Oczakow. At the bottom she had added, "Have I done well, my master?"

The empress always accused herself of ignorance; and one day when she was arguing with me on that point and I had proved to her that she knew by heart Pericles, Lycurgus, Solon, Montesquieu, Locke, and the great eras of Athens, Sparta, Rome, modern Italy, France, and the histories of all lands, I said: "As your Majesty insists upon it, I shall say of you what the valet of Père Griffet said of his master after complaining to me that he never knew where he had put his snuff-box, his pen, or his handkerchief: 'Believe me, monsieur, that man is not what you think him; outside of his learning, he knows nothing.'"

Her Majesty made use of this pretension of ignorance to laugh at doctors, academies, semi-learned men, and sham connoisseurs. I agreed with her that she had no knowledge of painting or of music; and I proved to her one day, rather more than she wanted, that her taste in architecture was second-rate. "Acknowledge," she said, showing me her new palace at Moscow, "that this is a magnificent vista of apartments." "It has," I replied, "the beauty of a hospital; but as a residence it is pitiable. The doors are too lofty for each room, and yet they are, necessarily, too small for such a long suite of rooms, which are all, just as they are at your Hermitage, precisely alike."

But in spite of some defects of architecture, her public and private edifices have made Petersburg the finest city in the world. Her tastes stand her in place of the "taste" which I refuse to her, for fear of thinking her invariably too admirable. She has, however, collected in her residences masterpieces of all kinds. She used to boast of her knowledge of medals; but I will not answer for that.

When her anti-musical ear prevented her progress in the mechanism of verse, which the Comte de Ségur and I tried to teach her in her galley on the Borysthenes, she said to us: "Now you see, gentlemen, that you only praise me in the mass; when it comes to details you think me an ignoramus." I said that at least she must allow she was mistress of one science. "What is it?" she asked. "That of seizing opportunity" [*celle des à propos*]. "I don't understand that," she said. "Your Majesty has never said, or caused to be said, or changed, ordered, begun, or finished anything except at the right moment." "Perhaps," she replied, "it may all look so, but examine a little deeper. It is to Prince Orloff that I owe the glory of my reign; it was he who advised me to send my fleet to the Archipelago. It is to

Prince Potemkin that I owe Taurica, and the expulsion of all sorts of Tartars who were always threatening the empire. The most that can be said of me is that I trained those gentlemen. To Maréchal Rumiantzeff I owe my victories This is what I said to him: 'Monsieur le maréchal, we are coming to blows; it is better to give them than take them.' To Michaelsen I owe the capture of Pugatcheff, who came very near getting to Moscow, and perhaps farther. Believe me, I have had *luck;* and if people are satisfied with me, it is because I have had a little firmness and consistency in my principles. I give great authority to those I employ; if they abuse it sometimes in my provinces that join the Turks, Persians, and Chinese, so much the worse, I wish to be told of it. I know very well they say to themselves: 'God and the empress would punish us; but one is very high up, and the other is very far off.' Such are men; and I am only a woman."

At another time she said to me: "I'll wager they serve me up in your Europe very badly; they are always saying I shall be bankrupt because I spend money. Well, you see my little household keeps a-going." She was fond of that expression; and when we praised the order and punctuality with which she did her work, she often answered: "One must have method in one's little household."

The force of her mind showed itself in what was very improperly called the weakness of her heart. The favourites never had either power or influence; but when her Imperial Majesty had trained them herself to business, and had tried them by the communication of such business as she was willing to disclose, they were useful to her. This use was always honourable on both sides, giving the right to say and to hear the truth. I have seen Count Momonoff, who practised that virtue perfectly, constantly ready to sacrifice his favour to it. I have known him to contradict, oppose, protect, recommend, insist, and resist; and I also know that it was taken kindly. and admiration was felt for his fidelity to friendship, his loyalty and his constant desire to do good for good's sake.

She said to me: "My so-called extravagance is an economy; the money stays in the country and comes back to me some day. I have some little resources still left, but as you tell me that you would sell, gamble, or lose the diamonds I might give you, here are some worth only a hundred roubles round my picture in this ring." She had all sorts of ways of giving. Besides the sort of profusion of which I have spoken, which was that of a great and powerful sovereign, she gave with the generosity of a noble soul, the beneficence of a kind one, the compassion of a woman, and also, for the purpose of rewarding, like a man who desires to be well served. I do not know whether it was the thought she put into it, or merely the style of her soul, but she gave with a singular grace. For instance, she wrote to Count Suwaroff: "You know that I never promote any one out of his turn; I am incapable of doing such wrong to men older in the service; but you have made yourself a marshal by the conquest of Poland."

She always carried with her in travelling the portrait of Peter the Great, and she explained to me: "It is that I may ask myself at any moment of the day, What would he have ordered, what would he have forbidden, what would he have done, were he now in my place?" She assured me that what made her like Joseph II. (besides the charm he put into every hour of his intercourse with her) was his resemblance to Peter the Great in activity and the desire to be instructed and to give instruction; and also in his devotion to the State. "He has a serious mind," she said to me, "and is also very agreeable; he is always occupied in useful things; his head is forever at work." Alas for those unjust persons who have never rightly valued his worth.

The empress was much beloved by her clergy, although she had diminished and limited their wealth and authority. When Pugatcheff, at the head of his brigands, roamed the country and entered the churches, sabre in hand, commanding that prayers be offered up for him alone, a priest took up the Holy Sacrament and went to meet him. "Increase your crimes, wretch," he said, "and slay me here, bearing in my arms Our Lord Jesus Christ. I shall pray for our great empress."

One could never say a word of harm of Peter the Great or Louis XIV. before the empress, nor the slightest little thing against religion or morals; she would scarcely allow of anything the least risky, though carefully veiled, although she might laugh under her breath at it. She never allowed herself to jest either on such matters, or about persons; sometimes, in presence of the one whom the joke concerned, she would touch upon it very gently, but she always ended by giving pleasure to the man himself. I had much trouble one day in getting myself pardoned for a remark I made at the expense of Louis XIV. as I was walking with the empress at Czarsko-zelo. "At least," I said to her, "your Majesty must allow that the grand monarch required an avenue one hundred and twenty-five feet wide in which to take his walk beside a canal of the same width, and that he knew nothing, as you do, of a wood-path, a brook, or a meadow."

I have had occasion already to remark upon her courage. Just before entering Barczisarai, our sixteen little Tartar horses were unable to hold back the great carriage with six places in which we made our entrance to the Crimea, and were forced to run away with it down the slope of a hill with a precipice on one side; there was every reason to suppose that our necks would be broken. I should have been more frightened myself but that I wanted to see if the empress were so. She was perfectly calm, — as if she were still at the breakfast-table we had just left. I looked also at the emperor, who was putting a good face on an ugly matter. The sixteen little horses all fell down, one on top of another, as I had expected, and that saved our lives. But what an upsetting might have taken place in Europe! Sixty millions of inhabitants were within one minute of changing masters. I heard the touching "Allah! Allah!" of our Tartar escort, invoking Heaven to preserve the life of its new sovereign.

The empress was very hard to please in her reading; she would have nothing sad, or too refined in quintessence of mind or feeling. She liked the romances of Le Sage, Molière, and Corneille. "Racine is not the man for me," she said, "except in 'Mithridates.'" Rabelais and Scarron had made her laugh in former times, but she did not recollect them. She had very little memory for frivolous or useless things, but she never forgot anything that was interesting. She liked the Plutarch of Amyot and the Tacitus of Amelot de la Houssaye and Montaigne. "I am a Gaul of the North," she said to me; "I understand the old French, but I do not understand the new. I have tried to get something out of your clever men of isms; I have had them come to Russia, and have sometimes written to them, but they bore me, and they never understand me. There's no one like my kind protector Voltaire. Do you know, it was he who brought me into vogue. He paid me well for the pleasure I have taken all my life in reading him; he has taught me a great many things while amusing me."

The empress neither liked nor really knew modern literature; she had more logic than rhetoric. Her frivolous works, her comedies for instance, always had some moral purpose, such as criticism of fashionable people, modes, sects, and above all *martinistes*, whom she thought dangerous. All the letters that I have from her are filled with grand, strong, and vividly luminous ideas; sometimes with keen criticisms, especially when something in Europe had made her indignant; besides all this, much gayety and good-nature. Her style has more clearness than lightness; and her serious works are profound. Her history of Russia is, to my thinking, worth more than the chronological tables of Président Hénault; but little shadings, the charm of details and colour were not her forte. Frederick the Great had no colour, but he had all the rest, and he was better read than Catherine.

She said to me sometimes: "You want to laugh at me; now what have I said?" It was usually some obsolete French word, or one ill pronounced. For instance: "Your Majesty said *baschante* instead of *bacchante*." She promised to correct that, and then immediately made me laugh again at her expense, for, while granting a favour to some one, she made a stroke of three at billiards, which allowed me to win a dozen roubles.

Her greatest dissimulation was in not saying all that she thought and all that she knew; but nothing sly or insidious ever came from her lips. She was too proud to deceive; and if she deceived herself she would get out of it by relying on her luck and her superiority to events, which she loved to master. Some thoughts, however, of the reverses that befell the reign of Louis XIV. at its close did cross her mind, but they passed like clouds. I am the only one who saw that for a single quarter of an hour the last declaration of war with Turkey made her think humbly that nothing in this world is stable, and that glory and success are uncertain. But she left her apartment that day with the same serene air she had worn before her courier departed, and with the same confidence by which she inspired, from the first, her whole empire.

Her traits of humanity were of daily occurrence. I remember her saying to me one day: "I made my fire this morning so as not to oblige my servants to get up too early, because it is so cold. There was a little sweep in the chimney, who never supposed I would get up at half-past five; he screamed like a demon; I put out the fire as fast as I could and begged his pardon." It is known that she almost never sent any one to Siberia, where, however, they are very well treated; and she never condemned any one to death. The empress often appealed to the judges against their judgments; she would urge them to examine and prove whether or not she was wrong; and she frequently furnished the means of defence to accused persons. I have, however, detected a sort of maliciousness in her, a look of kindness, sometimes a benefit, given to embarrass those of whom she had reason to complain, but who were persons of merit nevertheless; such, for instance, as a grandee of the empire who had talked too freely about her. Here is an instance of her despotism. She forbade a man of her Court to live in his own house, saying: "You shall have in mine, twice a day, a table served for twelve persons; the company you are so fond of having in your own house you may have in mine. I forbid you to ruin yourself; but I order you to continue the same extravagance here, as it gives you so much pleasure." [The prince does not give the name, but this was doubtless Prince Narischkin.]

Calumny, which has not respected the most beautiful, the best, the most feeling, the most lovable of queens, whose soul and conduct I am, more than any other, able to justify, will doubtless, without respect for the greatest of sovereigns, strew thorns upon her grave; it snatched away the flowers that should have covered that of Antoinette; it will tear away the laurels from that of Catherine.

The inventors of anecdotes, the libellers, the false ferrets of history, the evil-intentioned, the malignant by profession, and all the heedless people seeking to say a piquant thing or earn a little money, may try perhaps to lower her celebrity. But she will triumph over all. People will remember of her what I have *seen* myself as I journeyed two thousand leagues beside her through her States; they will remember the love and adoration of her subjects, and in her armies the love and the enthusiasm of her soldiers. I have seen the latter in the trenches, braving the balls of the infidels and the rigour of the elements, consoling and animating their hearts with the name of Matouschka — their mother and their idol.

I have seen what I would never say of the empress during her lifetime, but what my love for truth has made me write on the morrow of the day when I learned that the brightest star that lighted our hemisphere has disappeared.

X.

1800–1809.

LAST YEARS IN VIENNA.

TWICE I was chosen and very nearly ordered to take command of our army in Italy against Bonaparte. They sought me, as it were, in my bed, where laziness kept me away from all base efforts required to succeed in such directions. Each time I learned that the four pensioners who have lost us that beautiful land, were preferred before me. Enchanted that I was thought of to save it, I felt a momentary pang at the fall of the visions of victory in which I had let myself indulge. But I have the good sense to grasp eagerly and give up tranquilly whatever expectation promises, so that it does not cost me very much to be deprived of it.

I have myself to blame, moreover, for not having made all the needful applications. The first time, a woman made me promise I would take no steps to command the army of Italy. I consented because, at that time, I chose to give the name of baseness to what I might really have done very nobly. I heard afterwards that the grand vizir [Thugut, Austrian prime minister] expected this very thing. I was not his man; I would never have allowed an adjutant to be given to me to govern me; I would never have let my plan of campaign be made by puppies and postilions, who, carrying news from the army to the vizir, shut themselves up with him in his vaulted den of intrigue, concocted operations, and returned to the army with orders that they themselves had given. Though I might not have had full success, I will answer for it that the enemy would not have had much either, and the spirit of our army would have been preserved.

All this, however, did not prevent me from offering my services later, to serve with whom, or even under whom they chose; nor did it hinder me from expecting and awaiting a battle where, as I ardently hoped, I might end and glorify my career. I have since heard that Lord Grenville, being in Berlin at the time when Belgium, two years after its capture, began to bestir itself, sent a letter to our vizir requesting that I might be placed in command of the army of the Rhine. The emperor was not even told of this.

At another time the Comte de Castellofero asked for me on behalf of the King of Sardinia, who was, he said, dissatisfied with the Austrian generals, and wanted some one "of the school of Loudon." The king, he said, would only allow his contingent to be commanded by me, and he offered to give me the same patents and instructions as the emperor. Thugut smiled pleasantly, seemed about to consent, but turned the conversation and soon made his exit. "What are you about?" said the Chevalier Eden (a third in the triumvirate with Razumoski and the vizir) the next day to Castellofero. "They tell me you want to say who shall command the armies — and who indeed? the Prince de Ligne, who would exterminate those of Piedmont and Austria in one campaign."

The stupidity or the malice of persons in favour, the miserable selections they have made, their neglect of brave and enlightened men, have at last destroyed my military fervour, which until now I could never have thought possible. I have broken the dearest idol of my heart — Glory. Almost I have resolved never again to put myself under fire. I never boasted of my battles or of certain distinguished actions during my twelve campaigns; I wept and laughed to see in Italy and in the Low Countries four poor ignorant men in command, all of whom I had had under my orders, and to none of whom, except Clerfayt, would I have given three batteries to command. Of all the public puppets on the stage of this war, the best would have been Clerfayt, if his fear of responsibility had not too often paralyzed his numerous means.

All those who have lost the Low Countries and Italy, and who are working to lose the rest, and all those who have played a good or a bad part in these wars, have been under my command and little expected themselves to be preferred before me. I am sorry to find myself avenged; this is not the vengeance that I want. I own that I stand here, in the midst of alarms, hoping to avenge myself by being useful. I shall perhaps find a corner in some redoubt, or in the ranks, if they attack, where for the last time I may do myself honour by rendering some great service.

Never have I desired to fire a shot within the empire. I would have left all that to the Prussian protection, so-called; but I could have won back our captured countries. In Italy I would never have separated my columns to make combined attacks; I would never have gone too far from my neighbours, my supplies, my reserves. Many scouts, patrols, outposts, light troops, detailed maps, friendliness to inhabitants, activity in knowing every road, promptness in surprising, persistency in harassing the enemy's little outposts to get an air of superiority to the enemy, — for the *tone* which one gives to a campaign does much, — all this I should have watchfully attended to.

Instead of that — here I am, tranquil and happy. I enjoy the present without going over continually all that I have just said I could have done, and which might not have succeeded as well as I imagined. I am here alone on my mountain, writing in my pretty little belvedere that I call my little Belœil; and it compensates me for that which another than myself might never be consoled for having lost forever.

A jest can do much harm. It was a foolish speech that kept me from being employed in the last war of all. I said, when they gave the favourite Godoy the title of the Prince of the Peace, that Thugut ought in like manner to be called the Baron of the War. That speech flew like wildfire, and seemed so just (Thugut having refused all the advantageous conditions proposed by France) that he never forgave me for it.

The Archduke John might, as I told him, have become a Créqui through the loss of the battle of Hohenlinden, just as the latter became a great general through Conserbrick. He has military erudition, much application, and, as I believe, a strong character. If the Archduke Charles [both were sons of the Emperor Leopold, brothers of the Emperor Francis] had another physique, his perseverance, his intelligence, his firmness would have been doubled. He might have equalled Condé and Eugène. He is brave, he is good, he has mind, with facility of conception and grand military views; but distrust of his health makes his imagination uneasy, and often stops him short under a dread of never being cured. May flattery not spoil this prince! He has great talents and he has done great actions. I am afraid, however, that the feebleness of his nerves will be communicated to his character. He is a general and a soldier both; that is what is wanted in war; but he is not an officer, that is what is wanted in peace; his changes and defences are not worth much then.

Francis II. has good impulses both of heart and judgment. What he needs is to be well surrounded, or else not surrounded at all. He inclines towards justice and even beneficence, and believes he has, and wishes to have, firmness. Those about him wish him to be hard. An Emperor of Germany who lets himself be made Emperor of Austria by an Emperor of the French is an officer who retires with a pension.

When I was in Berlin in 1804 the king of Prussia [Frederick William III.] received me with cordiality and distinction at Potsdam, where he sees no one. How bitterly cold it was at the review of his guards and garrison, which he showed me! After it he said: "Come and warm yourself at my fire. We will go up this little staircase, which is not brilliant." As it certainly had no pretensions to being so, I replied that the safest and straightest way was always the best. "And now we will go and breakfast with the queen," he said.

The Queen of Prussia [Louisa] is beautiful as the finest day and the purest sky. What loveliness! what grace! She recalls to me, with features more regular and a skin as exquisite, the unfortunate Queen of France. Her hands are particularly beautiful; they remind me of Marie-Antoinette's, and she is just about the same age as when I saw the queen for the last time in 1786 — how smilingly unconscious then of what was just before her! God grant that no sorrows shall ever come near this queen, who has succeeded her in beauty and goodness.

And the sisters of the Queen of Prussia, how charming they are! I went to see that Court at Anspach. The king is shy, without much to say in the beginning, and being rather vacant in company, where he walked about all by himself, I attacked him in conversation. He took hold of it wonderfully and talked war and service well. He has a military air, precise, firm, and kind; and when seated on a stone on which Gustavus Adolphus had breakfasted, he pictured the scene himself unconsciously. I spoke to him with fire of the Thirty Years' War. It seemed as if I communicated a little to him, for he had an air of regretting that the vile, distrustful, criminal policy of all the Courts had prevented him from doing what honour and self-interest dictated to the whole empire at the time when they allowed the Electorate of Hanover to be invaded.

I asked the King of Prussia, at the review at Potsdam, who was a fine young officer who defiled before us. "That is my brother William," he replied; "I will present you to him presently." He also presented me to the officers who had fought in the Seven Years' War, told me about their wounds and their actions, wanted us to talk together of that war, and listened with interest. I was introduced in succession to all the members of the royal family. Prince William has a most charming face, and is interesting and attractive. Prince Henry not as much so, but a fine man. Both are good and trusty and brave, I will answer for it. Prince Louis-Ferdinand of Prussia is a hero of romance, history, and fable. He would have been a demigod, when such existed,—Mars, Adonis, and Alcibiades, all in one; human kindness, grace, and ease. What military talent! what noble valour! and what humanity!

"I see," Frederick William said to me, "much cordiality between your officers and mine, and it gives me pleasure." "I wish, Sire," I replied, "that in order to vex the mischief-makers of Europe, and especially Mischief-Maker No. 1, Bonaparte, all the world could hear you say so. Our two Courts would be more respected. I beg your Majesty to hang the first general, minister, courtier, whoever he may be, who dares to say that we are natural enemies." "Oh! I am often told that," he replied, with charming *bonhomie.* "I wish," I continued, "that the emperor would do the same, and I shall tell him so on my return (and so I did); for what is Germany," I added, "if it is not you, Sire, and he? Same language, same interests; outside of us there is no nation. Mischief-Maker No. 1 — the Elector of Hanover, Trèves, Cologne, Mayence, and in a week, if he chooses, of Baden, Würtemburg, and Bavaria, whose troops he has already incorporated with his own, making those three sovereigns majors in his regiments — is the Emperor of the West."

The king smiled, but the smile was bitter. "People have confidence in M. de Hardenberg," I said; "I think him a true gentleman." "That is why I took him," he replied. "Sire," I said, "let your two Majesties clasp hands by letter, and be ready in case of attack or further humiliation. Let none of your ministers, nor any of the cabinets know of this, but send sealed orders to every Prussian and Austrian general on the frontiers, not to be opened till they are told to open them; those orders to contain your Majesty's commands to march the Prussian troops in an hour, and sweep the enemy out of the Electorate of Hanover, while the emperor gives the same order to recover Switzerland."

Young Frederick William III. did not smile this time; he approved, reflected, and seemed very grave for a moment. Then he said: "You saw what I have just done for Sir George Rumbold [the English minister at Hamburg, imprisoned in 1804]?" "Yes, Sire," I said, "and I wish they had hung him, to make you and all Europe more angry." The king gave a short laugh, and then said: "I am sorry those devils of Englishmen committed the meanness of seizing the Spanish vessels without a declaration of war. There's another piece of luck for that man" (meaning Bonaparte).

Louisa Queen of Prussia

"Yes, Sire," I said, "but it will not counterbalance the Duc d'Enghien."

One is less free with a king at the head of his Potsdam garrison than with the same king roaming about the world, whom one sees in his bath, and who, while professing to be a knight, has been nothing up to this time but a knight errant. That is what made me say to him one day in Berlin, when he had wearied me with his chivalry: "Sire, your intentions are superb, but they will not be executed unless you combine with your three comrades, and say: 'On the honour of gentlemen let us swear an eternal alliance.'"

It is now two months since I talked with him thus in Berlin. Every one was hot enough then; so they were in Petersburg, and nearly so in Vienna. Müllendorf, a brave and charming octogenarian with whom I drank three bottles of champagne daily, was even more so than all the young men. What has come of it? Rumbold is given up; everybody has returned to ice, even about the new kingdoms that are being formed. In war, politics, and love if the right moment is missed it never comes again. So much the worse for Europe.

Bonaparte is all things in one: Cæsar, Alexander, Pyrrhus, and Scipio. He is a prodigious being. But there is not a word of his quoted which shows either feeling or elevation of mind. When I read how he loves ceremonies and to be arbitrary he makes me think of Paul I. Why does he have a wife and children? they are not for such as he. If he took for himself only one hundred thousand francs a year, and had no other shows than reviews (of which I approve), if he listened, if he answered, he would be one of the greatest men that ever lived. The Duc d'Enghien has killed him; vanity has killed his glory; his imperial mania has lowered the Alps; Saint-Cloud has destroyed Marengo;

his throne has toppled over his tent; fable has crushed history.

In 1807 I went to Dresden out of curiosity to see him. This journey and what I said of it was not viewed with favour in Vienna, although I did not allow myself to be presented to him.

[The following letter gives an account of this event.]

The Prince de Ligne to Prince Auguste d'Arenberg.

TÖPLITZ, July 20, 1807.

Well, here I am! I have seen him, and for fear of being partial, having perhaps been pretty well treated by him (though he does not look obliging), I am the only one of the reigning or ex-reigning princes who has not been presented. They amuse me, those confederated princes, with whom I dine daily. He has forced them to come here, all but your nephew Prosper, who is making war, and the reigning Prince of Lichtenstein, who is cutting his teeth. I told them they looked to me as if they were there in the valley of Jehoshaphat awaiting the Last Judgment; to which they responded with a big empire laugh in chorus, and said, "Touchours aimaple!"

I cannot say of *him* what Ali said of Azor, either from his face, or the intonations of his voice, or his expression, for I listened to what he said in the gallery, rubbing shoulders with the crowd. But he has the air of a man of war, with firmness and deliberation rather than genius, of which he has never had the aberrations. A Saxon lieutenant-colonel who never left him at Friedland, told me that he was on foot upon a height under fire of a battery, whence he saw everything so well that, pencil in hand, he wrote his orders on cards which his aides-de-camp carried to the generals. Suddenly he saw a movement that the

Russians wanted to make. "Ha!" he said, "I think they mean to manœuvre; I'll show them tactics;" and with that he instantly took advantage of the opportunity.

On arriving he bathed; during which time he sent off various couriers and talked with several of the ministers; the next day he was on horseback at five in the morning, without other suite than a few aides-de-camp (for he has no guard), and was off to the hospital to talk to his wounded of the Prussian campaign; then to see the fortifications, and afterwards the cadets, to whom he sent no notice of his coming, and whom he questioned and corrected on very difficult points of mathematics.

I met Talleyrand just as he arrived, and went up the stairs faster than he. He had not stopped a moment between Königsberg and Dresden. You can imagine his pleasure at being received by me; for he and you and I are the only Frenchmen now left in the world, and you and I are not Frenchmen. He would rejoice if you were here too. They served us at a long table with thirty covers, where we supped *tête-à-tête,* and at one in the morning I left him, out of discretion but against his will, and came back here.

He told me that the Emperor Napoleon (I suppose I may permit myself to call him so) was never so great as at Osterode, where, with nothing to eat but bad lobsters, in a horrible house surrounded with the carcasses of men and horses covered with manure, everything against him, even his own army (though no one dared to show it), he swore to suffer all in order to humiliate Russia.

They have been very well satisfied with the frank behaviour of Poniatowski, who could not have been blamed even if things had turned out differently. He is expected to arrive in Dresden to-day with Molachuski, Stanislas Potocki, etc., for the organization of Poland, in which they mean to mix a little of the constitution of May 3 with the sovereignty granted to the King of Saxony under the title of Duke of Warsaw.

That name made me laugh, and I asked Talleyrand if it was a copy of the Duke of Dantzig. He told me they had given it out of delicacy to us, in order that the malcontents of Galicia might not think the kingdom of Poland was re-established and begin to ask concessions of us.

Jérôme is King of Westphalia and has the possessions of the King of Prussia, and of Hesse, Fulda, and Brunswick; pensions are given to the three latter princes. Talleyrand is expecting Vincent [Baron Vincent, Austrian ambassador to France] to treat of Braunau and other such matters. He says he is under the greatest obligations to him for his prudence and the way he has kept at arm's-length all bitterness and semi-suggestions of war which threatened to embroil everything.

The King of Prussia at Tilsit, with the Legion of honour and a moustache, blushed and stammered and looked like an aide-de-camp of the Emperor Alexander. The latter said on the day of the signature: "This is the anniversary of Pultawa; a day of good omen to the empire of Russia."

Napoleon, who likes better to magnify himself than to increase his territory, to conquer rather than acquire, preferred that interview to marching to Riga on the one hand, and Grodno on the other. I don't know what he will do or will not do about the Turks. But he said: "I wished much good to Selim, because he was my intimate friend."

Alexander embraced Oubril on his arrival, and when the English cabal caused him to be dismissed he gave him a pension of twenty thousand roubles "for good luck." Just make coalitions after that! If we had only so much as stirred, the French would have made peace with Russia.

I cannot see how it is that pretended zealots regret the exhaustion of Russia and the nullity and abasement of Prussia, which is now reduced to fourth rank. However, I do not think this new mapping out of Europe very dangerous. It will not last longer than its author. A pen made it, and a pen will unmake it if some one knows how to hold it.

They are marching Spaniards against the King of Sweden, who came to demand that Louis XVIII. should be restored. England is not thought of at all; she can do what she likes.

People always say when they want to finish a letter that the post is just starting. I do not want to finish mine, but the reason for ending is true this time, and I can only tell you, dear contemporary, how dear you are to me by taste and good taste, and through gratitude for a friendship in which I trust with very tender and lasting attachment.

PRINCE DE LIGNE.

When Paul I. was Grand-Duke of Russia, I stood as well with him, and this is very remarkable, as I did with his mother, whom I often reproached for not drawing him nearer to her. He always behaved in her presence like a courtier under a cloud. He used to tell me evil things of his nation and declare they were tricking the empress; he really believed that all we saw and did in Taurica was a fable. I said to him in reply: "There certainly were some shams about it, but also a great deal of reality. How can you expect, monseigneur, that a woman should fathom everything, climb mountains, and look on the other side to see the reverse of the picture." "Of course it is impossible," he said; "and that is why these beggars of Russians want to be governed by a woman." The grand-duchess lowered her eyes and we were all three rather embarrassed for some minutes at the remark having escaped him.

By nature the grand-duke had gentle tastes, and especially those of a country life. But as soon as the fancy to make war in times of peace seized him he went with great strides into madness, though never with the cruelty of his father. He was gay in society, true to his friends, and had much liveliness of mind. It was just before his travels that he first began to show suspicions, especially towards his mother. He thought she wanted to keep him out of Russia. His suspicions of being poisoned in Italy, and even by me at Bruges, when the beer disagreed with him and gave him the colic, are well known. He was just as amiable to me afterwards, though more distrustful, and less just on the parade ground, and even in society some years later. When the empress spoke to him he would make a cold, respectful bow and retire. "Why, monseigneur," I said to him, "do you put on that air of a disgraced courtier? See the pleasure the grand-duchess, who is an angel, gives the empress when she answers her with that winning manner. The empress is at her ease with her; but you are neither at your ease yourself nor will you let her be."

He showed me the letters he had received from M. de La Harpe, — those that he was then receiving, and all he had received for six years past. They had put him so much *au courant* of everything that when he went to Paris he made no blunders about names or things. The empress used to laugh a little at the correspondence whenever La Harpe, quitting his literary people, began to write about Turkey and politics. She said to me one day, "M. de La Harpe is teaching monseigneur to reign;" and then she added a fact only too well proved later: "These gentlemen, these men of letters know nothing about governing, but that 's their way."

Two-thirds of Catherine and one-third of Paul, before the latter became hopelessly insane, would have made the greatest, best, and most fortunate of sovereigns. I think he always felt grateful to me for not having profited by the intimate friendship and confidence of his mother to abuse it and obtain the very considerable amount of the claim of the Massalskis which had been turned over to me; and this it was, I think, which induced him to grant me a pension of a thousand ducats. To give an idea of the love of justice which possessed that extraordinary being, who was driven out of his mind, I shall cite his action on that occasion. I wrote to him after his accession, and mentioned that, as it was very easy to show delicacy when one was rich and prosperous, I had never asked for the three thousand ducats which M. de Stackelberg (the only minister who had cognizance of the claim) had awarded me, although it was actually the cause of my first journey to Russia; and I also said that no record had been kept of that award. Fortunately for me, the old ambassador went to Petersburg. The emperor made inquiries of him, and the following day Stackelberg died of apoplexy. By the next post I received my pension. So that, with that and what I derived from Iphigenia's land in Taurica, I have more money from Russia which I never served, and more distinction from Prussia which I served very ill, than from Austria which I have served only too well.

I have seen in all their brilliancy the lands and the Courts where enjoyment and splendour most abounded. For instance, that of the last Saxon King of Poland [Augustus III.], or to speak more correctly that of the Comte de Brühl. I saw the last magnificences of that satrap, who, to ride one hundred yards, was attended by a hundred palatines, starosts, castillans, *cordons bleus,* and quantities of princes allied to the house of Saxony.

I have seen Louis XV. with the grand air of Louis XIV., and Mme. de Pompadour assuming that of Mme. de Montespan. I have seen three weeks of magic fêtes at Chantilly; theatricals and sojourns at Villers-Cotterets [country seat of the Duc d'Orléans], where all that was most agreeable assembled; I have seen the enchanted voyages to l'Isle-Adam, the delights of the little Trianon, the promenades on the terraces, the music in the Orangerie, the magnificences of Fontainebleau, the hunts of Saint-Hubert and Choisy, — I have seen them all diminish and perish utterly.

I have seen to their very last the noble days of the house of Lorraine, which did not fall from so high a place, it is true, but which still existed in all its splendour to the days of the little King Stanislas I. [Leczinski], who inherited the *bonhomie* and the jovial delights of the old Court of the dukes of that province.

I have seen the grandest magnificences of Europe in an icy climate where Catherine II. combined the luxury of Louis XIV. with that of Asia, the Greeks, the Romans, and the Arabian Nights.

I have seen Potsdam, Sans-Souci, and glory; a military reign uniting an august Court with a stern headquarters.

I have seen disappear, with Prince Charles of Lorraine, the charming Court of the Low Countries, gay, safe, agreeable, playful, convivial, hunting, breakfasting: I have seen all perish; even the little Court of the last Prince de la Tour (which albeit ridiculous was none the less magnificent), and of Manheim, Munich, Erlangen (in the days of the last Margrave of Baïreuth), and Stuttgard, the centre of fêtes, pleasures, and ceremonies, — all, I have seen them all disappear; even the little Court of Bonn, and that of Liège so brilliant under the princes of Bavaria.

But nowhere have I seen substituted anything that takes

the place of those great homes of the great seigneurs. They had ceased, it is true, to have their pages, guards, and gentlemen-at-arms; but they still had their footmen, their horses, their tables open to all, and their splendid entertainments.

Life is a circle; it often ends very much as it began; the two childhoods are a proof of this; only the interval between the two presents any difference. My autumn, prolonged by my constitution and character, impinging on my winter, is ending like my spring, owing in this case to an unexpected circumstance, namely, a revolution. Creditors and money-lenders are in my antechamber as they were in the days when I was forced to live on the meagre paternal pension. Sums of money which I borrow on some pretext of splendour, are used to meet real wants; very much as they were when I was twenty, and lost at faro the half of what I borrowed. So here I am, a poor gentleman of expedients, just as I began. I have known many who rose from nothing to be great seigneurs; with me, through external circumstances, it has been the reverse.

Another proof that life is a circle: I have a donkey, a sheep, and a goat, who come and breakfast with me when I am at my Refuge. They almost climb upon my bed; I think myself lucky when they only put their fore paws up to beg for bread. If I clap my hands they follow me at a gallop through the woods. When I was a boy of twelve I had a crow, a sheep, and a fox, who all three consoled me for the severity of masters always displeased with me. The crow pecked the legs of the dancing-master — he was the one I hated most. The fox was a rascal, who took the cotton from my governor's ink-bottle to smear his papers; and one day he spoilt the face of an ancestor of our family, whose portrait was lying on the floor while my father was arranging the room. The latter was frightfully angry, because, he said, my fox had intentionally insulted his great-grand-father. And thus our life goes round in a circle, and the beginning is the end, and the end is the beginning.

One might perhaps wish to grow old, not to live but to die, for an old man goes out like a candle.

How many reflections this book, the confidant of all my thoughts, has led me to make upon myself. I have written in it almost ever since I came into the world, certainly ever since I learned to write. The space within is growing smaller by degrees. But I write so little and at such long intervals that often I do not remember what is in it. In fact, a charming woman, full of intelligence, to whom I lent it, defeated me a while ago with one of my own arguments and laughed at me well for not remembering it was mine.

Perhaps I might here abridge what I have written into a few short words: Calmness within one's self; to rightly live, and to die well.

Life does visible homage to Providence in some things; for instance: the effect of time. That is why the ancients raised a statue to Time with this inscription: "To him who consoles." Without that quality what would be the result of great sorrows? Could men survive them? If the morrow, without our perceiving it, did not already bring some change, should we bear up? We find that though we thought and wished to die at the death of a wife, a father, a daughter (most terrible of all), or a mistress, we have insensibly returned to our way of life, our conversations, our gayety. The more or less time the consolation requires comes from the greater or less sensitiveness of our souls, or rather of our organs. But without this consolation our lives would be too cruel; the sum of ills would far exceed the sum of good. —

The above words were written as a matter of theory in

days of happiness. Yes, undoubtedly the sum of ills surpasses that of good. He whom we mourn was a glory to see, to embrace, to admire: he was all that was bravest in the world and most distinguished. Great God! what a blow was that to learn that earth had lost him! — Yes, we recover our senses and our way of living. But is there a day when a place, a thought, a memory, his name, a resemblance, does not plunge the dagger again into the breast?

No, time does not heal. It only closes the wound; it puts a compress upon it, which a trifle lifts; a word, an inflection, the tone of a voice, a gesture, a glance, a mere nothing, cause torrents of tears to flow when we are thus reminded. The nerves are then like an instrument which the wind, or the noise of a door will vibrate into sound; it is a sort of magnetism. According to the disposition we are in, and the manner in which we learn the death of one we love, our lives may depend. It is a chance if we do not die upon the spot. Sometimes we cannot believe our misfortune; we think we dream; we await the one who has passed out of sight. Alas! an icy cold succeeds this species of delirium: a total suspension of our faculties, a forgetfulness of all, of ourselves even; and then a dreadful weight, of which it is impossible to rid our souls. Anxiety may banish sleep, but happy they who have causes for anxiety! When the worst has come, the body, exhausted by the struggle, takes a sort of rest. But, for one quarter of an hour's sleep, Great God! what an awakening! Before we have roused our still numbed senses we know we are unhappy; and when we begin to feel the cause, when we learn it as it were anew, that state is worse than death.

[From this point the picture of the prince's last years must be continued in the words of those who knew him and were with him during that period, namely: Comte Ouvaroff, attached to the Russian legation in Vienna in 1807; the Duc de Broglie, son-in-law of Mme. de Staël, who was sent to Vienna after the battle of Wagram in 1809; and the Comte de la Garde, who was present during the Congress of Vienna in 1814, the period of the prince's death. They have all given very lifelike pictures of him. The works from which these pictures are taken will be found described in the list of authorities in Vol. I. of this edition. Comte Ouvaroff speaks first.]

It was in 1807, when attached to the Russian embassy in Vienna, that I first had occasion to see the Prince de Ligne. Young in years, but by tradition and taste passionately in love with what is now called the *ancien régime*, I could not be presented to the veteran of European elegance without feeling a sort of enthusiastic quiver. I had so often heard his name quoted, I had read it on all the pages of the eighteenth century among those of Voltaire, Catherine, Frederick and the Emperor Joseph!

A man who for so long a time had made the world talk of him seemed to me, a mere lad, as if he were, in all probability, a dilapidated relic, a sort of decrepit Nestor. Imagine therefore my astonishment when I found the Prince de Ligne, at seventy-two years of age, in very nearly all the vigour of his best years. Tall in figure, and very erect, having preserved his eyesight, his hearing, and above all a good digestion, much sought after in society, devoted to women, resplendent in elegant frivolity, the prince piqued himself on treating young men as comrades, and the delight with which I found myself admitted to their number can be imagined.

The prince had preserved his hair and a great deal of it,

which he wore powdered, so that his handsome face, though a trifle wrinkled, showed no signs of decay. His military uniform became him, and the cross of Maria Theresa hung nobly on his breast, together with the Order of the Golden Fleece. He had lost part of his property in the Belgian revolutions, and had spent the rest. Out of an immense fortune, part of which he had settled on his youngest son, the prince had only kept a modest little house on the ramparts of Vienna, called, by courtesy, the hôtel de Ligne. There were assembled every evening his charming family of two married daughters, and a third who was then a *chanoinesse;* thither flocked nightly all that Vienna could offer that was choicest, — old ladies of exquisite tone and grand manners, or young ones full of charm and attraction; sometimes a knot of Englishmen who (as the prince said) were travelling for their own pleasure not that of others; sometimes a group of Russians, whom he welcomed in preference. Very few Germans ever came there, unless they were relics of the old days of Joseph II. or certain great seigneurs of the Low Countries, exiled liked Virgil's sage, or, like the host himself, far from their domestic penates.

To these always eager visitors were added a few distinguished *émigrés:* Comte Roger de Damas, the Marquis de Bonnay, with others like them; and amid these varied groups a man was seen with fiery eyes and a swarthy Southern skin. This was Pozzo di Borgo, whose charm of conversation, very different from that of the Prince de Ligne, drew every one about him, while his original mind, passionate and wholly of the present day, brought finely out the eminently eighteenth-century mind of the Prince de Ligne.

In that little gray salon, modestly furnished, and so narrow that it was difficult to find standing-room when the company assembled, there appeared one evening Mme. de

Staël, a radiant meteor, stimulating public curiosity, from whom we later drew much pleasure. At first the Prince de Ligne was not much inclined in her favour. The dramatic exaltation of Corinne seemed to him slightly ridiculous, and her innovating ways as to salon doctrines were repugnant to him. Moreover, in France before the Revolution, he had seen little of M. Necker, and liked him still less. Mme. Necker had bored him intensely, and his only remembrance of the Swedish ambassadress was that of a woman whose ugliness was not doubtful and who meddled with politics and "made phrases." Deeply attached to Queen Marie-Antoinette and chivalrously in love with her, any contact with the Genevese minister must have been displeasing to the Prince de Ligne. It needed all the amenity of his nature and the exquisite delicacy of his manners to admit in Mme. de Staël (a proscribed fugitive in 1808) a rare and exceptional nature, and one which, by the eminent qualities of her heart even more than by the lofty aims of her mind, had a right to universal good-will.

By a mutual unspoken compromise of good taste, never was a serious word on the events of 1789 exchanged between them. *There*, certainly, was absolute incompatibility; never could they have agreed on any point, no matter what, that concerned the Revolution. Prince Auguste d'Aremberg (Comte de la Marck), the friend of Mirabeau and the Duc d'Orléans, who sympathized on those grounds with the ideas of Mme. de Staël while his social position and antecedents drew him to the Prince de Ligne, seemed the point of intersection between this pair of opposing minds, the god Thermes, as it were, watching that the territory of both should be scrupulously respected.

It would be difficult to express the infinite pleasure we all derived from the charming spectacle of this intercourse.

The Prince de Ligne was never more delicately witty, more winning, more felicitous, and never was Mme. de Staël so brilliant; although in the prince there was always a faint, imperceptible tone of irony, which, without ever wounding Mme. de Staël, presented a kind of passive resistance, which was not without attraction for her. When Corinne soared to the seventh heaven with an explosion of inimitable eloquence the Prince de Ligne would, little by little, lead back to a Paris salon. When he himself would frivolously indulge in the perfumed talk of Versailles or of Trianon, Mme. de Staël, with brief and concise words after the manner of Tacitus, would allude to the end of that society, condemned to die by its own hand. Spectators of the scene were drawn first to one and then to the other; but no one would have wished to help them to agree, of such good taste and good quality was the struggle. Let me hasten to say that in these charming combats there was nothing prepared, nothing artificial; here were two different natures exhibiting themselves spontaneously; two able players tossing back the ball from one to the other courteously. Lively sudden expressions, easy talk, almost careless, from one to the other as it came, extreme care to avoid all asperity of speech, mutual *bonhomie*, if I may use the word, — these were the leading features of those delightful fireworks whose wonderful rockets still linger in our memory.

The Prince de Ligne and Mme. de Staël were both passionately fond of playing comedies, and both played them very badly. The prince took no more important part than that of the notary who comes in at the *dénouement*, or the lacquey who brings letters, but whenever he did appear he always persisted in remaining on the stage, saying in a low voice, "I am not in your way, am I?" After Mme. de Staël's arrival several plays were set going; among them,

"Les Femmes Savantes," in which she took the famous part of Philaminte. Comte Louis Cobenzl, friend and compatriot of the Prince de Ligne and well-known for his embassies to Russia and France, played Chrysale with a talent and fire that might have made a consummate actor envious. His sister, Mme. de Rombeck, a warm friend of the Prince de Ligne and an inimitable and gracious mixture of heart and mind, of gayety and reason, played Martine, while Arthur Potocki and I, being the youngest of the troupe, were *rigged* in a wonderful way in huge perukes, and thus disguised, Arthur played Vadius, and I Trissotin. The piece was performed with some completeness and gave pleasure. Mme. de Staël did not escape without a few covert and mischievous allusions. At another time she played a piece of her own, called "Hagar in the Desert;" it is printed, I think, in her collected works. The Prince de Ligne, taking me aside after the performance was over, whispered: "Cher petit" (he often called me so), "were you not enchanted? do you not think the play excellent? But will you just tell me its name?" "'Hagar in the desert,'" I answered, ingenuously. "Oh, no, my boy, you must be mistaken; is n't it the 'Justification of Abraham'?"

This delicately malicious wit [*malicieux*], so gayly ironical, was united in the Prince de Ligne with a sweetness of nature and an equability of temper that were quite unparalleled. Serious considerations did not affect him long. *Insouciant* rather than philosophical, he let his days, already counted, roll by without regrets; no one would have had the courage to trouble the security, true or false, of this old and charming child. Political ideas had little hold upon him. He hated the Revolution because it had drenched the salons with blood, ravaged Belœil, and struck down all the objects of his tenderness and veneration. But he went no farther.

Paul I,
Emperor of Russia

One could even see in him a sort of leaning to Napoleon because he was rebuilding much that had been demolished by the Revolution; though in speaking of him to M. de Talleyrand he said with a contempt that was purely aristocratic: "But where did you make the acquaintance of that man? I don't think that he could ever have supped with any of us."

The great, incurable, solitary wound in his heart was the death of his son Charles, killed on the retreat from Champagne. This light-hearted man, so experienced in life, so accustomed to losses, was seen, many years after the catastrophe, to weep at the name of that cherished son. No one ventured to pronounce that name in his presence; his voice betrayed his grief; his eyes would fill with tears. There was something singularly affecting in the sight of this old man, Voltairean and *viveur*, as we say in these days, who would not be comforted because the child of his heart was no more.

As a writer the Prince de Ligne had no merit except that of facility. [The reader of these volumes, which contain a large part of his works, can judge if this opinion is correct; also whether the levity so constantly attributed to him by younger and succeeding generations was the leading quality of his nature.] Nearly all his letters were piquant; but printer's ink did not suit his style of writing. The edition of his Works ruined the Dresden publisher, who was forced by contract to publish everything that came from his pen. He wrote, at hap-hazard and on all sorts of subjects, between thirty and forty volumes. From this unreadable jumble, which he himself admitted to be such, Mme. de Staël has had the talent to extract one very pleasing volume, to which she has added a preface, full of good taste and wit. I could myself swell this literary budget of the Prince de Ligne (which can never go down to posterity) with a quantity of detached articles on the Queen of France, the Duc de Choiseul, the Duc d'Orléans; and I possess a great number of his letters both in prose and verse, but nothing of it all can add to the literary credit of the writer.

He has often told me a number of very amusing details about his childhood and youth, with anecdotes about his father, who was the most haughty and fantastic of men, and hated his son cordially. The latter was allied from his youth with the princes of Europe, including Voltaire. Frederick II. sought him; the Empress Catherine admitted him to her inmost circle and made him travel with her. With what enjoyment he used to tell us of the charming evenings at the Hermitage and at the brilliant Court of Petersburg. The Prince de Ligne retained a true attachment to the empress. He often told me that she was one of the most accomplished women he had ever met. "She was," he said, "prudent, reserved, imposing, when occasion demanded; an empress, measuring her gestures and her words, while at the same time she was a type of grace, naturalness, and true kindness. When she laid aside her air of studied gravity, with what indulgence, what charming gayety, she would lend herself to my nonsense!" We have all read the prince's letters to the Marquise de Coigny, relating his journey to the Crimea with the empress, and those to Ségur on his campaign against the Turks with Prince Potemkin.

The Prince de Ligne had spent a part of his life in making war, if not with great distinction, at least with the most brilliant bravery. He played a real part in the Seven Years' War, was a friend of Loudon and Lacy, and became intimate about that time with Prince Henry of Prussia, whom he visited many years later in his philosophical retreat at Rheinsberg. There the veteran prince-hero loved to make long disquisitions on his military life, — disquisitions often repeated, and so wearisome to his listeners that the Prince de Ligne said once: "When Prince Henry launches upon the Seven Years' War you may know it is going to be the Thirty Years' War instead."

On the death of the Emperor Joseph II. the military and political career of the Prince de Ligne came to an end. He was never employed again; but he retained, with his high social position, his titles and dignities. In the eyes of all civilized Europe he appeared to do the honours of Vienna, and he was, beyond a doubt, the centre of a circle to which we may look in vain for anything analogous in the present day. The most indefatigable of *flâneurs*, he was everywhere; at the theatres, the dance halls, the Prater, — very much in society, and a little at Court. In Vienna every one, grandees and people, saluted him with pleasure; they would see him at a distance, coming either on foot, wrapped in a semi-military cloak, or in his gray carriage with its white horses, on which, beneath a prince's coronet, were blazoned the arms of his family, — or, a bend gules, surrounded with their motto: *Quocunque res cadunt, semper linea recta.*

A great number of the witty sayings of the Prince de Ligne (many of them never said by him at all) have been collected; the most piquant of them, known only to his intimates, are now forgotten. "When I was twenty years old," he once wrote me, "I had chosen my career. I hoped to play a great rôle in war; but as for Courts, I was contented with that of confidant and supernumerary. When the play is so short and the audience so ill-composed, how can one be fool enough to wish for anything else?"

At the time when we were all at Presburg for the coronation of the Empress Maria Louisa the Prince de Ligne said to me one day: "Be ready at such and such an hour, and I will take you to see the last great lady of France and Europe." It can well be imagined that I was punctual. At eight o'clock in the evening we got into the carriage, and after driving far through the dark and crooked streets of the town we stopped before a house of rather dismal appearance. We had some difficulty in getting up the staircase by feeling our way. Finally, in a vast salon, very poorly furnished and scarcely lighted by two wax candles, we found Mme. la Comtesse de Brionne, Princess of Lorraine, who united in her person the white ermine of Bretagne, the proud motto of the Rohans, and the escutcheon of the Balafré, over which the noblest races of Christianity have waved their banners.[1]

Afflicted with paralysis of the hands and feet, and half lying on a reclining chair, Mme. de Brionne preserved, at nearly eighty years of age, the traces of her dazzling beauty. The sound of her voice, slowly accentuated, her noble, regular profile, her gentle, but imposing glance, remain to this day deeply engraven upon my memory. Here was a queen dethroned, a Hecuba. After the usual visiting topics I managed to make the conversation turn on France of the olden time. Then, as if by a fairy wand retrograding us fifty years, we were back in the midst of Versailles, in the midst of Trianon. The past, so old, so completely vanished, was the present, — the present in flesh and blood. 'T was a dialogue of the dead; but the dead were full of life and were each renewing the other's youth. Closing one's eyes one might fancy one's self in the Œil de Bœuf, or the little apartments. All the Versailles of that long past time re-

[1] "Roi ne peux, prince ne veux, Rohan je suis." (King I cannot, prince I will not, Rohan I am.) Le Balafré was Henri de Lorraine, Duc de Guise.

turned to the light of day, coquettish, gallant, dainty, joyous, and, oh, bewildering thing! the two octogenarians, intoxicating themselves with this fictitious reality, began to talk as if the monarchy were there, living and moving before their eyes, and Louis XV. still the king of that enchanting fairyland. He had once been deeply in love with Mme. de Brionne, from whom he never obtained anything, it was said, but friendship. During the minority of her son she had herself exercised the office of Grand Equerry; time was — or was it that very morning? — she had left the cabinet of the king, portfolio in hand — ah, yes! he was so handsome, so gracious, that king of Lawfeldt and Fontenoy! They forgave him Mme. de Châteauroux, but there was small indulgence for Mme. de Pompadour. As for Mme. du Barry, the prince scarcely ventured to name her, on account of memories. We made a journey (on this occasion) to Chanteloup, and were firmly convinced that if the Duc de Choiseul, the intimate friend of the comtesse, had not been driven away by the cabal of the Duc de Lavauguyon, who made the king (take notice, *the king*), believe that M. de Choiseul had poisoned the dauphin, he would still have been at the head of affairs instead of being exiled to Chanteloup, and this revolution would have come to naught. We did not spare the gentry of the long robe, nor of the parliament, and, above all, not the encyclopedists.

There was much talk about a certain jostle of a hoop, given, methinks, by the Duchesse de Grammont to Mme. du Barry, which led the prince to say, "See what it is to have a panier and no consideration." They blamed the little Maréchale de Mirepoix for consenting, great lady that she was, to be so accommodating to the king's mistresses. The Maréchal de Richelieu, they considered, would have been perfectly agreeable if he alone, of all Versailles, had not persisted in retaining the red heels and the rather stiff, affected manners and formal compliments of the previous reign. I was made to observe that the Duc de Choiseul had a singular way — all his own — of wearing his *cordon bleu*, and of putting his hand in a certain manner into his half-opened waistcoat. All that was highest in Versailles, all the great ladies, with their beautiful trained robes and their paniers, their rouge and their *mouches*, all the handsome young men, powdered, perfumed, and spangled, came and sat with us there in that poor salon that was almost denuded.

There was something fascinating and bewildering in it all, which was not unlike that scene in "Robert le Diable" where the dead come out of their tombs and dance with the living. In point of fact, my head did swim with the wonderful evocation; and I only came back to myself when, on leaving the house after spending two hours in that magic circle, I asked the prince to tell me who was a lady, a young lady, not pretty and very silent, who had kept her eyes bent on her tapestry and had taken no part whatever in the conversation. That, he said, was the Princesse Charlotte de Rohan, niece of Mme. de Brionne, who was thought to have been privately married to the unfortunate Duc d'Enghien only a short time before he was murdered in the moat at Vincennes.

Those words fell like a thunderbolt, before which vanished the enchanting phantoms with whom I had lived for the last two hours; an unspeakable emotion took possession of my breast as I thought how in a remote little town of Hungary three persons, struck by fate in ways so different, should have met as if to give me, a young foreigner, an epitome of two centuries at the confluence of which it was my fate to be born.

[The Duc de Broglie is less sympathetic, but he sees things from another point of view.]

In 1809 I was sent to Vienna immediately after the battle of Wagram; it being customary during that and the other campaigns to send a messenger from Paris to general headquarters weekly, with all current information for the emperor [Napoleon], then at Schönbrunn.

I reached Vienna, where I spent three weeks. As the French army still occupied the city, I was lodged by the military authorities in the house of Prince Nicolas Esterhazy, who received me with politeness and soon after admitted me to his family. After the departure of the French army he insisted on keeping me longer and overwhelmed me with attentions and kindness. The three weeks that I spent in his hospitable house were full of charm. I divided my time between my excellent hosts and the house of the Prince de Ligne.

This house, situated on the rampart, was literally a bird-cage. It consisted of a dining-room on the ground-floor, a salon on the next floor and a bedroom above that; the last two being reached by a sort of trap-ladder. Each room was furnished with a few straw chairs, a pine table, and some other little articles of the same magnificence. It was there that the Prince de Ligne received every evening, and even, on occasion, in the mornings, a small number of persons with whom the pleasures of conversation took the place of all things else. He regularly gave supper to those who came; and that supper consisted of a miserable chicken, spinach, and hard-boiled eggs. The evenings, often the mornings, were passed in interminable conversations, in which the events of the Court of France under Louis XV. and Louis XVI. were related in a tone conformable with the spirit of those frivolous periods; the prince comparing the battles of the Seven Years' War with those of the Revolution and the Empire; which provoked even a young man of my age to take a part and say his word, either bad or good.

The family of the prince was very pleasing; it consisted of his three daughters: the Princesse Clary, the Comtesse Palffy, and the Princesse Flore, afterwards the Baronne von Spiegel; also his granddaughter, Christine, now the Comtesse Maurice O'Donnell, the natural daughter of his son.

The time that I spent in this gentle and peaceful company seemed very short and pleasant. I saw before my departure a touching sight, — the return of the Emperor of Austria to his capital after the very painful events of the preceding campaign and the melancholy peace of Vienna. The greeting that his people gave him was tender and respectful; it was that of a true family receiving its father after a long series of misfortunes; sparing him all blame, which, indeed, were it even well-founded (which is doubtful) his people deserved as much as he..

In 1812, being again in Vienna on a mission [to convey the news of the Beresina], my sole refuge was the perch of the Prince de Ligne. There I was received with open arms, and it was from that amiable family that I learned positively what I had already divined, namely: that in the present state of public opinion no one in the highest society would have dared to receive a Frenchman unless obliged to do so by duty to the State, or by official position.

XI.

1814.

THE CONGRESS OF VIENNA.[1]

A STAY of several months in Vienna during the memorable period of which this book will treat gave me opportunities for observation from which to gather material that did not come within the reach of all the spectators of that great drama.

It was under the guidance of the Maréchal Prince de Ligne, my relative and friend, that I gained access to everything that was best worth knowing. His rank and station, his seniority of years, his military and literary reputation, and the personal esteem and friendship with which he was honoured by the sovereigns assembled in Vienna and by all the other illustrious persons there collected, gave him universal acceptance and consideration in the highest circles of the place. His society was courted by all; sovereigns, princes, great captains, and men distinguished in art, literature, and science crowded his little salon. The advantage of being guided by such a man and of constantly listening to his remarks upon men and things are among the considerations that have led me to think that the following pages will be of interest to a reader.

The Congress of Vienna bore the character of a great solemnity for the celebration of the tranquillity of Europe.

[1] Taken from "Fêtes et Souvenirs du Congrès de Vienne," par le Comte de La Garde. Paris et Bruxelles: 1840.

It was a Festival of Peace, intended to restore the political equilibrium which the struggle of armies had so long interrupted. The nations of Europe, convoked in the persons of their sovereigns, and negotiating together by means of their most enlightened ministers, was a unique spectacle, fitly concluding the extraordinary events that had led to it.

The Congress was already under way on my arrival in Vienna about the middle of October, 1814. It was then supposed that it would speedily be dissolved; but, pleasure or business, I cannot say which, ruled otherwise. Months went by and the sessions continued. Sovereigns met and discussed their national interests like brothers amicably settling, as Catherine the Great was wont to say, the affairs of their "little households;" and the Abbé de Saint-Pierre's philosophical dream of a universal peace seemed about to be realized. It is Dr. Johnson, I think, who says in reference to the great wall of China, that the grandson of the man who has seen it will have reason to be proud of that circumstance. So I, for my part, am proud of having been at the Congress of Vienna, although I bore no part in it, and had not the honour of previously knowing all the illustrious persons who formed that most memorable assembly.

When I first went to Vienna in 1807 the Prince de Ligne received me and presented me at Court and in society. The revolution in the Low Countries had deprived him of his property, a loss he bore with philosophic fortitude. The Emperor Francis II. made him the commander of his own regiment of Trabans (halberdiers) and a field-marshal in 1808; and he always presided at the council of the Order of Maria Theresa. During the last twenty years of his life he devoted himself wholly to literary pursuits, and published his Works in thirty-four volumes, some of which have attained considerable celebrity; especially those in which he describes the events in which he took part, and the distinguished individuals whom he knew personally.

The day after my arrival I went to pay my respects to the prince, who readily agreed to be my guide and instructor whenever circumstances threw me in his way. "You have come," he said, "just at the right moment. If you like fêtes and balls you will have enough of them; the Congress *ne marche pas, il danse.* There is, literally, a royal mob here. Everybody is crying out: 'Peace! justice! balance of power! indemnity!' As for me, I am a looker-on. All the indemnity I shall ask for is a new hat; I have worn mine out in taking it off to sovereigns whom I meet at the corner of every street. However, in spite of Robinson Crusoe" (his nickname for Napoleon, who was then at Elba), "a general peace will really be concluded by this Congress of all the nations of Europe who are now exclaiming, '*Cedant arma togæ.*'"

While we were talking about Paris, my family, my journey, my plans, a servant announced that his carriage was ready. "Come and dine with me to-morrow," he said, "and I will take you in the evening to the Ridotto, where reason wears the mask of folly." The prince kept up the good old fashion of dining early, and I went to his house on the rampart at four o'clock. We were soon summoned to dinner, at which all his charming family were assembled. Like the suppers of Mme. Scarron ["Madame, another story! the roast is lacking!"], the prince's dinners certainly needed the seasoning of interesting conversation. He himself did full justice to the very light fare that was served; but he so possessed the art of occupying the minds of his guests that it was not until they rose from table that the ethereal nature of the meal was apparent to them.

On returning to the salon we found that visitors were

already arriving. Nearly all were persons of distinction from various parts of Europe, who obtained their introduction to this living monument of a past age for the purpose of saying, "I have seen the Prince de Ligne." Making his escape after a time from one of these dull groups, the prince came up to his grandson Comte Clary, son of his daughter Christine, with whom I was talking. "I once wrote to Jean-Jacques Rousseau," he said to me, "a letter which began: 'I know you hate importuners and importuning;' there are people here to-night to whom I would like to give that hint, but they are too dull to take it. Let us get away to a society that is more to our liking: follow me." So saying, he slipped out of the room with the agility of a page, and laughed heartily, when we were seated in the carriage, at the trick he had played on the would-be wits, and their disappointment when they found he was not there to listen to them.

At nine o'clock we reached the Burg, the Imperial palace where the Ridottos were held. The ballroom, which was brilliantly lighted, is surrounded by a gallery leading to the supper-rooms. In it were seated groups of elegant women; some in dominoes, some in fancy costumes; bands of music, stationed in different parts of the hall, played waltzes and polonaises alternately. In the adjoining rooms some of the company were performing solemn minuets with German gravity, which added a comical element to the scene. Vienna, as the prince observed, was now presenting an epitome of Europe, and the Ridotto was an epitome of Vienna. Impossible to imagine anything more remarkable than this assemblage, masked and unmasked, amid which the rulers of mankind were walking about and mingling with the crowd without the slightest distinction.

"Take notice," said the prince, "of that graceful, martial

figure walking with Eugène de Beauharnais; that is the Emperor Alexander. And that tall, dignified man with the lively Neapolitan on his arm is the King of Prussia; the lady, who is making him laugh, may be an empress or a grisette. And there, in that Venetian suit, the stiffness of which scarcely conceals his affability, is our own emperor, the representative of the most paternal despotism that ever existed. Here is Maximilian, King of Bavaria, in whose frank countenance you can read the expression of his good heart. Those two young men over there are the Prince-Royal of Bavaria and his brother Charles. The latter has the head of an Antinous; but the other, Louis, whose tastes are all for literature and the fine arts, promises to give Bavaria, one of these days, a noble reign. Do you see that pale little man with an aquiline nose, near to the King of Bavaria? That is the King of Denmark, whose cheerful humour and lively repartees enliven the royal parties — they call him the *Lustig* [merry joker] of the Sovereign Brigade. Judging by his simple manners and the perfect happiness of his little kingdom, you would never suppose him to be the greatest autocrat in Europe. But he is, for all that. In Copenhagen the royal carriage is preceded by an equerry armed with a carbine, and the king as he drives along can, if he pleases, order any of his subjects to be shot. That colossal figure leaning against the column, whose bulk is not lessened by the folds of his ample domino, is the King of Würtemburg, and next him is his son, the prince-royal, whose affection for the Grand-Duchess of Oldenburg has brought him to the Congress, rather than the settlement of public business that will soon be his own. All this crowd of persons who are buzzing round us are either reigning princes, archdukes, or great dignitaries from various countries. With the exception of a few Englishmen (easily distinguished by the richness of their clothes), I do not see any one without a title to his name. And now I think, having sufficiently introduced you, you can work your own way. Come to me if you get into any trouble; I am always here to pilot you."

In these souvenirs I note down only my personal recollections; it is no part of my plan to record political events; however important and interesting they may be, history has made them too well known to need further detail.

The Prince of Hesse Homburg and Comte Woina brought me news that preparations were making for a splendid tournament to take place in the Imperial Mews; which would be, they declared, the finest spectacle ever witnessed. All the engravings and descriptions of the tournaments of Louis XIV. had been collected and consulted. The Comtesse Edmond de Périgord (before her marriage Princesse de Courlande), who was one of the twenty-four ladies appointed to preside over the fête, told me that the dresses would surpass in magnificence all that was recorded of the luxury of the women in the days of the Great Monarch. "I really think," she said, "that we shall wear all the pearls and diamonds in Bohemia, Austria, and Hungary. Family jewels that have not seen the light for a century will be worn on this occasion." "Next to the ladies — always the first attraction," said Comte Woina, "I am sure that our superb horses will come in for their share of admiration; some of them can passade a minuet as gracefully as a Court cavalier."

The next morning I went to see the Prince de Ligne, being anxious to avail myself of every moment that he was willing to give me. It was rather late when I arrived, and I found him just stepping into his carriage with the Prince de Lambesc (so famous in the early part of the French Revolution). They were going to Schönbrunn, to pay a visit to

Napoleon's son, and asked me to accompany them. I was obliged to decline on account of an engagement. "I shall be going again to-morrow," said the Prince de Ligne, "and if you would like to go then I will announce you to-day to Mme. de Montesquieu; for I perform, *ad honores*, a sort of grand-chamberlain duty to the little duke who was born a king." "At what o'clock shall I wait upon you?" I asked. "At eleven," he answered, and we parted, I for a gallop on the Prater.

When I called to keep my appointment I was told that the prince had not left his bed, but I was ushered up into the library, which he had turned into a sort of chamber, and there I found him sitting up in bed and writing, for his active mind never wasted a moment. "You are very punctual," he remarked. "Louis XVIII. says that punctuality is the politeness of kings, and I have always remarked that it is a quality which never fails to please. Let me finish what I am writing and I shall be at your service. I always jot down my ideas as they occur, lest they escape me."

Presently he said, having occasion to refer to a book: "Be so kind as to hand me that volume — there, on the third shelf." I did not see the book at once, and hesitated. Thereupon the prince sprang up and, holding by the top of the book-case, reached the book himself and then lay down again. I was amazed at this feat of agility in a man of eighty. Observing my look of astonishment, he said: "I was always active, and my activity has sometimes been of great service to me. When I accompanied the Empress Catherine to the Crimea, the imperial galley rounded the Parthenion promontory, where stood, it is said, the temple of Diana which Iphigenia made famous in the olden time. We were discussing the various versions of that fact, when the empress, who was walking up and down the deck with her customary majesty and slowness, said to me, pointing to the shore: 'Prince, I give to you that disputed territory.' I immediately jumped into the water, uniform and all, and swam ashore; then I turned and called out: 'Since your Imperial Majesty permits it, I take possession;' and that rock has been mine and bears my name ever since; so much for a little agility!"

Thus talking, he dressed himself, and as he put on his brilliant uniform with his half-dozen Orders he remarked: "If illusion would once more hold her mirror before me, how gladly would I exchange all this for the plain uniform I first put on as ensign in my father's Wallon regiment. I was seventeen then and I thought thirty very old, and now at eighty I think myself young. Censorious people say I make myself too young — well, I take care to be young enough. Few lives have been happier than mine; I have never been troubled by remorse, ambition, or envy; and so until I step into Charon's boat I shall consider myself young in spite of those who declare me old." This was said while he dressed, in that charming tone of light-heartedness that characterized the Prince de Ligne, and of which those who never knew him can form no idea.

As we left the house we met a visitor, one of those pedantic persons by whom he was beset. The prince got rid of him civilly, and then remarked: "How I hate those people whose learning is nothing but words. They are walking dictionaries and have no merit but memory; the world is the best book after all." We drove to Schönbrunn in a carriage that seemed to be as old as its owner, though not half so well preserved as he. On the way he talked of Mme. de Staël. "If," he said, "when she asked Bonaparte whom he thought the greatest woman of the age he had tickled her harmless vanity and said, 'You,' instead of coarsely saying, 'She who bears the most children,' I venture to say we should not now be driving to Schönbrunn to see his son. It cannot be denied that Corinne and her Genevese coterie had a great deal to do with his downfall."

As we passed through the courtyards, which are very spacious, the prince showed me the spot where a young political fanatic attempted to murder Napoleon soon after the battle of Wagram. "Such crimes are unpardonable," he said, "but one cannot help admiring the cool courage with which that young fellow met his death."

We were received on the grand staircase by a French lacquey wearing the Napoleon livery. He knew the Prince de Ligne and went immediately to announce him to Mme. de Montesquieu, who soon made her appearance and politely apologized for not being able to admit us at once. The young Napoleon, she said, was then sitting to Isabey, and she feared that the sight of the Prince de Ligne, of whom the child was very fond, would distract his mind. "Will you have the goodness therefore," she added, "to take a turn in the gardens? and I will end the sitting as soon as I can." "Willingly," replied the prince, "for I want to go over the château and gardens with my relative here, whom I have the honour to present to you, madame." "As this gentleman is introduced by you, monsieur," said Mme. de Montesquieu, "I shall be happy to receive him at any time. When you have seen all you wish, come in without the ceremony of being announced." "It would have been well," said the prince as we walked away, "if I had waived that ceremony the first time I came out here, for when the child heard the announcement of the Maréchal Prince de Ligne, he exclaimed: 'Is he one of the marshals who betrayed my papa? If he is, he shall not come in;' and it was hard to persuade him there were other marshals than French ones."

We passed through a long suite of handsome rooms, in

which there was nothing remarkable, until we reached a little cabinet, on the walls of which were a number of drawings by the various archduchesses. "It was here," said the prince, "that Napoleon when at Schönbrunn used to spend many hours alone in reading and writing; that portrait of Maria Louisa was the first he saw of her, and in all probability it was in this room that he formed the idea of a marriage which had such influence on his destiny." . . . As we were returning to the house after visiting the grounds, the gardener called our attention to an enclosed little plot. "That," he said, "is the Prince of Parma's garden. He plants the flowers himself, and comes every morning to gather a bunch for his mother and his *maman-quiou*, as he calls Mme. de Montesquieu."

The moment we entered the prince's room he jumped from the chair on which he was sitting and ran to embrace the Prince de Ligne. He was certainly a most beautiful child. His brilliant complexion, his bright, intelligent eyes, and his fair hair falling in curls over his shoulders made him a charming subject for such a painter as Isabey. He was dressed in the hussar uniform, and wore the cross of the Legion of honour. Bearing in mind Rousseau's remark that no one likes to be questioned, least of all children, I contented myself with stooping to kiss him. He then ran hastily to a corner of the room and brought back a regiment of wooden soldiers, given to him by the Archduke Charles, and these he manœuvred, while the Maréchal drew his sword and commanded the evolutions.

Mme. de Montesquieu, whose love for the child fully justified Napoleon's selection of her, told us several very clever remarks made by the little prince which tend to show that certain qualities are hereditary. "A striking instance of his using his mind," she said, "occurred yesterday when Admiral

——, who accompanied the emperor to Elba, came to see him. 'Are you not pleased,' I said, presenting the admiral, 'to see this gentleman, who left your papa only the other day?' 'Yes,' he said, 'I am very happy to see him, but,' laying his finger on his lips, 'I must not say so.' 'Your papa,' said the admiral, lifting him in his arms, 'desired me to give you this kiss.' The child, who happened to have a toy in his hand, flung it down and broke it; then he burst into tears and cried out, 'Poor papa!' What could have been passing in his mind at that moment?" said Mme. de Montesquieu. "Perhaps it was the same train of ideas that made him resist being taken from the Tuileries. He cried out that his father was betrayed and he would not leave the château. Catching at the curtains and clinging to the furniture he said it was his father's house and he would not leave it."

We went to look at Isabey's work. The likeness was excellent, and the picture had all the grace that characterizes the miniatures of that admirable artist. This was the portrait which Isabey presented to the emperor on his return from Elba. "What particularly interests me in it," said the Prince de Ligne, "is that it closely resembles his great uncle Joseph II. when a boy. I should like to compare it with a portrait of Joseph which was given to me by Maria Theresa. That likeness, though a matter of accident, seems to me of good omen for the future." Then he paid a few well-deserved compliments to the artist. "I came to Vienna," said Isabey, "in hopes of painting all the celebrated personages collected here; and I ought to have begun with you." "On account of my seniority?" asked the prince. "No," said Isabey, "as a model of all that is illustrious in the present day."

The Empress Maria Theresa was now announced and we paid our homage and withdrew, leaving Isabey free to show her the portrait which she had come to see. "Ah!" said the prince as we were driving away, "when Napoleon received at Schönbrunn the submission of the city of Vienna after the battle of Wagram, and reviewed his victorious troops in these very courtyards, how little he dreamed that the son of the conqueror and the daughter of the conquered would be held as hostages by the nation whose destinies were then at his disposal. How extraordinary the fate of that man! Not content to be king, his ambition was like that of Alexander and he sought to be Jupiter. I have seen many instances of good fortune and adversity in my long life, but none to compare with this on which the world's attention is now fixed. If the reflections we make on all we see and feel were always present to our minds, how wise we should be!"

I could not help asking him how it was that throughout so many important campaigns his military experience and talents had not been put into active service. "Ah!" he said, with a laugh, "I died with Joseph II." "Say like him, rather than with him, prince, for Europe declares him immortal." "His is the immortality of genius, and mine, if I have any, will be that of the sybil—lasting age." As we were crossing the glacis between the suburbs and the city, we met an open carriage, in which sat a gentleman of portentous proportions. "Halt!" cried the prince. "Let us make our bow; here is another king by the grace of God and Robinson Crusoe." It was his Majesty of Würtemberg.

At a party given by the Princesse Bagration the fashion of drawing a lottery, one of the favourite amusements of the Court of Louis XIV., was revived. All the sovereigns sent presents to the princess, which made the prizes; and the fortunate men who won them presented them in homage to some lady in the company. The Grand-Duke Constantine won two vases, which the King of Prussia had ordered from Potsdam, and these he presented to our hostess. The Emperor Alexander's prize was a mosaic box which he entreated the Princesse Marie Esterhazy to accept. The salon was so crowded that I did not see my friend Prince Alexander Ypsilanti until he went up to receive his prize, a sable tippet, which he presented to Princesse Hélène Suvaroff, daughter of the grand chamberlain of Russia, Narischkin. When I had last seen Ypsilanti he was only a cornet in the guards. He was now a major-general, brilliantly decorated, but lacking an arm, which he lost at Bautzen. Princesse Hélène was just as I left her in Petersburg, always "fair and good," as they name her there. We were all three delighted to meet again. "We have so much to say to one another," said Princesse Hélène, "come and breakfast with me to-morrow at twelve, both of you, and then we can talk at our ease."

The breakfast was delightful. We talked over all the news of Petersburg and the friends we had left there, the *bon-mots* of Prince Galitzin, the sternness of the Grand-Duke Constantine, and the droll sayings of her father the grand-chamberlain Narischkin. When it became Ypsilanti's turn to speak it was quite evident that, in spite of his brilliant position, all his hopes of future glory turned to Greece, whose subjugation he mourned and longed to avenge. I saw plainly that Princesse Hélène was encouraging these dreams. Like all the rest of the Russian nobility, she cherished a hope transmitted to them from generation to generation as a sacred inheritance. "The time is coming," said Ypsilanti. "I have letters from all directions calling for me; from the islands of the Archipelago, from the two principalities, and from higher places still. Mine shall be the blood to fill the cup." "Why delay?" cried the princess. "Could you wish for a higher glory than to be at twenty-three the regenerator of an oppressed people? This is the era of youth outstripping middle age. Think how Alexander wept at the tomb of Achilles and mourned that he had never achieved anything as great. What is there comparable to the independence of Greece?" [Alexander Ypsilanti fulfilled his desire. He initiated the revolution of Greece in 1821, which, though it failed under him, was carried on by his brother Demetrius. He himself, after a cruel imprisonment, died in Vienna, shattered by his sufferings.]

I was beginning to share their enthusiasm; as for Ypsilanti, his face was a presage of emancipation; Greece was on the point of being liberated, when, to our surprise, General Comte Ouvaroff entered suddenly without being announced. We then turned to subjects of a less heroic kind, for, though gifted with many excellent qualities, the worthy general was by no means famous for conversational powers or depth of information. Presently, however, the servants announced the princess's carriage, and she invited us all to drive with her on the Prater.

A few days later I met at the Prince de Ligne's M. Novossilsoff, a well-known Russian statesman, held in great esteem by the Emperor Alexander. He was a member of the provisional government of Poland, and was talking with the prince when I arrived over the affairs of that country. The subject is one of deep interest to me, for the happiest days of my life are those I have spent in Poland, and the feelings I have for that unfortunate country are deep indeed. The conversation turned chiefly on the constitution which it was now proposed to give the Poles; M. Novossilsoff was one of the commission appointed to draw it up. "The Polish nation," he said, "are forever letting their minds turn back to the brilliant past of their history; they want their country to have once more the proud independence it enjoyed under the Batoris, the Sobieskis, the Sigismonds, never reflecting on the vast changes in the political situation which Europe has seen since then, and which, with their geographical position, make it impossible that they should be again what they once were. Poland is now linked to us, and must content herself with the inevitable fate that awaits her politically. If we allowed her to be completely independent she would make an Asiatic nation of us." "Burke said," observed the prince, "that the partition of Poland would be paid for dearly by those who made it; and he might have added those who defend her, for Napoleon's interference in her concerns has helped in no slight degree to lose him his throne. I hope your Emperor Alexander will have a better fate; but all depends on the adoption of proper measures secured on a firm foundation. A people as proud as the Poles may bear being conquered, but they will never endure being humiliated. You may conquer them, but you can never subjugate them, except by a just and generous policy." "My dear prince," replied Novossilsoff, "you need not fear that the Poles will have reason to complain of any system of policy from us. Read this memorandum; it contains the constitution we propose for them; the notes on the margin are all the emperor's, written by his own hand; you will see how strong our desire is to meet the wishes of the Polish nation. The institutions, if secured on this solid basis, will in turn secure the peace of Europe." "Well," said the prince, "if the foundations of the edifice are proportioned to its weight and sufficiently solid they will, no doubt, be durable; but if not, you may fear the vengeance of men who are driven to desperation."

At this moment Comte Arthur Potocki, a young friend of the prince, came in. Being a Pole and an ardent enthusiast for his country, his presence put a stop to further remarks from M. Novossilsoff, who folded up his papers and presently went away. The prince invited the count to come and dine with us at his "Refuge," as he terms his country-house on the Kalemberg — otherwise called the Leopoldberg — just outside Vienna. The prince was greatly attached to Comte Arthur, whom he called his Alcibiades. The latter declined the invitation because he was engaged with Princesse Lubomirski to take part in some *tableaux vivants* to be given that night at Court under the direction of the painter Isabey. We were also invited as spectators, but as the performance did not begin till eight o'clock the prince considered that we had time to dine at the Refuge and return.

The Kalemberg is a lofty hill in the vicinity of Vienna from which a broadly extensive view is obtained. The house [an old monastery] is small, but neat and pleasing in appearance. Over the portal of the entrance the prince had caused to be carved these words: *Quo res cadunt, semper linea recta.* "Here," said the prince, "I find rest and relaxation; especially at present, for, no matter what our own inclinations may be, there is a certain stiffness which we are compelled to impose upon ourselves in presence of so many crowned heads and important personages. Here I can live my own life."

When we reached the extremity of the garden he opened a door which led into a summer-house overhanging the Danube, from which was a view of the whole city of Vienna. "It was from this spot," he said, "that John Sobieski began his glorious attack upon the Grand vizier."

At three o'clock we sat down to a dinner on provisions which the prince had ordered to be sent out with us in the carriage. Never will my grateful memory forget the charms of that repast! How bright the colours were in which he pictured the noted persons who, in the course of his long career, had honoured him with their friendship. He had a way of treating every subject of which he spoke with a grace and charm imparted to the merest trifles. I listened with the deepest attention to all he said, and I felt myself transported to the scenes to which his imagination gave such vivid colouring

When we reached the palace that evening we found that Comte Arthur Potocki had secured seats for us next to the Princesse Esterhazy and Prince Leopold of Saxe Coburg. The performance began by extinguishing the lights while an orchestra, of harps and French horns only, played an *ouverture.* The *tableaux* were three in number: A Spanish conversation; Louis XIV. at the feet of Mme. de la Vallière; and a picture by Le Gros representing Hippolytus defending himself to Theseus against the accusations of Phædra. These pictures, represented by the most distinguished men and women at Court with magnificent and appropriate costumes and arranged in the most masterly manner as to light and shade by Isabey, naturally caused great admiration. It is impossible to convey an idea of the magic effect to those who did not witness the exhibition. [*Tableaux vivants* were then a novelty; these were among the first ever shown.]

The lights were now replaced, and while the next series, called "dramatic romances," were being prepared, all kinds of refreshments were served to the company. There were, as before with the *tableaux,* three romances. The first was the well-known idyll: *Partant pour la Syrie, le jeune et beau Dunois,* composed by Queen Hortense and sung by Mlle. Goubault, daughter of the Dutch minister, Baron Goubault, now Governor of Brussels. Her voice was very pathetic, and she sang the air with exquisite feeling, while

Comte Schäufeld and the Princesse Philipstadt expressed the scene with pantomimic action. They were supported by a full chorus of both sexes; and the beautiful grouping, especially during the marriage stanza, together with the admirable training of the chorus, produced a perfect enthusiasm among the audience.

I was too far from the Emperor Alexander to hear what he said to Prince Eugène, who sat between him and the king of Bavaria, but from the expression of the prince's face, it was evident that the emperor was paying a just tribute to his sister's talents.

The next "romance" was Compigni's, *Le Troubadour qui chante et fait la guerre.* This was performed by Comte Schomberg and the Comtesse Maressi. The third was another composition by Queen Hortense: *Fais ce que doit, advienne que pourra.* This was as well sung and expressed as the two others by young Prince Radziwill and the Comtesse Zamoïska, the beautiful and accomplished daughter of the Maréchal Prince Czartormiski. The author's name was called for, and its announcement received with unanimous applause.

"The truth is," remarked the Prince de Ligne, "that Mlle. de Beauharnais wields a sceptre that will never break in her hand. She remains a queen by the grace of her talents, after ceasing to be one by the grace of God. As for me, I not only applaud these marks of genius, but I delight in paying homage to fallen greatness, when persons in that situation have proved themselves worthy of the station they attained."
"I saw so much of Queen Hortense," said Prince Leopold, "during my frequent visits to Paris, that I can bear ample testimony to the truth of what you say. She was very young when brought into a Court resplendent with military glory, but her amiable nature was not in the slightest degree

affected by this brilliant change in her fortunes. Neither imperial splendour nor her own regal honours made the least alteration in her; throughout she kept her modest, unaffected ways. I do not believe that the loss of those honours have caused her any regret. She was born with a gift for the fine arts, which her superior education, and the means at her command, have fully developed. You are right in saying she wields a sceptre of which she can never be deprived. She sings exquisitely, plays delightfully on several instruments, composes, as we have just heard, charmingly, and draws most beautifully. No woman ever danced better. But what all strangers in Paris felt most in the days of her greatness was the courteous consideration which she and her mother showed to them. They both seemed constantly anxious to smooth the peculiar difficulties of position which some of us could not avoid feeling at the Tuileries."

"I like," said the Prince de Ligne, "the frank homage that you pay, dear prince, where it is so justly due. I love to admire wherever admiration is possible; I have no patience with those who are always seeking a motive for acts of kindness outside of kindness, as if they did not believe that amiable qualities can come of native impulse."

The habit of meeting one another every day in Vienna produced a most friendly and intimate feeling among persons of many diverse countries. Vienna is a small city, and its places of public resort so many that people were no sooner parted than they met again. The Prater is, however, the grand meeting-place, — not for persons of social distinction only, but for all classes. Besides the Court carriages, of which three hundred were provided by the emperor for the sovereigns and their suites, there were throngs of equipages belonging to foreigners of all nations, who flocked to Vienna for this great occasion. The English ambassador, Lord

Stuart, drove four superb horses; the Emperor Alexander and his sister, the Grand-Duchess of Oldenburg, took their airing in a simple curricle; in a large landau, emblazoned with his arms, sat the English admiral, Sir Sidney Smith; after him came the Pacha of Widdin in a tangle of hackney coaches, mixed with the carriages of the archdukes, who, in all their amusements, behaved as private individuals, and assumed their rank only for ceremonial functions.

The scene was also enlivened with the beauty of various very interesting costumes, Oriental, Polish, and Hungarian, and above all by the becoming cap of the wives and daughters of the Viennese burghers, which displays their fair hair and pretty features to the best advantage. But most charming of all were the beautiful women of the Court, in their elegant equipages, drawn by splendid Hungarian horses: the Comtesse Fuchs, the Princesse de Courlande, the beautiful Duchesse de Sagan, passionately devoted to all that is heroic and grand, the Comtesse Kinski, the sincerity of whose face gives it a charm it has long since ceased to derive from the bloom of youth.

It was interesting to observe the friendship shown by the Emperor Alexander to Prince Eugène Beauharnais, of which he had lately given him so many proofs at the time of his mother's death. It was rare to see the emperor without the prince. Every day he went regularly at twelve o'clock to the prince's lodgings in the Wieden Kaisergarten, and together, after walking twice around the ramparts, they generally went to see some of the many sights Vienna afforded at that time, ending their day on the Prater. The amiable qualities of Prince Eugène might make it unnecessary to look for any other reason for this friendship. The noble nature he had always evinced was a sure guarantee of his future conduct. But to a lofty mind like that of Alexander the misfortunes that had come upon his friend were the real magnet that drew them together. Alexander's noble and handsome face would have been almost awe-inspiring, had it not been for an expression of sweetness that tempered its dignity; the good-humoured attention with which he listened to all that was said to him captivated every one. Those who had the honour of his intimacy adored him, and the simplicity of his manners, combined with his easy politeness and gallantry, won all hearts in Vienna.

To avoid the awkward questions of precedence liable to arise among so many sovereigns unless positively settled in advance, the Emperor Alexander proposed that age should determine the matter. This was heartily agreed to, and the monarchs took their rank as follows: King of Würtemburg, born 1754; King of Bavaria, 1756; King of Denmark, 1768; Sovereign of Austria, 1768; King of Prussia, 1770; Emperor Alexander, 1777.

For some time after my arrival in Vienna I had been so much engaged that except for a few formal and necessary visits I had scarcely been to the French Legation, though some of its members were my intimate friends. France was represented at the Congress of Vienna by the Prince de Talleyrand, the Duc d'Arlberg, and Comte Alexis de Noailles. I was invited to dinner by M. de Talleyrand, and looked forward with some impatience for the event, as I had not seen that now famous man since my boyhood. The Comtesse de Périgord did the honours of her uncle's house The prince received me with that gracious affability which in him is second nature. "So, monsieur," he said, "you could not pay me a visit till I came to Vienna!" Besides the members of the embassy the only persons present at the dinner were Prince Razumoski, the Duc de Richelieu, and General Pozzo di Borgo. The latter, whom I now met for the first time, seemed to me to combine with a considerable fund of information the shrewd judgment that characterizes his countrymen [Corsican]. From the beginning of his career he had been the declared enemy of Bonaparte, and he did not now conceal the satisfaction that he felt at his downfall. He pointed out, and very clearly, the causes and circumstances that had led to it. The conversation turned, after a time, on the affairs of Saxony. M. de Talleyrand maintained the rights of that country with dignity and sound arguments. "It has been her fate," he said, "to be dragged into quarrels that did not concern her; the results of which have proved fatal to her. Augustus the Strong by allying himself with the czar drew Charles XII. into Poland, and Augustus III. by taking part in those wars of Frederick II. lost all and retired to Warsaw. Saxony may be more fatally involved now than she ever has been before; yet it is constantly being said here that the king is saved in spite of his cession of Lusatia and other places. The king may be saved, but the kingdom is not. What will Saxony be when Prussia gets to the suburbs of Dresden?"

Although there is an air of coldness and reserve in the person and manner of M. de Talleyrand, every one pays court to him, his apparent coldness seeming to increase the value of his notice; people are proud to obtain a smile, or a word of approbation. He possesses that flexibility of talent which without effort or assumption enables him to shine on great occasions, and yet in social intercourse to give ineffable grace to trivial conversation. Justice has never been done to M. de Talleyrand's kindness of heart; perhaps because he never does a service for the sake of ostentation, and he is always the first to forget his benefits. I happened to speak of him one day to Achille de Rouen, who was on terms of the closest intimacy with him. He said to me: "History will be as lavish of praise on M. de Talleyrand as some of his contemporaries have been of blame. When a statesman has made and kept so many stanch friends and so few enemies, through a long and most difficult career, history must pronounce him to have been wise and moderate, his character honourable, his talent lofty. It is impossible to know him and not love him. All who have the happiness of his real acquaintance judge him as I do. He is an indefinable mixture of dignity and simplicity, of sound sense and graceful trifling, of sternness and urbanity. In being with him one learns unconsciously the history of ancient and modern times and the most interesting Court anecdotes; his conversation is a perfect portrait gallery."

Good taste is not so superficial a quality as it is generally considered. The concurrence of many essential things is required to form it, such as delicacy both of mind and feeling, acquaintance with the habits of good society, and a certain tact in harmonizing the whole; but at the same time the sentiment must be superior to the condition of its possessor, for no one is at ease in elegant prosperity unless he has a mind that can rise above its influence. This definition of a valuable quality can be applied to fêtes and entertainments as well as to persons; and it may therefore be allowed to precede the account of a spectacle, unique of its kind, the splendour of which was greatly enhanced by an exquisite display of good taste.

Many weeks had been spent on the preparations for the tournament, to which I was engaged to go with the Prince de Ligne. It was held in the Imperial riding-school, the great hall of which, in the shape of a long parallelogram, was surrounded by a gallery supported by twenty-four Corinthian columns, from which hung the shields of the knights, emblazoned with their arms and devices. In this gallery benches rose gradually one above another, commanding a full view of the arena and able to accommodate about a thousand spectators. Several officers under the direction of the grand-master of ceremonies waited at the doors and took the invited guests to their appointed places. Ours were between the Bavarian minister and the Spanish envoy; next to us sat Prince Nicholas Esterhazy in the uniform of the Hungarian hussars richly embroidered with pearls, which in itself was a sight to behold, inasmuch as it was valued at four million florins.

At each extremity of the hall were two ranges of decorated seats; one for the monarchs, empresses, queens, archdukes, and sovereign princes; the other for the four-and-twenty ladies whose knights were to prove in the tourney that they were the fairest of the fair. In the gallery above these seats were the orchestras, and I need scarcely say that all the distinguished musical performers then in Vienna, and there were many, lent their aid. The whole front of the gallery was occupied by ladies distinguished for rank and beauty. Behind them were two rows of princes, ambassadors, and noted foreigners, the court dresses and uniforms presenting a solid mass of gold and diamonds and precious stones, while the turban of the Pacha of Widdin, the caftan of the Mauro-djian, and the czako of Prince Mauni-Beg Mirza gave variety to the scene. I was continually asking the Prince de Ligne the names of those I did not know, until finally I could not help exclaiming: "Prince, the whole world is here!"

The two emperors sat with the empresses beside them, and all the other monarchs and reigning princes took their places in the order of rank. They were all in full costume

Alexander I.
Emperor of Russia

and presented perhaps the greatest spectacle that Europe could offer. It was hoped that the Empress Maria Louisa and her son, young Napoleon, would have been present; but Maria Louisa felt the delicacy of her position, and rightly believed that the only way to preserve her dignity under misfortune was to live in retirement. But the Prince de Ligne informed me that she had been to several of the rehearsals, accompanied by her father and younger sisters.

Punctually at eight o'clock a flourish of trumpets announced the entrance of the twenty-four ladies, who were conducted to their seats by their champions. One might have imagined on seeing them that all the wealth of Austria had been lavished on their adornment. Their velvet gowns were made after the fashion of Louis XIV.'s reign, modified by the taste of the wearers but literally covered with pearls and diamonds and other precious stones. The dresses of the Princesses Paul Esterhazy and Marie Metternich and the Comtesses de Périgord, Rzewuska, Maressi, and Sophie Zichy were valued at more than twenty millions. The ladies were divided into four parties distinguished by the colour of their gowns, which were black, crimson, rose, and blue. The cloak and scarf of each knight corresponded with the colour of his mistress. The knights were dressed in Spanish costume, richly embroidered in gold and silver, and their plumed hats were looped with pearls and diamonds.

After the ladies were seated, while martial music resounded through the hall, the twenty-four knights, the flower of the Austrian nobility, made their entrance mounted on splendid horses, twenty-four pages with their banners preceding them, and thirty-six esquires with their shields following. The whole cavalcade advanced to the sovereigns, whom they saluted with their lances, then turning at a gallop they offered the same homage to their mistresses, who, rising from their seats, returned the salutation. After which they twice rode round the circle and withdrew; four of them immediately returning to begin the exercises. Turks' and Moors' heads were fixed on stakes and each knight passing at a gallop bore one of them away on the point of his sword. Some caught rings on their lances; others, armed with short javelins, hurled them with great dexterity at the figure of a Saracen which served as target, and then with another javelin hooked at the end they picked up as they passed at full gallop the one they had previously hurled. Another party, carrying sabres, cut in twain an apple suspended by a string, and then, in passing a second time, halved the pieces again. This required great dexterity, and the knight who excelled all others was a son of Prince Trautmansdorff.

Finally, the whole cavalcade of knights and attendants appeared again and executed various manœuvres, ending in a sort of minuet, which displayed to the utmost advantage the intelligence and beauty of their horses. The prizes were then awarded by the ladies, and the knights having again saluted them and the sovereigns, rode once round the circle for the last time and then withdrew. In a short time they returned to lead out the ladies, and from this moment they became the sole object of attentions, for the sovereigns eclipsed themselves by wearing dominos and mingling with the crowd unheeded. The supper was most sumptuous, thousands of candles sparkled in crystal chandeliers, and minstrels, accompanying themselves on harps and zithers, sang strophes and roundelays to beauty and valour.

Thus ended a spectacle the like of which will in all probability never be seen again, for the same conditions can never recur. It was a sight that will not soon be forgotten by those who saw it.

"Is it true," I said to the Prince de Ligne a few days later, "that you are the author of a song on the Congress which is echoing in the boudoirs of even the empresses?" "I am told," he replied, "that the verses are attributed to me; but I do not forget the way in which the Comtesse de Boufflers rewarded Tressan's vanity. However, like other people, I have heard the song sung and have sung it myself; I have even copied it out in my own handwriting, and if you like to have it, there it is."

LE CONGRÈS D'AMOUR

Après une longue guerre,
L'enfant ailé de Cythère
Voulut, en donnant la paix,
Tenir à Vienne un congrès.
Il convoque en diligence
Les Dieux qu'on peut réunir;
Et par une contredanse
On vit le congrès s'ouvrir.

Au bureau de Terpsichore
Dès le soir, jusqu'à l'aurore,
On agitait des débats
Sur l'importance d'un pas.
Minerve dit en colère:
"Cessez au moins un instant,
Si vous ne voulez pas faire
À Vienne un congrès dansant."

Venus et la Jouissance
Qui savaient bien que la danse
Ajoutait à leurs appas,
Voulaient qu'on ne cessât pas.
"La Sagesse doit se taire,"
Dit, en riant, le Désir;
À Vienne l'unique affaire
Est de traiter de plaisir.

À ces mots on recommence,
Les Dieux entrent en danse.

Mars, Hercule, et Jupiter
Valsent un nouveau landeler.
Soudain Minerve en furie
Dit en courroux : " Moi, je crois
Qu'à ce congrès la Folie
Présiderait mieux que moi."

" Taisez-vous, mademoiselle,"
Lui dit l'enfant infidèle.
" Laissez ces propos oiseux,
Et livrez-vous à nos jeux:
Assez long-temps sur la terre
Votre sœur nous fit gémir,
Laissez-nous après la guerre
Respirer pour le plaisir."

À l'instant à la barrière,
Pour entrer dans la carrière,
S'offre trente chevaliers,
Le front couvert de lauriers.
On lisait sur leurs bannières
Ces mots : *loyal et fidel ;*
Ce sont les chargés d'affaires
Du congrès au carrousel.

Enfin de tout on se lasse ;
Les bals, les jeux, et la chasse
Avaient été discutés
Et resumés en traités.
" Que ferons-nous davantage ? "
Dit l'Amour. " Donnons la pai
Et cessons ce badinage
En terminant le congrès."

While I read it the prince was finishing one of those little notes which he usually signed with a line ——, saying that it saved him the trouble of a signature. " Like the Arab," he said, " let us thank God who has given us a pen for a tongue and paper for a messenger. These lines," showing me a paper containing a poem of some length, " I am sending to the Grand-Duchess of Oldenburg, who laid me a wager yesterday I could not write before noon to-day a hundred lines on a topic she would give me. I accepted the bet and have won it, but I sat up all night, and I might have added to my note what Voltaire said to Mlle. Clairon, 'I have toiled for you, madame, like a youth of twenty.'" "Has the Duchess of Oldenburg," I said, "time to think about poetry? I thought she was too much taken up with her attachment to the Prince-Royal of Würtemburg." "Oh!" said the prince, "that affair is coming to a happy conclusion; I was told yesterday that the dispensation from the Greek Church has arrived and the marriage will soon be officially announced."

At this moment the pretty Titine, the Prince de Ligne's adopted granddaughter, came in to say that visitors were awaiting him below. "I will come in a few moments, my dear," he replied; then he added to me: "I, like others, furnish my contingent to the Congress; but people seem to take me for one of the curiosities of the diplomatic fair, and I am obliged to entertain persons who are not worth the trouble. Because I am gay, I am expected to fatigue myself in amusing those who are not so. However, like a good soldier I do not quit the breach, or rather like a good actor I remain upon the stage till the curtain is down; and though I am not one of the committee our good emperor appointed to the duty of making the visits of the sovereigns as agreeable as possible, I do all I can to further that purpose. I am the talking puppet, and I help the acting ones to perform their greater part in the comedy."

On the morning of the 8th of December I was informed that the Prince de Ligne was dangerously ill, and I hurried at once to his little house. There I found his family, with Dr. Malfatti, his physician, and Comte Golowkin, a friend of the prince, best known by the failure of his mission to China.

[He was one of the party which accompanied the Empress Catherine to the Crimea.] Dr. Malfatti blamed the prince for having left the court fête several times without his cloak to put ladies into their carriages; by which imprudence he had taken a severe cold that developed erysipelas in the nape of his neck. Comte Golowkin, who had no more faith in doctors than Molière, endeavoured to encourage the prince, who seemed to be rather cast down by the tone and words of the doctor. "I have always belonged to the incredulous," he said. "Once when the Empress Catherine urged me to take medical advice I said to her: 'I have my own method of treatment; I send for two friends; I physic Ségur and bleed Cobenzl, and I get well directly.'" "Times are changed since then," said the doctor, rather nettled; "that was thirty years ago."

His three daughters never left him for a moment. His mind seemed full of projects; he wanted to see his "dear Belœil" and the old battlefields once more; far-off memories came to him; he talked of the days when he climbed the knees of his father's dragoons and listened to the tale of their battles under Prince Eugène. On the night of the third day his illness made terrible progress, and when Dr. Malfatti came in the morning he said: "What ails me, doctor, is the difficulty of dying." Then he added: "I have always admired the end of Petronius who died listening to beautiful music and noble verse; but I am happier than he, I die among friends, in the arms of those I love. If," he said, looking at his daughters, "I have no strength to live, I have still enough to love you." They burst into tears and kissed his hands. "What are you doing, children?" he cried gayly; "do you take me for a relic? Wait, wait, I am not a saint yet." This little jest touched them more than complaints or tears would have done.

The Comtesse Palffy gave him a drink ordered by the doctor, which procured him several hours of quiet sleep from which he woke with all his natural cheerfulness. His children began to feel some hopes. But towards evening he was seized by violent fever and delirium, with moments of apparent sinking. At midnight his strength revived, and sitting up in bed he made a motion as if to draw his sword; his large eyes flashed, and he cried out in a strong voice: "Forward! Vive Maria Theresa!" Then he fell back exhausted and died without struggle or suffering.

The impression produced by his death is indescribable. During the few days of his illness a crowd of persons stationed themselves about his door to get news of him from hour to hour. For long years the Viennese had considered him as their particular property; their mourning was a true grief, and they made his funeral as imposing as the obsequies of a sovereign, although it was not officially commanded. It took place on the 13th of December, 1814, with a pomp and following till then unknown for private individuals.

His company of Trabans in full uniform marched to right of the car; the emperor's guard to left. A man-at-arms on horseback wearing armour, with a crape scarf *en bandoulière*, followed, holding his sword with the point reversed. Next came a horse caparisoned with a violet veil studded with silver stars. Behind the horse walked his whole family, and after them a truly unheard-of crowd of marshals, generals, and princes from all the countries of Europe; among whom we remarked the Prince of Lorraine, Prince Augustus of Prussia, the Duke of Saxe-Weimar, his intimate friend, Prince Philippe of Hesse, Prince Eugène de Beauharnais, Princes Schwarzenburg and Ypsilanti, the Comtes Colloredo, Radetski, Neipperg, Giulay, Ouvaroff, de Witt, the Duc de Richelieu, Sir Sidney Smith in full admiral's uniform, who had solicited the honour of commanding the last battery. After these came the whole garrison of Vienna, infantry and cavalry, four batteries of six cannon each, and all the Austrian field-marshals, who clung to the honour of accompanying their comrade for the last time.

The procession moved to the church of the Écossais, where the service was performed. On the rampart (close to the breach made by the French) stood, with bared heads, the Emperor Alexander and the King of Prussia, who had come to render homage to the old friend of the Empress Catherine and Frederick the Great.

When the church was reached three salvos of twenty-four cannon thundered from the ramparts. The service over, the same procession, but without the cannon, marched to the Kalemberg, where the prince had asked to be buried in a little chapel which he himself had built.

XII.

SCATTERED THOUGHTS.

ALL those who write Thoughts or Maxims are charlatans, who throw dust in people's eyes. There is nothing so easy as to make a book of that kind. I mean to try. We are bound to nothing; we can take or leave the work as we like. That exactly suits me. But nearly all such writers say trite, false, or enigmatical things. They ought to give matter not for dissertation or interpretation, but for thought.

A maker of Reflections often thinks more of being applauded than of being understood, and lets himself off in little sparkles which dazzle but give no light. There is a sort of mechanism of definitions, synonyms, antitheses, comparisons, resemblances, and differences, which makes, if we want it, a reputation easily. Detached thoughts are the easiest of all forms for a man of intelligence; but, like most easy things, they require all the more intrinsic value. It is in literature as it is in music: vanquished difficulties may prevent our perceiving whether the performer is a good musician, but a simple air does not allow us to mistake.

La Rochefoucauld has more reputation than he deserves; sometimes he is even wrong in being right; his tone is a little *précieux;* I wish he had been more a man of the world. But the Hôtel de Rambouillet spoilt every one.

La Bruyère is too vague; though he seems to be making portraits I do not think them good likenesses. Besides, he paints only Frenchmen, never men in general. We ought to be able to find our own portrait, and say: "Oh! that is I; that happened to me; how true that is!" I look in vain for this sort of faculty among makers of Reflections, who mostly write in a false key, because they are not men of the world.

When Theophrastus wrote his "Characters" he was eighty years old. I began this present work at nineteen, and I think I had already seen more worlds, countries, Courts, and armies, and had had more experience of life than he.

Some people reflect to write, others write in order not to reflect; the latter are not such fools; but those that read them are, I think.

I am a little of the second class; but, to justify my readers and myself, I ought to say that if I write (to occupy my time), it is because I am accustomed to meditate, observe, and withdraw into myself; and because of this I have, without seeking it, a budget of thoughts, of which I want from time to time to relieve myself. I write more from inspiration than reflection. There is a world of people to whom I shall seem neither clear nor agreeable nor wise. If I do seem so to any it will only be in lands and with persons where, and among whom, I have chiefly lived, who have learned about the same things that I have learned, being brought up in the same way and living under the same circumstances. I am, therefore, doing very wrong to publish these Thoughts, for we should not only be heard, we ought also to make ourselves understood.

Man is an instrument on which it is well to know how to play. There is almost one for every individual, and we should seek for it.

I do not like to hear the term "honest men" given to those who do not steal because they are rich or afraid of being hanged; and I declare that they are worthy of being hanged who do not do all the good they can, who love themselves at the expense of others, who are not capable of enthusiasm, admiration, compassion, friendship. It is usurping life to limit ourselves to doing no harm; the dead do as much, and exact nothing for it.

No one is bad enough to feel ingratitude from mere indifference; but we try so hard to attenuate benefits, we seek so many motives for them, we think we find so much self-interest in our benefactors that, little by little, we become ungrateful without perceiving it.

The least dishonest self-interest is that which, after examining matters under the two faces they almost always wear, does not take the side that suits it best until convinced that the other party will not be too much injured. That proves at least that the person has discussed the matter with himself; and so long as he thinks himself an honest man he is so still to a degree.

Why is Justice always represented with a sword and scales? I should like to put a veil upon her sometimes. It is often justice not to do justice. There is a justice of severity and a justice of kindness. If, after well weighing in those scales, and even lifting high that threatening blade, the veil should hinder her from seeing all that should be punished, methinks that Justice might be more just. But if, seeing all, she pardoned, that would be mercy. I do not wish her to pardon always, but I do wish that her inquiry and her judgment should not be made with the will to punish. There are so many imperceptible little shades to distinguish, of which it is difficult to render an account, but which, nevertheless, do allow of justifying an action, or lessening the penalty. There is much intelligence in kind interpretations; they presuppose more penetration than there is in blame; for what is best in man is often hidden in the depths of his soul.

I think I have said a hundred times what I think of ingratitude, which seems to me a monster. But we ought to ask permission to render services, because if benefits which we do not want from persons for whom we do not care are to be rained upon us, we are constrained to be under obligation all our lives to those persons; often without much reason for gratitude, and often, too, without esteeming those persons as individuals. Can there be a greater embarrassment? — we must either fail in gratitude or truth.

The pleasure we receive from praise is never equal to the pain of criticism. We take one for a compliment, the other for truth.

We are often deceived by confidence, but we deceive ourselves by distrust. He in whom we show confidence, although it may be little deserved, is flattered, and will try, perhaps, to be worthy of it; but he whom we distrust unduly will never forgive us. After distrusting persons we come to distrust things. We consider to be impossible that which is only difficult. We persuade ourselves that even the most probable events will not take place; after which, we distrust ourselves and are no longer good for anything.

As soon as we are enough considered in the world to play a part in it we are set rolling like a ball that never again recovers stillness.

The world is itself a ball that God sets rolling. It does not always go well, but it goes, and will go ever. People say: "If that man who fills his office so well should die, what could be done?" His place is filled and all goes well as before. We say: "If we do not do such a thing this year, what will happen?" Nothing. "If this or that change does not take place in the Administration the country is ruined." Not at all, it gets out of it. We must do, and make others do, each man his own duty. And if we do not do it, it comes to pretty much the same thing.

The passions of the vicious are put an end to by the hangman; those of the virtuous are more to be feared. We have seen lovers commit crimes, zealous ministers bring on wars, and pure, though narrow minds not balk at revolutions. Who says passion, even for good, says danger. Passions are not born in us. If you ask: "How can a passion be stopped?" I answer: "Why begin one?" 'T is a sentiment, heated by imagination which stiffens itself against all obstacles; 'tis an ephemeral volcano. Rarely do we meet with those veritable conflagrations of heart and mind which are really passions.

That which proves the emptiness of reputations is the facility of making dupes. I will bet that M. de Voltaire would have been taken in if, at a dinner at his house, I had previously prepared a fool to play the part of a man of intellect. Two fools even, who had no other cleverness than to be each other's partners, could dupe the world. That is why one ought to distrust the dinners of clever men. To judge a man as he is, we ought to take him as he jumps out of bed. If, before he gathers together his ideas and revives his spirits, he shows wit, conception, repartee, force, or naïveté, that man is certainly a man of intellect.

The thing that costs us most in pleasing is to hide that we are bored. It is not by being amusing that we please. People are not amused even when they are amusing themselves. The thing is to make them believe they are being amused.

It is not always necessary to be right in order to please; there is a way of being wrong that is sure to succeed. In fact, there are very agreeable crookednesses — provided they are not put on.

It would be sad to believe that the man who comes nearest to the animal, who foresees least, thinks little, who has neither soul, mind, education nor memory, nor hope, nor fear, should be the least unhappy of human beings. What a difference between the tranquil state of a Bavarian or Suabian peasant smoking and drinking round a tavern table and that of Prince Eugène after his victory at Zenta, or that of M. de Voltaire at the first representation of "Mérope"! One thing makes up for another, and all things can be bought in nature. But the nobler race of the two is that which makes great outlay — it brings returns.

We ought to coerce our humour more, and ask ourselves often, especially as we grow older, whether we have not done wrong to speak, and see, and *disapprove* as we do. If we paid more attention to this there would not be half so many grumblers in the world, especially among women. We are always dissatisfied. We like to complain wherever we are. We are constantly declaiming against some one or some thing. "What a nation!" we say. "What a climate!" "What an age!" "What a life!" Is this the congenital uneasiness that we feel within us, or is it self-love? Perhaps both. We are only well-off where we are not; and we try to make ourselves believe we are worth more than that which surrounds us.

There are fewer hypocrites now than there were in former times because we have rather left behind us the desire for respect.

The dog that lives most with man contracts part of his defects. He is corrupted because man educates him; he is base, cringing, fawning, and cowardly. Leave him to his instinct and he will be only faithful.

Do not thaw the frigid peoples; they have their good side, and what you give them will only spoil it. Patience, fidelity, obedience are worth more than enthusiasm, which is never sure or durable; for once that it may be well directed it will be so a score of times ill. Better that a nation should have no opinions. The one that has them is subject to storms, and if the natural philosopher does not put the lightning-rod in the right place the thunderbolt will fall on his head.

I know no nation so gentle (but without amenity), better, more trustworthy, and less cruel than the German.

Enthusiasm and fanaticism: one belongs to grandeur of soul, the other to pettiness of mind; one is on fire for fame and glory, the other for a sect, a mode of thought, or a man who does not deserve it. One is ardent in good faith; the other is often prompted by secondary causes. The first leads onward, the second is swept along. The first was fired by the name of Liberty before its theory was examined or its results experienced. None but the second would have uttered the word *equality*. The first derives from pride; the second from self-conceit. Enthusiasm which does not give itself time to reflect may have crimes to repent of; but fanaticism denies itself no crime.

Great geniuses (they are called, I think, philosophers), after saying evil of God whom they do not know, say it of sovereigns whom they know but little better. There are two ways to punish them: first, by not punishing them at all, for they are usually fools who desire the celebrity of misfortune; secondly, by forbidding the liberty of the press. But it is better that governments should have writers in their pay, to foil and ridicule these pretended teachers of the human race, who, in their self-claimed love for the public welfare, are seeking nothing other than their own.

I don't know how it comes to pass that Free-Masons are at present in the world. They have much that is high and much that is low. It is interesting to see visionaries among them. Maybe they have good reason to be enthusiasts, for I am convinced that what is done by the body of Masons (of whom I am one) is nothing in comparison to what some of them know and are seeking to know. It is not possible that so ancient a society should have maintained itself without some vast meaning hidden under it. Meantime, when it consists merely of good company (which is very rare) it produces emulation, acquaintance, agreeable intercourse, and excellent pleasantry. Free Masonry requires eloquence, memory, presence of mind, bravery of body and soul, gentleness, patience, moderation, sobriety, prudence, charity, generosity, love of one's neighbour, imagination, compliance, gayety.

Going back to their origin, which is perhaps mythical, we shall find the cabalistic knowledge of the Jews; the

talent for architecture and the rallying cry of the poor Templars; the most abstract science that exists, that of Numbers; all those sciences inclosed by the Egyptians in their pyramids; and, without doubt, The Great Work, the science of Universal Medicine (Healing); with a thousand other discoveries yet to make. Reverence it all, divine and recognize these mysteries; or else, see nothing in them — as you choose. The Rosicrucians and pretended magicians, with their apparitions, etc., have spoiled the whole thing; which, from being a laudable and interesting Institution, has been made ridiculous and dangerous, and divided between two classes, the makers of dupes and the dupes themselves.

We do not pay enough attention to the People. We ought to think of amusing them — and in so doing amuse ourselves. We spend immense sums on suppers for two hundred persons, and full-dress balls, at which everybody yawns more than they dance. If we had violins in an open square for the People, or better still, out in the country; if we gave them something good to eat and drink, and amused them with a show, a race, a fête, a masquerade, something which gives pleasure to look at, we should certainly spread joy among the masses. If we gave prizes and revived the taste of the Ancients for the innocent pleasure of games, fusing together the city folk and the country folk, we should gain the blessing of thousands of joyous beings. We ought to have public promenades well-kept; and a member of the government should be charged with Pleasure, as being a matter most interesting to the administration. The mixing up of classes for the time being, the good-will which would certainly prevail in the midst of it all, the air of liberty, the music, the songs, the joviality would break the uniformity of dull lives, to which we are now so stupidly habituated.

Père Griffet was the first to make me know Frenchmen. He painted them to me such as they have now become. Afterwards, seeing them for myself, I remarked the brutality, the malignancy, the hardness of what is called the little people — the populace. There is no other which has the cruelty of childhood joined to that of all the other ages. The first prompts to crime like that of barbarians, the second, cold-blooded cruelty, leads to the abominable murders of the present day.

It is not always sad persons who think the most of sad things. No one thinks more than I do of woes and death. No one is more expectant that evil things will happen. But I reckon as happiness everything that is not misfortune. To be prepared for evil, to be shocked by nothing, to make one's self preparatives, curatives, or preservatives, and to fear nothing, that is happiness.

How I detest persons who are always seeking a selfish motive in a fine action; who cannot make themselves believe in it. It is admirable, as I think, to admire. If I find something that deserves admiration I hasten to give it, all the more because it seems to me that I uplift my own existence. I am proud that one of my fellows has done a great thing; there is glory enough for all.

They cast ridicule now-a-days on the spirit of chivalry, and laugh at those who seek gun-shot wounds in foreign lands; also, they forget fast enough those who have borne them. Honour departs. If it were replaced by pleasure, that, at least, might be a consolation. But no, people are dulled; and it comes from the same source — want of energy. The pretended philosophy of the age is only apathy, and it is destructive. It is those who have the loftiest souls who usually have the most taste and talent for enjoyment. They have impulse. Others vegetate, and only burden the earth with their dull existence.

What, or who, is it that marks in the world what we call energy? It is almost always he who knows but the name of it. The world is full of false braves; parliaments and State assemblies are often false braves, who prod the Court; they advance because others draw back, but they recoil hastily if others advance. There are scarcely any but jugglers among them now; and reputation, in the present day, is getting to be a trick of legerdemain.

The cry is "To arms!" I rush myself. I fly to glory. I sacrifice my pleasures, my tastes, my passions; my repose — of which no one feels the value more than I. But, through a series of involuntary contradictions to myself, though swept along in this whirlpool of chimeras, I do not cease to be an observer. Though an actor in the scene that is being played, I take all that is happening, and all that is done around me as a kick in an ant-hill.

What else are we, poor human beings? How much space do our innumerable armies occupy in Space? If ballonists were philosophers, they would rise into the air and laugh with all their hearts at our confused meanderings on the surface of the earth, and consider my comparison to an ant-hill a very just one.

Never say "the policy" of Prussia, England, France, Spain, Holland, etc. It is private interests, ambition, revenge, or the more or less logic or temper in the man or the woman who wields the influence, which causes the course of conduct that is laid to the account of some mysterious and profound diplomatic calculation. It is thus that personal egotism has almost always lighted the flames of war. The Place des Victoires, where the nations were seen enchained, was the cause of one war. The gloves of the Duchess of Marlborough played a great part in another. The jokes of the King of Prussia on a sovereign lady, a mistress, a great and a little minister, brought about the league that so nearly flung him from his throne.

We must not make a monster of that finest of evils, War. I have seen so many noble traits of humanity, so much good to repair a little evil, that it is not possible for me to look upon war as altogether an abomination, provided they neither pillage nor burn and no other harm is done than to kill off those who would perish a few years later less gloriously. I have seen my grenadiers give their bread and their kreutzers to poor families in a village that an accident (foreign to the war) had reduced to ashes. I have blessed my fate in commanding such men. I have seen the hussars return the purses of prisoners and open their own to them. It seems as if the soul were exalted. The more courage a man has, the more he feels. In all things it is emotion that is sublime.

Fame is sometimes a courtesan of the lowest type, who attaches herself in passing to those who are not thinking of her. They are surprised by the favours they receive without doing anything to obtain them. At the end of a generation they are believed to be superior to those who deserved such favours and never obtained them. It is unfortunate for virtue that so many noble actions of obscure persons remain unknown, and that we cannot go back to the hidden authors of great results. We might perhaps be able to disinter a few; it would be a novel way of writing history. We could relate the great effects and portray those who pass for having produced them, and then, side by side, make known the hidden causes and the ignored agents. This would be subterranean history, if I may so express it.

Better not to have glory in times and countries where few people know what glory is. It will fade at once. Three classes of persons contribute to this: enviers, detractors, and non-appreciators. See the times of the Great Condé in France, and those of Prince Eugène in our own country. As there were other heroes and glory enough for all, no one disputed theirs. That age held honour high. Sorrow to him who wants his laurels among those who have none; he will be crushed. What consoles us for not winning fame is that the greatest men are often denied it. I have heard it said that Frederick, King of Prussia, the great Frederick, was a coward!

It is often for want of being enlightened about their duties that persons fail in them. This is why there are so many unconscious criminals, and the reason why narrow and limited persons are so dangerous; the impulsion of character leads them astray.

We must come into the world general, painter, poet, or musician. When one of our colonels promoted by the Court said to Guido Stahremberg: "The emperor has made me a general," "I defy him," he replied, "he appointed you a general, and that is all."

M. de Turenne was well aware that the gazette would say more than he did about the battle of the Dunes when he wrote: "The enemy came to us and was beaten; I am rather tired and will bid you good evening." It is very easy to be modest like that. It does not belong to everybody to be modest. Modesty is either vanity or silliness when real merit is not behind it.

An eccentric man is often a pretty good devil. His eccentricity is founded on the certainty he feels about his own character. That feeling makes him indifferent to conventional manners. He may have plenty of faults, but he certainly will never be false or cringing.

Why are there so few natural persons in the world? There are many who, being capable of true sentiments, make themselves factitious ones to try if in that way they can produce more effect. They are well punished by their pains and their restraints. They lose by calculating a success that they might have won by nature.

Philanthropy, or rather philanthropomania is a singular invention. Do we need a Greek word, a sect, assemblies, and works in order to love our neighbour?

It is thought that quizzing renders a person ridiculous. Yes, so it does; but the person is he who uses it; the more wits the quizzed one has, the less will he seem to think that vulgar style could be used against him. There are many things we ought to baffle by not observing them.

Those who are least suspected of philosophy are often those who have the most of it. True philosophy is pleasure; it should enter into our duties. Fulfil those, and then breathe only joy; enjoy all things, games, fêtes, theatres, good living, good society, folly, if you will, and even follies. But always with good taste, even in our errors. There are some people whom all things become because they have grace and tact. We feel that they are better than their faults, and that they know as much about themselves as their censors; we therefore await their return to better things.

We say nothing new, we think nothing new. The same conversations come over and over again. We know beforehand the replies that will be made. I am annoyed with myself in seeing the little circle of thoughts in which I turn. It is enough to make one dislike one's self; and I can imagine a person taking a resolution never to speak again.

It is the laziness of men of intellect that I like. But lazy fools are like the valets in an antechamber; they soon become liars, slanderers, eavesdroppers, and bullies.

I do not like learnèd persons unless they are so without intending it or knowing it. There is nothing easier than to become one. Shut yourself up at home for six months if you want to know, and you will know. It is better to have imagination than memory. What, after all, are these ambulating dictionaries? Learnèd persons know words only. I never see them learnèd in things. The best book is the world.

Is it not cruel that we know nearly everything except that which we most need to know? We know the history of plants, animals, stars, the globe, but not that of man.

In order to behave well, be careful not to reflect; follow the impulse of your instinct. Every man has his own

Seize it on the fly; let it decide your course. It is through inspiration that you will do what you ought to do.

Passions depend on the life we live and the position we have taken. If Charles XII. had been born obscurely what would he have done with his passion for war?

A flash of genius is almost a flash of madness. If Frederick the Great, Charles XII., Eugène, and Condé had been truly wise we should never have heard of them as we have.

I love kindness; but do not push it so far that you are forced to become harsh. This happens to governments, tutors, and masters in relation to servants.

I do not believe in tutors, schools, or convents, but I do believe in nurses; if they take care of the health and the gayety of the little creature intrusted to them, they will make his happiness and that of all dependent on him.

There are differences between a dogged man, a self-willed man [*têtu et entêté*], a firm man, and a man of character. The first maintains, right or wrong, what he thinks, and listens to nothing; the second does what he likes without looking back to see if he is right or not; the third, without the doggedness of the first or the wilfulness of the second, chooses his side in advance of the event, whatever it may be; and the fourth is all his life what the third may not always be — and he undertakes more.

We change our sentiments because our health and our sensations have changed.

Imagination has more charms in writing than in speaking. Its great wings must fold on entering a salon. If too vivid, too ardent, it must be checked; too much fire chills a conversation, too much wit is wounding, too much intellect humiliates. To please, we must know how to come down to the level of the greater number.

Of Myself — perhaps this is scarcely worth speaking of. I am about like the rest of the world, — better than some think, less good than others think. Content with myself in great things, as to which I defy people not to do me justice, I have perhaps been too careless of the judgment of others in little things. "Must a man's reputation depend on a quantity of persons who have none?" I pity or I joke at those who judge me askew. I laugh when I see I am not understood as to certain essential parts of my nature. Well, what can I do better than laugh if persons whom I like reproach me for want of feeling, and those whom I have taken persevering pains to oblige accuse me of levity? In spite of it all, I make some one ungrateful from time to time. I do not know if I do good, but, at least, I never do or say or think evil.

I defy sorrow for myself. If those I love have sorrows I share them; but then their pleasures are mine. I have them for myself, I have them for others, I have them for all the world. Save for that sensibility only — to which the compensation of Good outweighs all Evil — I care little for anything; I feel the vanity of nearly everything; I see so plainly the nothingness of all things that I have no merit in being neither malignant nor vain. I am too easy-going to be the first, and too proud to be the second. I forgive or I forget; and if friends are rare I make up by quality for quantity. My soldiers, for instance; I find in men of war the most attachment.

Either I see all things in good, or, I put all things at

their worst. If something fortunate happens to me I have enjoyed it in advance and I enjoy it after. If I meet with some little misfortune I say to myself that I expected it would have been greater, or else that it cannot last; I have always the hope of a change, and hope in itself is a good. If troubles continued I should see less regret in quitting life, for this world is only a passage. If my situation grew better I should feel that happiness the deeper.

I give light food to my mind, not too strong because the mind is as susceptible as the stomach to indigestion. Philosophy, literature, and verses, — that is what I need. I am too old to educate myself any longer, and not old enough to educate others; besides, that is not my vocation. That which seems the most frivolous is often the most essential. I listen because I know that that gives pleasure; I never care to make myself listened to, because I know that that humiliates. If I am with those who bore me, I think of something else without their perceiving it; when persons are worth the trouble, I do all I can to please them.

If I am obliged to reflect, and some painful thought comes to me about the loss of my best days, I say to myself: "When the very few years of active life I have still to spend in the pleasantest of ways have all gone by, I shall enjoy the peace my soul will have, and my successes in my gardens and country works will compensate for all the rest." But I do not give myself the time to reflect; I am busy; or else I drop insensibly into gentle idleness, thence to sweet reverie, and so to sleep and dreams.

But there is a way, a very hard way of becoming superior to events. It is to buy it by a great sorrow. If the soul is wrung by the loss of all we hold most dear I defy all other griefs to touch it. Fortune lost, ruin total, persecution injustice, all is insignificant.

When any one tells you a piece of news bet a hundred louis it is not true; you will make your fortune in a month; for once that you lose, you will win twenty times. People will tell you they have seen, read, heard — bet on. In the first place, people fib immensely; next, they want the appearance of knowing everything; besides which, they see, read, and listen badly, and are deceived, or deceive themselves. Therefore go on betting and you will be the better for it.

It is easy to be agreeable when all things encourage it. But if we can show wit when thwarted or wearied in society we have it really.

Why do we not say to ourselves, "I am happy"? We ought to take two days in the week for saying, each to himself: "Let me look at my life. I am well in health. The ten or twelve I love almost wholly, love me. I am rich. I play a part in life. I have consideration, people love me; people esteem me. Such and such a happiness will be mine. I enjoy this and also that, and before long the other." Unless we make this conscious recapitulation we get *blasé* on our happy condition; we change; we are less content; we regret the regiment, or the government that we have no longer. If we had said all along, "How happy I am to have all I have," we should have it still, for we should still feel its blessing.

Nothing annoys me more than to meet persons who think there is an underhand meaning to everything. Independently of a class I abhor — namely, those who diminish the glory of a fine act by imagining selfish motives, — persons who see some other thing in what is said and what is done, a reason, a malice, a satire, or what such fools call quizzing, a word and a thing both vulgar, — such persons, I say, seem to me odious.

In order not to lose your head when the house takes fire, say to yourself sometimes what you would do and what orders you would give when it happened. If you are surrounded in war or tormented at Court, do not wait till your enemies crush you, but prepare with self-possession to do what you cannot do without self-possession, namely, get out of the difficulty. I should like to see a school for Presence of Mind, with professors for coolness, foresight, and resource, in place of law and history, which any one can read without their aid. Such professors of theory and practice could soon put self-possession into their pupils' minds by having it themselves, and might succeed in making excellent heads prepared for all emergencies.

I know sensible people who believe in a little genie, a guardian demon of a good kind; and certain pretty women have assured me that all they have done that was best in life was done by the advice of their Sylph. I cannot flatter myself that I have a Sylphide, but what is very certain is that all the good ideas I have ever had in my life and the good decisions that I have taken (sometimes under very embarrassing circumstances) have invariably come to me at six o'clock in the morning, when I wake for a few moments. Sylph or Sylphide, I can conceive of such a being. My sleep has been peaceful because my soul was calm when I went to bed. This influx of calmness ought to give our minds the ability to judge well. I advise others, because I have had such good out of it, to take counsel with themselves only at their waking.

The only thing in which we have made an advance is in knowing better than they did in the days of Socrates that we know nothing. Information and education have been pushed so far that our greater knowledge of the for and against has, necessarily, increased doubt.

Laziness is so completely the instinct of animals that they are always lying down unless hunger or fear compels them to move. They are like the Turks, who never walk.

What will Posterity say, and what idea will a youth who studies history get on reading these headings of the present day: "Progress of the Human Mind," "Regeneration of Mankind," "System of Universal Happiness," "Fraternity or Death," "Terror the Order of the Day," "List of the Guillotined," "Report of the Killed, Wounded, and Dead in Hospitals"? With reason and, above all, good faith, what anguish might not have been spared to the poor human race! Read, if you can without shuddering, the origin of the infernal Troubles which for eight years have made earth itself quiver and blush; you will see there that the first sparks of the conflagration came from the pride, the folly, and the ignorance of a few unworthy individuals.

Is there not something more than love and friendship? It seems to me that something may exist. But I know very well it has no name. As for friendship, it is plain that that is a cold, cold sentiment — we are often bored by friends. As for love, it is so warm, so warm, that it passes quickly if successful; quicker still, if it is not. What then *is* this state of tenderness, so superior to all else, yet resembling nothing? All that is not she we love, all places where she is not become a weariness; with her, the soul is ever smiling, if that expression is allowed me. This alone can be called passion; and I think it must be that which comes but once in life. 'T is sympathy, the mingling of atoms, the blood magnetic — yes, true magnetism. It is all we want. It is the greatest happiness.

If you are dissatisfied with marriage do not blame the sacrament; blame the barbarous fathers and the false interpreters of God who prevent true hearts from meeting in this world, and in the next if they do not love here their unfaithful husbands. Parents, Priests, Notaries! if the name of God does not move you, let that of humanity do so. You are about to unite two unhappy persons, who will create others as unhappy. The health, the gayety of their children is at stake; and they themselves will seek outside of marriage a consolation for the desolation within.

It is because I love decency that I detest what is called such. See how marriages are arranged. A young girl is taught that she must not look a man in the face, nor answer him, nor ever know how she came into the world. Suddenly one day a notary in black appears, and a man in a coat embroidered on every seam. Her parents say to her: "This is your husband, you are to pass the night with monsieur." Such are the auspices under which marriage begins for her. Chastity departs; what chastity will henceforth keep that woman from granting out of feeling to him she loves what she has been forced to grant from duty to him she does not love? Thus it is that the most sacred bond of the heart is profaned by parents and notaries; the first call it union, the second a contract; both have created indecency and the principle of corruption; neither have considered love.

See that young victim of religion and avarice launched into the world and its dangers. The more the graces presided at her birth, the more she attracts desire on the part of men, and envy on the part of women. She is about to be judged severely. If she has a fancy she is lost; if she has a passion, she is wretched; if she has neither she is called insipid — unless, indeed, she has a really superior mind. If she has neither a good nor a bad reputation she is soon neglected by her husband, who is vexed that she is not the fashion, but would, nevertheless, be more so if she were. What vengeance is there for that poor little woman? Ill-humour to her husband? — he will avoid her and never see her. Shall she take a lover? — they will lock her up. The wonder is that there should be so many virtuous women in the world.

That which justifies the weakness of women in respect to us is that men demand it of them. Moreover they have nothing to do. Why not occupy them? They sit at home with their arms folded. They know their reign is short, and they put their little moment to profit. Why not employ them in negotiations, as they are physically too feeble for war? They have more self-love than men, and they would employ it in persuading sovereigns and ministers. Mme. de Königsmark was an ambassador. An embassy would be for their declining life. Work in the offices would occupy their tempestuous years until they were twenty-five. They have secrecy (when they are interested in anything), shrewdness, wiliness, ambition; what more is needed to succeed in diplomacy?

In vain shall I do justice to women's sagacity, sensibilities, charms, and even virtues; it must be acknowledged that we have spoilt them by calling them queens of society and the best and most beautiful part of creation. The first term is vague, the other is true when they are gentle, not reserved, not exacting, and concerned only in making the happiness of husband and friends. But the habit of being flattered makes them cry out against all works in which they are discussed. Mercy, my ladies, for mine! I will flatter you one after the other, if you wish it, but as a body, you must accept from me a few truths, though a trifle severe.

What can a feeble sex do, if it has not been trained in youth to a knowledge of morals [*exercé à la morale*] when it desires to follow that path without a rule, when it seeks to rise above itself, and yet has not the strength to know enough to compare and judge; a sex which never travels, and has seen little, and read badly, which mistakes imagination for education, rigidity for virtue, the desire to know for knowledge, and obstinacy in an unwise course for character? The education of women, the want of proper direction of their reading, the bad choice of the books they do read, often full of very false philosophy, all this does injustice to women who think and desire knowledge, and often puts them at a disadvantage with other women who have less mind than themselves.

After having said, read, written, and heard much of women, what is the outcome of good and evil to be put to their account — without seeking to be either spicy or gallant in our reply?

Here is mine, in good faith. They are more amiable than we, more genial, more feeling, more spiritual; they are worth more than we are. All the imperfections with which we reproach them cannot do the harm that one of our defects can do; and besides, as I think I have said elsewhere, we are the cause of them by our despotism, injustice, and self-love. Look at their reigns when women are on the throne. It is false that men govern them. They have too much ambition, which once in a way they are able to satisfy, to share their authority. I have seen this twice, and closer than any other man, and I can be believed. Look at a dowager, or an heiress in her castle; she does more good than her predecessor, the deceased seigneur. I am not speaking now of distinguished women, who by the loftiness of their souls, the spirituality of their minds, the refinement of their organizations, and their perseverance in educating themselves, rise higher than the most distinguished men. But follow through the course of their lives one hundred persons of each sex and you will find twenty per cent more virtues in the one than in the other.

We moralists are not any better than those who read us We belong to that class between foster-mother and maid, called, I believe, child's nurse. She is often as ignorant as those she holds in leading-strings. Still, one would fain hold the leading-strings of the world (which is only a big child), to keep it from falling, burning itself, and above all, from crying, screaming, tearing and spoiling things.

That which alone suffices to make us believe in the immortality of the soul is the injustice of the strong. How is it possible that the divine Being who has made such glorious things could be so able, universal, and great without being just? And how can He be just if so many worthy sick and disabled persons have no other state of good to hope for? It may be that the obtaining of that state depends on bearing with patience the one in which they suffer.

There is this to be said on the prosperity of evil minds, that perhaps it is only outward. The rich are robbed, the gluttons are sickly, the libertines exhausted, and slanderers fear that the evil they say may be brought home to them.

Putting things at their worst, I should say to sceptics: It is as difficult not to believe as to believe. What does it cost to believe? All is supernatural. Nothing can be explained. Let us repair the wrong we see in the world by doing good to the sorrowful, not permitting that any should be unhappy; consoling the afflicted, humiliating no one, honouring old age, defending the orphans, consecrating our voices to the defence of oppressed innocence, sacrificing our lives to our sovereign and friends, acknowledging benefits, forgetting wrongs, enlightening others who neglect their duties for want of knowing them, shedding abroad upon society that security, that amenity of morals and manners that make the comfort of this life and the inward peace of the soul which scepticism is endeavouring to take from us — what is all this, I ask, but the Gospel, pure and simple? Can there be a better morality, with more philosophy and more policy than that?

Assured of eternal happiness in the other life we can let the moment come to go there without either desiring it or fearing it. Exempt from all anxiety in that respect, we must be happier in this life; there will be no evil humours, no illness, nothing to trouble the general harmony; if all are advancing towards Good there can be no evil men; there will be no wars; each will cultivate his own blessings and increase his wealth to share it.

If any one inclines to shake your little system of Morality by asking if you are sure your soul is immortal, answer: "What is that to me?" If it is, I see, through the practising of my Law, the heavens opening around me; *but* I do not choose to be told that those who do not believe in immortality will therefore commit all crimes; I declare those who say that as wicked as if they themselves committed them. It seems to me that virtue brings its own reward in this life. The soul is in hell if, looking inward, we are conscious of crime. See the faces of jealous, avaricious, cowardly, and ambitious persons; there alone is a warning greater than Gehenna, the pagan's Tartarus, the molten lead of Christianity, and all the pots of boiling oil in the world.

The doctrine of Zoroaster, revived among Christians in Manichaeism, is an error far more reasonable than many others. Rather than believe in nothing, liking the marvellous, needing it, it is believable that celestial, aërial, and terrestrial Spirits should direct the Universe; and so perhaps the influence of planets is believable. If the latter influence were true we should be brave under Mars, gallant under Venus, eloquent with Mercury, tender and delicate under Virgo, just under Libra, strong with the Lion, adroit with Sagittarius, capable of friendship with the Gemini, discreet under Pisces; but how about Aries, Taurus, Capricornus, and Cancer? Should we have to consult them all before attending to our business or marrying? Better renounce each, and live in sloth and celibacy.

Let the ancient splendour of our religion be revived. The primitive Church has left us its vestments and ceremonies, imposing when intelligent persons employ them. This it was that made the charm of the old mythologies; those religions were in the hands of poets; Homer, Pythagoras,

Virgil, Ovid, Cæsar, Cato, Cicero, were the doctors of their Sorbonne. They uplifted or comforted the soul, promised the hero the rank of demi-god, the philosopher another body young and fresh, and a state of happiness after death, and so forth. But what do our ignoramuses who have managed to get a parish among us tell you? "Read a few tiresome books, mutter a few ill-written words, be present at such an hour in an unhealthy, ill-built Temple, and you will be canonized," — not one word of morality, or the practice of Good. They say to you: "Fast, pray, sin, and come and tell us about it." Yes, no doubt, observe the rules of our religion, but *also* read the Fathers of the Church and the "Imitation of Jesus Christ," one of the greatest books of the world. If you are not convinced by it be persuaded; and if you are not persuaded make believe that you are, and pray that you may be.

To abase the soul, narrow the mind, and mortify the body was never the intention of a God so powerful, so noble, so magnificent. Not to recognize Him proves the impoverishment or the parching of ideas. If what we learn of Jesus Christ seems to us more reasonable, more true than probable, the answer is that he is easy to follow if interpreted rightly. There is no danger in believing, but much perhaps in doubting. Mystery for mystery, since mystery there is in every way, better let ourselves go to that which by means of a good morality and certain ordained practices comforts the soul and sustains it in the last moments of life.

INDEX TO VOL. II.

www.ingramcontent.com/pod-product-compliance
Lightning Source LLC
Chambersburg PA
CBHW021729110726
47902CB00005B/1405
9783337169831